Dear Reader,

For years, I've wanted to tell a story inspired by Edgar Allan Poe's "The Fall of the House of Usher." I adore its chilling gothic atmosphere: the strange siblings, the unnerved interloper, and that bleak stone manor house beside an even bleaker lake. However, Poe's genius aside, there isn't a great deal of meat in the story to base an entire book on. So for a while, the ingredients for this book—the twins, the friend, the house, the lake—existed only in my head and not on the page.

That was until I went to visit family in Ireland. In Roscommon, we stayed in a friend's house that backed onto a beautiful lough (Irish for *lake*), and once again, the bones of that story came back into my head—and this time, they wouldn't leave. Not only that, I recalled stories about the Bean Sí, a wailing harbinger of death, and her association with water. Slowly, the pieces of the story began to fit together.

The title *Our Wicked Histories* refers not only to the split-second mistake that costs our main character, Meg, her friends and causes her endless sleepless nights. It also relates to the equally dark personal histories of her acquaintances, as well as England's wicked treatment of Ireland during the Great Famine, an episode of history that isn't taught in British schools.

Meg's story asks what we might be willing to forget in order to achieve our goals and where the line is drawn between ambition and accountability, and it reflects on the mutability of memory.

Thank you so much for reading what will be my second book. Now, it's almost Halloween, and the sky is darkening. Time to allow Wren Lake to pull you into its murky embrace . . . and remember, fear death by water.

AG

Amy Goldsmith

RANDOM HOUSE
CHILDREN'S BOOKS

TITLE:	Our Wicked Histories
AUTHOR:	Amy Goldsmith
IMPRINT:	Delacorte Press
PUBLICATION DATE:	July 30, 2024
ISBN:	978-0-593-70395-3
TENTATIVE PRICE:	$19.99 US / $26.99 CAN
GLB ISBN:	978-0-593-70396-0
GLB TENTATIVE PRICE:	$22.99 US / $30.99 CAN
AUDIO ISBN (download):	978-0-593-86606-1
EBOOK ISBN:	978-0-593-70397-7
PAGES:	384
TRIM SIZE:	5-1/2" x 8-1/4"
AGES:	14 and up

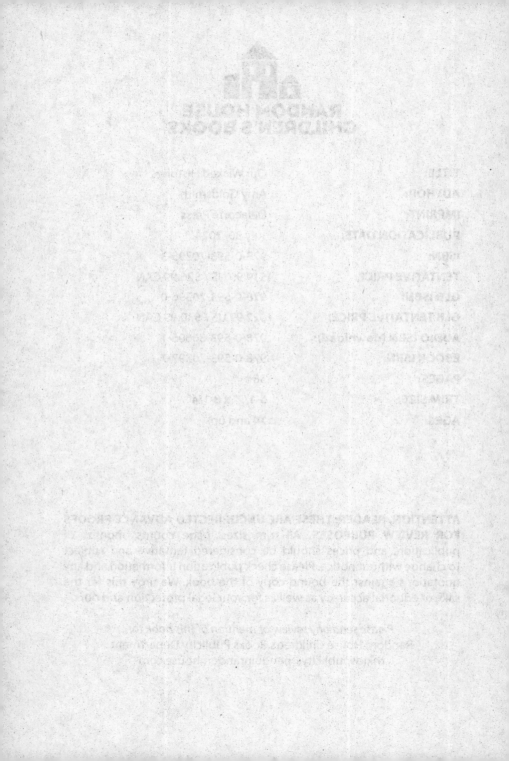

OUR WICKED HISTORIES

BOOKS BY AMY GOLDSMITH

Those We Drown

Our Wicked Histories

OUR WICKED HISTORIES

AMY GOLDSMITH

DELACORTE PRESS

Text copyright © 2024 by Amy Goldsmith
Jacket art copyright © 2024 by Marcela Bolívar
Interior art used under license by stock.adobe.com

Visit us on the Web! GetUnderlined.com

Educators and librarians, for a variety of teaching tools, visit us at RHTeachersLibrarians.com

Library of Congress Cataloging-in-Publication Data
Names: Goldsmith, Amy, author.
Title: Our wicked histories / Amy Goldsmith.
Description: First edition. | New York : Delacorte Press, [2024] | Audience: Ages 14+ | Summary: After a disastrous accident at her school's Midsummer Ball leads to Meg's suspension, she agrees to attend a Halloween party at her old friends' ancestral home in Ireland in order to make amends, only to discover that the estate has a sordid past of its own.
Identifiers: LCCN 2023001477 (print) | LCCN 2023001478 (ebook) | ISBN 978-0-593-70395-3 (hardcover) | ISBN 978-0-593-70396-0 (lib. bdg.) | ISBN 978-0-593-70397-7 (ebook)
Subjects: CYAC: Secrets—Fiction. | Murder—Fiction. | Ireland—Fiction. | Horror stories. | LCGFT: Horror fiction. | Novels.
Classification: LCC PZ7.1.G6515 Ou 2024 (print) | LCC PZ7.1.G6515 (ebook) | DDC [Fic]—dc23

The text of this book is set in 11.3-point Adobe Garamond Pro.
Interior design by Cathy Bobak

Printed in the United States of America
10 9 8 7 6 5 4 3 2 1
First Edition

For Ciara and Rory, the light of all lights

RAIN SPATTERED AGGRESSIVELY at the oval window as the plane sped furiously down the runway at Shannon Airport, the sky overhead a flat, foreboding gray.

It had been a short flight, shorter than I'd expected, and part of me was disappointed it was already over; that brief buzz of holiday excitement generated at the airport squashed now I'd actually arrived.

Ever since the front door of the flat had thunked shut behind me this morning I'd been dogged by a nagging sense of unease; the idea that something would prevent me from getting here—canceled trains, sick pilots—or worse. It was as if the sword of Damocles had swayed precariously above my head as I edged my way over the Irish Sea.

After all, I'd waited three long months to be here.

I checked the time on my phone. Just after two in the afternoon and already the weak October light was failing, obscured by sullen black clouds. Mum had warned me that Ireland was notoriously wet, but I hadn't expected it to be so bleak.

I'd landed a few hours after Seb and Lottie, which meant a long, awkward taxi ride alone but I didn't exactly have much choice. There was no way the likes of me was flying British Airways business class like the Wren twins.

Out in the taxi queue, I absently thanked my driver, a rotund man in his fifties with a wealth of gray hair and a strained checkered shirt, as he put my case in the back, gallantly opening the door for me.

He made an impressive effort at small talk at first—clumsy attempts to discover why someone my age was making my way down the west coast of Ireland alone—but finally got the hint after five entire minutes of my monosyllabic answers, leaving me to pull on my headphones guilt-free and sink back into my thoughts.

A tight coil of anxiety twisted snakelike in my gut as we sped along narrow, empty roads dotted here and there with cozy-looking bungalows. I'd never traveled abroad before, having to awkwardly bow out of recent school trips to Verbier and Zanzibar, the cost of which was more than my mum earned in an entire year—even *with* the scholarship subsidies. So when Lottie's invite arrived, pinging into my inbox at eleven a.m. on another tedious Sunday, I'd almost opened my window and screamed down at the street in joy, Scrooge-style. A chance to spend the autumn midterm in Ireland at the Wrens' ancestral home. The fact I even knew someone with an *ancestral home* still made me snort-laugh.

Before everything went down at the ball, Lottie had been banging on for ages about the amazing Samhain party she was planning (the idea of a regular Halloween party was far too pedestrian for her) and if that sounded pretentious that's because it *was*. Everything about Charlotta Ophelia Chatto-Wren, art darling of the exclusive Greyscott's Academy was unapologetically pretentious.

But it wasn't the party I was excited about. No—it was the chance I'd been offered. A shot at being let back into her circle, and more importantly, let back into Greyscott's. A sliver of light let out by an opening door.

November 12.

The date of my upcoming suspension hearing was etched permanently in my mind. Crashing down upon me with a wicked screech in those still moments before I fully woke, when everything seemed normal for a few precious seconds. This trip was my first, and probably only, chance to tilt the balance in my favor.

I dragged myself back into the present. Honestly, I was impressed by the rain—it hadn't let up the whole journey; the rhythmic swiping of the windscreen wipers almost lulling me to sleep as lush green fields swept past. Beneath the fizz of excitement, there was a gnawing hollow ache in my stomach that had rooted itself there the night of the summer ball and had never left. It would be the first time I'd see everyone together—the first time I'd see Seb after the night that had changed everything—

"Shite—*shite*!"

The driver's frenzied cursing broke into my thoughts as the taxi swerved, then rocketed dramatically up onto a grass shoulder, throwing me forward before coming to a bumpy stop before a low flint wall, the engine flatly cutting out. I only narrowly avoided greeting the front seat with my head. My heart shot into my mouth and my breath came fast. I wrenched off my headphones.

"Hey—what—what *happened*? Did—did we hit something?"

I tried to catch the driver's eyes in the mirror but they were squeezed tightly shut, his breathing erratic and wheezy, his skin a troubling shade of gray as one hand clutched at his chest.

"Hey—*hey*! Are you okay?"

Above the steady swoosh of the windscreen wipers I could hear something else. A low broken sobbing. Clumsily unclipping my seat belt, I struggled round to look out of the rear window in the direction of the sound, squeezing my eyes half shut, afraid of what I might see and praying nobody was badly hurt.

A woman was crouched on the grass only a meter or so behind us, her dark slender shape silhouetted starkly against the glowering sky, head bowed and buried in her hands. Her hair was long and darkened by rain, falling over her face and down the sober black dress she wore in straggling tendrils. She was absolutely soaked to the skin.

I fumbled for the door release but it wouldn't budge.

"Shit—did we—did you hit her?"

That sobbing continued. Low and undulating and *heartbreaking*. Now so loud it was as if she were sat in the car with us. I had to resist the urge to clamp my hands over my ears.

"Do—do you think she's hurt? Should we check?"

I forced myself to take another look behind me. Well, she was sitting up—that was good. And there were no obvious signs of any injury. No gallons of pumping blood or limbs hanging at weird angles, thank God. She was probably just in shock.

Still, the crying continued, louder and louder, an unpleasant low, rasping quality to it. Even though she didn't look hurt, I knew from the gruesome emergency service documentaries Mum loved that she might still have some nasty internal injuries. We needed an ambulance.

Other than his ragged breathing, the driver remained silent. Was he in shock too? Or worse—having a heart attack? He wasn't exactly the picture of good health—what if he had a medical condition? *Oh God.* Panic unfurled its dark wings within me and I scrabbled for my phone in the depths of my backpack. My fingers fumbled to unlock it. Was the emergency number even the same over here? I began to key it in, hands shaking, that dark feeling of impending doom stronger than ever. Wow, what a way to start the trip.

Without warning, the car's engine abruptly revved up again, pulling off the grass shoulder with sudden violence and, with a screech of brakes, back onto the road.

"Hey!" I said, dropping my phone into the footwell and hurriedly clipping my seat belt back on. "Wait a minute. Shouldn't we go back and check on that woman? I think she was hurt. She was crying back there—"

It hadn't *felt* as if we'd collided with anything. Only swerved to avoid her. But we should have at least checked if she was okay—

Ironic really, pretending to be citizen of the year after everything I'd done—The taxi driver cleared his throat.

"What? What are you on about? It was just some old drunk, that's all."

His easygoing banter had entirely evaporated, leaving him cold—borderline unpleasant—his tone unnecessarily cutting.

"She was upset, not *drunk.* She was right behind us. You must have heard her crying?"

"Feck all is what I heard," snapped the taxi driver. Eyes widening, I stared at him in the mirror. He met my gaze with a frown, as if daring me to say more, continuing to drive on at breakneck speed. Then, with another squeal of complaint from the brakes, he turned sharply off the road and started down a bumpy tree-lined drive, gravel crunching beneath the wheels.

It was dark here.

The twisted elms that lined the drive crowded over us, creating a wizened tunnel. Through the thick crowd of branches I could make out a flat body of water in the distance, brown as gravy and distinctly uninviting. A lake.

"Anyway, we're here now," the driver muttered. "If you're that convinced in what ya saw, you're more than welcome to take a walk back once I drop you off."

But I said nothing because there, at the very end of the weed-strewn drive, stood Wren Hall.

It was nothing like I'd imagined.

In my head, I'd envisioned some grand estate from a Jane Austen movie adaption built of pale buttery stone with stately windows that twinkled in the sun and grand Ionic columns either side of a vast door. It *was* the Wren twins, after all. The same Wren twins whose parents were Greyscott's most generous donors, a fact I discovered after jokingly pointing out the family resemblance in the stern ancestral portraits that hung in the main lobby of Greyscott's.

But this Wren Hall looked as if it had been wrenched out of a Gothic novel, bleak and rambling and wreathed in ivy. Mean-looking windows were crammed haphazardly into the gray pebble dash walls. Several turrets stuck out at asymmetric angles, some crenelated, some tiled. The unrelenting rain cascaded over the roof—most of which was covered with a thick slimy moss—pouring into the broken guttering beneath.

The gravel driveway was littered with potholes and cracked urns filled with dead vegetation. From the iron sky above, to its stubborn dark reflection in the large lake, to my own reflection, captured in the dark tint of the car window—everything was *gray.*

For a second or two, I toyed with the idea of asking the driver to take me back to the airport but, after his alarming 180 in attitude and erratic driving skills, getting out of the car seemed the lesser of two evils right now.

He pressed a button that released the trunk.

"There we are, then."

"Don't worry, I'll get my case!" I said with cheery passive-aggression, thrusting a wad of euros in his direction, then hauling myself out onto the drive, slamming the door behind me.

I heaved my cheap plastic-shelled case out of the trunk and dumped it beside me, shutting it with purposeful violence. The car immediately sped off, scattering a wave of stones in my direction, and leaving me alone in front of Wren Hall.

The drive was offset, arriving at the side of the house as if added as an afterthought. A pathway continued through a wooden gate on my left, wedged open by weeds, and led down a narrow passageway flanked on one side by the walls of the house and a high, straggling hedge on the other. Feeling oddly watched, I dragged my case past dark little diamond-paned windows set at odd angles into the wall, their leprous frames peeling paint, until I emerged at the front of the house.

Here a ragged lawn ran down to a steep bank, its grass a tired yellow, and disappeared into the thick reeds of the lake. It stretched out far into the distance, the water ominously still and encircled by a dark crescent of forest on the far side.

Wow. Perfect for a swim.

Peeping above the reeds closest to the house, were a series of rounded white objects. Curious, I wandered over to take a closer look.

At some point the lake must have burst its banks and begun encroaching upon the house as—emerging from the waters like an advancing army—were several stone statues. Greek-inspired— a couple were missing heads—and draped with slimy algae. I tried to smile at the sight but, honestly, the overall effect was more unnerving than anything.

Still, with this weather it was hardly surprising. A cold wind blew dead leaves around me in a swirl as I turned to face the house.

I steeled myself.

Come on, Meg. I'd come this far. After the most desolate summer break of my life, followed by the six slow and interminable weeks of suspension from Greyscott's, where the walls of my tiny bedroom seemed to close in on me more and more each day, this was my chance to be anointed back into Lottie's hallowed inner circle and, arguably more importantly, back into Greyscott's itself.

I took a final glance at the lake, its waters still, almost expectant, and turned back to the house.

A stone plinth set above the door helpfully informed me the house was built in 1768. *Properly* old, then. It was encouraging to see someone had at least tried to make it seem welcoming. Lottie, no doubt. Flanking the heavy wooden door and sheltered beneath a rickety tiled porch were two enormous jack-o'-lanterns, candles merrily flickering away within, accompanied by a large wicker basket filled with exotic-looking squash. Orange fairy lights dressed with fabric autumn leaves twinkled around the door and, from several of the first-floor windows, tea lights glowed warmly inside jewel-colored jars.

Above me, the upper windows of the house stared, blank and dark, out over the lake. I squinted. Was that movement behind them? Were all the others here already? An involuntary shudder racked me.

Get it together, Meg! They're expecting you.

I was damp and cold and in a new country—completely out of my element, that was all. I'd be fine once I was inside, finally catching up with Lottie beside a roaring fire, porcelain teacup in hand—Earl Grey with a slice of lemon. The Wrens enjoyed the finer things in life.

Fat spots of rain began to plop on my head so I hastily followed the house round, past a series of murky old greenhouses that leaned against the house, their black frames skeletal against the starkness of the sky, until I found what must be the kitchen door. It was old and heavy, the utilitarian blue paint scratched and peeling, a pane of wire-latticed safety glass in the middle. Beside it, just as Lottie promised in her last message, was a large urn filled with brackish rainwater and weeds. Wincing, I lifted it, spilling a glut of foul-smelling brown water over my new Converse. Muttering curses, I snatched the key from the ground.

It was unremarkable. Just a regular bronze Yale, a plastic tag proclaiming KITCHEN hanging from it. Despite not seeing the slightest hint of a person for miles around, I still gave a stealthy glance around before inserting the key into the lock and opening the door.

I didn't step inside immediately.

The kitchen beyond was vast and gloomy. Shadows thickening to darkness in its corners. A thick odor of dust slunk out, immediately irritating my nose. It was as if no one had stepped foot in here for decades.

"Hello?" I called out, but my voice was immediately swallowed by the vast emptiness beyond.

So, reluctantly, I stepped into the house.

2

"NO, SEB—I SWEAR I heard someone—"

A welcomely familiar voice drifted down a corridor off the kitchen followed by a clattering of footsteps. My shoulders slumped in relief.

"Meg! You're *here*! Amazing! I didn't think anyone would arrive for ages."

Lottie emerged into the kitchen; a whirlwind as ever. A dizzying tornado of cloying designer perfume, silken fabrics, and hair. She clasped me in a fierce hug, then held me at arm's length to examine me, her blue eyes huge in her heart-shaped face. A perfect face. A face that had over one hundred and one thousand followers on Instagram at last count as she posed beside her latest creation.

I couldn't help but grin back, brushing an arm nonchalantly over my face as I furiously blinked back tears.

Those long months apart had been a *punishment*.

I'd been drawn to Lottie like an errant magnet from the first time I saw her. The girls at Greyscott's—the prestigious private

arts school I'd miraculously earned a scholarship to—were an intimidating bunch. Out of uniform, they dressed in eye-blisteringly polished streetwear or carefully curated vintage accessorized with their mum's old Birkin.

Lottie had been strolling out of the principal's office the first time I saw her, chased by effusive praise, while I sat waiting for my introduction session, wide-eyed and chewing my nails, frankly overwhelmed by the grandeur around me. The vast expanses of expensive dark wood. The glistening diamond-paned windows and deep, luxurious pile of the wine-colored carpets. Greyscott's was worlds away from the seventies-built brutalist secondary I'd just left; the gray-tiled corridors forever permeated with the delightful combo of sweat and cheap gravy. She'd caught me staring and rolled her eyes playfully in the direction of the principal, a smirk on her face.

Seeing her for the first time had been like being caught in a pair of dazzling headlights. Her hair fell in wild dark corkscrews to her waist and her eyes were a sparkling blue set above cheeks spattered with freckles. In a sea of carefully contoured faces, she wore zero makeup other than a bold flick of black eyeliner.

"Ah, and here she is," said the principal, Mrs. Cholmondeley, as her eyes alighted on me. She was a formidable woman in her forties, forever dressed two decades older in fussy silk blouses and navy pumps, her ash-blond hair set with so much hairspray it never moved. "Our newest recruit. Meg, meet Lottie. She's our redoubtable head girl and will be glad to show you the ropes here." Turning toward Lottie, she added, "Meg's starting school on an art scholarship, clever thing."

I'd given Lottie an apologetic smile, already uncomfortable

with being a burden, and was surprised when her face broke out into a ready grin. She'd taken my arm in hers, and within minutes I was standing within a circle of her friends like some kind of awkward museum exhibit.

"Meg's come from Catford Comp," she'd announced to them, almost proudly. "So like, a proper South Londoner."

Her friends, with their canvas totes scavenged from fringe-art shows and tattered Reeboks, seemed far less intimidating than most of the other girls milling past. And, as I was soon to discover, Lottie herself wasn't only beautiful, insanely rich, and talented, she was also kind. Seems like some people really did have it all.

Standing before her now in the kitchen as she smiled sunnily at me, it was as if the ball had never happened. And, not for the first time, I desperately wished that was the case.

"Yep—made it! Honestly, I was bricking it on the flight. First time I've ever flown, y'know."

She gave me an indulgent grin. "*Bricking it.* That's hilarious! We've only just arrived ourselves. Mama insisted we meet her for lunch in Dublin before we came here—you know what it's like. *God*, it feels like ages since I've seen you!"

I couldn't exactly point out that it *had* been. Literally. That she'd pretty much ignored my pleas to meet and talk it out for those endless months after the ball.

Okay, Meg, and what exactly did you expect *her to do?*

Forcing those thoughts away for the moment, I drank in my surroundings.

The kitchen we stood in was large and rustic—and fancier than the exterior of the house belied. The walls were rough, white-washed stone and a huge and complicated black range dominated one wall. Beneath our feet were terra-cotta tiles and a rough-hewn wooden table sat beneath a window, laden with bags. Desiccated bunches of herbs and gleaming copper saucepans hung from the low ceiling beams.

Lottie glanced over her shoulder and I slowly followed her gaze to where Seb was struggling down the corridor, yet more bags hanging off his shoulder, his mouth set in a grim line.

"Seb!" she chided. "Don't look so grumpy. Look who's here!"

He ducked through the low-beamed doorway into the kitchen, and my heart stuttered to an immediate stop as his eyes met mine. They were the same eyes as his sisters—although much darker— and set into a face almost as pretty.

"Huh," he said, his gaze immediately sliding away from mine. My heart plummeted. An elevator in free fall. "So you actually came, then. Means I lost a bet. I told Lots there's no way you'd show."

I forced an awkward grin. Okay, so not everyone was going to be pleased to see me, I knew that. I'd known that the moment Lottie extended the invite. And I knew I'd have to graft to earn my way back in, but some things were worth working for.

"Well, why wouldn't I?" I said, with a short laugh. "Free holiday, right?"

He gave me a thin tight smile, entirely devoid of humor. *"Right."*

The pit in my stomach deepened. That precious pearl of hope I'd curated this entire time, that he might be secretly glad I was here, already crushed to dust. He clapped me harder than was necessary on the shoulder and then, before I even realized it, had slipped several of the bags he was carrying onto my arm, each one likely worth more than the entire contents of my suitcase. "Well, since you're here, perhaps you wouldn't mind dropping these upstairs for us?"

Lottie rolled her eyes.

"Don't be a twat, Seb. That's what Eimer's for. God, the poor woman's desperate for something to do."

Before I could say anything, he'd already stomped back into the gloom of the corridor, stooping slightly to contend with the low ceiling. I stared after him, open-mouthed, still holding the bags, my face steadily growing more and more hot.

Lottie stared at me for a moment, eyes wide with alarm, then swiftly recovered, giving an uneasy laugh.

"Here—give me those, lovely. Honestly, Seb can be such an arse. He knows exactly why you're here. I filled him in on the drive up here."

I cleared my throat, composing myself. Calm and collected. That was who I was now—who I had to be.

"Um, well, thanks."

"And it will all be *fine*," she continued, taking my arm. "I promise. Everyone knows how much I want us all to be tight again. You know, I want to get the group back together—the way things used to be. This break will be a clean slate for all of us. Now, let me show you your room—and more importantly, the *studio*."

I trailed Lottie down a series of dark narrow passages papered with aggressively large orange florals until we emerged in a cavernous entrance hall, its polished black and white tiles gleaming like an expensive checkerboard. A glorious chandelier swung high over our heads, its brittle brilliance dimmed by dust, while an impressive staircase of polished dark wood swept to the upper floors. Flanking either side of the staircase were two roughly carved hooded figures, their heads bowed and hands clasped together in prayer.

Lottie caught my gaze and chuckled. "Creepy, right? The newel posts, I mean. They're *meant* to be saints. Can't get away from the religious shit over here."

As we climbed past them up the stairs, I admired the dark oil paintings lining the walls in ornate gilt frames. Most depicted stormy naval battles or stern-looking men in which I dimly saw Seb's likeness. Several of the larger frames had been entirely covered with black dust sheets.

"What's up with those, then?" I nodded. "Not safe for work?"

Lottie chuckled. "They're mirrors. Eimer likes to keep them covered. Some old Irish superstition—can't recall exactly why now. Eimer's our housekeeper, by the way. She's been working here so long she's part of the furniture. I tend to just let her get on with it, to be honest. There are proper mirrors in all the bedrooms, don't worry."

The second floor was gloomy. And even though it was only a little after four, all the wall lights were already on. Fussy things in bulbous glass lampshades, they glowed a feeble orange. Lottie nodded toward a shut door immediately to our right at the start of the corridor.

"So—main bathroom—but honestly, avoid that one. There's something wrong with it—" She paused uncertainly for a moment, catching the confused look I gave her. "Um, with the drainage, I mean," she continued. "Smells like a swamp. There's plenty of others."

We walked past a series of identical closed doors until Lottie stopped and threw open the last.

"And this is you! Sorry about the desiccated state of the towels—they're literally as stiff as a board. No tumble dryer, can you believe it?"

I took in the room. It was dated but still grand—about the size of my entire flat back home. There was an abundance of expensive-looking vintage furniture, gilt-edged and lion-footed, and a generous bed covered with a dusty tapestry overhang that made me glad I'd packed some antihistamine. Positioned against one wall was an incongruously rickety school desk. A large pinboard was nailed to the wall above, patched with faded sunspots. The wallpaper, depicting scenes of blankly smiling teddy bears, was a little eerie but I could live with it for a few days.

"Let you into a little secret," said Lottie. "This used to be Seb's room when we came here as kids."

Weird—pretty weird—but since I was staying here for free, I couldn't exactly complain. I wheeled in my case.

"Swanky."

Lottie pulled a face. "Oh, c'mon, Meg. It's really *not*. But Daddy simply refuses to spend any more money on this place. It's been pretty much abandoned for years. Tragic really. But the plans I have for it for when it passes to me . . . An artists' retreat, I reckon. Speaking of which, I haven't shown you the best bit yet—c'mon."

She led me up a much meaner, steeper flight of stairs, concealed behind a door farther down the corridor. I gasped as I emerged. Money had clearly been spent *here*. All the rooms on the top floor appeared to have been knocked into one gigantic white space. Huge glossy shelving units covered one wall, groaning with top-brand paints and canvases and easels, and a pricey-looking marble-topped island dominated the center of the space. Directly opposite, a regimented line of windows stared out over the lake and the forest beyond.

"Amazing, huh? *So* much better than the space back home. I'm planning to come here next summer and set up a little commune, if you're in?" She nodded at the windows, rain running down them in busy rivulets, and screwed up her nose. "Hoping the weather will be better then."

I marveled at the space and the view. "Bloody hell, it's *gorgeous*, Lots."

She gestured at two closed doors at the far end of the studio.

"Another bathroom and then Seb's room. Right, I'll leave you to unpack. Come down when you're ready. Seb found some whisky in the kitchen—as my dad always says, 'Sun's over the yardarm'—so we'll toast to making amends."

3

AFTER LOTTIE'S FOOTSTEPS had receded down the stairs, I ducked back into my room to unpack. A tattered postcard was still affixed to the pinboard above the desk. It depicted the lake outside but on a far better day, the waters now inviting, glistening blue in the late summer sun. The words COME ON IN—THE WATER'S DIVINE! were printed over the image in effusive bold type. Had this place been some kind of holiday retreat once? Granted, I was not exactly a holiday connoisseur, but even in the height of summer I found it difficult to believe people would actually *pay* to come here.

The drawers of the dresser were empty apart from a long-dead spider so I shoved my clothes away, the only exception being my Halloween costume, still in its garment bag, which I carefully hung on the wardrobe door.

Afterward, I found myself drawn back to the window. The view was something else. Certainly beat staring at the dirty-white stucco of the flat next door to ours every day for the past three months. The dark crowd of the forest stretched out endlessly beyond the lake, the low-lying mist blending the trees into sky. And rising up out of the midst of it all like some enchanted wizard's lair was a tall stone tower. I made a mental note to ask Lottie what it was.

Before heading back down, I decided to take another peek at the studio. Lottie had briefly mentioned it when we'd spoken last week so I'd packed some paints in case I did get the chance to start something. It had been months since I'd been able to paint. Any spark of creativity I might have had dampened by that dark, ever-present swell of guilt.

Jogging back up the stairs, I shut the door quietly behind me and drank in the vast space once again. It was airy and light, its layout similar to the converted double-garage Lottie used as a studio back in London. In one corner stood a large easel, covered by a cloth. Curious to see what Lottie had been working on, I lifted a corner and peered beneath.

In the London art scene, she was already going places. You could scoff and say it was only because of her connections that she'd become as well-known as she had—pieces about her already cropping up in edgy art zines and websites—but you couldn't deny her talent. She was known for her violent explosions of fluorescent color, like a manically cheerful Rothko, painting giant canvases in joyously bold stripes.

But *this*? I'd never seen her paint anything like *this* before.

At first glance the canvas was covered with nothing more than a swirl of earthy colors. A murky array of slimy greens and foggy indistinct grays, so different from her usual bold shades. Clearly, they'd been chosen to mirror the landscape beyond the windows. The work appeared mostly abstract, but as I peered closer, I could pick out small details. There, in the background, etched in black, was Wren Hall, a haphazard box, stark against the sky. Below it, the mossy green-yellows of the grounds merged with slimy brown waters of the lake.

In the foreground of the painting—I don't know how I missed it at first—was a woman: her face half turned to the observer, her skin as wan and as gray as the sky behind her. Her hair was an odd shade of black green—like sodden seaweed—and it fell down her back in dripping rattails. Her eyes were huge and black and full of sorrow, twin voids of nothingness.

I wasn't sure if I was afraid of her or sorry for her.

Unlike Lottie's usual bold style of painting, this work had a soft, dreamlike quality to it, although in this case, *nightmarish* worked better. And in keeping with that was an odd sense of déjà vu. A feeling I'd seen this woman before—

"Bloody hideous, isn't it?"

I jumped about two feet into the air and gasped, whirling around guiltily.

Sebastien leaned against the doorway, arms folded, his gaze directed at the painting. "I mean, admittedly, I've never been the biggest fan of her work, but she's outdone herself this time."

While I secretly agreed—I couldn't see anyone sane wanting to actually hang this in their house—I felt a stab of righteous indignation for my friend. "Doubt you could do better," I retorted lamely.

Seb kept his gaze trained on the painting. "A three-year-old with a box of crayons could come up with something more *appealing*. Meg—why are you here?"

I blinked at the directness of the question. He still wouldn't look at me. I stalled a little. "Because Lottie invited me—obviously. She said—she said she'd spoken to you about it and . . ." I trailed off.

It was so difficult seeing him. I'd known it would be. He finally looked at me as I spoke, his generous mouth curled into a hint of a sneer, his dark eyes blazing with distaste, although his posture was still relaxed.

"I know all that. What I meant was, why the hell did you agree to it?"

So, I'd prepared for Sebastien to not be pleased to see me—after all, he'd spent the last three months acting as if I no longer existed on this earthly plane—but I hadn't expected him to be so outwardly hostile.

"You *know* why. I've tried telling you enough times. I want to—I want to apologize, to make things right and—"

And get back into Greyscott's because my future depends on it.

There it was. The selfish truth I couldn't voice.

He stepped fully into the room, closing the door carefully behind him. Instinctively, I backed away.

"Do you, though?" he asked. "Do you *really*? I mean, you've never struck me as the apologetic type before." His voice was low, almost menacing, now. "Maybe that's part of your charm. But it's fucked up enough that Laure's on her way here, and then you decide to show up too. I have to hand it to you, you've got balls. If I'd have known—Lottie didn't bother telling me she'd invited you until we were five minutes away from the bloody house—but if I'd have known, I would never—"

"You're saying you want me to leave, then?" I threw it out, calling his bluff.

"Yes," he answered with impressive speed, the relief on his face palpable. My heart cracked at the sight of it. "This trip was always going to be interminable but now we have the added joy of you two kicking off at the drop of a hat. I mean, haven't we all gone through enough lately? Look, I'm more than happy to sort your flight—call you a taxi—even book you a room at a hotel if there's a long wait—"

"Shit, Seb . . . ," I said, genuinely shocked.

Stupidly, I'd allowed myself to hope that my actual physical presence here would stir something in him and that there'd be a good explanation for why he'd let the last few months pass without a single word. That he'd felt the same way I had these past months. Like some of the pages of me had been violently ripped away, the edges left ragged and bleeding. It was a kick in the gut to see there was no emotion at all in his dark eyes except annoyance.

"I—I didn't think it would be that much of a problem—" I stuttered, my eyes prickling with tears.

Hold it together, Meg. Hold it together.

Below us came the sound of the front door slamming and distant voices raised in greeting. Seb shot a guilty look at the closed door, then took another step toward me. This time, I didn't move away.

The scent of him wrapped around me with disconcerting familiarity. Woody and expensive, like a fancy tree. He held me with his eyes. Such an unusual shade: indigo or midnight blue or—

"No—no. You knew *exactly* how much of a problem it would be," he murmured, his eyes blazing all over my face. "I think that's part of why you came." His hand, warm and soft, reached out to encircle my wrist. I jolted at his touch. "Take the flight. I'll call you a taxi now." He slipped his free hand into his pocket, pulling out his phone.

I stared at it, my throat dry. Recalling all the times I'd prayed he'd pick the damn thing up, every message I'd sent him, unread and ignored. My eyes flickered to his lips, the bottom one insolently full. As if noticing, his grip on my wrist tightened a little, his breathing hastening. I waited a moment longer before I spoke.

"I'm not going anywhere." My voice was slow and deliberate as I wrenched back my hand to push him lightly in the chest. "I know it might be hard for you to grasp—but this isn't about *you*, Seb, it's about *me*. And if my presence here's a problem for you, well, you've made your bed, now I guess you'd better lie in it."

He glared at me; mouth half open as if about to say something else. But he didn't, only whirled away, his footsteps thumping violently down the stairs.

4

FEELING SMUGLY TRIUMPHANT, I trailed Seb out of the studio and down the stairs, in the direction of the voices.

"Aha, there they are!" shouted Ollie, fifteen decibels too loud, as usual, his stocky polo-shirt-clad figure lounging against the wall. "Sneaking about in dark corners already. Bloody hell, Seb, you don't waste any time."

Sebastien said nothing, only shot him a look that would fell a horse.

"God, ignore him," drawled the girl next to Ollie, tiny and dark-eyed, dressed in beautiful silk-printed trousers and a delicate camisole, her sleek black hair flowing over her shoulders. "Guess who took full advantage of the duty-free on the flight over?"

Oliver Chetwin and Saira Rani. The golden couple of Greyscott's. So long as you ignored Ollie's fondness for day drinking and a propensity to cheat. When I first met them, I'd wondered what Saira, immensely intelligent and not to mention stunning, saw in him—until I saw the pictures of his home, that is. Oliver's family was *old* money. Even from the little I'd seen, a Halloween party at his ancestral pile in rural Buckinghamshire would have been an entirely more welcome prospect.

"So, you going to give us all a tour, then, Lots?" Ollie asked, glancing at Lottie.

I hung back a little, counting neither of the new arrivals as particularly close friends anymore, especially Ollie, whose bluntness was the stuff of legend.

"Let me get you all a drink first," replied Lottie, that familiar serene, everything's-fine smile plastered on her face, clearly relishing her role as host.

Saira caught my eye, and I braced myself for the worst. But instead of the cold hostility I'd been expecting, I saw a glimmer of nerves.

"Meg," she said stiffly. "It's been a while."

Relieved, I murmured in agreement as Ollie cast a sly look in my direction. He didn't offer a welcome, his eyes only glazed over, as if I weren't worth acknowledging.

"Laure not here yet?" he asked pointedly.

I felt my face heat at the mere mention of her name. It was like a hot pin, pressing unwelcomely into every nerve of my body. I was dreading her arrival. That familiar swishing mane of red hair, the high-pitched fake laugh at literally everything Sebastien said, the constant referrals to things I couldn't afford, the faux-innocent questions she'd mercilessly fire at me.

"No, not yet," said Lottie, taking an antique coffeepot off the stove, pouring coffee into tiny green hand-thrown cups, then adding a splash of whisky. "I think she's arriving with Charlie and Joss—they should be here soon, though."

26

"We've been volunteered by Lottie to get supplies for the party tomorrow," announced Seb, knocking back his coffee. "There's a taxi on its way. Meg, if you're still reconsidering, you can come with—then carry on to the airport?"

Lottie immediately looked at me, brow furrowed.

"What? Meg's not going anywhere, are you? She's got no reason to reconsider anything, Seb."

I beamed at her while Seb glowered, but he said nothing more.

Last September, when I first stepped through the towering doors of Greyscott's, an anxious and insecure mess, Lottie had immediately taken me under her wing, aggressively welcoming me into her group of friends.

I'd first heard about the scholarship from Mum and she'd been surprised at my initial reticence to apply, her excitement immediately turning to confusion the moment I didn't jump with joy at her suggestion.

I thought you'd be over the moon? I mean—think about it! The quality of teaching—the connections you'll make—it has a bloody Leading Arts Award! It's a world away from that crappy polytechnic down the road.

But I'd walked by Greyscott's in the past. I'd seen the sleek cars that pulled up silently outside the gates, engines purring; the gleaming teeth and subtle cosmetic tweaks of its pupils. There was a fusty old-fashioned uniform—black blazers and ties and the like—but that didn't stop the students accessorizing it with Gucci trainers or Chanel flats.

And when Mr. Selmeston, the art teacher at my old comp, vigorously supported my application to Greyscott's sixth form (no doubt glad to be rid of me after the "incident" involving his overly "hands-on" reputation and a tin of black paint), I was surprised to find myself invited to an interview. Less than a week later, I'd sat before the principal for the first time, her neck dripping with silver-clasped pearls, an actual Rolex balanced delicately on her birdlike wrist.

"You must understand, your family's financial situation doesn't matter to us," she said, smiling, revealing even white teeth. "Neither does your past. Here at Greyscott's, we believe everyone deserves a fresh start. You'll be a blank slate here—tabula rasa, as they say. The raw talent of our pupils is what we're interested in—the potential and the journey." She smiled again, her eyes black and as flatly emotionless as a shark's. "You see, we want to see what you're capable of."

So, when the letter of acceptance flopped onto the doormat a week later, my hands trembled, not only with excitement but with fear. That persistent voice that always told me I wasn't good enough, louder than ever.

But from the moment I met her, Lottie had been hell-bent on proving me wrong.

All right, I wasn't *stupid;* it was obvious there was a degree of charity in it. Lottie was desperate to be considered edgy. She never failed to mention how she only ever wore castoffs and thrift-store finds for sustainability (although I'd quickly noticed that most of them were still vintage Westwood or McQueen), accompanied by a battered old pair of DMs. She was an old-school type of rich who quietly sneered at anyone who wore their wealth too blatantly. On the weekends, she was always suggesting meetups in the not-*quite*-gentrified parts of London, taking us along to some pop-up street-art exhibition or poetry readings in seedy East End pubs.

I knew her friends were wary of me—suspicious of the tatty cuckoo in the nest—but they'd never been outright hostile.

Not until I got on the wrong side of Laure Westridge, that is.

"You'll totally *love* Laure," Lottie had said, holding on to my arm as she led me into a bijou coffee shop in Wimbledon Village a couple weeks after I'd started at Greyscott's. "Literally *everyone* loves Laure. She's kinda like the mother hen of our group. Y'know, the one who gets us all home on a night out, holds our hair out of our face when we're vomming in the loo—that kind of girl."

And, initially, I *did* love Laure, who arrived fashionably late weighed down by shopping bags. There was a brashness, an openness to her that made me think she was a little like me. Her accent not quite as polished as the others, her teeth a little too white, her laugh a little too raucous, the labels on her clothes always too obvious. And she was hilarious too.

"Hey—scholarship!" she'd joked, approaching our table with plates of cake. "God, we're all so excited to be your friend, you've no idea. We *love* normal people. Shit, last week I had to partner with Violet Von Berndt in chemistry—she's Germanic royalty, you know—I nearly slit my wrists out of boredom."

And to begin with, Laure and I had got on brilliantly. Somehow it was easier, more natural between us than it was between Lottie and me (who even after a week or two of friendship, I still regarded with a kind of distance-creating awe). Laure's family were new money, she openly joked, and would never truly be accepted by the likes of Ollie and Lottie. Because of that, I'd gravitated to her lack of airs. The way she'd bring Lottie back to earth or poke good-natured fun at her pretentiousness. Sure, she'd ask disarmingly blunt questions about how someone like *me* came to be at Greyscott's, but I didn't mind at first. I mean, I had nothing much to hide.

But then Sebastien had come along—and ruined it all.

5

"SO, WHICH OF us are venturing into—what's it called again?" asked Seb, his pleasant good-guy persona now solidly back in place before an audience.

"Knockhaven. And *all* of you," said Lottie. "Eimer and I need to start getting this place scrubbed up, ready for the party tomorrow."

"Sam-hain," drawled Ollie. "I mean, *really*? Couldn't just be Halloween, no? So pretentious, Lots."

"It's not pretentious, it's traditional," snapped Lottie. "And it's pronounced *Sow*-en not *Sam*-hain. Jesus, get some culture, would you? It's the night the barrier between the living and the dead is—"

"Wah-wah-wah," interrupted Ollie. "An excuse for a piss-up is what it is."

I mean, he had a point. Lottie and Seb's parties were legendary at Greyscott's for both their scope and ambition. For the last one they'd re-created Burning Man in a paddock behind their house, convincing their parents to secure a free outdoor bar run from a VW camper-van. Things had gone a bit awry when one of Ollie's friends thought it would be a good idea to set fire to a neighboring farmer's hay bales in the name of authenticity, but it had been memorable, all right. This party was looking a little less wild, though, considering there were only eight of us on the guest list.

"Okay, what do we need?" asked Saira, pen in hand, forever organized.

"Uh, whatever," Lottie said with a shrug. "Some booze, I guess. And kettle chips, dip, pizza—lots of Coke—the *liquid* kind, Ollie."

A horn blared sharply outside alerting us to the presence of the taxi.

Ollie jumped in the front first, always ready to bore the ear off anyone who couldn't escape. Thankfully, the journey was only fifteen minutes, during which I shifted my body as far away from Seb's rangy form as it was possible to get, staring obstinately out of the window as bleak brown fields and isolated farmhouses flew by.

Eventually the taxi pulled up in a parking lot wasteland of large department stores. Seb pointed at a gray flat-roofed supermarket.

"That's us."

We split up once inside, with Seb and Ollie taking a cart for the booze while Saira and I focused on the rest. I paused at the aisle of brightly colored Halloween decorations and Saira firmly shook her head.

"Don't even think about it. Lottie's got her own idea for decor. Can you imagine her face if we returned with a load of plastic crap from the supermarket. That'll buy you a ticket to her four-hour TED Talk on the demise of our oceans."

I smiled. She wasn't wrong. "Yeah . . . snacks it is, then."

We wandered down the aisles, tossing Doritos and cheese puffs into the cart.

"So," Saira continued, more carefully, "Lottie says you're planning on making some grand apology for what went down at the summer ball. Big of you."

If that had come from anyone except Saira, I'd think they were being sarcastic, but Saira was earnest to a fault. I looked at her plainly.

"You think?"

She nodded, not quite meeting my eye.

"The others might've been oblivious to it all, but I know what Laure can be like. I love her, but she can be a real bitch, sometimes. I almost cheered that night when I heard—when you— y'know. As soon as I found out she was all right, of course."

I attempted a smile, but the fractured memories of the night her words conjured were still too painful for any pretense of humor.

"Obviously, I'm sorry," I said, my face involuntarily heating at the first public acknowledgment of what I'd done. "I mean, it was such a stupid thing to do. But . . . I have this suspension hearing coming up, and if she and her parents keep pushing for my expulsion—well, I can't see a scenario where it goes my way. If I can speak to her, properly—explain myself, and apologize— maybe I have a shot at staying."

Saira threw a load of vegetables in the cart and chuckled. "Oh, I *see,* so that's what you're up to? Devious—respect it."

I frowned a little. Now that the words were out, they didn't sound quite right. As I paused, wondering whether I should clarify further, Saira continued drifting down the aisle. "So, what else do you reckon we need? Cheese board? Who doesn't love cheese?"

"I swear Joss is lactose intolerant—"

"Exactly," she said. "God, why Lottie had to invite the original Basic Bitch is beyond me. I mean, does anyone *actually* like her?"

I had heard from multiple sources that Ollie did, but that definitely wasn't appropriate to bring up in a supermarket cheese aisle.

A clown, its face painted a ghoulish white, teeth long and yellow, suddenly loomed up at us from behind a basket of discount biscuits.

"Your mother knits socks in hell!"

I recoiled. "Ugh, Jesus Christ—*do* one, Ollie."

He pulled the rubber mask off his head and dumped it in the cart along with several boxed bottles of eye-wateringly pricey champagne.

"What's *that* for?" Saira said, eyeing the mask.

"Thought you could wear it in bed tonight." He paused, pulling the pathetic hangdog expression I was eternally surprised Saira fell for. "I forgot to bring a costume."

"Lottie'll go mad if you wear that," observed Saira coolly. "You know what she's like when it comes to her bloody *aesthetic*. Don't you remember the invite? Everyone's costume was meant to be handmade and original."

"Well, tough shit. Not all of us have as much free time on our hands as she does."

"Okay, but expect to be erased from all her social media.

Damn it—forgot batteries," muttered Saira. "Meg, you carry on, meet you back at the car."

"So, plan is," began Ollie as soon as we were all squashed back into the taxi, "to find a traditional Irish pub—one for the road—as they say. Before we all march back to be bossed around by Lottie for four hours straight." Ollie turned to the taxi driver. "Hey, mate, drop us at one, would you?"

Beside me, Saira rolled her eyes but said nothing.

The taxi soon pulled into an empty parking lot off the main road. The pub itself was ramshackle and dark; the stucco that coated the walls like thick royal icing painted a drab blue, the roar of some sports match blaring from under the door. Overhead, the clouds hung low, pregnant with rain.

"Twenty quid everyone goes quiet and stares at us when we walk in," I muttered, reluctantly following everyone out of the taxi.

"God, it's going to be like Cornwall when everyone looked at me like I was from a different planet, isn't it?" replied Saira resentfully.

"Nah, not when we have the illustrious Lord *Wren* with us, surely?" said Ollie, confidently approaching the door.

I gave him an incredulous look. "Maybe I studied an alternate history to you, but I'm fairly sure the likes of *Seb's* ancestors wouldn't have been particularly welcome among the locals back in the day."

"What the hell are you on about?" Ollie snipped back.

"She means the famine, you dick," replied Saira good-naturedly.

"I've got to make a call," muttered Seb, rummaging through his jacket pocket and hanging back. He'd been quiet since we'd left the house—in an attempt to make me feel guilty for existing no doubt.

The rest of us braved the dim interior, commandeering a table in the corner, directly beneath a dartboard. In the background, soft trad music wheedled away.

"Hottest one gets the round in—off you pop, Meg. I'm gonna go to the gents," said Ollie, swiftly disappearing.

Giving Saira a sympathetic shake of the head, I made my way over to the bar. There were a few old men standing at it staring at some match onscreen, stoically sipping pints, their faces solemn. While I stood there, rummaging in my backpack and hoping I actually had enough euros left on me for a round, hushed conversation continued around me.

"Dermot swears he saw her, y'know, on the road up by the old Wren place. And then, less than an hour later, he spins out of control and that poor elderly lass with him takes the brunt of it. He's been driving that taxi for nearly thirty years now—thirty *years*—and not a hint of an accident. I mean, when was there last a collision out on that road? Now, what does that say to you?"

I froze, my purse halfway out of my bag.

The old *Wren* place?

In a flash of memory, I saw the license in my taxi driver's car, blue-tacked to the dash. Gray hair and a steely blue gaze. *Dermot O'Malley.* A coincidence?

Fiddling with my purse, I deliberately avoided making eye

contact with the person behind the bar, hoping to hear more. Was this about the accident I'd had on the way here? Guilty heat flushed my face. *Had* someone died? Should I say something? But, I hadn't seen anyone elderly—or even any other cars—only that woman on the grass, sobbing.

No.

There was no way I could be sure it was the same Dermot. And Wren Hall was down a turning off a major road. They could be talking about anyone.

"Did anyone else hear it?" muttered another of the men, his voice hesitant, wary. "That accursed noise, I mean? There'll be another one soon—there always is."

"Aye, our Clodagh said the foxes were baying something awful last night but any fool knows foxes don't sound like that. And I was terrible restless. Nothing's been the same round these parts since that Donnelly lass—"

A shadow loomed up behind me.

"Excuse me, barkeep, what is the proverbial *craic*?"

The conversation immediately stopped and four cold pairs of eyes slid to look at Ollie. As ever, he didn't even notice.

"What's taking so long, Meg? Run out of cash already?"

I sighed.

"Ollie, do you live to offend absolutely *everyone*?"

For a moment he looked almost hurt. His blandly good-looking Labrador features creased into a frown. If the bartender was offended, she hid it well.

"Ah, visitors, is it? Your first time here?"

"That's right," I said quickly, before Ollie could speak again and got us all kicked out. The barkeep, only a little older than us and with quick blue eyes, nodded to the rain-spattered windows.

"They say it would be a grand island if it were roofed."

Not sure I entirely understood, I grinned politely and ordered three halves of Guinness—I'd never tried it but when in Ireland—and a Diet Coke for Saira.

"You staying in the village, then? Not much to do for people your age, I'd say."

"No, we're at Wren Hall, actually," said Ollie. "Guy we're staying with owns it."

I watched the men exchange dark looks over Ollie's oblivious golden head. One of them spoke, his tone gruff and unfriendly.

"Oh, is that right? You're telling me James Wren has decided to pitch up and show his face around here again? The balls on the man . . ." Ollie looked momentarily confused, finally picking up on the hostile vibe enveloping us.

"No—no, just Seb—his son."

"Should have filled in that fecking lough years ago," muttered one of the men. "Drained and cemented the whole damn thing."

Did they mean Wren Lake? I looked at the man who had spoken, curiously. But as I debated asking him what he meant, the bartender cleared her throat.

"We're closing in ten minutes, now. Just so you know, lads."

Hint taken, we meekly headed back to the table.

"Is Seb okay?" wondered Saira. "He's still outside. He seems . . . kinda quiet."

I sipped at my Guinness, wincing at the sharp metallic taste. Ollie downed half of his immediately, wiping the foam from his lips. "I don't think he's overjoyed to be here. From what I can gather, he had other plans—but I think the 'rents asked him to keep an eye on Lottie."

Keep an eye on Lottie? Why?

I swallowed down another sip of the Guinness. It was stupid of me, and I'd told myself repeatedly exactly how stupid, but that hope I'd harbored of Seb being pleased to see me—openly or secretly, I didn't care which—was proving hard to extinguish. And the idea he didn't want me here at all—that he hadn't messaged me in over three months because he hadn't *wanted* to, that for him out of sight was *truly* out of mind—had never even occurred to me.

"Other plans?"

Ollie pushed back a handful of his floppy blond hair. "Yeah, things have been a bit intense lately at his place. But as usual, whatever Queen Charlotta wants us plebs to do, we all obey—"

"The house is a total shit tip, though, isn't it?" We all jumped slightly as Seb appeared, pulling back a stool with a loud screech. "And all it does in this bloody country is rain. I mean, if we all had the time and energy to go somewhere on a plane this week, I hear Ibiza's still warm at this time of year."

"C'mon, Seb," said Saira. "It'll be fun when everyone arrives. The old crew back together again . . . some drinks, some music . . . we'll have a good laugh. And as for the house—well, at least it's perfect for Halloween!"

But even she didn't sound convinced.

Ollie returned to the bar to call another taxi and while everyone finished up, I popped to the bathroom.

Pushing open the door, I saw the room beyond was dark. I fumbled for the light switch and the fluorescent tubes overhead flickered on with a loud insectile buzz. The walls were lined with dark green subway tiles and, annoyingly, all the stall doors were shut so it was difficult to see if any were occupied at first glance. But the lights had been off—no one was in here, sitting in a stall in the dark—so I pushed open a door at random.

Quickly, I used the toilet. As I pulled up my jeans, I hesitated, hearing something. At first, I thought it was someone quietly laughing, and looked up in alarm—an image of some stranger leaning over the top of the cubicle and staring down at me inexplicably popping into my head.

Then I realized the sound was someone crying. A soft sound, hesitant and hushed. It brought to mind the woman I'd seen earlier on the roadside—so thin and pale—her head buried in her hands as harsh sobs racked her body.

Whoever it was continued to cry as I washed my hands. Had someone come in here after me? Surely no one had been here all along, sitting crying quietly in the dark? The thought made me shudder.

"Hello?" I called out experimentally.

Immediately, the sobs subsided, as if whoever it was had heard me, but soon returned, louder now, bitter and gasping.

"Hey—hello?" I said again, wandering down the stalls, pushing gently at the doors, trying to locate the source of it. "Are—are you okay?"

A final, gasping hiccup echoed through the space. Then: silence.

It was an unnatural, immediate silence that stretched on for too long, as if whoever it was were holding their breath. Then came the slow deliberate click of a latch unlocking. I swallowed.

The bar patron's words came back to me. *The foxes were baying something awful last night but any fool knows foxes don't sound like that—*

There was a strong smell in here. Acrid and floral. Like an elderly lady's perfume. A vase of flowers that had been left for too long and had started to decay.

Abandoning my stall search, I turned to face the mirror that ran above the length of the sinks, currently reflecting nothing except my pale face, the tiles, and the closed cubicles behind me. I glanced over my shoulder again to look at them, to check they were the same as their reflection. Of course, they were. Why would I even *think* that? My eyes flicked back to the mirror.

Mirror, Mirror on the wall. Who's the fairest of them all?

I couldn't explain why, but suddenly I was afraid.

Back in primary school there was a dare we all used to take part in. You had to stand before the stainless-steel mirrors (safety first!) in the girls' bathroom and, looking yourself directly in the eye while your friends watched on, whisper "Bloody Mary" thirteen times.

Bloody Mary—
Bloody Mary—
Bloody Mary—

Thirteen times. And in quick succession. Then, if you did it right—and if you *believed*—it was said that she would appear in the mirror, watching you, sore-eyed and lank-haired and *reaching* for you. Wanting you to take her place forever in that lonely space behind the glass while she took hold of your body. I swallowed and looked down, losing my nerve.

Ridiculous.

Christ, I wasn't ten years old anymore.

I forced myself to look up again.

Just my face, looking like a ghost myself, wan and insubstantial, the silver blond of my hair blending into the pallor of my skin. The only color was the warm hazel of my eyes. Huh. Was I really so bored I'd resorted to freaking myself out in an empty bathroom? Self-consciously, I adjusted my hair in its loose plait, tucking a few stray strands behind my ear.

The cubicles were the only thing reflected behind me, not some wild-eyed dead queen. All was well. Nothing was hidden; all the doors were wide open, revealing nothing—well, except for the one farthest from the door. The darkest one.

I blinked.

Wait. Hadn't *all* the doors been closed a second ago?

The crying had started up again, no more than soft, occasional hiccups, as if whoever was there was now listening.

A brief rush of noise; low chatter and soft music as the bathroom door swung open with a bang and a couple of heavily made-up girls clattered past me in towering heels. Friday night evidently starting early.

"Aoife, for feck's sake—get ahold of yourself—we've all told you he's not worth it, now." The first girl kicked open the door to the end stall and half fell while the sobbing rose in volume, more dramatic than ever. The other girl turned to me with a wry smile. "Gobshites and booze—don't mix 'em, ey?"

Smiling back with relief, I made a hasty exit.

Seb was now the only one standing by the table, evidently waiting for me.

"Sorry," I muttered, unable to look him in the eye. "Is the taxi here already?"

He gave a dismissive nod.

"I guess you're staying, then?" he asked. "It's not too late—we could pick up your stuff from the house and then you could go from there? I mean, if I were you, I'd jump at the chance—"

I exhaled slowly and deliberately. I was *tired* of this already. Should I just do as he said? Make him happy? The vibe at the house was already tense and Laure hadn't even bloody shown up yet. Maybe we could chat once they all got back to London. And there was no guarantee Laure would even speak to me, let alone forgive me. As I'd expected she'd blocked my number immediately after the ball. Sure, I needed her on my side or I didn't stand a chance at my suspension hearing, but was getting back into Greyscott's *really* worth all this?

Yes.

Yes, of course it is.

On top of that, there was how hard Mum had saved to help me get over here in the first place. Flights weren't cheap. Anyway, going back would also mean accepting the charity of the Wrens, and I'd already done enough of that.

So I walked past him, deliberately nudging him out of my way.

"Fuck *off*, Seb," I muttered good-naturedly.

6

"SORRY WE'RE A bit late—we stopped at a pub on the way back and well, that was *wild*," said Saira as she heaved the shopping bags up onto the kitchen island.

"No worries," said Lottie, now dressed in paint-splattered dungarees. "Gave Eimer and me a chance to deal with the delightful mold issue downstairs. Hey, did you notice anyone behind you? Swear I heard a car pull up a second ago."

Down the hall, the front door slammed once again and a loud voice rang out through the house.

"What is *up*, bitches!"

"Ah, so Charlie's here, then," said Seb, attempting to shove multiple pizza boxes in the tiny freezer beneath the fridge.

I grinned at the sound of his voice.

Six-foot-plus and as willowy as a supermodel, with a bleach-blond buzz cut and a penchant for high-end fashion, Charlie looked coldly beautiful but was one of the warmest people I'd ever met. So much so, I sometimes felt as if we'd known each other all our lives. Except for the fact he lived in a multimillion-pound town house in Chelsea while my mum and I were squashed into a one-bed flat in Catford. Behind him stood Joss in low-slung tie-dyed joggers and an improbably small crop top, her bee-stung lips pursed in an unimpressed pout.

"Hey, guys. Weren't you two meant to come with Laure?" asked Lottie, her tone uncharacteristically cool.

Charlie shook his head. "I mean, yeah? I turned up at her house like a right prick but her housekeeper said she'd already left. Thought she'd be here, to be honest. Was ready to give her a piece of my mind."

I gave Charlie a bone-crushing hug. He'd been my single remaining lifeline to Greyscott's since the incident, and while he'd been sensibly reluctant to get drawn into any deep conversation about that night, his steady companionship had been more than enough. As for Joss—we *weren't* friends. She was one of the many at Greyscott's who would never accept me. To her credit, she'd always treated with me with outright hostility, alternating between entirely denying my existence or sweetly spraying poison in my direction. A position I'd always actually preferred to Laure's hot-and-cold mind-fuckery.

Lottie looked concerned. "That's *weird,* though. Why isn't she here yet if she left before you guys? I'm gonna give her another call in a bit. Hope she's not got on the wrong flight or anything."

"Stuck out in the wilds of Ireland without a phone signal. That would be a Halloween horror story," snorted Ollie.

"Guys, grab yourself a drink and make yourself comfortable," said Lottie, remembering herself. "Seb can show you where you're sleeping. Meg, give me a hand making dinner?"

I nodded gratefully, following her to the kitchen. Even before

I started at Greyscott's, I'd never had a friend like Lottie. Before I met her, I'd always found myself pushed to the shadowy peripheries of friend groups after an incident in Year 8 when I'd inadvertently almost made Juliette Gower swallow a tooth. *Anger issues,* the principal had said, grim-faced and drawn, as Mum and I sat nervously in his office. But Lottie hadn't known about that, didn't know about any of my flaws, so when I met her I found myself letting my guard down with dangerous haste. Still, it wasn't easy between us at first. I was overeager; like a puppy desperate to please, so keen for her to like me it made things awkward.

"Pasta?" mused Lottie. "*Nice* save. I mean, what kind of monster doesn't like pasta?"

She busied herself salting a huge pot of water on the stove then continued rummaging through the bags. "Bloody Saira and her raw diet. Where's the chicken nuggets and oven chips? Still, we can knock up a salad with some of this. Here—"

She passed me a knife and I began chopping up tomatoes, the two of us drifting into silence. Despite all her kindness since I arrived, there was still an unusually stilted atmosphere between us I was keen to break.

"Look—"

"Lottie—"

We started at the same time, then laughed, breaking the tension.

"I'm so glad you came," she said quietly, fixing me with her dark blue eyes. "I know it can't have been easy after—after everything. I mean, everyone thinks it's brave of you. And we *will* fix this, I promise. We'll convince Laure to have the school drop the hearing. We won't leave here until we do."

She reached over to squeeze my hand, and my stomach cramped with appreciation. Despite my fears about seeing Laure, I was pathetically grateful to be here. Grateful I'd been offered another chance at Lottie's insistence.

She had been the one to call me the morning after.

I'd tumbled out of my sweaty pit of a bed, mouth dry and head pounding, desperately scrabbling for my phone. I'd never forget that sour, heated rush of disappointment followed by crushing guilt when I saw her name.

The *wrong* twin.

Regardless, I'd appreciated it then, and I still did. She'd been the *only* one to get in contact in the direct aftermath. Even Charlie had waited over a week before replying to my messages. Besides those two, no one else had spoken to me since.

"Well, it's been great so far," I lied cheerfully. "I mean okay, Ollie's never been my biggest fan so whatever, but it's been amazing to see you and Saira and Charlie and—"

"And Seb?" Lottie prompted.

I swallowed.

"Of course, Seb. Of course."

I mean, it wasn't a *lie*.

Like so many at Greyscott's, I'd admired the glorious Sebastien Wren from afar, long before he even knew my name. Watched him confidently recite T. S. Eliot in English, earnestly pushing his dark glossy curls out of his face as he offered sensitive insights I had never even considered. I wasn't the type of girl to fawn over guys, but I'd found myself *staring*, chin in hand, twisting a lock of hair lazily around my finger, as he earnestly discussed Phlebas the Phoenician with Ms. Jacobi while everyone else checked their phones under desks.

Despite the fact I'd finally managed to blag my way into Lottie's group, he of course hadn't even known I'd existed until he'd found me that rainy October morning in Lottie's studio almost a month after the start of the school year, sitting on the floor, painstakingly painting sprays of baby's breath for my first end-of-term project.

"Oh—shit, sorry—didn't realize anyone was in here. Was looking for my bike actually—"

I'd stared at him, open-mouthed, all the confident and witty responses I'd planned in the event of an accidental run-in with him immediately fleeing my brain. While I knew he was Lottie's twin, I never expected to find him stood in the doorway to the studio, dressed in gray joggers and an old sweater, his hair still mussed from sleep. It had been odd to see that side of him, out of the formal Greyscott's uniform of blazer and tie, no longer wearing the dark-framed glasses that gave him his unattainable Clark Kent look. I'd blushed hideously, my face heating to volcanic levels.

"Wait, you're one of Lottie's friends, right?" he continued, when I remained silent. "What's with all the flowers? Are you like a florist or something? Didn't realize they offered vocational shit at Greyscott's?"

"They *don't*," I replied, half smiling. "No need, is there? Not when most of their cohort can rely on Daddy's contacts for an internship at *Vogue*. It's for my art class."

"Ohh, *now* I know who you are." He smirked. "You're Lottie's latest project."

I raised an eyebrow, unsure whether or not to be offended. "What's *that* supposed to mean?"

"Only that my sister loves to *help*."

With a dismissive shake of my head, I ignored him and carried on. It wasn't that I was shy so much as Sebastien was incredibly hard to talk to. Or so I'd thought at first.

At Greyscott's, he was one of the untouchables, him and his friends wandering the halls like Greek gods. I'd always viewed guys like that with disdain. Sure they weren't interested in girls like me, but that worked both ways. I mean, personally, I had no desire to date braying sports bores. But Seb, as the cliché always goes, was different. Quieter than the rest of his group—studious and less sporty. There was a clever, independent streak in him that I was drawn to; an elegance about him that set him apart from his slightly bullish companions. An appealing arrogance as he pushed our teachers, asking questions they always vowed to "find out for him."

Admittedly, though, the first thing I noticed about him was his face. It was delicate, and sharp, but with an open and pleasant warmth about it, a smile always playing about his lips. His eyes, a blue so dark they were almost black, always seeming to be observing sympathetically. There'd been a few rumors about him— inevitably centering around some callous breakups—but I figured losing someone like *him* was always going to hurt.

"Well," he said, ignoring me to focus on his reflection in the huge mirrors that lined the studio, primping his dark curls. "Good chat, um—wait, what *is* your name?"

"It's Megan," I said, continuing to focus on painting delicate white petals on the enormous canvas as if I wasn't bothered by his presence at all. "And you're Sebastien."

"I see my reputation precedes me," he preened.

"Your reputation as Lottie's *less* talented sibling, you mean."

He chuckled. "Can't argue with that. So what exactly *are* you doing?"

"It's my take on liminal spaces," I muttered, a little embarrassed. "Where the city meets the countryside—it's—complicated."

He smiled. "Liminal spaces, hey? I like it. Well—I've gotta be off, but maybe I'll catch you later, *Megan*."

Part of Lottie's generous nature was demonstrated by how she gave me a key to the converted garages her studio was housed in, whether she was around or not. She spent a lot of her weekends assisting at one of our art teacher's private galleries for an internship and I was hopelessly grateful for the space. There was zero chance of me getting anything done properly in my cramped box of a flat without making Mum and me high as kites on paint fumes, something Lottie seemed to understand without being obvious about it. The next weekend, when she had given me free rein of the studio again, I'd walked past Seb in the lounge, engrossed in some video game. I considered stopping and casually saying hi but was also worried he'd have forgotten who I was.

Ten minutes or so later came a polite rap at the door.

I wrenched it open with a flourish, ready to welcome Lottie, who said she'd be dropping by, but behind it stood Seb, holding a bunch of baby's breath wrapped in cheap supermarket cellophane, a yellow 30-percent-off sticker marring their beauty further. I flushed with an unwelcome heat at the sight of him, the shade deepening even further as he thrust the bouquet out toward me.

"There you go, Miss Florist."

He never appeared shy or awkward, and right then he looked inordinately pleased with himself.

"Er . . . thanks? What are they for?" I babbled like an idiot.

"I don't know—impulse buy down at the shop. I thought you might be here today and they reminded me of you," he said, his eyes flicking to my hair, which was currently tied up in a checkered rag. I dyed it pale silvery blond—*moth's wing*—according to the box. I was naturally blond anyway so it didn't cost the earth to maintain. Everyone knew the first rule of the art set was it was essential to look different.

"I—uh—I like your look."

"Oh . . . thank you?" I muttered again, trying to act like it was no big deal.

It was a *massive* deal.

Nobody had ever bought me flowers before. *Nobody*—not even a relation, let alone someone that looked like *Sebastien*.

"Although," I couldn't help adding, "common consensus is that gypsophila smell like cat pee."

"Told you they reminded me of you," he said with a grin. Then a forlorn look crossed his face. "But yeah . . . I picked up on that in the car, but by then it was too late to take them back. I kinda hoped you wouldn't notice until I was gone."

I smiled at him and he smiled back and, despite the smell, I kept the flowers in a pint glass in my bedroom and, when they started to wilt, pressed them tightly within the pages of a book.

7

AN HOUR LATER, we all sat down together to eat at the long trestle table in the kitchen. Lottie and I had beavered about making the vast stone room as welcoming as possible, jamming the ancient, yellowed candles and tea lights we'd scavenged from drawers into wine bottles and jars thick with dust. The enormous stove that dominated the room proved a reliable source of heat and once we'd arranged the mosaic-patterned bowls of pasta and salad on the table, it looked almost cozy.

Lottie sat at the head of the table, Seb at the other end, while the rest of us took up the sides. Ollie cracked open a bottle of cold pinot grigio, generously sloshing it into blue-tinged recycled glasses, whether we wanted it or not.

"Well, this is pretty fucking civilized, isn't it?" remarked Charlie, breaking off a hunk of garlic bread. "I'd imagined us all sitting cross-legged on the floor in front of a pile of pizza boxes."

"If only," lamented Seb, picking at his food

He was wrong, though. The food was delicious. The

caper-flecked ragú on the right side of spicy, the pasta silky and perfectly al dente. But I could barely stomach it. My eyes constantly flicking to the door in anticipation of Laure's arrival. Schrödinger's Laure. Both wanting her here, but also not.

"I'm so pleased we're all here," said Lottie warmly. "The old crew back together again."

Ollie drained his glass and followed my gaze to the door. "But we're not all here, though. Not yet."

"Yeah—anyone hear from Laure?" asked Charlie.

Lottie shook her head. "Nope, nada. She didn't pick up when I called earlier. I'm hoping she's just having issues with her phone. I mean, if she's on a plane we won't hear from her until she lands. There's still a couple of flights due in tonight. If I don't hear anything by tomorrow, I'll try and get hold of her mum—find out what's going on."

Ollie cast me a dark glance as he sloshed more wine into his glass.

"Maybe she caught wind of the *guest list* and changed her mind."

"*Ol,*" said Charlie, his tone a stern warning. "We're here to patch things up, not drag up the past."

"Oh, cool, so we're supposed to just act as if nothing happened?" Ollie's eyes fixed on me, cold and gray. "No offense, Meg, but after all that shit you pulled at the ball, I didn't expect to ever see you again. I mean, I don't think anyone did. Am I right? Seb?"

Seb said nothing at all, just exhaled loudly, doggedly twirling his fork in the pasta.

I'd have to face it at some point, might as well be now.

"Look, you may as well know, the reason I came, was to attempt to sort this all out. To *apologize* to Laure—to you all. Not to cause any more problems."

"Ah, got it. So to weasel your way back into Greyscott's?" said Joss, casually aiming her fork in my direction.

I blinked at her, heat immediately blasting through my veins. Okay, so she wasn't entirely wrong, but trust her to twist it into something unpleasant and dark.

"The *hell*, Joss?" said Lottie, shocked.

Joss only shrugged. "We all know she isn't really sorry. Look, Meg, if you want my opinion—"

"Which I don't," I interjected.

"—I think you're better off studying somewhere else anyway. Somewhere you actually fit in. Sorry, but that's the truth."

Had to love Joss for voicing the things most people thought but would never dare say. I forced myself to keep my tone cool.

"Somewhere I fit in? Wow. What's that supposed to mean? Why don't you enlighten us all on your views of class segregation?"

My heart thumped in my chest at the sound of my acid-coated words.

Joss wasn't one for backing down, though.

"You know *exactly* what I mean," she drawled. "Stop being so tedious. Somewhere you're not desperately trying to be something you're *not*. I mean, somewhere you can actually *afford*, for starters."

I could feel the anger already burning in my gut, threatening to spill over like a bucket of liquid fire. I clutched my hands into tight fists in my lap, nails digging into my palm in painful crescents, exhaling thinly.

Cool it. All you're doing is proving her right.

"And what is it you think I'm trying to be? Successful? Because I got a scholarship, Joss. And in actual fact, I think that means I belong at Greyscott's more than most people."

Joss gave a cold little laugh and helped herself to more salad.

"Yeah, you keep harping on about that, but we've all heard the rumors about how you *really* got it. And frankly that was based more on your mum's talents than your own."

Rage frothed, hot and vicious. A spiteful, childish little rumor started by Laure, or so I'd heard. Say whatever you wanted about me; I could take it. But *not* my mum.

"Keep going, Joss," I snapped, gesturing at her. "At least have the balls to say it. I mean, come on—what talents are you talking about?"

I got up, the chair screeching across the flagstones, adrenaline kicking through my veins. The sight of Joss's smug, cool composure making my heart thump harder than ever. She snorted. "Uh-oh, here we go. They say you can take the girl out of Catford—"

I felt a placating hand on my shoulder, gently pressuring me back to sit on my chair. Charlie. I cast a grateful look at him.

"*Guys,* let's keep it light, hey?" he said, his voice uncharacteristically stern. "Whatever happens, we're all here to get back on track, right? Like things used to be."

Ollie snorted. "Not much chance of that when Lottie's decided to invite the most contentious mix of people ever. Who else you got coming, Lots? Stalin? Your racist uncle?"

Lottie rolled her eyes. "Actually the only people *I* see causing an issue are you and Joss."

"Just wait till Laure gets here, then," muttered Joss ominously.

"Yeah, I wonder what's keeping her?" mused Saira.

And then the lights went out.

Nobody said anything for a couple of seconds, the only sounds our combined hastened breathing and the steady patter of the rain against the windows. Then Charlie gave a dramatic little shriek.

"Shit, you never told us this place was *haunted*, Lottie!"

There followed a few halfhearted chuckles.

Other than the soft glow of the fairy lights outside and the candles we'd placed on the table that were valiantly trying to illuminate the vast expanse of the kitchen, it was utterly dark. The familiar glow of streetlights we were all used to back in London was entirely absent here.

Seb was the first to locate the flashlight on his phone, lighting his face from below like a ghoulish kid at a campfire.

"Fuck's *sake*—this house is a train wreck," he griped. "We need to start the generator."

Lottie was already out of her seat. "Yeah, yeah—I'll get it. Won't be a minute. Meg, come with?"

Gratefully, I followed her out of the kitchen and into the damp chill of the night, down the side alley that led to the back of the house, the light from our phones bouncing crazily off the hedges. Drizzle welcomingly cooled my still-hot face.

"The electricity in this place is *screwed*. Always has been. Don't think anyone's touched the wiring since World War Two. We've a backup generator, thankfully. I forgot how often this used to happen."

Together we huddled into a rickety shed that housed a complicated-looking machine seemingly composed only of rusting wheels. I tried to ignore the monstrous amount of spiderwebs we'd walked through, brushing my skin with their eerie silk, focusing my flashlight solely on the generator.

"This thing's practically an antique. Luckily, Eimer said it was all oiled and checked before we arrived. Right—keep the flashlight on me a sec?"

I watched as Lottie began turning a crank with impressive strength, causing the wheels in the machine to slowly rotate, hissing viciously as they did.

"Good workout, huh?" she said cheerfully. "Give us a shout when you see the lights go back on."

I turned obediently to the house, its window still blank and black. The absence of light seemed threatening somehow, swallowing us all whole. I couldn't recall ever being someplace where the darkness wasn't mellowed by the warm orange glow of streetlights.

Movement caught my eye. I squinted hard into the night. A shadow was slinking silently toward us across the gravel, long and slim—someone coming out to lend us a hand, by the looks of things. Although I wasn't sure who, their features obscured by the larger shadow cast by the house. I hoped it wasn't Joss, primed for round two.

"You okay? Thought you needed a break from the table," Lottie said over the hissing of the machine, and I twisted around to face her. "Once Laure arrives and you guys make it up, things'll be *much* easier—promise. I am *so* sorry about Joss. But you know what she's like. The girl would start drama with the dead—"

A loud pattering drowned the end of her sentence as a sudden torrential downpour tumbled from the sky, scattering the gravel outside. Rain streamed down the walls of the shed, sending insects scuttling out of their hiding places. I turned back again to see where the person on the drive had got to, but there was no one there—they must have been forced back to the house.

Lottie stepped away from the generator, breathing hard, wiping her hands on her paint-splattered tee.

"Why haven't the lights come back on? The outage must have tripped the fuses. . . . Do me a favor, Meg. As you go into the kitchen there's a door on your immediate left that leads to the basement—so mind the stairs. The fuse box is just on the left as you open the door. Shout at Seb if you can't find it. I'll give this a couple more turns and see you back there."

Er, hell *no*.

Not the basement. You *never* went into the basement of old dark houses. Everyone knew that. But everyone was in the kitchen, it wasn't like I'd be alone—and if it was right at the top of the stairs . . .

Besides, what was I going to say? Sorry, Lottie, I'm too *scared*.

I *was* scared, though. Something about the house gave me the creeps. I knew it wasn't a rational fear, only a feeling—a bad vibe, as Laure would say. Funny how knowing all that didn't stop the creeping dread I had.

Pulling my sweater half over my head, I sprinted back through the downpour to the kitchen. Beyond, the room was now utterly dark.

Flashing my phone's light around, I started as I saw the dining table had been deserted, the candles all extinguished. Everyone must have retreated to the lounge where Ollie had laid a rather reckless fire before dinner. With a sigh, I focused my light on the wall beside me.

The door was smaller than average, a low oak beam above it, set directly into the wall. I twisted the handle and it swung inward with a loud crack, revealing a steep set of concrete stairs leading down into an inky pool of darkness. A cold, fetid draft that stank of stagnant water swam up from below. I shivered. However much I liked Lottie, nothing would have compelled me to go all the way down *there* in this darkness. Quickly, I located the fuse box on the wall, only a step or so down as she'd promised.

Opening it, I began flicking all the switches into the up position, hoping it would do the trick. After only a few seconds, I stopped.

There was a sound coming from below. From the depths of the cellar.

It was slow and squelching. That was the only way to describe it. The kind of sound you might make after walking through a deep muddy puddle in the wrong kind of shoes.

I froze, my hand poised on the fuse box, unable to do anything for a few moments other than listen. Was someone *down* there? I considered calling out, but frankly, if someone *was* down there I definitely didn't want to meet them. Not *now*. And not in the dark.

I flicked another switch, pausing again as I realized the sounds were becoming more distinct. Heavier and louder. As if someone was slowly trudging up the stairs. Wildly, I waved my phone in the direction of the noise. But it didn't help, the pale beam of the flashlight not powerful enough to illuminate the solid darkness at the bottom of the steps.

Were the others playing a joke? Was that where they all were? Trying to scare me?

"Who's there? Ollie?"

Outside the wind howled, forcing another waft of mildewed air up from the darkness. No, no one was hiding down there, not if they were sane. Swallowing, I focused on the fuses. Three more, then the lights would come on and I could get out of this place and chill by the fire and—

A hissing suddenly exploded in my ear. I gasped and stepped back, dropping my phone and missing my footing on the steep stairs, almost tumbling all the way down them before catching myself just in time. Flattening myself against the wall, I straightened up, heart pounding, my whole body shaking.

What the fuck *was that—*

My phone had come to rest a few steps below me. Too many steps down. Illuminating the gray concrete of the basement ceiling and several unpleasantly large cobwebs. And what *was* that—

It *looked* as though someone was climbing the bottom step. Their body hunched over like a scrawny spider, not walking but crawling on spindly limbs. Long dark hair trailed to the ground concealing their face: thin, overly long fingers scrabbled at the cement. The hissing was more distant now, emanating from them, I was sure of it. My brain might have been enthusiastically filling in the gaps, but I could just about make out their eyes—dark, *so* dark—glistening moistly like wet onyx.

Gasping, I flicked the final switches on the fuse box and behind me the kitchen erupted into golden light, pouring welcomely over the threshold to the basement and revealing nothing but a rusted-looking washing machine and a basket of old sheets spilling over onto the bottom step. Swallowing, I leaped down the steps to retrieve my phone, ran back, and slammed the door behind me.

"The hell were you doing in there?" said Charlie, grinning uneasily from where he sat at the table.

I blinked. Everyone was back, seated in the exact same places they had been before the lights went out, the candles dancing merrily away among the now-demolished bowls of pasta.

"Wait—did you guys just get back?"

"No," said Ollie with a hint of annoyance. "We've been sat here in the dark waiting for you to stop fumbling around in there like a psycho."

But the table had been empty. I'd *seen* it—hadn't I? I rubbed my sore eyes.

Behind me, Lottie burst through the kitchen door, making me jump several feet.

"All sorted," she said. But even she looked out of sorts. Her eyes overly bright; her voice too cheerful. I noticed her hands were shaking. "You all right, Meg? You look as if you've seen a ghost."

Was she deflecting? Was she as afraid as I was?

"Of course," I replied, embarrassed. "Of course I'm all right."

My dreams were troubled that night. I drifted in and out of sleep, a soft sibilant sound trickling into my consciousness like smoke.

I was back in the taxi on the way here, jolting over the curb again, stopping inches away from the wall, my head ricocheting off the seat.

But this time I wasn't alone. Someone sat beside me in the back. Someone I couldn't bring myself to look at. Someone sobbing, their head buried deep in their hands, and I thought how it was a very good thing their face was hidden because I didn't want to look at it—didn't want to see it at all—

The car was filled with a strong smell that made me want to gag. A bitter floral perfume. Flowers left to rot in a vase; their petals blackened, stems slimy.

I recalled the principal's words as I sat in her gleaming office, full of hope.

We want to see what you're capable of.

Cold bony hands pressed something into mine.

Exactly what *was* I capable of?

What's the worst thing you've ever done?

A sodden piece of paper. A postcard.

Come on in—the water's divine!

Breath against my ear, sweet and unpleasant, like wine-dark meat fallen behind a refrigerator and long forgotten. Their voice ragged; the words half formed, mumbled through rotting, flapping lips.

The image changed, flashing to familiar words inked on familiar skin in looping script.

Fear death by water.

I WOKE EARLY to a silent house. Knowing there wasn't much chance of getting back to sleep after that delightful little dream, I pulled on some sweats and headed downstairs.

In the kitchen, I put on a large pot of coffee, then threw on my coat, hoping a walk down to the lake would clear my head. I wasn't used to having all this space at my disposal. Back in London all we had was the local park—a tiny square of green in the middle of the estate that was always full of drug dealers and dog crap.

Outside, a damp mist fogged the air, but the sun was valiantly trying to peep through, lending the grounds a soft, ethereal quality.

It was beautiful..

Although, even in the gentle morning light, those drowned statues still looked unnerving: arms aloft, eyes staring blindly at the sky. I wandered as close as I dared, my feet leaving deep indents in the soggy turf of the bank.

Beyond the yellowed reeds, the water was brown and

dense—like thick gravy. I noticed a pale face reflected in the water, wavering in the breeze and positioned directly behind me. I jumped.

"They're not actually meant to be *in* the lake, y'know?"

Turning, I saw a girl around my own age with a pretty, open face and thick fair hair gathered in a loose braid. She chuckled.

"Sorry, didn't mean to scare ya. It's the rain—the ground is so saturated there's nowhere for it to go. Y'know, there's about two months of the year where it actually looks like a proper patio with the benches and statues and all. The rest of the time it's horror movie central." She paused and gave me a shy smile. "I'm Emma. I help out around here."

I remembered Lottie saying someone helped out at the house. I thought she'd said *Eimer*, though—perhaps Emma was an Anglicized version, a nickname locals handed out to tourists who they knew would butcher the real thing? I might not have known much about Ireland but I did know they had some tricky-to-pronounce names. Or Lottie might have just mispronounced it. For all her progressive virtues, I wouldn't put it past her.

Eimer or Emma aside, I'd expected her to be a good deal older. But judging by the number of fields I'd passed on the journey down, I supposed there wasn't much in the way of work around here.

I smiled back at her. "Meg. Good to meet you—thanks for all you've done so far." I followed her gaze down to the lake. "I think it looks kinda cool. Do you stay here too? At the house, I mean?"

Her sharp green eyes widened.

"No, no. I never would. Between you and me—this place is

meant to be *cursed* or whatever, but the Wrens get all uppity when you mention it. Y'know, there's a local legend that says a bean sí lives in the lake—supposedly a woman that starved in the famine."

Cursed? *Wow.* I tried hard not to smile. "A *what,* now?"

Emma grinned at my confusion. "A banshee—an Irish spirit found by water. She's meant to be seen sitting by the lake, combing her long hair, and crying and all that."

Crying?

I felt all the heat leave my skin in a chill rush. It must have been clear on my face as Emma gave me a teasing grin.

"Why, seen her, have ya?"

I laughed uneasily. "So what exactly *is* a banshee? Like, some kind of goth mermaid?"

She chuckled.

"Not far off, I suppose. Until she starts screaming, that is. Y'see, if you hear the shriek of a banshee, it means"—she looked around and lowered her voice, the smirk still on her face—"that someone is going to die."

That poor elderly lass—

Thirty years and not a hint of an accident

"Well, I guess there aren't many days that go by without someone in the world dying," I said, trying to keep the conversation light and failing.

Emma chuckled again. I decided I liked her.

"Someone in *earshot* of the screaming, I mean. Still, it's only a story—made up to scare little kids, y'know, keep 'em away from water." She waved a hand, dismissing the subject. "You're an early riser now?"

"Must have been all that screaming," I teased. "So how long have you worked for the Wrens?"

She gazed back out onto the lake. "My family have worked for them for years—ever since the place was a B and B, way back in the eighties. The lake was a bit of a draw, back then, y'know."

"So you must know Lottie and Seb pretty well?"

I took a longer look at her, at her thick blond hair and pretty smiling face and began wondering exactly *how* well.

"Yeah, you might say that. It was easier between us when we were younger and"—she wrinkled her nose a bit—"and our differences weren't *quite* so clear. We'd have a grand ole time in the summer as kids—what with the run of the place."

She turned, raising her head, to look in the direction of the strange tower I'd seen from the window, looming up out of the forest like a stone colossus.

"What *is* that place?" I wondered aloud.

"That there's the Wren Folly," she replied. "It was built around the same time as the house for rich people to fanny about in. No one goes there anymore, though. Not if they've any sense in them. My dad says it's structurally unsound—place is a death trap."

She paused as if wanting to say more but didn't. *No one goes there anymore?* Sounded a bit Scooby-Doo to me. I half smiled, unsure if she was having me on, but she wouldn't meet my eye.

"Anyway, I best get on—I've plenty to do. You all have an exciting evening planned, I hear. Hope yer banshee stays in the lake tonight."

I nodded, awkward now. She was only our age—it didn't seem right that she was spending her time doing a menial job like this instead of being at school. I felt a sudden solidarity with her. We weren't the same as these rich kids. We knew what it meant to work a crappy job all summer because we had to. But then again, here, and now, I *was* one of them. That was what I wanted, wasn't it? That was the whole reason I was here. To guarantee that version of me. Successful, a well-regarded private school on my résumé. No longer living in the crappiest parts of London.

With a wave, I headed back up to the house as Emma continued in the opposite direction, toward the gate. I paused as someone emerged from around the side of the house.

I groaned.

Jogging toward me at a steady speed was Seb, clad in sports shorts and a T-shirt despite the finely falling rain. As he got closer, I raised a hand coolly in greeting, immediately focusing my eyes back on the house. He wasn't the only one who could act like someone was invisible.

To my dismay he slowed his pace and stopped before me. There was something trucelike about his posture as he caught his breath, his chest rising and falling, sweat gathering at the neck of his tee, a gentle film of rain sheening his face. I looked away again. Honestly, it felt safer.

"Hey, it's really something out here, isn't it? On the rare occasions when it's not raining, that is."

Something was the word.

I could see the absolute beauty in it—it was impossible to deny. That serene wash of green on gray. But there was a harshness about the landscape too. Ditches deep with brambles and nettles. Yellowed clumps of reed that disguised the treacherous incline of the bank. Even the trees looked cruel. Spiny, deciduous giants. Seb turned and gestured down to the water, his posture easy and familiar, as if the last three months had never happened.

"Those statues used to scare the shit out of me when I came here as a kid. One night, I'd stayed up late watching *Dawn of the Dead*—y'know, the zombie one—and then literally pissed the bed imagining those statues were coming out of the lake to get me."

I laughed despite myself. "Yeah, I can see that, actually. And it's *cursed*, right?"

He snorted. "Not unless you're a local. Although I imagine it's filled with some proper weird shit. Google 'giant catfish'—in fact—*don't*, if you ever want to sleep again."

Why are you being so nice? I wanted to ask. *What's changed overnight?* He cleared his throat, still staring at the lake.

"You're looking really well," he said, deliberately waiting to continue until I looked at him, his eyes twinkling with what appeared to be genuine warmth. "And honestly, it *is* good to see you." He cleared his throat. "I'm—I'm sorry about yesterday—about dinner."

I stared at him, taken aback. "Why? You didn't say anything."

Which had actually surprised me, given how he'd acted earlier; I'd expected him to relish the opportunity to twist the knife. Now he looked away, his words hesitant.

"It's more of a general apology, I guess. I was pretty floored when you showed up. It—it caught me off guard. What I wanted to say—what I should have said—was that if you really did come to try and smooth things over, well, that's pretty fucking brave. I know stuff can't have been easy for you—since the ball."

Understatement of the century.

"So Laure should be arriving today, right?" I replied pointedly.

"Yeah—I mean—that's the plan. You're really going to apologize to her?"

Will you forgive me if I do? Will things go back to how they were?

The words almost tripped off my lips. Honestly, I wanted to *know* what he thought. After all, he hadn't said a word to me since that night. Not when I needed him to. Had that one impulsive move genuinely changed everything for him? Was that why my calls—at first tentative, quickly turning desperate—the next day went totally unanswered? Why my messages were all left on read, completely ignored?

Where was I even meant to start?

I shuttered my face. No. I couldn't and wouldn't go through it all again. I wouldn't let myself.

"Yeah, I mean of course I genuinely *am* sorry. I definitely intend to try and work things out. See if there's, uh, a way forward for us . . ."

He nodded toward the lake. "Nice. Well, I better get in there before I start thinking about catfish again and change my mind about this swim. Catch you later."

I watched for a few moments as he continued toward the lake in a languid, easy jog. His footsteps thundered over the small wooden jetty as he reached over his head and discarded his T-shirt in one easy motion. A glimpse of his skin, tan and glistening, before he executed a perfect dive, splitting the serenity of the water.

Face hot, I turned back to the house.

9

IN THE END, I decided to forgo the coffee and head back to my room for a nap. I'd slept so badly the night before that my head felt unpleasantly heavy, the threat of seeing Laure later hanging over me like a thunderous cloud.

When I woke sometime around noon, I headed up to the studio rather than downstairs. I wasn't feeling up to an audience that included Ollie, Seb, and Joss just yet. To my delight, the lights were on and Lottie was busily painting while Charlie sprawled in an armchair.

Other than a brief break for lunch with the group, we whiled away the rest of the swiftly darkening afternoon chatting over endless cups of tea. Except for the carefully chosen innocuous topics of conversation and my frequent nervous glances at the door, it *almost* felt like old times.

It was fully evening when Lottie finally put down her paintbrush. From the brief glimpses we'd gotten, her work seemed in the same dour vein as the painting I'd found the day before.

"Right, I reckon it's time to get ready. I'm going to start setting up downstairs—see you all in about an hour."

Nodding, we parted ways. I headed back to my room, only to be summoned to the door by a sharp rapping less than a minute later.

Saira stood behind the door, holding up a couple of dramatic-looking wigs, one sleek and straight in a bold shade of emerald, the other riotous curls of mint green. "I mean, you don't even need a wig with that hair—it's fab—but . . . do you want to get ready together?"

I smiled, opening the door wider to let her in. *"Please."*

I'd always gotten along with Saira. Quieter and more studious than the rest of Lottie's group, she could be a little intense, but as I'd got to know her better over the course of last year, I'd quickly discovered her deliciously wry sense of humor. She'd always seemed a little wary of getting too close to me, as if she never fully trusted me, but I was grateful she appeared to have relaxed a little. Maybe things were going to work out after all. I looked down at the enormous garment bag she carried over her arm.

"Whoa—what are you going to be?"

She grinned. "You'll see."

A few minutes later, the door burst open and in walked Charlie with an enormous silver case of makeup. "Right, which of you ladies wants to get *beat*?"

He looked, predictably, amazing. A glittering and glamorous bride of Dracula, with a river of sleek black hair that swooped right down to the floor. Smoky eyes and a glimmering red lip completed the look. He plonked himself down on the bed before us and opened the case. Endless tubes and compacts of high-end makeup sparkled like treasure within.

"What do you think of this place, then?" he asked. "Gotta admit, it's not exactly what I imagined when I pictured Lottie's ancestral home."

I didn't want to betray Lottie. I was grateful to be here, and under different circumstances it might have been fun. I mean, if the sun ever decided to shine it would be almost pleasant here— almost. But I couldn't lie.

"It's a little . . . creepy, isn't it?"

"Say that again," agreed Saira darkly, rummaging through the enormous case of cosmetics. "Not to mention damp . . . and cold . . . and gray and dusty. I don't think anyone's been near this place with a duster since it was *built*. It's setting my allergies right off."

Charlie snatched a rainbow-colored palette away from Saira. "You know the drill. Outfit *first*."

Saira rolled her eyes. Dutifully moving away from the makeup case, she lowered her voice, looking at us both with a cautious dark gaze.

"Hey, did you guys hear anything weird last night?"

"Yes!" Charlie said, leaning forward, his eyes shining. "Like someone crying? To be honest, I thought it was you, Meg."

"Me?"

"Yeah, after all that shit at dinner. Joss always goes in hard. And you've had a lot to deal with, this year. I notice more than I let on, girl. But if it wasn't you, then who? Lottie, maybe? Seb says she's been under a lot of strain lately."

Visions of the sobbing woman from last night's nightmare

crowded into my head. *Had* it all been a dream or had the crying been real, twisted into monstrous shapes by my sleeping mind? I recalled what Emma has said this morning with a shiver.

She's meant to be seen sitting by the lake, crying—

Immediately, I dismissed the thought. If anyone had been crying last night, it certainly wasn't a bloody mythical creature.

As Saira left to get changed in the adjoining bathroom, Charlie chatted away while effortlessly touching up his look, and my thoughts circled back to Lottie.

I remembered Ollie had said something similar about her at the pub, but for some reason, it just didn't ring true. I mean, what kind of strain could she possibly be under? Lottie had the perfect life. Immediately, guilt flushed through me. Lottie was my *friend*. Possibly my only friend right now, other than Charlie and maybe Saira, and if it *had* been her crying last night, then I needed to check she was okay, not roll my eyes. Since she'd been the only one to support me after the ball, it was the least I could do. I made a mental note to chat with her later.

Saira bustled back into the room in an enormous pink cake of a dress. An elaborate white pompadour sat upon her head, and around her neck was a livid red line of scarring, dark blood oozing from it and convincingly drenching her gown.

"Tah-*dah. Let them eat cake!* Do you love it?"

"Hell yes!" screamed Charlie. "That dress is *ridiculous*! Where'd you get it?"

Of course, none of this lot would be wearing mass-produced cheap polyester. *Oh* no. Thankfully, I'd put some proper thought into my outfit.

"My aunt's a costume designer at the Old Vic. Think this is actually from *Les Mis*. God, it's going to be annoying to move in all evening, though—the amount of . . . scaffolding underneath."

Grabbing my costume from its garment bag, I took Saira's place in the bathroom. I had worked hard on making my costume both scary and, admittedly, hot. I'd found a floor-length gown of emerald sequins on eBay for a few quid and had spent long evenings with Mum tailoring it into a formfitting ball gown, with a low-cut velvet bodice and a shimmering gold underskirt. To top it off, Charlie had sent me a link to a beautiful headdress that he'd sourced online, wound with delicate gold snakes. The perfect finishing touch.

"Shit, Meg," said Saira as I emerged. "You look *insanely* beautiful. Seb is going to quite literally fall in love."

"Err, that's definitely *not* the plan," I said quickly, sitting beside Charlie on the bed.

He set to work, packing on as much green glitter as my eyelids could take.

"*Yes*, Medusa!" exclaimed Charlie, sitting back to examine his work. "But make it sexy. Bring that Gorgon chic."

We collapsed onto the bed, snorting with laughter.

"So you're really going through with this?" said Charlie eventually. "You're really going to apologize?"

I said nothing for a moment.

Mum, despite all her dance-mom pushiness at getting me into Greyscott's in the first place, had *not* agreed with my plan to get back in the group's good graces. I'd had to share it with her, of course, after Lottie invited me. My evening shift at Wicked Chicken wasn't going to cover my flight costs.

"Jesus, Meg, why are you apologizing?" Mum had sniped. "That girl had it coming! And as for the rest of them, they *ditched* you—all of them, even your precious little Lottie—at the first sign of trouble. Pretended like you didn't even exist! That's *not* what friends do, Meg. That's *not* how they act."

I recalled her, outside on our tiny balcony, her dark eyes ringed raccoonlike with kohl as she flicked away the ash from the end of a cigarette, forever rolling her eyes at the injustices of the world. I'd wanted to agree with her then—but it felt so much like failure, crashing and burning in front of her, after all she'd done, after all I'd had to listen to—that I couldn't.

So instead I'd explained to Mum how it was all calculated on my part. Pushed home that whole it's-for-*my*-future-I-don't-actually-care-about-them angle. But deep down I'd always known the truth. Because what I really wanted was for them all to forget it had ever happened. To baptize me, to make me pure again, wash away my shame and make me one of them once more. I was irrevocably under the Wren twins' spell even after everything that had happened, and not even my own mother could do anything about it.

That first autumn term, it had taken another month or so of awkwardly trying to wedge myself into Lottie's circle—*we* got on great but I could tell her friends weren't so sure—before I received my first official social invite, outside of going round to her studio. Some new art zine was launching at a bar in Dalston—Lottie's parents were connected to the owner—and somewhat unsurprisingly she was being featured in its debut issue.

We'd all agreed to meet outside the venue, and of course I was unfashionably early. I peered through the window of the neon-signed bar. The crowd inside the venue was intimidatingly fashionable, their laughter spilling out onto the street. Self-consciously, I adjusted the loose black slip dress Lottie had loaned me (with the price tags still attached, hence the double take I did as I carefully unpinned them) and shook back my hair. I belonged here now; I was part of this crowd. The only thing that would give me away was myself—

"Heeeey, scholarship!"

I turned around. Laure was clacking down the street toward me in a pair of vertiginous designer heels and a tightly laced hot-pink minidress, a relieved smile on her face at the sight of me. I almost winced for her. This was so *not* the look for tonight. I'd already clocked everyone inside was in chunky trainers or Birkenstocks.

I smiled. "Well, you certainly brought the glam."

She looked me up and down, took in the oversized denim jacket I wore over my dress, then glanced through the bar window. Her face fell.

"God, it's too much, isn't it?" she lamented, gesturing to her outfit. "I mean, Lottie said it was a launch event with free champagne and stuff, so I—"

"Nah," I said quickly, "*individuality* is what's important. You've gotta do you, Laure."

She eyed me warily, tugging down her dress.

"Sorry to keep you waiting, guys," said Lottie breathlessly, appearing behind us with Saira and Charlie in tow, effortlessly casual in DMs and dungarees, her hair loose and unstyled. "The Uber driver couldn't find anywhere to stop."

"No Seb tonight?" asked Laure. She said it in an offhand way, but I picked up on the disappointment in her voice.

"Um, I think he and Ollie are dropping by later," said Lottie dismissively, as she craned her head through the busy bar window. "Right, come on then, girls, what are we waiting for?"

Inside, the bar was ear-splittingly loud. The lights were a low, heady shade of red and copies of *Pulse,* the art zine Lottie was featured in, had been fanned out on every available surface of the room. We trailed Lottie, pausing behind her awkwardly as she air-kissed various acquaintances, to the bar, where we sensibly ordered glasses of sparkling water and lime.

As expected, Lottie immediately began networking with various journalists and photographers like a seasoned pro while Saira excused herself to have another one of her long, terse phone calls with Ollie. Laure was deep in conversation with some older guy at the bar, so Charlie and I wandered over to an empty table and sat down. I flipped through a copy of the magazine, idly wondering whether everyone featured inside was as well-connected as Lottie.

"All right, Charles."

I looked up. Joss, of course. I'd met her a couple times now—she was in Lottie's friend group as well, after all—but she hadn't yet warmed to me the way the others had begun to. Now it seemed she was studiously ignoring me as ever. Thankfully she bypassed our table and headed to the bar.

"What *is* her problem?" I breathed.

Charlie laughed. "Joss is all right. She doesn't look it, but she's genuinely the most insecure person ever. You guys have more in common than you think, y'know. She's been a scholarship baby since I've known her—which is forever. Only never bring it up in front of her—she'll literally kill you."

An hour or so later, after several awkward conversations with strangers who only seemed interested in what school I was from, the bar was packed solid and the DJ filled the small room with pounding bass. Stifling a yawn, I glanced around, wondering if it would be okay with Lottie if I left yet.

Then I caught sight of Laure, slumped on a stool at the bar, a tall glass of what I sincerely hoped was only Diet Coke in front of her. Beside her, the same older man who sequestered her earlier now appeared to be talking *at* her rather than to her, his gaze focused on her dress in a hungry way I didn't like.

Reluctantly, I made my way over.

"Hey, Laure, everything okay?" I forced myself to say cheerfully. I liked Laure but she could be oddly snappy sometimes. The guy beside her was in his midthirties at a guess, bleary-eyed and weaselly. He looked me up and down and, evidently not liking what he saw, glared at me. Laure barely lifted her head, just gave me a defeated side-eye.

"Excuse me, love, your friend and I were in the middle of a conversation," he said with a patronizing little chuckle, nudging closer to Laure. She sat up, edging slightly farther away from him.

"Yeah, we're maybe gonna head somewhere else," she agreed, shaking back her hair, and looking at me defiantly. "Not sure if this is my kind of crowd, y'know?"

"I *really* don't think that's a good idea," I said firmly, now wedging myself between them and immediately taking in the strong smell of liquor and Laure's chaotically smudged eyeliner.

But the guy wasn't ready to give up yet. He gave an exasperated little laugh.

"Listen, I don't know what your problem is, but you can't just interrupt like that. Your friend and I were about to go and get better acquainted, so if you don't *mind*—"

I ignored him and passed Laure my glass of water. "Here— drink this. I think you need it." I lowered my voice, remembering something she'd said earlier and the hope in her eyes as she'd said it. "Laure—what are doing with this loser? Isn't Seb coming here in a bit? You don't want him seeing you like this. Come on, let's go sort you out in the bathroom."

At the mention of Seb, Laure seemed to come to her senses, offering me a weak smile and staggering up from the barstool. "Oh yeah, shit, I forgot." She turned to the weasel-faced guy. "Um, thanks for the drink and all, but . . . but I think you've got the wrong idea."

His face hardened immediately. "Yeah, well if you come in here dressed like a little slut, don't be surprised when you're treated like one," he sneered above the music, causing everyone standing nearby to look.

The way Laure's face crumpled was painful to watch. Incensed, I whirled around, that dark fire within me immediately let loose. "Oh really? Well, here's some advice for you too. If you're going to chat up minors," I snapped, impulsively pouring Laure's untouched drink into his lap, "don't be surprised when you end up on some kind of register, *pervert!*"

And of course at that exact moment, the music snapped off in preparation for the magazine founder's speech and everyone's eyes alighted on me.

"You *know* the boys will have put zero effort into their costumes," commiserated Saira as we all clattered down the stairs.

I sucked in a breath as we entered the lounge. Lottie had an artist's eye for decor. Silken cobwebs were festooned about the beams of the low ceiling, while tea lights twinkled away merrily in orange glass. On the large antique sideboard, a myriad of candles wept wax over vintage green-glass bottles labeled POISON. Ominous cello music drifted from ancient speakers contending with the storm outside, which rattled the sash windows with a rhythmic regularity. Stacked artfully around the fireplace were an array of jack-o'-lanterns, their faces carved into unpleasant rictus grins.

"All that's missing is a couple of Lottie's creepy-ass paintings," murmured Charlie with a smirk.

Ollie was in the kitchen, troubling the bowls of crisps, a can of lager in his hand already. He was dressed as a clown in extremely flammable-looking polyester and a cheap red wig. As we entered the room, he gave a slow clap.

"Bravo, ladies, *bravo*."

"Wow, I've never seen a costume so fitting," I innocently remarked as I strode past him to the fridge for a can of Diet Coke.

Ollie glowered at me; his thick white face paint cracked under the low lights.

"Same. Snaky bitch."

"Medusa was a *victim*, actually—raped by Poseidon and then punished by Athena just because it happened in her temple," I replied smartly, slamming the fridge door.

Joss was lounging on the sofa in the main room, tapping at her phone. She was dressed as a nurse in a tiny white PVC dress and red PVC stockings, a cursory bit of blood dripping from her lip. She looked undeniably amazing.

"Fucking *hell*, Joss," muttered Ollie appreciatively. I winced for Saira, entering the room directly behind me.

"We're not *American*," I remarked cattily. "Halloween costumes are meant to be *scary*."

Joss rolled her eyes. "Bitch, sit here, put a tray of medical equipment in front of me and I'll show you just how scary I can be."

Moments later, Seb dashed into the room, slashing a very realistic sword dangerously close to Ollie's face.

"Yield, foul fiend."

He was dressed as a highwayman, complete with tricorn hat and immensely sexy frock coat. I cursed myself for the images that flashed before my eyes. I would need to be *very* careful tonight and keep well away from any booze.

"What's Seb's excuse, then?" drawled Joss, not even looking up from her phone.

We all quieted as Lottie walked in behind him. I stifled a gasp, an odd flash of recognition jolting through me.

She looked *terrifying*.

Her trademark bouncy curls had been replaced by a drab, wet-look wig that trailed to the ground. Her face was bone pale and gaunt, her skin somehow green-tinged, her eyes circled with pink, as if she'd been crying for years, crystal tears rolling down her face.

"Some of my finest work to date, I think," murmured Charlie appreciatively.

"I mean, yeah, Lottie, it's . . . disturbing," remarked Joss thoughtfully. "But what in the actual *fuck* are you meant to be?"

"I was going for the local angle," replied Lottie, her smile incongruous on such a sinister face. "I'm a banshee."

10

"INTERESTING CHOICE," I managed, unable to tear my eyes away from her. She looked so *somber*. So entirely different from how she normally did—cheerful and irreverent—a wide smile always ready on her lips. "I mean, I heard earlier this place is meant to have a resident banshee."

Lottie stared at me, the black lenses that covered most of her eyes giving her a terrifying blank look. Her tone was unusually sharp.

"Oh? What exactly did you hear?"

I shrugged. "Just that there's some old local legend about a banshee in the lake out there. You look good, though—admittedly terrifying, but good."

But she didn't. She looked like my *nightmares*.

Lottie grinned, revealing disconcerting yellow pointed teeth. Just prosthetics and makeup, that was all.

"Right—everyone, over here. Let's take a snap for the Gram."

After Lottie had directed us through several carefully curated photos, Seb cornered me in the kitchen while I busied myself re-filling bowls of snacks.

"You look . . . you look nice. I mean, kinda *disturbing*—but nice. Medusa, right?"

After two hours of prep I had better look at least *nice*. I nodded blithely, deliberately not returning the compliment and tucking a length of bright green wig behind my ear. It worked—it usually did. He continued. "Um, do you want to go somewhere and talk? Properly? I hate that it's—it's so awkward between us right now. And I know it's mostly my fault, but if we can sort this out—well, don't you want that? . . . I want that."

A bright flare of hope flashed within me, causing an almost physical pain. Every sensible part of me was screaming out a warning, but I couldn't ignore my stupid heart. I met his eyes, dark behind the mask, and allowed him the slightest of smiles.

"Uh, sure. Let's just get these stupid games out of the way first, yeah? Lottie's been planning all this for ages—you know she'll be properly pissed if we both disappear now."

As if on cue, we heard Lottie calling our names. Raising an eyebrow, Seb and I returned to the lounge.

An hour of apple-bobbing and blindfolded turnip-carving later (during which Ollie very nearly lost a finger), the party atmosphere had already begun to wane. Laure's absence hung large over the house like a shadow. Seb sat sequestered in a dark corner of the lounge, our planned chat apparently forgotten, tapping away at his phone, grim-faced, while around me, Saira began clearing away some of the detritus.

Joss tottered back into the room holding some kind of board in her hand.

"Hey, guys—guess what Ols and I found!" she called far too loudly.

Saira looked over at me and rolled her eyes. "I'm really hoping that's a cheese board."

"Better than that—it's a fucking *Ouija* board!" Joss chirped. "Your parents have got some *weird* shit in their cupboards, Lots. Perfect for tonight, though, right? Who's in?"

She plonked the board on the glass-topped table beside the dying fire and brushed her hair out of her eyes. "Come *on*!" She demanded. "It's *Halloween*. Perfect time to call up some spirits."

"Nice find," said Lottie, thin-lipped.

"I reckon some of us have had too much contact with spirits already," said Charlie beside me, a grin on his face.

Minutes later, we were all huddled around the low coffee table before the fire. The Ouija board was a dusty old relic from the seventies made from a large slab of cheap plywood, the letters of the alphabet as well as *yes* and *no* and numerals zero to nine all spelled out in gaudy gilt lettering.

"Everyone needs to put their finger on the mouse and invoke the ghosts," whispered an evidently drunk Seb in a foreboding voice.

"It's called a *planchette*, you lemon," corrected Charlie, giving him a playful nudge.

"Honestly—I'm not keen on this," admitted Saira. "I don't think you should mess with this kind of shit. It disturbs the natural order of the universe and—"

"Then don't do it," interrupted Ollie unkindly. "Sit out and watch again. Y'know, take your general attitude to life."

I itched to say something in her defense, but I knew Saira wouldn't thank me for it. I realized Lottie had been very quiet for the last hour. Maybe she was more worried about Laure than she let on. At once, I remembered Charlie's comments—how Lottie had been under strain lately. I hoped it wasn't because of me, the tension I'd caused the group. Once again, I resolved to catch up with her later—alone.

"All right, let's go!" Joss cleared her throat. "Tell me, what spirits are present in this house tonight?" she asked, putting on a dramatically reedy voice.

We all watched, snorting, as the planchette clunkily moved between the letters.

"*V-O-D-K—Guys!* Are you taking this seriously, or what?" shouted Joss.

Lottie tutted irritably. "Yes. Don't anyone *actually* move it— you're meant to just relax your hand and place a finger on top. It'll move all on its own—*especially* tonight, of all nights." She looked around the table, catching the eye of each and every one of us. I gave a thin shiver. "Spirits of Samhain, make yourselves known. Tonight when the barrier between our world and yours is at its thinnest, let us know of your presence."

Ollie stifled a snort, but the room around us seemed to darken somehow, the fire burning lower, the candles dimming as Lottie took charge. Her manner was entirely serious, sharp, and sober, the greasy gray strands of her wig dancing over the board, her voice hypnotic and low.

"I know of a spirit, lost here when the house was first built, and tonight I summon her. The woman who died in Wren Lake during the famine, drowning both herself and her child. Whose spirit now haunts the lake beyond the house."

I caught Charlie's eye and raised a brow.

"Shit, that's dark," he murmured amiably. "Made up or not."

"Spirit, we summon you here tonight," Lottie continued, oblivious. "We wish to make amends."

"Typical Lottie," I whispered back. "Social justice for everyone—including ghosts."

"Can you hear us? Will you accept our apology? Can we ever make things right?"

Across from me, Seb cleared his throat, shifting uncomfortably.

Rain began to hammer at the windows, making me jump. The planchette swung easily over the board, with far less resistance than before, pointing to the word *NO*.

"Fair enough," muttered Charlie, but this time, the light-heartedness of his tone was absent.

Lottie seemed wrong-footed by this. Perhaps someone had hijacked her planned response—Ollie, probably—it wouldn't surprise me. Still, she persisted.

"Spirit—tell us—where are you? Where do you . . . reside?"

The planchette swung again; smooth and regular, dancing between letters.

ILIVEINTHEWEEDS

"In the *weeds*?" muttered Joss. "Well, what the fuck does that mean?"

An image of the lake flashed before my eyes, green-choked and dark.

"The housekeeper told me the lake is haunted, earlier," I said quietly. "It kind of makes sense?"

"Eimer also avoids walking through circles of mushroom because she thinks the Fae will spirit her away if steps in them,"

Seb said irritably, then nodded at me. "You ask it something now."

"All right." I cleared my throat. "So, um, spirit—what are you? I mean, what kind of spirit are you?"

"Creature from the black lagoon, by the sounds of it," said Ollie, who was immediately shushed as the planchette began to swing easily about the board again, with increasing speed.

"H-A-R-B-I-N-G-E-Q"

"Harbin-Geq?" snorted Ollie. "The fuck is that—"

"Sssh," hissed Saira, all her previous concerns apparently forgotten as she stared intently at the board. "*Harbinger.* Obviously, it meant to say harbinger."

"*Okay,* but my question remains—"

"Shut *up,* Ollie," snapped Lottie, whirling toward him with uncharacteristic venom. She looked unnerving in the flickering light of the fire, the makeup making her eyes look sore and red, her lank wig swinging in front of her face. Rain continued to spatter hard against the windows, completely drowning out the weak crackle of the fire. Some of the candles had burnt so low they'd winked out, filling the air with smoke.

"Now you, Saira. A question each. That's the deal."

Saira shifted beside me. "Deal? I don't know if I want—"

"God's sake, just *ask* a question, Si, it's not *real,*" droned Ollie, rolling his eyes.

"Fine—um—so why are you here . . . spirit?"

There was no movement of the planchette for a few moments. Then it began to move, more determinedly than ever, shifting from letter to letter with great speed.

YOURWYCKEDHISTORY

"The hell?" laughed Saira awkwardly. "What's that meant to mean?"

"Your wicked history," murmured Seb. "I . . . I don't know." He caught my eye. Something about the words made me shudder. Was someone here playing games? Trying to make me feel worse than I already did?

I glanced over at Lottie. She was smiling now. An awful kind of smile I'd never seen before, fevered, almost drooling. Her breath was fast.

"Who's next? Who's *next*? Charlie? Quick, it's here—while it's here."

Charlie's calm and amused voice went some way toward settling my jangling nerves. "All right, cool it. Spirit, how about you tell us all the lottery numbers for tomorrow? I quite fancy Christmas in Barbados and—"

"Charlie!"

Charlie pursed his lips and frowned.

"Jesus, Lottie, *chill*. Thought we were meant to be having fun? Fine, spirit, do you mean us any harm? Please tell us you're a nice spirit."

Ollie stifled another snort. But again, the planchette immediately began to move. I had to hand it to whoever was moving it—and for some reason I was sure it was Lottie—they could think on their feet.

FEARDEATHBYWATER

"The hell?" said Charlie, stifling a yawn. "Not exactly answering my question there, spirit."

"It's from T. S. Eliot," said Seb dryly, catching Lottie's eye. "How convenient."

"Your turn," she shot back coldly.

Seb gave a loud dramatic sigh. "Okay, great. So, spirit, how about you tell us your *name.*"

"Saira, you are *totally* moving that—"

"Fuck *off*, Ollie. I'm not doing anything, I swear—"

We all watched as the planchette glided over the board, pausing clearly at five separate letters.

LAURE

There was silence for the longest moment. No doubt all of us spelling the letters out in our head, checking they were right.

It was Seb who broke it.

"Wait—what the actual hell? That's too far. I mean, that *isn't* funny. Who the fuck thinks *that's* funny?"

His eyes immediately alighted on me and I felt the fury spark white-hot in my veins. Lighting the kindling that had been left smoldering by him *ignoring* me for most of the night.

"What? It wasn't me—"

"Did I *say* it was?" he threw back, his tone cold.

"Don't fucking look directly at me when you say shit like that, then—"

Charlie's cool hand was immediately at my back. "Hey—calm down. He didn't say it was you—"

"Oh, stop making excuses for her," drawled Joss. "We all know she's off her head. I just *love* how we've spent the last day or so conveniently forgetting about what happened at the ball when she—"

I stood up so quickly my chair toppled over, hitting the stone floor with a loud clang. I hurled the planchette over her head where it smashed against the wall. Saira flinched.

"When I *what*? Why don't you just keep your dumb mouth *shut*, Joss? You don't know anything. And you certainly don't know anything about me!"

That familiar Klaxon was going off in my head, louder than ever. *Stop it, Meg. Too far. Calm* down.

A bright flash of fear sparked in her eyes and I whirled round to find the door, immediately ashamed, my face burning. I needed to get away from her—away from Seb—from *all* of them. Out of the stuffy room, my eyes burning with the stench of woodsmoke and sticky liquor. It had been a mistake to come here. Everyone clearly wanted to forget all about what had happened—forget about me—and move on—so why was I here? Why was I the one hell-bent on bringing it all up? Why was I doing this to myself? The best thing I could do was *leave*. Leave before Laure got here. Leave and forget them *all*.

Barreling toward the kitchen door, I wrenched it open and collided into something solid and damp.

Shocked, I staggered back a few steps, almost tumbling down onto the cold kitchen tiles.

A ghost stood in the doorway, dressed in an old-fashioned high-necked gown of white silk. A dress I'd seen a million years ago. A dress that had billowed out like a jellyfish as it plunged into freezing dark waters, like that line from *Hamlet:*

Her clothes spread wide; and, mermaid-like, awhile they bore her up.

Her face was wide and moon-white, her eyes a bright, unnatural silver. Weeds were threaded through her pale red hair that clung damply to her skull. Behind me, I heard a stifled gasp.

"Laure?"

INSTEAD OF BEING reviled after my outburst at the launch party as I'd feared, I actually ended up drawn more closely to the center of Lottie's gravity. Moments after my gaffe, I'd escaped, red-faced and heart pounding, to the restrooms, where a grateful Laure had allowed me to fix her makeup.

"I *always* get it wrong," she muttered resentfully as I carefully reapplied her eyeliner. "It's like—sometimes I swear Lottie deliberately misleads me. I mean, she told me to wear something glam tonight, so I did and now I look like an absolute—"

She was nervous, I realized. She didn't quite fit in here either. In a way, we were kindred spirits tonight. I caught her eye in the mirror and smiled.

"You look objectively amazing, Laure," I said honestly, "and anyone who thinks otherwise is a pretentious twat."

"So . . . literally everyone here, then," said Laure, that mischievous defiance back in her eyes.

"Exactly," I replied.

At that moment the bathroom door bounced open, crashing against the wall, the pounding music pouring in, the speeches now done with.

"Fucking *hell,* Meg!" Lottie bounded in, a gigantic grin on her face. "You know the guy you threw the drink over was the financial backer of this whole magazine, right?"

"Er, no, actually," I said, instantly nauseous but also thrown off by Lottie's expression of glee.

"And you literally called him a pervert in front of everyone! We are in *awe*! Oh my God, you should have seen how quickly he left with his tail between his legs. . . ."

"I mean, isn't that bad—that he left?" I said, still confused.

Lottie only shrugged. "Bad for *him*—if he pulls out I'm sure Daddy can find someone else. Fact is, you're an actual legend, Meg. Come and have a little glass of fizz with us—Seb and Ollie have just got here."

She cast a sympathetic look down at Laure. "And are you okay, babe? You seem a little . . . overserved."

Laure tossed her silky hair back as she admired her reflection in the mirror.

"Never better."

The rest of the evening flashed past in a series of joyous snapshots as my status as one of Lottie's friends became fully cemented. Laure's hand in mine as we headed back out to the party. Watching even Ollie laugh in admiration as Lottie recounted the whole story. Saira's disbelieving head shake as I recited what the guy had been saying, embellishing it only slightly. And Seb—his glittering dark eyes meeting mine before Laure dragged him away to some dark corner—that inscrutable smile upon his face.

"Fucking ace costume, Laure," drawled Ollie, pouring her a drink as we stood in the kitchen forming a crescent around her, everyone immediately in her thrall as usual. "For a second there I thought you were *actually* dead."

Laure accepted the drink, placing it beside her on the counter. "I know, right? Bloody rain certainly helped my look. Bastard taxi driver wouldn't come down the drive—said it was too waterlogged—so I had to lug my case through the storm. Anyway, here I am! The party has *officially* started."

In the warm orange light of the kitchen, the close realities of Laure were a relief to see: The patches where her pale makeup had been washed off by the rain and her freckles showed through. Her ever-present Cartier bangles chiming against her wrist, the expensive handbag strapped across her shoulder by a chain.

Still, the tension in the room was soupy and unpleasant. I hadn't missed the occasional little glances people were giving me, as if they expected me to prostrate myself before her on the cold stone floor, tearfully begging for her forgiveness the moment she arrived. I mean, yes, of course I regretted what happened, but it's not as if I wasn't provoked—

I rubbed my eyes. *No.* I wasn't that person anymore. I *wasn't,* and this was my one and only chance to prove it.

As if reading my mind, Laure directed her laser-sharp gaze to me.

"Nice to see you here, Meg," she said icily, clearly not meaning it at all. "Although, if I'm honest, I wasn't expecting to see you—ever—actually. Guess it's clear where some people's loyalties lie. . . ."

"Good timing, Laure," said Joss with a cruel smirk. "Meg's only just finished her latest tantrum."

Lottie only rolled her eyes in my defense and headed back into the lounge trailed by Saira. Ollie and Joss both stared at me expectantly. Despite preparing for this moment, despite knowing exactly what Laure would be like, I still had no idea what to say. No idea what order the words should come and how they should sound.

In the end, it was Charlie who broke the silence.

"Well, I'm going out for a smoke. Meg—wanna come?"

We stood beneath the shelter of the porch awning, leaning against the damp stone wall of the house. My head was swimming unpleasantly.

"Fuck, Meg, you really are a live one. I forget sometimes."

A lighter flared in the darkness. Hot tears of shame sprang into my eyes. I'd wanted to show them all that I wasn't that person anymore, but already I was living up to everyone's worst expectations. Disguising my sob as a cough, I leaned into Charlie as he flung a fragrant arm around me.

"I know, I *know*," I said. "And I know I shouldn't let Joss get to me. Plus Seb's such a *prick* sometimes. I didn't spell out her stupid name. I mean, why would I? And then the moment she shows up I'm expected to kneel before her and kiss the ring?"

Charlie shrugged. "Babe, I think people just want to lose the tense vibe, y'know? And Joss is never going to be your greatest fan—you're too similar—so you've gotta learn to just ignore her."

I took a deep, shuddery breath. He was right. And I *was* different now, wasn't I?

"Don't you think Seb seems a little on edge tonight, though?" Charlie continued thoughtfully. "I know he had some kind of history with Laure. I don't think you're the only one not exactly overjoyed she's here."

The comment, spoken aloud, burnt the air, the words turning immediately to ashes. I didn't expect it to hurt so much.

I chose my words carefully. "Did he, though? I thought it was just rumors—like, wishful thinking on her part."

Charlie shrugged. "Seems it depends on who you ask. Look, it'll all blow over tomorrow. Everyone's had one drink too many and is being a dick. Fifty quid says it was Ollie or Joss who spelled that out, what with their sparkling sense of humor."

"But that *costume*—I mean, did you notice her dress? It's exactly the same one she wore at the summer ball. Same hairstyle—same *everything*. She's clearly come here trying to make some kind of a fucked-up point—"

Charlie nodded sagely. "But that's *Laure*. She lives for the drama. We know this. All we can do is rise above it. Like a heavenly phoenix." He turned to me, dark eyes meeting mine. "You *know* you need to apologize—you can keep your reasons to yourself—but it does need to happen."

He was right. It wasn't just about proving I had changed. Callous as it sounded, I had to think of my future too. If I had any chance of getting back to Greyscott's, of getting my friends back—my *life* back properly, then I needed Laure on my side. I needed her to forgive me at the hearing, to not press charges. I also knew I needed her to not think I had any interest in Seb.

Fucking Seb.

And I *was* sorry. Genuinely. For her, for what I'd done to her, what I'd risked happening. I'd never intended to hurt her, let *alone* endanger her life. It had been one stupid, reckless, impulsive second.

But admittedly yes, I was also sorry for myself, for everything I'd ruined that night. Most of all I was ashamed that yet again, I'd let my anger take charge. That deep down I was still *that* person, however much I tried to distance myself from my past. That I'd started this chain of events that had led to my ostracization and I had no one to blame but myself.

I took a deep gulping breath. It was time to force my anger and my anxiety aside and do the right thing.

The night of the ball had been one of broken promises.

The grounds of Greyscott's looked magnificent. As usual, no expense had been spared for the end-of-year ball; this year's theme "A Midsummer Night's Dream." The crowning of head boy and head girl—something even my last school, a failing secondary, had considered an archaic practice—centered on Oberon and Titania. Lottie of course had protested noisily against the whole thing, labeling it an outdated, anti-LGBTQ+ popularity contest—despite currently *being* head girl.

Fairy lights glittered like stars, strung up along the neat box hedges and Italian cypress trees that lined the lawns, while thousands of glowing tea lights floated in the river along the edge of the grounds. Trestle tables of expensively curated "faerie food" from luxury caterers had been set up along the walls of the building while students wafted about in diaphanous silk and satin dresses; their hair accessorized with custom-made circlets and tiaras, fairy wings studded with pearls and diamanté.

I'd caught a glimpse of Sebastien as I'd entered. He was on the social board, of course, and was busy directing staff about in the jokey I'm-just-like-you-man way he had. His hair was messier than usual, his curls appealingly left to do their thing, and he wore a blazer of midnight-blue velvet that matched his eyes.

I forced my gaze away. It was too easy to stare.

I'd been pleased with the theme—it had been an easy one to dress up for on the cheap. Mum and I had made my dress from yards of black lace we'd bought at the market and stitched it with plastic pearls to resemble constellations. All right, so it wasn't a genuine McQueen or Alaïa, but under these lights it would be hard to tell.

"You look like some dark goddess," Seb had whispered in my ear as he took my ticket, his hand brushing mine a second too long. "It's perfect for you. I love it."

I could only stare at him, the casual collected words I had held for him in my mouth scattering over the ground.

He'd messaged me earlier, asking me to meet him at nine by the gate to Greyscott's Copse. I'd stared at the screen for ages, wondering about the intent behind the words. And I was fairly certain I'd guessed right. Seb rarely messaged, instead preferring to just show up. At the studio. At the bike shed after I'd finished tutoring. He showed up outside my work the other night.

Anywhere he thought I'd be alone.

I fished my phone out of the pocket I'd sewn into my dress and read the message again, checking it was real and that the words weren't going to fly from the screen. I was a ball of tightly wound anxiety tonight. Seb was the strongest contender for Oberon, of course. He had everything going for him, not least his grades. Would it mean something if he and Laure were crowned together? She was a good all-rounder, and it could hardly be Lottie again. The idea of me being crowned was absolutely laughable. This wasn't like those ridiculous teen shows on Netflix where the geeky poor girl somehow always rose to attain the rank of homecoming queen or whatever. I *saw* the pitying looks the professors gave me. People with backgrounds like mine were never fully accepted at Greyscott's. No, *that* would be one fairy tale ending too far.

Cut to later, when the night was quiet and the lights had slowly started to wink out. At this point, I could only ever remember snapshots, increasingly blurred around the edges as time went on. But they would replay again and again in my head, all the same.

As she fell in, her silken gown slipping between my fingers, I'd expected more noise. Screams—an enormous splash—distant sirens—*something*. But it had been ominously quiet. She'd slipped in without a word, the dark waters immediately covering her head as if she'd never been there at all. Then she resurfaced, and for one frozen moment, she looked beautiful, her pale skin lit up by the candles still floating in the water, her red hair drifting around her like spun gold.

I'd wished, for an insane second, I could paint her.

The very image of Millais's *Ophelia*.

We want to see what you're capable of.

The principal's words when I started at Greyscott's. But not *this*. She could never have meant this.

And then the screaming started.

I was never sure if it was her or me or both of us.

Moments later, a strong hand clamped around my wrist and dragged me away.

Back in the house I could feel the frazzled energy of a party that had clearly run its course. Ollie was comatose on the sofa in the lounge, his bright red clown wig slid over his eyes, mouth hanging open and snoring loudly, while Charlie and Lottie began expertly balancing things on top of him—a can of Coke, an empty tube of Pringles, several dusty books—snorting with drunken amusement as they did so.

Saira was quietly leafing through a magazine, while Seb, Joss, and Laure were nowhere to be seen.

A cold feeling of dread slunk along my skin. It was *that* time of the party. The time people's inhibitions lowered and they disappeared into quiet corners where they wouldn't be found.

I walked along the passage to the entrance hall, trailing my fingers along the damp wallpaper, and peered up the stairs.

Did I go upstairs? Right now, I had the intense feeling I'd find something I wouldn't like. Seb had looked amazing tonight; anyone with eyes would want to corner him, lead him away, sequester his time. Maybe it was something I *needed* to see, though. A painful truth that would drag me out of this malaise. Show me the things I couldn't stop imagining in my worst hours—

I crept lightly up the stairs.

I knew I wouldn't find them on the second floor—they would be in the studio—or worse, Seb's bedroom.

I know he had some kind of history with Laure.

Cautiously, I opened the door that led to the studio. If they were up there, surely I'd hear voices by now, unless—unless they were—

Stop it—

The wide expanse was lit by soft moonlight but deserted.

Then I heard it, the low, deep rumble of Seb's voice. Coming from the far end of the studio—from his bedroom. The masochist in me paused for a few moments more, balanced on the staircase, deciding I wanted to be sure of what was going on, one way or the other. Laure's voice cut in—high and harried, her words sharp. They sounded as if they were arguing. Then came a sudden thump—a fist on a hard surface—Seb's voice louder, allowing me to make out a few words.

"You need to be *careful*, Laure. You don't know what she's capable of."

12

HAD SEB BEEN *talking about me?*

Before that familiar, sweaty sense of shame could come over me again, I swiftly made my way back downstairs to the kitchen, in need of a strong drink or an entire box of Maltesers—preferably both—only to find Emma there, dressed in sweats and busily emptying trays of crisps and empty soda cans into a black trash bag.

"Hey—here, let me give you a hand with that," I said, feeling immediately guilty. People doing things for me always made me feel awkward. I could never be cool with it—unlike the Wrens, used to luxury travel with dedicated butlers and people waiting on them hand and foot. Emma gave me an amused sideways glance. "Ah no, you're all right. Go enjoy the party."

I nodded in the direction of the lounge. "Have you *been* in there? This party is most definitely over."

She laughed, and we spent the next ten minutes chatting and cheerfully rinsing the glassware (unsurprisingly, there was no dishwasher) while jamming food back in the fridge.

"I reckon I might check out the folly tomorrow," I said. "It looks like you'd get some good views from up there. I'm surprised Lottie's not taken it over already."

Was it my imagination or did Emma seem to freeze for a moment or two, her expression inscrutable?

"Aye, you can see the sea from there on a clear day. But I'm not sure we even have the key—no one's been there in years, y'know. Like I said before, the place is a death trap. Put your foot through a floorboard and the whole place might collapse around you."

"Oh, okay," I said, disappointed. It looked pretty sturdy to me, but I wasn't exactly an architect.

"Ah. Here you are. Seb tells me you've got something to say to me?"

Laure entered the kitchen, her sleek red hair now pulled into an artfully messy topknot. The imperious tone in her voice set my teeth on edge. The way she looked at Emma and me, cold-eyed and dismissive, like we only existed to serve her.

You need to apologize.

Beside me, Emma muttered something about taking out the bins—no doubt sensing the doom-laden energy that had descended over the entire room—and for the first time since the ball I found myself alone with Laure. I rearranged the tense expression on my face into what I hoped was a warm smile.

"Yeah, um, it would be great to catch up, actually," I lied. I poured myself a large measure of vodka out of pure nerves and took a hasty swig. "It's been a minute. Do—do you want a drink?"

Laure stared at me in thinly veiled disgust and shook her head. Close up, she looked so different from how I remembered her.

Thin now—gaunt, even—cheekbones sharp, a nervous energy in her dark eyes. She said nothing else, clearly waiting for me to begin.

I put down my drink, trying to compose myself.

"Hey, look, I never wanted us to become . . . whatever we've become," I said slowly, forcing myself to look at her. "When we first met, I wanted us to be friends—we *were* friends. I liked you; you know I did. I thought you were funny and smart and *real* in a way that none of the others are. I thought"—I cleared my throat awkwardly—"I thought you were like me."

She gave a short, unpleasant laugh and shook her head, as tight and neat as a guillotine blade falling.

"I'm *not* like you."

I exhaled in frustration. I knew she wouldn't make this easy. Time to serve her some cold hard facts, then. "Okay, so my family doesn't have money. But just because I wasn't born with everything handed to me on a plate like you lot, that doesn't make me a bad person or *lesser* in any way or—"

Laure laughed sharply. "C'mon, *Megan*. This is so old now. You know I don't care—that I'm not shallow like that. All of us accepted you immediately. No, the reason I'm not like you is because *I* have a spine."

I rubbed my hands over my face, conscious of how tired I suddenly felt. Already, I just wanted to put it to bed. To speak plainly. I glanced behind her, checking we were alone.

"What? What are you talking about? Look, is this still about Seb, then?"

Laure pushed her hair behind one ear, breaking her gaze. I knew I'd hit close to the truth.

"Yeah, all right, I'll admit it. It *was*—to begin with. And I don't deny I was a bitch to you toward the end, Megan. But the way you waltzed in and started taking everything I had—I can't be fake like that. I couldn't sit back and pretend I *liked* it."

"I didn't *take* anything. Seb and I were never together."

Laure rolled her eyes, then stalked over to the kitchen door, quietly closing it. Returning, she lowered her voice. "I'm not an *idiot*, Meg. Let me guess, he told you to keep whatever happened between the two of you quiet, right? I know how he operates—it's always the same."

I bit my lip, my face heating. Laure tilted her gaze to the ceiling. There was something oddly defeated about her, so different from the Laure I used to know.

"I figured as much. Look, I know what you really want, Meg. And I *am* prepared to forgive you—completely. I'm prepared to tell the principal to drop the hearing—I'm prepared to downplay everything you did. Whatever needs to happen to reinstate you back at Greyscott's. The only thing I need *you* to do . . . is to fully admit the truth."

I stared at her, unable to comprehend what she was saying. The calm ease with which she had granted my every wish.

"Wait—wait, what? *Really?* Laure, are you serious? *Th-thank you.*"

Whatever needs to happen to reinstate me?

And there it was, an open invitation to my old life, crammed once more with possibilities and connections and friends. A life with a real *future*. With gallery openings and well-connected parties. With Lottie and Charlie and Saira—

With *Seb*.

My thoughts were racing into the distance. Our final year; all our friendships now fully cemented and unbreakable. The opening night of my first exhibition at some small bougie gallery in Shoreditch. Seb on one arm, bespectacled and proud, Lottie on the other—patting my arm, my rock—

"Are you listening, Meg?"

There was an openness in Laure's expression I'd rarely seen before, tinged with some unreadable emotion that I thought might be sadness. Part of me wondered whether this was some cruel joke. Whether she'd jump up, thump the table, and yell, *Ha, psych, bitch!*

"Yes . . . yes, of course. What—what do I need to do?"

Laure stared at me for an uncomfortable few seconds before answering.

"I need you to tell the truth. All of it. Everything that happened. Every single detail of that night."

I was a little confused. I mean, I'd already admitted the worst of it to the principal, shame-faced and shaking. There were witnesses, after all. But the words came pouring out of me, pathetic in my gratitude.

"Of course! Of *course* I will. I'll do whatever I need to. It was a stupid moment of madness and I am honestly so, *so* sorry. Laure, I'm trying to change—I'm different now, I promise."

Laure gave another resigned shake of her head. So far removed from the loud, barbed comments I was used to. She looked exhausted—haunted, almost. For the first time, I felt concerned for her. Genuinely. Always living in Lottie's glamorous shadow. And I hadn't missed the way she'd looked at Seb this evening. Gone was her self-satisfied smirk. She'd looked like a kicked dog trailing after its master.

And for a moment, I thought maybe I should have taken Seb up on his offer. That the best thing for me—for everyone—would be to hop on the next plane and forget about them, forget about Greyscott's. Hadn't I caused enough drama? Maybe it was time to forget Lottie's circle, forget all the luxury, and more importantly, the opportunity afforded by Greyscott's. After all, wasn't Laure right? Hadn't she been right all along? I *didn't* belong here. I didn't belong with any of them, and least of all with Seb. I was playacting at this. Pretending. And it would never get easier.

But then I recalled our art tutor at Greyscott's, Monsieur Desjardins, an eccentric, soft-spoken man in his sixties.

You are *capable of greatness, Meg. I believe it wholeheartedly. Your connection to your work in undeniable—your originality. The only question is, can you bear the journey?*

And Mum, slight and wan, her eyes forever ringed with dark circles from her night shifts at the school. *I don't want you to grow up like me, Megan; don't want you working two dead-end jobs just to make the rent, not when you don't have to—not when you're so talented. Whatever happens, we'll make this work.*

Laure was looking at me, her face pale, her expression a mixture of thinly stretched patience and sorrow.

"I'm still not sure you're *getting* it. If you want me to forgive you, you need to tell the actual truth about that night, Meg. About what really happened from the moment you turned up. And you need to make it all public." She pulled a hand down her face and blinked, her usually sharp green eyes dull and wreathed in shadows. "*All* of it. Look, I'm off to bed. Take some time to think about it, all right? We can talk some more tomorrow."

13

AFTER LAURE LEFT, I needed some air. Her willingness to seemingly grant my every wish had left me almost trembling with adrenaline. Despite the coolness of the weather, my skin felt feverish, my mind unsettled, jumping haphazardly between thoughts, and outside it looked as if the rain had finally relented.

Slipping my jacket over my thin dress, I wandered down toward the lake, my boots sinking into the saturated grass.

This trip wasn't exactly going the way I'd expected.

I'd thought about nothing else for days, running every possible scenario through my head at least a dozen times.

I knew what to say if Laure rejected my apology—as I'd expected her to.

I knew to keep well away from Seb and I knew to stay close to Lottie and Charlie.

But already, *nothing* was working out how I'd planned.

Laure's response had left me unmoored. I hadn't dreamed she'd forgive me so easily. And I hadn't expected to encounter this . . . changed version of her.

Still, the fact remained, without Laure's forgiveness, after the hearing I would drift away from all the glamour and light of Greyscott's like a ghost, with nothing to show for it other than a permanent black mark against my name. Whatever she wanted me to do, I knew that I was prepared to do it.

A trio of mossy stone benches sat before the lake, arranged in a semicircle. I perched on one and stared out onto the glossy dark waters, a gentle breeze rippling the surface like a phantom hand, the moon benevolently glowing overhead. I exhaled slowly; it was a serene sight, and for a moment I had a desperate urge to paint it—as if the act would somehow erase Lottie's dark and spoiled vision, which haunted the studio upstairs. Even the statues seemed at peace, sunk deeper than ever before, only their blind eyes visible, silently keeping sentinel over the house.

Come on in—the water's divine!

Somewhere close an owl hooted and the night breeze stirred the fir trees, sending a scent of balsam over the waters. I took another deep calming breath. Charlie was right. Everyone was drunk—Ollie and Joss were properly wasted. Hopefully, after we got some sleep, my outburst would be forgotten and this would all blow over tomorrow. I'd idle the morning away in the studio or go for a walk up to the folly, clearing my head; then Laure and I could sit down and talk it all out, like she wanted. Maybe we'd even reconnect and things could be like they used to. Maybe we could be—

I glanced back at the lake, my thoughts scattered by a soft splashing. Just a bird, probably, wading into the water—a heron or whatever.

My eyes drifted to the statues, all facing my way, curious, their bodies mirrored in the waters below them. I knew they were just statues—ten of them, I'd counted that morning—but something about them made me feel *watched*.

Unnerved now, I counted them again. I must have been wrong before—there were clearly eleven. One straggling a little farther out from the rest, and darker in the moonlight.

Strange. The first one I'd counted—when I looked back at it—now seemed closer to me than the others, its head now fully above the water. Just my imagination, of course. It was a male wearing a wreath of laurel leaves, his brow lowered in a frown, sightless white eyes seeming to glare at me.

I blinked and looked across the lineup again.

No—wrong again. He wasn't the only one whose head was above the water. The statue farthest back was now submerged only up to its neck. A woman, her hair long and slick, the hollows where her eyes should be staring sightlessly in my direction. The statues must have been arranged in a rough semicircle to mirror the benches, the ones at the ends closest to the bank.

For a brief mad moment, I considered running up to the studio and grabbing a canvas and my paints. If I could somehow anchor the statues in a portrait, then maybe they'd stay *still*.

I rubbed my eyes and yawned. *Lord*, I was tired. Hopefully, everyone would have passed out by now and I could climb into bed without any more awkward conversation.

When I opened my eyes again, a thin chill slipped down my spine like ice water.

Somehow, through some trick of the moonlight maybe, the statue that had been farthest looked closest now, barely a few feet away from me, the woman's pale thin shoulders clearly visible above the water. Her face seemed better carved than the others, her features intricate and almost . . . familiar, with thin tendrils of hair falling over her shoulders, her brow lowered—

No. No, no—

Impossible.

I needed sleep, that was all. There was no way—

"Hey you."

I almost screamed. Whirling round and nearly toppling off the bench into the weeds on the bank.

Seb stood behind me, his curls a dark tangle free from his tricorn hat.

"*Shit*—you scared the crap out of me."

He gave me an apologetic smile. "Sorry." He sat beside me on the bench. I shuffled over, giving the statues one last, wary look. All were still safely submerged in the lake. Something to do with the currents, probably.

"My turn to apologize, I guess," I conceded. "I shouldn't have blown up at you like that earlier. Guess we're all a bit tense. At least we're all here now, right? Glad Laure made it."

He gave a flippant nod. "I mean . . . do you really feel that way, Meg? You've always been so honest it's kinda brutal. Because I wish to God she'd never got on that plane."

His words, so directly spoken, shocked me. I stared out into the dark water of the lake, remembering his earlier, fevered conversation with Laure, the warning he had given her.

"Seb . . . ," I asked slowly, "what really went down between you and Laure? Are you—are you back together?"

After all, a lot could happen in three months.

There was a long pause, and immediately, I wished I could breathe the words back in. Seb didn't like discussing Laure. Everyone knew it. They were always civil to each other around the others, but . . .

"I don't really want to talk about it too much," he said, his voice low. "It's not fair to her. And it *was* mostly my fault, I guess. She just got in a bit too deep and . . ."

He trailed off and rubbed a hand over his eyes.

"And the truth is, I didn't feel the same. And no, we're not back together. Whatever it was, it's—it's done."

We sat for a few moments in a silence that wasn't totally awkward. There was a thickening in the atmosphere between us that I was sure he sensed too, a darkening, an unfolding. My hand itched to reach out for his, warm and familiar. I longed to rest my head on his shoulder, to bury myself in his arms, because I knew how good it felt to do those things.

After the magazine launch, word spread throughout Greyscott's and I spent the next few weeks fully enveloped in the warm sunshine of Lottie's group, instead of anxiously circling the chilly outer reaches. Ollie and Saira were now happy to partner with me in the classes we shared (on the rare occasion Lottie couldn't), and even Joss had softened the stinging jibes.

As for Sebastien, the next time I saw him wasn't in the studio but in English class. Lottie was off doing some head girl shit, so I sat alone at our usual desk, got out my notebook, and began writing the date. I glanced up in surprise as a shadow fell across the desk and someone slumped down into the seat beside me.

"Wrong twin, I know," he murmured with a crooked smile, shrugging off his blazer. "But Lottie ordered me to keep you company, being the new girl and all."

He smelled delicious, citrusy and shower fresh. Confused, I looked toward the back of the classroom, where he usually sat, and saw Ollie mugging away at us. A cold rage washed over me; was he *mocking* me?

"There's really no need, y'know," I replied coolly. "*You* might not have noticed, but I've been here for at least two months now. I'm not the new girl anymore."

He only shrugged, glancing around the room, where we were now attracting a fair bit of attention. "Well, there's no seats free now, so guess you're going to have to put up with me." He leaned closer, lowering his voice, a dark smile on his face. "Besides, I *have* noticed."

Laure was sitting directly behind us and I caught her eye, hoping for some sympathy, but I was surprised when she glared at me, her gaze so hard and so cold I recoiled. Clearly I'd made a misstep—through no fault of my own.

"So, Megs, what's the worst thing *you've* ever done?"

Turning back, I blinked at him, surprised. "What kinda question is *that*? Because I come from a public school, you think we spend break times having knife fights?"

He chuckled, then nodded at the board, where Mrs. Jacobi had written in sprawling letters *What's the worst thing that happens in* Hamlet?

"Ophelia's death," I said confidently.

"Falling out of a tree into a river, then deciding to just lie there like a sim in a swimming pool with no ladder?"

"She *drowned* herself—have you even read this? The entire play is about death."

He chuckled again. It was beginning to irritate me. I wasn't here for his amusement. "Talking of Ophelia, do you know the painting by Millais?"

I stared at him, his deep blue eyes still playful, my interest piqued. "Yes, actually. I saw it at the Tate when I was a kid—it's what got me interested in art."

The time I first saw her, I almost cried. Lying there, resplendent but solemn in the water, more beautiful than anything I'd ever seen. Even the flora of the riverbank seemed to lean closer desperate to drink in more of her face.

Her clothes spread wide; and, mermaid-like, awhile they bore her up.

We'd started studying *Hamlet* this term, and that line of Gertrude's monologue had haunted me ever since I'd read it.

Even before that, though, since that chance meeting at the gallery, I was hopelessly under Ophelia's spell. My bedroom crammed with cheap blank canvases Mum picked up for me at the store, my hands and clothes forever smeared with color: Prussian blue. Rose madder. Vermilion. Burnt umber. The names like spells in my mouth.

"Yeah, I know it. Let me guess—you're gonna tell me your dad owns it or something?"

This time Seb laughed aloud. *"No."*

"*Well,* Meg?"

Crap. I shot a panicked look at Ms. Jacobi, my face heating. I had literally no idea what she'd just asked me and I'd been working so hard in all my classes, keen to give the impression I was grateful to be here. At that exact moment, accidentally or not, Seb chose to reach down and retrieve something from his backpack, one hand gently brushing my thigh as did so. My face heated more.

Vermilion. Alizarin. Amaranth.

"I . . . I—er—I wasn't listening—sorry."

Beside me, Seb smothered a snort of laughter, pushing back his hair and staring intently at his paper. *"Brutal."*

Thankfully, Mrs. Jacobi only glared at me and moved on.

I managed to focus for the rest of the class, and Seb surprised me. He shouldn't have, I'd seen him work magic in English before, but he was a great study partner, insightful and articulate, happy to fiercely debate the crucial issues, such as who would make the ultimate Shakespearean power couple (King Claudius and Lady Macbeth) and who had more game, Troilus or Mercutio (Troilus).

But once the bell buzzed for the end of the lesson, he left with nothing more than a brief wave, jostling a braying Ollie out the door. Laure, however, was waiting for me with a face like a pug dog who'd unknowingly chomped into a lemon.

"Hey . . . Everything . . . okay, Laure?"

Rather than give me her usual bright smile, she looked at me as if I were something unpleasant she'd found on the bottom of her limited-edition Jordans. I blinked, a chill seeping through me.

What exactly had I *done*?

She lowered her voice. "Seb and I have history, Meg. I don't know if you realized, but he's off-limits. Besides, he's Lottie's twin—don't you think that's fucked-up of you?"

Partly because of the absolute hypocrisy of her statement and partly because sitting next to Seb had raised my blood pressure to a probably unhealthy level, I wasn't about to take this lying down.

"Wait—what the hell? Are you blind? *He* sat next to *me*."

She shrugged, fluttering her lash extensions at the ceiling. "So? You could have moved. Instead you spent the entire hour giggling at everything he said like some kind of demented manatee—"

"Wow, Laure, I *really* think you've got the wrong idea."

Guilt swiftly replaced anger. She totally didn't. It had been the most memorable hour of education I could remember, other than the time Logan Sullivan projectile-vomited all over my math book in Year 2.

Still, Laure's one-eighty—from bubbly bestie to imperious ice queen—was a little alarming. She sighed, as if having to even speak to me was a chore. "Look, you do you, Meg, but if Lottie asks, I'm going to have to be honest."

That was the first moment I realized my time at Greyscott's wasn't going to go as smoothly as I'd hoped.

A cold wind rippled the waters of the lake, pulling me back to the present and away from Seb's touch.

"What do you mean?" I pushed. "What do you mean 'she just got in a bit too deep'?"

Obviously I had an idea, but I wanted him to explain, to speak the truth aloud. There were many (*many*) positive things about

Seb, but he had an annoying tendency to speak in riddles, to always leave things half said.

He huffed out an awkward laugh. "I meant exactly what I said. Look . . . Meg, there's something else you should know—"

A few meters away from us, where the rickety wooden jetty stood, I noticed a light, flickering and insubstantial but there all the same. Who else would be out here so late at night?

"Hey," I said, interrupting Seb. I wasn't so sure I wanted to hear what he was about to say anyway. Not tonight. "What's that? Do you see that light?"

The light was flickering closer to the water now. Seb got off the bench, his movements slow, staring at the guttering flame. I followed him, half curious, half terrified.

There was someone up ahead, walking down the rotting boards, someone slender and submerged in shadow. Seb broke into a jog. As I walked, I watched in silent shock as whoever it was slipped into the still waters of the lake, barely making a sound, the candle they held still glimmering in their hand. I hesitated at the edge, not trusting the ancient boards above the dark water.

I caught my breath. Now that I was closer, something about the figure was familiar. The light from Seb's phone illuminated the water, creating a silver pool around the person wading determinedly into the depths.

"*Lottie?* Lottie—what the *hell* are you doing?"

She was carrying what looked like an armful of purple flowers, the same ones Saira had thoughtfully picked up in the supermarket yesterday. I hadn't noticed before, but now I realized they were hyacinths. Some had already slipped from her grasp and were floating out onto the water. Her long wig trailing behind her and her pale makeup conspired to create an eerie sight.

There was a loud splash as Seb plunged in. She continued to silently sink into the black waters of the lake without a word while Seb swam after her.

"Lottie!" I screamed, not knowing what else to do. Nothing could have compelled me to enter that water. Not at night. Not in the dark. Nothing.

"Lottie, what are you *doing*? Come back!"

Beams of light waved around behind me as the others ran out of the house, flashlights aloft, at the sound of my screaming.

"Go get some towels," I yelled at Saira.

When I turned back to the lake, Seb was wading out of it, dark hair plastered to his pale face, Lottie's slender body lying in his arms, alabaster pale.

14

IT WAS AFTER three a.m. before we all finally got to bed, when the house finally stilled.

Lottie had been fine once we'd carried her back inside and she'd warmed up. Drunker than I'd ever seen her—or maybe something more than drunk. There'd been a strange distance in her eyes I'd never witnessed before. Like she'd witnessed something so terrible she'd never be able to relate it back to us.

The temperature of the water must have been a shock to her—her skin was freezing and almost blue when Seb first pulled her out. She was whimpering—wailing—silent tears streaming down her pale face. More like a banshee than ever.

We'd sat her by the fire for a while, to warm up. Seb taking charge, pulling off the sodden parts of her costume and wrapping her in a voluminous hotel-style robe. His actions—the smoothness, the grim determination on his face—surprised me.

As if he was used to it.

But that was ridiculous.

Because it was *Lottie* we were talking about. Sunny, ever-upbeat Lottie. Lottie, who sailed through life without a problem in the world. Lottie with the beautiful, tiny, yoga-teacher mother and handsome banker father.

She's been under a lot of strain lately.

Back in the house, she got ahold of herself with admirable speed, and once she'd warmed up, Seb had helped her upstairs.

Most of the others made their excuses immediately after, the mood somber now, but I sat for a few minutes by the fire, enjoying its dying warmth and wondering if Seb would come back.

What had he been about to tell me out there?

Exactly why he'd ignored me, hopefully. Had he been *so* disgusted by my actions that night? I couldn't exactly blame him. *Hadn't* blamed him, however low I'd felt in the months that followed. Did my lapses of judgment—of patience—repulse him?

Did he see something inside me, something dark and unpleasant, that he hated?

And if he did, could I blame him?

Chewing my nails, I stared into the fire.

Immediately after it happened, a foolish drunken part of me had expected him to come looking for me. Whether he was disgusted by my actions or not, he must have known the reasons behind them. Known he wasn't entirely blameless himself. And while I hadn't expected an apology, I'd expected some kind of . . . conversation. Not his complete disappearance. Not after everything that had happened between us that night.

The minutes on the mantel's carriage clock ticked slowly by, and yawning, I realized he wasn't coming back.

I got up, staggering more than I'd expected to. *Why* had I thought neat vodka was a good idea? I would never even have considered it had my nerves not being jangling like a deranged wind chime all evening thanks to Laure's imminent arrival.

She'd unsettled me when we spoke in the kitchen. More so than when she'd turned up at the kitchen door, looking exactly like she had the night she'd almost drowned.

The actual truth—

Every single detail of that night.

But what *was* that truth? What did she want to hear? Because there were some things that happened that night that I don't think I could ever share. That were as precious and as hidden as pearls, cloistered deep within their shell. Secrets I'd kept buried beneath still waters, keeping my own counsel, like the lake outside.

Greyscott's had been a little like the lake in that respect too. Still and calm on the surface but with a myriad of unpleasant things hidden beneath it. Deadly, if you weren't careful, if you weren't aware what was there waiting patiently to pull you down with it.

You see, on the surface, everything at Greyscott's was always *fine*.

Everyone and their family was doing just great, thanks for asking! No admissions scandals, no family dramas involving beautiful New Zealand au pairs, no absentee fathers with mistresses in every tax haven, no mums starting wine-o'clock before midday.

Unlike at my old school, everything was bloody perfectly *fine*.

And you knew there were things you just didn't talk about.

We never talked about how Ollie was failing multiple classes, forever sleeping in until midday thanks to his crushing hangovers or coke withdrawal, ashen-faced and distracted in those he did turn up to.

We never mentioned the alarming amount of weight Laure had dropped in the weeks before the ball. At the sudden surges of nervous energy she exuded.

We never discussed how Lottie wouldn't be drawn into any deeper conversations about her brother. About why someone as perfect as him only ever dated casually. Nobody talked about Ava Cheung, the previous head girl, someone he'd actually deigned worthy enough to parade on his arm, and who'd soon transferred to a sister school in Singapore beneath a thundercloud of whispers.

I trailed my fingers along the ancient wallpaper, tracing the lurid blossoms as I walked toward the staircase in a daze.

Moonlight shone brightly through the wide transom window above the main door, illuminating the checkerboard tiles of the entrance hall with a ghostly sheen. Odd for the moon to be so bright when the day had been so cloudy, when there'd been so much rain.

I stopped for a second as the room swam up around me, resting my arms on the newel post, my cheek against the cool smooth wood.

The saints.

I remembered Lottie mentioning them yesterday.

Can't get away from the religious shit over here.

I took a few steps back to look at them.

The dark wood they were carved from looked black in the dim light. When I'd first seen them, I'd thought they'd been praying, hands clasped, but now their hands covered their faces, as if they were hiding from some unpleasant sight. And hadn't I thought they were male before? I hadn't noticed the straggly dark hair, glossy and wet-looking, carved with immense precision, that slipped out of their dark hoods.

I stared for a few moments more, then tripped clumsily up the stairs to my room. But where I'd expected the landing to be, there were yet more stairs, and steeper this time, narrower. I'd climbed stairs like these before in long-ago visits to castles, twisting and treacherous.

The kind of steps I'd imagine to be in a tower from a fairy tale, in the folly. On the darkest side of the enchanted lake, across the wizened wood.

I kept on climbing; there was nothing else I could do. There was no going back now; it was too late, I'd come too far. Besides, it would be harder to go down. I needed to get to the top—to the studio.

The wind howled around the house, sending a chill through my thin green dress. I was still Medusa, defiled in a temple. Forever a monster.

I was so *tired*—when would I reach the top? Where did these stairs end?

Rounding the corner, I saw to my relief I was now in a small circular room with windows all around. A makeshift bed lay beneath one window. Above it, a perfect view of the lake: a pool of spilled blood in the moonlight; the faint white heads of the statues facing away from me, looking directing at Wren Hall.

Come on in—the water's divine!

And in the middle of the lake, standing impossibly on the water, her ragged dress billowing out behind her, was a woman. Unlike the statues, she was staring in my direction, staring directly at me, her eyes stunning silver in the moonlight, her lank hair thick with pond slime whipping viciously round her face, and her smile—a terrible smile—mocking, knowing, her teeth blackened and sharp.

Should have filled in that fecking lake years ago

Then she tipped back her head, her mouth opening impossibly wide, and began to scream. A scream so terrible, so full of anguish, so unrelenting that my eyes filled with tears and I had to jam my hands over my ears, sinking to my knees.

I need you to tell the truth.

It was a scream that told of everything bad in the world. Of a thousand injustices that no one cared about. Of endless secret cruelties.

Everything that happened.

Again and again, it vibrated about the forest, rippling among the trees, shaking the walls of the house. Drowning out the entire world until there was nothing left but darkness.

Every single detail of that night.

15

"GOD, THERE'S ALWAYS one who doesn't make it to bed."

Saira's vaguely disapproving voice jabbed into the tangle of my dreams—all of which dissipated like smoke in the dull morning light, leaving nothing behind but that *screaming*. I opened a single crusty eye. My mouth was as dry as the bottom of a moon crater. She sat across from me, casually scrolling through her phone. Blearily, I wiped my hand across my eyes, surreptitiously removing clumps of mascara-encrusted goo from my lashes, and sat up, taking a few seconds to collect myself. Why wasn't I in bed? Clearly I'd passed out on the sofa in the lounge in front of the fire, now long dead.

"Saira—hi. I was, um, helping Lottie, then must have dropped off. Is everyone else still asleep?"

Saira nodded. "Yep, I'm about to go for a jog. Wanna come?"

I suspected there was a good chance I would legitimately die if I did. "Nope, might head back to bed for an hour, actually."

"Probably a good idea—sounds like tonight might be another late one. Not sure if you heard last night, but Lottie was going on about some exhibition she's been invited to in some no-hope town down the road. As you might guess—we're *all* expected."

She tossed me a smirk before heading out of the room. After a halfhearted interlude of wandering around throwing empty cans into a trash bag, followed by a disappointing, pressure-less shower, I jogged up to the studio with a sugar-laden coffee. I wasn't exactly in a creative mood—my head was too full of noise—but I appreciated the blankness of the space, and the peace the view of the lake seemed to bring.

Before the windows were six large canvases, all turned to face the wall. It looked as if Lottie had been busy since yesterday. Curious, I turned the first of the canvases around.

It was the painting I had seen when I'd arrived. The strange woman half looking at the observer, half looking across the lake at Wren Hall, her smile secretive and somewhat cruel. It still unsettled me. The mood so drab and dour, so unlike Lottie's usual cheery splashes of color.

The next canvas was almost identical. The same miasma of brackish greens and leaden grays coated it; the house the same squat gray box—although this time a golden glow emanated from its windows, as if someone within had switched on the lights. The whole atmosphere was darker now, on the cusp of twilight. And the woman—this time she was no longer in the foreground, in the woods on the far side of the lake; instead, her slender figure was standing on the bank, her back to the observer, facing the house. The combination of her sober black dress and long hair from behind giving her a kind of grim-reaper effect, her limbs unfeasibly long and thin.

"I'm worried about her."

I jumped violently, cursing as I spilled my coffee over my sweater.

Seb stood in the doorway of his bedroom at the far end of the studio. Gathering myself, I turned to him. He looked tired; dressed in gray sweats, his black curls mussed from sleep.

"Sorry," he added, his gaze drifting toward the brown splotch on my chest. "Didn't mean to scare you."

"It's fine. And Lottie was just drunk last night . . . ," I said, automatically coming to my friend's defense. "Bet she's regretting those shots today. Bloody Ollie and his stupid drinking games—"

Seb ran a hand through his hair and directed his gaze to the window.

"It's not just that. . . . She's been different ever since we got here. I mean—" He nodded to the canvases. "Take *those*, for example. It's nothing like her normal stuff, is it? They're . . . fucking depressing."

"Yeah, but she's clearly been inspired by the view, which is"—I gave him a small apologetic smile—"frankly depressing."

He grinned and sank into one of the threadbare armchairs, eyeing my coffee. "God, I need caffeine. So, did you get a chance to speak to her last night? To Laure, I mean."

I blinked, unsure what to say, memories of the raised voices emanating from his room still fresh in my mind. What had they been discussing? And had it had anything to do with what Laure had said to me, later that night?

"Not properly," I hedged. "I don't think last night was the best time. I mean, I really can't afford to mess this up. But Laure and

I are planning on talking more today. We all know that if she doesn't forgive me for—for what happened, I'll be kicked out of Greyscott's and—and, yeah."

Seb yawned. He stretched and I looked away as his sweater rucked up, revealing the taut muscle beneath.

"I know. We *all* know. But the thing about Laure is, she's never satisfied. You'll apologize—but soon there'll be something else you need to apologize for. She'll hold this over you for as long as she can. You know that, right?"

And unfortunately I did.

Thankfully, Laure's outburst after English class appeared to be a strange one-off, and for the weeks that followed, Lottie's group continued to be an endless source of wonder. From being invited to glittering gallery openings (okay, we were there to serve drinks to rich old white men while wearing tiny black dresses—but even so) to raucous nights out in expensive clubs and bars where someone's dad always knew the owner, a different world had opened up to me.

Lottie herself was endlessly generous. Forever lending me designer dresses and expensive shoes the times my own high-street clothes wouldn't do—which was frequently.

As for Seb, after that awkwardness in class, he stayed away for a while, casually waving if I passed him while headed to the studio, usually when he was on his way out. I began to wonder whether he was waiting for me to make some kind of move. Or had our flirtation all been in my head? Was he like that with everyone?

He bought you flowers.

Had I played it too cool, then? Was it possible he thought I wasn't interested because of Laure or Lottie? Or both of them? More agonizing still was the fact that I couldn't bring it up to Lottie, who, even at this early point, I considered my best friend. I wasn't sure what she'd think. He was her brother, after all—it was bound to be difficult.

Still, every time I went to the studio, which in all honesty was now far more often than I needed to, I hoped he'd knock at the door.

Then, exactly two weeks after our encounter in class, as I was cycling up to their house—an enormous faux-Georgian mansion on a gated estate—I was overtaken too closely by an elderly lady in an SUV. The wheel of my bike clipped the curb, sending me flying over the handlebars and scraping the skin off the knuckles of my right hand, my head banging against the concrete pavement.

Dazed, I got up, and not really knowing what else to do, dragged my bike a few more yards up the road and turned into their drive. As I collapsed onto the gravel, meaning to take a closer look at the mangled wheels, I heard a car draw up alongside me, followed by footsteps pounding across the drive.

"Shit—what happened? Are you okay, Meg?"

I was mortified that Seb had found me in that state. So much so that I tried to downplay it. My head still fuzzy from when I'd hit the ground.

"Yeah . . . yeah. I just . . . fell off—a car got a bit too close—"

He took one of my hands in his, gently turning it over.

"Fuck, you're bleeding. Come on, let's get you inside. Can you walk okay?"

"Er . . . yes—definitely, yes." The idea of Seb attempting to *carry* me was way too much to bear.

Standing in their enormous modern kitchen, an airy space bigger than my entire flat, he rolled up his sleeves, then took my injured hand in both of his, gently, rinsing my scraped skin thoroughly under the tap. I noticed for the first time that he had a tattoo on his forearm, a line inked in delicate black script, the words somehow familiar.

Fear death by water.

"What's that from?" I asked.

He followed my gaze and shrugged self-consciously. "Just from a poem I like—it's called *The Waste Land*. Here."

He pulled out a stool from a vast marble island and gestured for me to sit while he rummaged through a giant first-aid box. Most of my attention was still taken up with trying very hard not to cry, thanks to the cocktail of shock, pain, and Seb's unexpectedly tender ministrations. He carefully applied a dressing to my skinned knuckles, then wrapped a bandage around them.

"There—all fixed. I can drive you home if you like, then take a look at your bike? Dad's a total bike nut—you might have noticed him skimming around in an unfortunate amount of spandex. He should easily be able to fix that wheel for you."

Okay, and *then* I'd cried.

I'd been so worried about being without my bike—my only means of getting around, as a car was far beyond both my mum's and my wildest dreams—that Seb's casual admission he was able to fix it for free triggered a relief I couldn't hide. I buried my face in my one good hand, embarrassed, as my shoulders shook.

"Hey." Seb's voice was gentler than I'd ever heard it—ever expected it could be. Almost a whisper. "Hey, look, it's all right. Everything's all right, Meg. You've just had a bit of a shock, that's all. Here."

His arms wrapped around me, broad and warm, and I gratefully melted into them. A perfect fit. He smelled delicious, the warm cedar of his aftershave filling my senses. Almost immediately, I stopped crying, returning his embrace, my arms twining around his neck as I buried my face in his sweater.

Seconds flowed by like quicksilver and both of us sensed the change; the moment our embrace turned from comforting to curious, his arms loosening from my middle and sliding down until his hands rested on my hips and pulled me closer. I breathed him in, not thinking, overwhelmed by the heat between us, then braved a look up at him, questioning.

In the late-morning sun, his eyes, lighter than I'd ever seen them, the blue of deep summer oceans and endless evening skies, blazed into mine, and there was no denying what was about to happen. As one hand slipped from my middle to brush a stray lock of hair away from my face, the other tightened—

Somewhere far down the hall, an entire universe away, a door clattered open and a voice called out.

"*Seb?* Whose bike is that?"

He stepped away immediately, as if burnt, busying himself packing up the first-aid kit. The twins' mother, as beautiful as her children, walked into the kitchen, still dressed in yoga gear that clung to her enviably lithe figure. I didn't miss the way her forehead furrowed at the sight of me. Did she know who I was? And if so, exactly how much did she know?

"Ah, hello. You're Lottie's friend, aren't you? And you're hurt, you poor thing—is that your bike out there?"

I nodded pitifully, a fresh wave of tears building behind my eyes.

After a few more excruciatingly polite enquiries, Seb finally told her he was taking me home. As he left to retrieve his car keys from the hall, his mum stepped closer to me, her hand gently slipping round my wrist, her cloying perfume filling my lungs.

"And how are they both getting on at Greyscott's? Lottie and Seb, I mean," she asked, as I looked down in surprise at where she held me. She glanced quickly—almost surreptitiously—over her shoulder, as if checking to make sure Seb wasn't still in the room. "It's so difficult to get the truth out of the staff most of the time. You see, our family contributes a great deal to Greyscott's financially. Sometimes I feel one of those two could kill someone and it would still be glossed over by the principal." She gave a weak little laugh, but there was an odd glint in her eye that unsettled me. Why was she even asking me this? They were literally model students. Lottie was head girl, for God's sake.

I gently pulled my arm away and offered her a polite smile. "Great," I answered truthfully. "They're honestly both doing great."

She opened her mouth again, but thankfully Seb returned, preventing any further awkwardness. After saying our goodbyes, we headed back outside to his car. At first, I'd been excited to sit inside it with him, but when he started the engine, deafening hip-hop immediately began blaring from the speakers, making conversation impossible. I wanted to ask him to turn it down, but I couldn't speak, could only replay the events of the last few minutes in my mind, starry-eyed and smiling.

He shouted a few pleasantries above the music, focusing on negotiating the tricky South London traffic and asking me where exactly I lived. Then the dream really shredded. I was embarrassed.

Embarrassed of my run-down neighborhood: Cartons from the chicken shop drifting down the road. The ever-present filthy old mattress in next door's front garden. The tatty net curtains hanging in our window.

So instead I asked him to drop me off on the high street, pretending I needed to get some painkillers from the pharmacy. I knew it would be impossible to find parking in the area, so I escaped his car with nothing more than a rushed wave.

Back in Seb's childhood bedroom, I lay for a while on the rickety single bed listening to the rain lash at the windows and staring at the walls, the corkboard directly opposite me.

Come on in—the water's divine!

Impulsively, I stood, crossed the room, and pulled the postcard off the board. It was softer than I expected, like ancient skin. I recoiled as I turned it over. The handwriting was faded, a delicate looping script.

> *Do you miss the lake?*
> *I miss you more. In the shade beneath the trees where nobody could see.*
> *I've thought about you every night since you left. Imagined you adorning my hair with hyacinths. Perhaps I shouldn't tell you that.*
>
> *Promise me you'll come back soon.*
> *E*

Immediately, I pinned it back up, embarrassed. This was Seb's old room, I remembered Lottie telling me. Why was I snooping around like a creep, reading his old love letters?

It was still early, and according to what Saira had said, the others were still in bed. I was impatient, though, to the point that I was considering going to find Laure right then. Her arriving in that dress the night before had made me more uneasy than I cared to admit. She had turned up unwanted in the fractured dreams I'd had just before waking. Instead of Lottie, it had been her wandering into the lake, her red hair streaming out behind her, and I'd been directly behind, my hands firm upon her frail shoulders. If I pushed down just a little, for just a minute or so—

I shook the image from my mind. A nightmare, that was all. Hardly surprisingly in this spidery old wreck. Deciding there wasn't much chance of getting back to sleep, I climbed back up to the studio.

Lottie was there this time, looking as fresh as ever in ripped black jeans and a vintage kimono, busily washing brushes in turpentine, her dark curls tied back from her face with a silk scarf.

"What a night!" she called over the sound of the tap as she noticed me. "Remind me never to follow Ollie's lead with the Fireball again."

I smiled. "Feeling better after your midnight dip?"

She leaned her elbows on the island and groaned. "Only my ego is wounded. Seriously, though, *so* embarrassing. I've not been sleeping very well—and that combined with all the drinks Ollie was mixing. I remember getting a bit overheated in the house because Ol had managed to stoke the fire to inferno levels, so I thought it was a great idea to go for a little swim to cool off. Completely forgot it was bloody October." She gave me a forlorn smile. "Unnecessarily dramatic, right? I spent hours in the shower, but I'm still finding bits of bloody pondweed in my hair."

I perched on the battered leather armchair, worried for my friend. Beneath her sunny smile, she was drawn and wan. If she had just been trying to cool down, what was with the candles and flowers? It had been like a—a ritual. Or something more sinister. An offering? Something linked to those huge, unpleasant canvases she'd been obsessively painting.

Come on in—the water's DIVINE!

"Lots, is that really all? Just . . . exhaustion?"

She sighed and slumped down in the chair opposite.

"Honestly, I don't know why I did it. But I couldn't get the idea of going in there—into the lake—out of my head. All evening, in fact. It was like it was *pulling* me to it—the lake, I mean. I've felt that since I got here, but last night . . . I know it was probably just the drink—but it was so *weird*. Especially after all that . . . Ouija board shit."

I snorted. "C'mon, that was everyone pissing about."

She looked at me then, her wide blue eyes framed with lush black lashes. Seb's eyes.

"Was it, though?" she asked, her voice hushed now. "I mean, some of those things . . . What was it? 'In the weeds' and that 'wicked history' stuff—all that seemed too weird to be made up by one of us."

I glanced out the window at the still waters of the lake below and gave an involuntary shiver.

Lottie followed my gaze, her mouth twisting in a grimace. "And since I've been here . . . it's all I can paint."

She leaned over and clutched my hand in hers, her grip clammy. "You know what it's like, don't you? Out of all of them, I know you understand—about how the—the landscape can be tied so closely to this." She gestured at the canvas. "To the point it's almost unconscious, like a tug, an undertow—like *drowning*, almost. But this, this is something else. I know this is going to sound strange, Meg, but do you believe in things like that?" Lottie continued. "Ghosts and spirits and things? A couple of times since we've been here I've heard this—this—"

"Crying?" I finished.

"Yes!" said Lottie, her eyes brightening in a feverish way I didn't like. She looked more than tired; she looked ill. Her face gaunt, her eyes circled with shadows. "You've heard it too?"

I nodded hesitantly. "Maybe . . . I wasn't sure if I was dreaming."

We thought it was you.

"There's a local legend—I first heard the story when I was a little girl—about a banshee, a water spirit, that's meant to live in the lake and plague the area," she said, her tone low and conspiratorial. "Anyone in town will tell you, if you ask, and most of them seem to believe it—no, more than that, to be *afraid* of it. It's a woman—lank-haired, emaciated, and dripping wet. And always crying. When you hear her scream, it means you, or someone close to you, is going to die."

An image flashed in my mind: *HARBINGER.*

I felt a glimmer of relief.

So it *must* have been Lottie last night, messing around with the planchette. But *why?* Perhaps Seb was right. Perhaps coming here had been a terrible mistake.

Oblivious to my thoughts, Lottie went on. "Centuries ago, not long after this place was built, locals say a woman drowned herself—and her kid—in that lake."

I frowned at Lottie. "Jesus, why?"

"It was during the famine. I suppose—I suppose she knew they were going to die and wanted to make it quick for them both. That's who she's meant to be—the banshee."

I forced myself to change the subject, desperate to lighten the mood.

"So, Saira was telling me we've been invited to some exhibition tonight?"

Lottie broke her fevered gaze, turning to stare out the window again.

"Yes, exciting, right? Daddy managed to squeeze me in last-minute, so I've got to go over this afternoon, lend them a hand with hanging these." She nodded in the direction of the series of large canvases. "Okay, so I know it's not exactly *London,* but I'm hoping to make some contacts for when I set up the retreat."

I nodded to the window, in the direction of the folly. "You're missing a trick not opening that. I mean, imagine the views from the top! Apparently you can even see the ocean from there."

A shadow passed over Lottie's face. She got up, turning her back to me and busying herself in the sink. "Yeah, it's definitely a *project,* but my parents reckon it's a complete ruin. Probably needs pulling down and rebuilding again before it's safe." She paused. "Have you managed to catch up with Laure yet? I'm glad she finally showed."

Catch up. Nice one, Lottie. Like we were firm old buddies who'd just lost touch.

"No—not properly. We chatted a bit last night, but we've probably got a bit more to sort out today. I don't think she's awake yet."

You need to tell the actual truth, Meg.

All of it.

I blinked against the memory, refocusing on the canvases. "So, can I see them?"

Lottie gave a firm shake of her head. "Nope, not yet. It's a surprise. You'll have to wait until this evening like everybody else."

The entire house reeked of burning fat. Downstairs, Ollie was busily cremating bacon on the stove, while Saira sat at the table nursing a bowl of granola and yogurt. Joss, dressed head to toe in black Adidas and sporting huge shades, and Charlie, face hidden within the depths of his hoodie, clutched mugs of tea on the couch.

"Bacon, Meg?" called Ollie, unusually jovial despite his heroic alcohol intake the night before. I suspected he was still drunk. I shook my head and reached for the plastic container of cornflakes.

"No, thanks. Where's the others?" I asked nonchalantly, trying not to read anything into the fact that only Laure and Seb were missing.

"Seb's out running, and I haven't seen Laure, so she must be still in bed," replied Charlie.

"Wait, no she isn't," said Saira, looking up from her phone. "Her bedroom's next to mine. I noticed the door was open as I came down. The bed didn't even look slept in."

"Hold up," said Joss. "Here's the *tea*! No wonder Seb's out for a run."

A sudden wave of nausea juddered through me, my skin clammy and tight, as I realized what she meant. The *implication*.

"Laure must be in the studio, then, apologizing to Lottie for all the noise she made with her brother last night," Ollie said, waggling his eyebrows.

"*Jesus*, Ollie—" muttered Saira in disgust.

"Must have been a good night," said Charlie, "because I'm pretty sure I heard some screaming."

I looked at him, surprised. In the light of day, I'd convinced myself that my strange dream had been nothing but that—a nightmare. He caught my eye, his expression dark. At that moment the kitchen door burst open and Seb came in, breathing heavily, his skin dewed with drizzle.

"There he is!" brayed Ollie. "We were just applauding your game, mate. Fast work, even for you."

"What?" breathed Seb, leaning on the counter and looking confused. "What's up?"

"You and Laure," Joss drawled.

Seb gave a nervous laugh. "What? What are you on about? I haven't seen her since last night."

You don't know what she's capable of—

For some reason that screaming came into my head again, and I spoke urgently.

"Joking aside, where is she, then? Laure, I mean? If she's not in her room or in the studio. . . . I was just up there—or down here?"

Joss shrugged, bored now. "Probably off somewhere on her phone again. You know Laure."

"All right, but did anyone else hear sobbing or screaming late last night?"

Saira slowly put down her spoon, staring at me. "Yeah, actually. It sounded pretty far away. . . . I thought I was dreaming. You don't think something's happened to her?"

I shrugged. "I don't know, but it's weird, isn't it? Laure's never exactly struck me as the adventurous type. The type to go wandering off on her own."

Saira got up. "Yeah, you're right, you know. We should go look for her," she said, an urgency to her tone that wasn't there before.

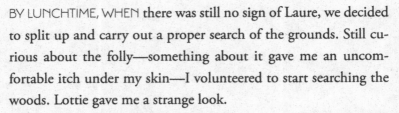

16

BY LUNCHTIME, WHEN there was still no sign of Laure, we decided to split up and carry out a proper search of the grounds. Still curious about the folly—something about it gave me an uncomfortable itch under my skin—I volunteered to start searching the woods. Lottie gave me a strange look.

"Are you sure, Meg? The paths are less than obvious. They've not been maintained for years. And the woods themselves are pretty deep and dark."

Seb rolled his eyes. "Let me guess, Eimer's influence again?" He mimicked a high-pitched Irish accent. " 'Those that wander too far in are never the same once they wander out.' The woods are *fine*. I'll come with you, if you like, Meg?" he finished, turning expectantly toward me.

I bit my lip, silencing the *yes* that had been about to jump out. Maybe it was unreasonable, but I was still annoyed at the insinuation that Seb had been with Laure last night—especially after he'd sworn to me that they were over. When she finally showed up, maybe we could compare notes and see just how long he had been playing us against each other.

Coolly, I declined and, donning my raincoat, headed outside alone.

Well, Lottie hadn't been wrong.

I followed the overgrown path that circled the lake, a mean little thing that, once I entered the forest, meandered, fainter and fainter beneath the trees, until I lost sight of it altogether and found myself in the semidarkness, the canopy of leaves lower than I'd expected, the trunks of the trees twisted together, blocking out the already weak daylight. As I tried to move faster in search of any kind of path, branches clawed at my clothes, as if trying to prevent my escape. A dim sense of panic began to form within me.

"Laure?" I called halfheartedly. Somehow I *knew* she wasn't here. I *felt* it. Who would willingly come here alone?

I forced myself to a stop, breathing hard and looking around me, unsure now of the direction I had taken to get where I was. The ground was thick with mud that oozed beneath my sneakers, stuck fast with dead leaves. I remembered a riddle from my childhood, one that my dad had told me, long ago, before he left.

How far can you go into a wood?

Only halfway. After that, you're walking out.

It might have been a cringey dad joke, but it also made sense. If I just headed in one direction, I'd emerge *somewhere*—with any luck, back onto the main road—or at least *a* road. Then I could use Google Maps again. At the moment, all the crappy signal here revealed was that I was a blue circle in an immense amount of green, which was not a great help.

Cursing Laure under my breath, I kept on walking, my progress slow, hampered by the mud. The silence of the wood, interrupted only by the occasional odd and jarring birdcall, bringing to mind all sorts of unpleasant things. That woman we'd nearly hit on the way down here. Her *sobbing*. And that screaming I'd heard last night in my dreams. Could it have been real?

Bean sí, Emma had called them. Unhappy spirits found by water.

What was it Lottie had said? *A woman drowned herself and her kid—wanted to make it quick for them both—*

Banshees.

Harbinger. Harbingers of *death*.

I shook my head with a grim smile. The hell was I thinking? Banshees weren't real—neither were hauntings. And while the story about the drowning was tragic, it had happened hundreds of years ago. All it was, was local legend and superstition. Drawing a steadying breath, I trudged on through the mud, dodging branches. At least the leaves were blocking the worst of the rain. Soon I began to glimpse something through the trees ahead. I increased my pace, hoping it might be a farm or a house where I would be able claw back some sense of direction.

Despite my excitement at seeing it from a distance, my heart sank when I realized I had only reached the folly. I felt as if I'd been walking for miles. It was a dour, formidable presence up close, surrounded by a leaning fence of rusted barbed wire half claimed by ivy. From the wire hung ancient signs made almost illegible by water damage, warning people to keep out for various reasons. THIS BUILDING IS PATROLLED BY SECURITY (chance would be a fine thing). THIS BUILDING IS STRUCTURALLY UNSOUND.

Curious, I located a lopsided gate in the fence and creaked it open, approaching the tower. The walls were coated with the same gray stucco as the house, the structure an unforgiving cylinder with an incongruous PVC door at the bottom, now dirty yellow with age. Remembering Emma's words about the folly being locked, I gave the handle a defeated tug and was surprised when the door swung easily open.

Inside, the darkness was absolute and had the musty, sour smell of places long abandoned, laced with stale piss. It reminded me of the deserted gun emplacements found on Wimbledon airfield, littered with empty beer cans, joint ends, and condom wrappers. Still, I had little choice but to go in. If I could get up to one of the higher floors, I could easily work out the direction back to the house and keep an eye out for any landmarks along the way.

Switching on my phone's flashlight, I stepped inside.

There wasn't much to see at first. Two plastic garden chairs sat beneath a broken window, both once white, now a filthy gray. On the floor was a sodden red blanket edged in itchy-looking satin spattered with mildew, and beside that, a wooden table thick with dust, upon which sat a cheap-looking composition notebook, the pages curled up at the edges.

I gave the book a tentative poke, half worried it might be hollowed out and filled with paper-eating spiders or something, then picked it up. It crossed my mind that it could be an old schoolbook of Seb's or Lottie's. Something we could laugh at back at the house.

Only a couple of pages had anything written on them—the rest were blank. The first page looked like the end of the journal, the previous pages hastily ripped out.

WHAT a summer we're having!

We went for our first swim together this morning. Already the sun was high in the sky and the water was so warm for this time of year. I can't say I'm ever wild about being in that lake. All those choking, slimy weeds and whatever else lives in it—you feel dirtier coming out than you do going in. Still, the view was pretty nice, and I don't just mean the scenery.

The lake's artificial, built around the same time the house and the folly were built for some rich old English aristocrat. Dad pretends to like the family that owns it, but I know he doesn't. I mean, it's not like he holds some ancient grudge because of things that happened centuries ago—unforgivable, wicked things. I know many still do, but Dad's not like that. It's more their attitude, he says. Says they act as if everything's disposable. As if everything only exists to suit them. I don't think him working on the grounds helps matters, to be honest. The date carved above the front door of the house acts as a constant reminder that some of our ancestors are actually buried here in the woods.

So the lake is nothing but a giant hole, dug by exhausted, starving laborers for rich people to fanny about it. Same as the folly. Dad tells me I'm forbidden to swim in it. Says it's unnatural and God knows what lies beneath it. Dad's rational and means man-made things, not that it's haunted as some say. Rusting machinery or hidden currents. All the same things they warn you to be careful about when swimming in quarries and the like.

I think.

Still, this hilarious dark expression comes over his face whenever he talks about it. There's some legend about a bean sí. I've overheard Darragh O'Brien say it's haunted by the spirit of a peasant woman when he's had one too many at O'Shea's. She's meant to have drowned her child and then herself before they died of starvation after her husband was killed in an accident building the folly. They say she's always looking for people to drag back into the lake with her to replace her kid. Sounds scary enough until you remember there's legends about literally every single body of water in the country.

I love coming here, though—to the house. It's about a million times better than our tiny place in the village.

And then there's him.

I was wary of him when we first met. As Sinead would say, he looks like the type who's only after a ride. He's pretty and so charming, with an accent like a fairy-tale prince. But he noticed me—kept making an effort to speak to me. And ever since that evening, the two of us alone in the folly, he's all I've been able to think about—

It stopped there, as if the writer had been interrupted. I raised an eyebrow. Looked like someone at least had had some fun here. Based on the notebook's age, a summer romance from back when the house used to be a bed and breakfast was my guess. The next page looked like some kind of poem, written in the same elegant hand, the pencil faded and faint, blotched here and there with mildew.

I live in the weeds,
The sun-starved ditches,
Dressed in nettles,
My voice the ebb of the bloated river.

And scratched out beneath:

WHAT ARE YOU CAPABLE OF?

Despite the weak sun shining through the thin glass panes, I felt a chill shadow run over me and I shivered, dropping the book back where it was. Whoever wrote those words hadn't intended them for me and yet . . . didn't they fit?

—*I didn't mean to do it—I pushed her but I didn't mean for her to fall in—I didn't know she couldn't swim—I didn't mean it—*

Against the far wall was a dated kitchenette and several Formica stools, everything colored in the tobacco-brown hues of the seventies. I made my way over to the window and forced open the plastic blinds, letting the dull gray light of the forest wash over the space. The staircase was in the middle of the room, a rickety metal affair that wobbled alarmingly when I touched it—more of a lighthouse-style ladder than the sturdy stone stairs of my dream. But the ceiling was low, and the next floor only a little way up, so, holding on tight, I half climbed, half hauled myself up through the square space onto the floor above.

Here was another seating area complete with a couple of busted old leather sofas—their yellowed insides spilling open like guts. As I paused, I heard a frantic skittering sound behind them so made the hasty decision to keep going up. The next floor was entirely empty except for dust. I wondered if I was high enough now to see above the tree line so I gingerly stepped out onto the floorboards, remembering Emma's earlier warning about the place being a death trap, and crept toward the window. Here, instead of the plastic blinds of the first floor, were a pair of old-fashioned wooden shutters, currently closed. Unlatching the rusting clasp, I wrenched them both open with an alarming creak. As I did so, I heard a heavy *flump* from overhead.

It sounded like something soft but heavy falling to the floor.

A *body*?

"Laure?" I called softly. I chided myself almost immediately. What would she be doing a mile away from the house, sitting alone in a dark abandoned tower? No doubt it was just the building settling. Something integral in its build shifting at the weight of my intrusion.

I turned my attention back to the window. I was just above the tree line now, but all I could make out from this direction was yet more forest, stretching on as far as the eye could see. I gave a small shudder. If I'd known the forest was as large as this, I would never have volunteered to search it. I edged carefully round to the opposite window and opened the shuttters on that side.

A soft wave of relief washed over me.

There, in the near distance was the solid gray block of Wren Hall, almost indistinguishable from the pregnant sky above it. Yet more rain on its way, then. Feeling relieved, I decided not to explore the rest of the tower—not alone, anyway—imagining myself trapped within its floors for weeks before anyone realized I was here.

Making my way back to the stairs in the center of the room,

I hesitated. Above the alarming squeaking of the floorboards beneath my feet, I thought I could hear something else.

It was the sound of someone sobbing.

Soft and barely distinguishable, but there all the same. Wasn't it?

No. Of course it wasn't. It was impossible. There was no way anyone else was here.

I raised my eyes to the ceiling. How many floors were above me? I recalled how the folly had towered out of the woods, like an accusing finger pointing directly at the sky. And I had only just made it above the tree line.

"Laure?" I called out. Sharper, louder. I didn't *want* to look upstairs. I didn't want Laure to be here. Why would she be?

But the sobbing continued, undeniable now. Low and morose, accompanied by a soft rhythmic creaking, as if someone were slowly rocking back and forth in misery.

I took a few steps over to the stairs and looked up into utter darkness. No. There was no way. Laure would not be sitting up there in the dark, surrounded by cobwebs and skittering things. She didn't *like* old things. Moaned about going to any bar or café that wasn't shiny and new. Strongly disliked the vintage trend. Scoffed at the very idea of wearing anything secondhand and refused to enter thrift stores.

Laure was *not* up there.

But if she wasn't, then who was?

I took a deep breath. Whoever it was, I couldn't just leave them. Could it be Emma, perhaps? Or was it somebody homeless? Maybe an addict? But would they really choose this tower, miles away from civilization—from the nearest shop—as a place to stay?"

Or . . .

This place is meant to be cursed.

Stop. I banished the thought from my mind. "Hey . . . Emma?" I called.

I stood on the first step, still listening intently to the sobbing, which had grown in intensity, undeniable now.

"Hey—look—I'm coming up," I said, more bravely than I felt.

My words were followed by a sudden series of quick thumps—the sound of someone running across the floor? Then, abruptly, the crying stopped mid-sob. There was utter silence for a few seconds, broken only by the howling of the wind around the tower, and then a laugh: low and cold and gleeful—and worst of all—close.

My entire body turned to ice at the sound and I half jumped down the stairs to the floor below, the whole tower seeming to sway as I landed. That laugh came again, following by the unmistakable ringing of quick footsteps on metal. Someone was coming down the stairs now, and fast.

Clinging onto the floorboards, I swung my body into the gap that led to the ground floor. As I did so, the light on my phone switched itself off, plunging the entire tower into darkness. I swallowed a scream.

I could just make out the white PVC door in the thin bars of light that crept through the closed blinds (*hadn't I opened them?*) and lurched over, desperate to get out now, but to my horror, the door wouldn't budge. I wrenched at it, hard, but still it wouldn't open. Outside, the sky darkened, casting long shadows in the cramped space. The footsteps on the stairs had quieted, but I fancied I could hear them still—soft and sly.

I knelt down to peer at the handle, trying it a few times as I did so. Impossibly, it looked as though the door was now locked. Had the latch inside fallen as it had shut behind me?

Cursing under my breath, I tried the handle again, harder, my hands sore as I yanked at it. It still wouldn't move.

"Shit, shit, *shit*," I muttered. From somewhere above I could hear muffled movement. Slower now. As if they knew there was no way I was escaping and they had all the time in the world. I thought of the woman on the lake from my nightmare—the banshee from Lottie's paintings. Impossibly tall, hatred radiating from her black eyes. There was no way anyone from the house would hear me calling. Panic started to flutter into my heart, painful, my chest aching. I glanced at the windows. The glass was thin. I could probably smash it, using the blanket for protection, but how was I meant to climb out without cutting myself on the jagged shards?

A muffled noise from close above me—a stifled giggle, a suppressed sob—forced me into action. I picked up the blanket, shuddering as hundreds of fat wood lice scattered sleepily away. Holding the stinking thing in my hands, I stared at the floor beneath.

There was a thick, dark stain, like dried red wine, spattered across the faded tiles.

There was no time to think about it now. Wrapping the blanket firmly around my fist, I wrenched the blinds away and struck at the thin panes of glass, my breathing stuck, until finally they shattered.

A dark shadow passed the window, momentarily blocking the weak light and making me flinch. Then the door opened with a bang, the gale outside blowing it almost off its hinges.

And standing illuminated in the doorway was Seb.

17

"YOU OKAY?" HE asked. "I was checking around the lake and heard glass shattering. The door was unlocked—could you not get it open?"

He looked genuinely concerned, his dark brow furrowed. I brushed past him, desperate to get out of the stifling confines of the tower.

"Seb, I don't want to alarm you, but there's someone *in* there," I said, shutting the door firmly behind me.

He laughed. "No *way*. No one's been in there for years. I thought it was all locked up. It was only when I heard you screaming that I came over. I mean, I get it. It's a creepy old place—especially in the dark."

Had I been screaming? I didn't *remember* screaming—

"Honestly, though, there is," I insisted. "I heard them crying and walking about—then—then *laughing*. I don't know if it's safe—but—but what if it's Laure, Seb? We have to check."

Seb's face sobered at this. So she'd not been found yet.

"You're right—wait here, then; I'll have a quick look up top."

Minutes later he returned, alone. As he emerged into the dim light, he looked different: paler, distracted.

"Well?"

He ran a hand through his hair. "Nope, like I told you, nothing up there at all—other than some alarmingly large spiders. We better head back to the house. Lottie's started freaking out."

I didn't argue. Seb had no reason to lie that I knew of, and there was no way I was going back in there myself. We walked for a while in silence as Seb confidently led the way through the forest, along paths I hadn't noticed, listening as the rain pattered peacefully around us.

"You're sure there was nothing up there," I ventured again. "I honestly did hear something—footsteps and what sounded like crying."

"Birds, probably, or foxes. I didn't look too closely, but definitely looks like the denizens of the forest are making themselves at home in there."

That *wasn't* what I heard coming down the stairs.

"You can't dismiss everything as animals, Seb," I muttered resentfully, feeling foolish. "It can't all be foxes and birds. Emma says the lake's haunted—and Lottie's mentioned it too. Now, I don't think it's something supernatural but—"

Seb stopped so suddenly, I collided into him.

He turned slowly to face me.

"*Who?*"

"Emma," I said, confused. "The housekeeper."

Seb immediately relaxed, his shoulders slumping. "It's

pronounced *Ee*-mer, not Emma. And there are a lot of superstitions around here. Well, a lot of things they love to tell the tourists. Complete crap, though. And as for Lottie—" He frowned. "Like I said, she's not been doing so well since she got here."

We walked for a while in silence. I wanted to know more about what was troubling Lottie but now didn't seem the time.

"So, was Wren Hall nice when you came here as a kid?"

Seb grinned good-naturedly. "Are you saying it's not nice now? Nah, I get it. It's definitely run-down. But yeah, back in the day it was nice. Still as dated, but in better condition. Y'know, the lawns freshly mown, the lake wasn't flooded and rampant with weeds. Lottie and I actually used to love coming here on holiday. We had the run of the whole place. Pretty different from London."

The trees were thinning out now, the house visible in the distance. I let out a relieved breath and then immediately recalled it as Seb stopped again, placing a hand on my shoulder.

"Hey, Meg. Before Lottie took her little dip last night, I was about to apologize. Not just for snapping at you last night but for—for everything." He looked away, raising his gaze above me. "I *know* I should have called you after the ball. And I wanted to. You know, you might not believe me, but I read every single message you sent me, listened to every single voice mail. And I'm sorry, I should have reached out sooner."

I raised my shoulder, nudging away his hand. Memories of the desperate messages I'd sent flooded my mind: my eyes sore and red with tears, my heart open and bleeding through my desperately typing fingers. The rawness of my pain seemed somehow embarrassing now.

"Why, though?" I asked. "Why didn't you?"

I regretted the words as soon as they met the air. Because the answer was obvious. He didn't care. Not enough, anyway. Didn't want to get tangled up in the mess I had made. And I'd gone, hadn't I? Erased from Greyscott's. No longer his problem.

His eyes alighted on mine, dark with guilt, and I felt that heat again, curdling in my stomach. I wanted to slide a hand down his cheek, to grab his hair, pull his mouth to mine. I wanted to tell him it didn't matter now. That he was here and I was here and everything was all right.

I wanted a million impossible things.

He ran a hand over his face.

"A lot of reasons, I guess," he answered. "I was embarrassed—*ashamed*—by how I acted that night. I know I was a prick—you were right. And then there was Lottie. . . . I basically needed to fix a bunch of things, but I wasn't sure how. I mean, all I really have for you is a load of crap excuses. But I hope you know—hope you believe—that I am sorry."

And would you ever had called me? I wanted to ask. *Would I ever even have heard from you again, if not for Lottie's invitation? Is the only reason you're acknowledging what you did . . . because I'm here now?*

It was toward the end of my first term at Greyscott's, as the nights grew longer and darker and a vast twinkling Christmas tree appeared in the entrance hall, when Laure finally revealed herself, her true colors unfolding like the wings of some nightmarish butterfly. By then I'd let my guard down almost entirely, basking in the warm feeling of being one of *them*. Enjoying the surprised (and still often derisive) looks I got as I stood chatting with Lottie by her locker. Luckily, being part of the art set had excused a lot—my eccentric way of dressing (*actual* thrifted castoffs), my lack of absolutely anything designer, my encyclopedic knowledge of the chicken shops of southeast London.

That day, Lottie, Charlie, and I had been sitting together on a pair of chesterfields that sandwiched a low oak table in the large common room of Greyscott's, eating lunch while sleet peppered the tall arched windows—superfood poke bowls, of course; no burgers here—and chatting about the preparations for the upcoming Christmas party. Laure had joined us a few minutes later, slumping down beside Lottie, a dark look on her face.

"God, I got roped into helping with the school website again," she muttered, rummaging in her bag and pulling out a single apple in lieu of a lunch box. She bit into it and looked at me, an odd, cold gleam in her eyes. "We were adjusting the staffing list. Have you got family at the school, Meg? Y'know a Sharon Green?"

My forkful of salad turned to dust in my mouth. I mean, I could have easily denied it. Green was almost as common a surname as Smith. But what kind of monster denies their own *mother*? I chewed for a while before answering, unable to meet her eye.

"Yeah. Uh, so that's my mum."

The gleam in Laure's eyes had brightened, becoming almost demonic. It wasn't exactly that I was ashamed of my mum. If anything, I was monumentally proud of her. As a single mother—my dad had buggered off when I was a kid, reduced to nothing more than a fiver scrunched into a cheap birthday card once a year—she worked two jobs to keep up with the mortgage on our tiny flat. But at the same time, I knew what people here would think. What they would say behind my back when they found out exactly what she did.

"Domestic supervisor," announced Laure, squinting at her phone. "Huh. What does that mean, exactly? She's not on the teaching staff, then?"

Opposite me, Lottie shifted uncomfortably in her seat. We all *knew* what it meant. Maybe everyone had always known. Maybe it was part of why Lottie had befriended me—out of pity.

"She's on the cleaning team," I said, forcing myself to look directly at Laure, challenging her to continue. "I mean, is there a problem with that? With her job? It's how I heard about the scholarship."

Laure snorted, pretending she was trying to keep a straight face, still not bothering to look up from her phone. "Cool, cool. There's no problem at all, it's just I've been wondering what that smell was, that's all. But that explains it. Eau de *piss*, right? Suppose it's an unavoidable hazard of living with someone who cleans the loos in this dump."

"Laure!" said Lottie, visibly shocked. I was gratified at the absolute lack of amusement on her face.

"What?" said Laure, wide-eyed. "C'mon, it's just a *fact*, Lottie. Meg's mother cleans the toilets. It's honest work—we're not nineteenth-century aristocrats who need to pretend all that stuff doesn't happen." She looked back at me, calm and measured, a condescending smirk on her face, and for the very first time, I *hated* her. "We still love you, though, Meg." She looked over at

Lottie again and grinned. "Maybe just keep an eye on your vintage Chanel when she's around, yeah?"

I could feel my face growing hotter and hotter, sweat moistening my palms. This was *exactly* the kind of thing that had kept me awake all night in the weeks before I started at Greyscott's. "I'm not ashamed that my mum works hard for a living," I muttered. "Besides, you're fine. Chanel's a little mumsy for my tastes."

I was pleased to see Laure taken aback. Clearly, she hadn't bargained on me having teeth.

Beside me, I heard Charlie audibly exhale and nudge me under the table.

"C'mon, Meg. We've gotta get to class." He shook his head at a still-smirking Laure. "Jesus, Laure. I've gotta say—you're everything that's wrong with new money."

I followed Charlie back into the main building in a daze, my thoughts racing.

Had I done something to upset Laure? The absolute 180 in her attitude toward me was ridiculous. Was this still over Seb's sitting next to me once in class—at Lottie's request? There was no way she could know what had happened that day in his kitchen. And besides, nothing *had* happened—not really. Or was it genuinely because I was poor? I understood the not fitting-in thing. It made sense that I'd be left out of the shallow bitchier groups where things like that mattered. But Lottie had made it very clear to me her crowd wasn't like that. And I *did* fit in—or so I thought. Had I been naïve to believe it?

Head spinning, I stopped in the bathroom before my next class, needing to compose myself before sitting in the same room as Laure again. As I sat in the stall, I heard the door creak open and voices drift through the space.

Lottie and Laure.

"She's so frickin' *annoying*, though," Laure was saying. "I don't know how you put up with her following you around like a lost dog all the time. It's pathetic."

My blood chilled as I waited, crushed, to hear Lottie inevitably deny me.

"Laure, c'mon," she replied. "What's happened between you two? I mean, why are you being such a bitch all of a sudden? She's not following me around—I *like* her—and so did you! And who cares about her background—that shit's so shallow. What matters is she's kind, not to mention a lot of fun—and when it comes to art, she's really talented. Not like some of the other wannabes in Desjardins's class."

My heart almost burst with happiness.

"Okay, fine, but you haven't heard the stuff *I've* heard about her lately," pressed Laure darkly. "I was chatting to someone who went to her old school. Apparently she was on her last warning there. She had anger issues. Probably why they were singing her praises—couldn't wait to be rid of her, I bet."

"Uh-huh. So, she's got a bit of a temper? She needs to be able to stick up for herself round here, especially with you bitching at her all the time. Why are you digging up dirt on her anyway?"

"I also heard something else—but I'm not sure if I should tell you—"

I rolled my eyes wondering what poisonous lie would drip from her lips next. Even Lottie audibly sighed. "Go on."

"Well, I have it on good authority, your studio is *not* what she's interested in when she's popping round yours. You know she's there more often when she knows you're not."

"Good authority, oh, okay? So what *is* she interested in? Let me guess, Dad's collection of rare Montblancs?"

Laure snorted. "Well, possibly, but I've heard she's got her sights set on Seb."

Lottie just laughed, but my skin grew clammy and hot.

How was it possible Laure *knew*?

I hadn't told *anyone*—least of all Seb. Had it been so obvious to him? Had he been laughing at me, at my pathetic crush on him, with Laure?

"Are you serious? I don't think they've spoken more than two words to each other in all the times she's been over. You know Seb, he's either out training or locked in the den, gaming. Besides, you know what he's like. Once he's into someone you can't shut him up and he's not even mentioned her name." She paused. "C'mon, Laure, be honest. The problem isn't really Meg at all, is it?"

When we got back to the house, things were tense.

"Right, I'm going to call the police," said Saira darkly, taking one look at us as we entered the kitchen without Laure. Joss and Charlie had also returned from their searches, and were seated at the table, listening as Saira continued. "This isn't like Laure. This isn't like her at all."

I chewed my lip. Had Laure changed her mind about our talk overnight and just gone home? Had she been toying with me yesterday? Holding the prospect of my return to Greyscott's out before her like some golden trophy before cruelly snatching it away again. I wouldn't have put it past her . . .

Joss stood and walked over to the latticed kitchen window that looked out onto the dark expanse of Wren Lake. "I didn't want to be the one to say it but . . . you don't think she went for a midnight dip and um . . ."

Saira shook her head, shooting me a small apologetic look. "We all know Laure can't swim. We found *that* out at the ball."

"People think they can do anything when they're drunk," said Charlie sagely. "I mean, look at Lottie last night—"

"But she *wasn't* drunk," I said absently, taking a seat beside Charlie. "Laure, I mean. I was talking to her late last night and she definitely wasn't drunk."

There was a moment of long, uncomfortable silence that was suddenly broken by the violent buzz of Joss's phone on the dining table. We all stared at the name that appeared on screen.

Joss picked it up and was silent for a few minutes, then gave a long exhale of relief. "Oh, thank *fuck*. She's fine. Says she's gone to a hotel to clear her head after last night. Needed some space." She thumbed at her phone in evident annoyance. "Jesus, the signal is shitty out here. I *just* got service—who knows when she even sent this. Could have saved us a lot of worrying if it'd come through earlier."

I ran a hand over my mouth, trying to hide my frustration. So she *had* changed her mind about talking, then. That, or she'd never had any intention of forgiving me in the first place.

Joss held up the phone so we could all see, then turned to Seb, a mischievous grin on her generous features. "Jesus, Seb. What did you *say* to her last night?"

Seb ran a hand through his curls and collapsed into a chair. I thought he'd be angry at the implication but he only looked genuinely relieved.

"What? Nothing? We barely even spoke. Thank God she's okay."

But Joss wouldn't let it go. "Oh, come *on*, Seb. I heard you both chatting away until the early hours. You forget your room's directly above mine. I can hear everything—well, almost everything. What did you say that made Princess Laure run off to some crappy B and B in the middle of nowhere?"

"And, hate to mention it again, but *I* heard screaming," murmured Charlie.

"Well, she's literally nowhere in this house," said Lottie, ducking into the kitchen, followed by Ollie, busily brushing what looked like several decades of dust from his hair. "We even checked the attic."

"It's all right," said Joss, her gaze still focused on Seb. "She just messaged—said she's gone to clear her head."

I watched the small tells in Seb. I knew them well. His pupils enlarging, his eyes darkening, his hands tightening on the arms of the chair, knuckles whitening.

"I wasn't talking to anyone late last night, Joss," he said, rising. "But even if I *had been*, you should learn to mind your own bloody business."

"Laure's my friend, so this *is* my business," Joss snapped back. "Everyone knew how shittily you treated her. It wasn't exactly a secret, now, was it? She didn't even want to come here." Her eyes flashed to Lottie. "But we all know why she did. Hardly *ethical*, is it, Lots? Forcing her to come and further Meg's fucked-up agenda by dangling your brother in front of her like *bait*."

"Jesus, chill out, Joss," said Ollie, who'd crossed to the fridge and was pulling out a beer. "Guy can't help it if Laure was obsessed with him."

"Ollie," said Seb, his voice sterner than I'd ever heard it. "That's enough, all right? Now we know she's all right, I'm sure we've got better things to do than sit around gossiping about her."

"Exactly," smoothed Lottie. "Like getting ready for this evening." She whipped the beer can out of Ollie's grasp. "And no more for you. Best behavior for the viewing."

Charlie gave a forced laugh of disbelief. "You can't be serious, Lottie. Don't you think we should wait for Laure to come back instead of immediately swanning off to a party? Message or not, she's clearly not in a good place. Did you *see* her last night? I mean, really a get a good look at her?"

I squirmed a little in my seat.

Lottie paled and Saira quickly took up the mantle.

"Yeah, I think Charlie's right. Something about this still feels wrong. We all know Laure. This isn't like her at all—to just up and leave without a word. To go to some random hotel alone in the middle of nowhere. How'd she even get there? Did anyone hear a taxi pull up? Because I didn't."

Lottie exhaled and crumpled into a chair. "God, you're right. What was I thinking? Joss—try giving her a call back? If she did just message, then she should have her phone nearby."

Joss picked up the phone and set it to speaker. The ring trilled shrilly in the cavernous room until eventually it clicked off and the robotic voice of the answerphone cut it, reading out Laure's number.

"So do we leave a message or what?"

But Seb held up a hand.

"Shh, a sec—ring it again, but don't put it on speaker," he murmured. With a confused shrug, Joss did exactly as she was told.

Then, from somewhere above us, we all heard it.

The repetitive vibration of a phone ringing on silent.

18

WE ALL LOOKED at each other for a moment in confused silence.

Then Lottie smiled, her familiar big grin breaking the tension in the room. "What is she *playing* at? She *must* still be here!" We watched her leave the room, her footsteps lightly running up the stairs, calling Laure's name.

"Weird," murmured Saira, looking over at Ollie. "Swear you guys just said you searched this whole place top to bottom."

Charlie headed over to the range and fired up the kettle. "Well, thank God for that. Now, who wants a cuppa?"

But a minute or so later, Lottie reemerged into the kitchen, empty-handed and pale.

"Her room's empty, but all her stuff's still there—all her clothes. I couldn't find her phone anywhere. . . . The hell's going on here?" she murmured. "Joss—that text was definitely from her?"

"Uh, yeah . . . you all saw it," replied Joss defensively.

"So she's definitely not upstairs?" interrupted Saira, speaking for us all.

"No," said Lottie quietly. "No, she's not. She's not in the house at all. Unless she's hiding . . . which would be . . . mad."

A lunatic vision of Laure crouching inside the wardrobe of an empty room flashed into mind. I shook my head, driving it away.

A loud crack of thunder broke the silence, shaking the house. The light in the kitchen seemed prematurely dark, shadows pooling inkily in the corners as the wind screamed about the eaves.

"Try her phone again," I prompted Joss.

Casting me a dark look, she once more put her phone on speaker and dialed Laure's number. Laure's face popped up on the screen, smiling widely, her arms slung around Lottie and Joss. This time, instead of ringing, the phone gave three low beeps and cut off.

"It's either switched off or she's not got any signal," snapped Joss, thrusting the phone back in her bag.

"Right, I'm calling the police," said Saira, her chair shrieking across the kitchen tiles. "None of this makes sense. She wouldn't just vanish without any of her stuff. Was her bag gone?"

"Wait—*wait*," said Seb. "Let's think things through logically. They're going to have questions when they get here—best we get things straight first. Who was the last person to see Laure last night?"

Get things *straight*? What did he mean? Laure *was* coming back, one way or another. I rubbed my eyes, the image of her pale face underwater filling my head. Silent in that drowning daze—

"*You* were," snapped Joss immediately. "Like I said, I heard you talking in your room."

"Yeah, we were talking," replied Seb slowly, visibly calmer now. "But then she left to go downstairs and find Meg."

I nodded, forcing myself to be calm. A deep red wave of guilt crawled over me as six pairs of eyes focused in on me.

You haven't done anything wrong. Not this *time.*

"That's right, and we chatted for a bit in the kitchen. She seemed sound, though. Looked a bit tired maybe—but she didn't seem upset or anything, and she wasn't drunk. I told her how sorry I was about—about how everything went down at the ball." My words sounded strangled and pathetic. Too small. Barely filling the ragged black hole of guilt I'd created. "Then she said she was going to bed."

Saira nodded. "All right. Does anyone have any rough idea of timings?"

"Why does it matter?" said Charlie, passing out mugs of tea, his manner relaxed. "We were all pissed. She obviously got upset over something someone said and headed off for some space. She's gonna show in a few hours."

"Headed where, though?" asked Saira quietly. She cast a meaningful glance at the window where the heavens had opened and rain was lashing in chevroned sheets down the glass. "She doesn't know this area. And then there's her phone. How'd she text Joss without it?"

Seb nodded in silent confirmation.

"I don't know about the rest of you, but my signal here is dodgy as hell," said Joss. "She could have sent it before she left and it's only just got through."

Saira rolled her eyes in exasperation and turned back to me. "But we literally just heard it vibrating somewhere in the house. Meg, what time did she head up to bed last night?"

I had no idea. "I don't know—I'd overdone the vodka by that

point. But it was just before Lottie's little swim." I frowned at little, irritated at Saira's apparent decision to appoint herself detective.

"Come on, it's clear what happened," said Lottie. "Seb pissed her off *yet again* and she's stormed off somewhere, messaged Joss before she went then left her phone because she didn't want him to contact her—or just forgot it—"

"For the last time, I *didn't* piss her off!" seethed Seb.

"Oh yeah? So what about that screaming?" interjected Charlie, a dark look on his face. "I know I wasn't the only one who heard it last night?"

"Come off it, Charlie. If you legit heard actual screaming, why'd you just roll over and go back to sleep?" said Seb, his arms folded.

"Probably just the house," chimed in Lottie. "It's ancient. The wind gets through gaps in the brickwork, in the window frames, and makes the weirdest noises."

"Okay, fine," said Saira. "But none of this explains why her phone is here and she's not? Sorry, but this is as weird as all hell. I'm calling the police."

Saira put her phone on speaker and placed it in the middle of the table. It rang for a few seconds, then the line seemed to cut out, replaced by a flat burr. She frowned and pressed redial. This time it didn't even ring. There was a long minute of static silence and the call cut out. Picking up her phone, Saira repeated this several times.

"The hell? Someone else try?"

"Service must be down, or something," said Ollie after a few more fruitless attempts. "I'm guessing there's no Wi-Fi. You got a landline somewhere?"

Lottie shook her head. "Even if we did, the bill won't have been paid for God knows how long. *Shit.* What do we do?"

Looking back, I think the cracks in our group truly started to show at the Greyscott Christmas party—my first glimpse of the school's wilder excesses. The party was being held in the enormous auditorium, with its vaulted ceiling, polished walnut paneling and elaborate frescoes foiled in gold; the floor beneath us a dangerously smooth expanse of silver-veined marble. A ten-foot Christmas tree stood regally in a corner, festooned with gold and red angel-hair tinsel, garlands of popcorn and cranberry, and antique glass baubles—no pound-shop gaudiness here.

The theme this year—I'd quickly discovered there was *always* a theme at Greyscott's; the principal was a sucker for one apparently—was the Nutcracker Suite. Thankfully, Lottie had kindly messaged me a Pinterest board once I'd confessed I had no idea what that actually was. All around me drifted rosy-cheeked sugar plum fairies in yards of pastel silk and glittered tulle, and bleary-eyed soldiers in red velvet frock coats. Unlike most, I'd had to get the bus here, so I'd dressed low-key in a thrifted black military jacket over a white silk slip.

The choir were performing as I walked in, singing something hideously complicated in what must have been Latin as my eyes darted about the gleaming room for someone I knew.

"Edgy as ever—love it, girl." Charlie popped up beside me, dressed in an exquisite suit cut from silver velvet, a lace-edged silk shirt beneath. I smiled at him.

"Yeah, I would have worn my mouse king outfit but some of us had to use public transport," I quipped. "Where are the others?"

Charlie rolled his eyes. "Ugh, despite this being the season of goodwill, *something's* going down. . . . From what I can gather, Lottie and Laure have had some kind of bust-up. Laure's off crying on someone's shoulder—taking a wild guess here—probably Seb's. Honestly, the drama never stops. I live for it." He passed me a silver flask. "Here—Christmas gift to the gang from Ollie. In case you need something stronger than soda to get through the night, which if the last ten minutes has been any indication, you most definitely will. C'mon, let's go find Lots."

He pulled at my elbow, guiding me through the crowds, but my mind was still caught on his words.

Laure's crying on Seb's shoulder? An image flashed across my vision—Seb comforting me in his kitchen, the look in his eyes before his mum had interrupted us. *Surely he wouldn't have done that if . . .*

Swallowing my fears, I followed Charlie through the party.

Lottie was indeed with Saira, along with Ollie and Joss, dressed as a soldier herself in a beautifully tailored dress coat of burgundy that flared out at her waist and tight leather pants, her long black corkscrew curls left loose to flow down her back. She hugged me as I approached, murmuring into my ear, "God, you look amazing, babe. There are so many try-hards here."

I frowned against her shoulder. It was unlike Lottie to be so cutting. Part of the reason I admired her so much was that she rarely ever bitched about people—the kind of person I aspired to be. Still, she did seem a little on edge tonight. Her eyes overly bright, her face tense and drawn.

"Where's Laure?" I asked innocently.

Lottie rolled her eyes at Charlie. "Ohh, news travels fast, hmm?" She turned back to me, taking my hand and leading me a few paces away from the others.

"Basically, I had words with her about how she spoke to you the other day. It was so *not* okay, Meg. Honestly, I know I should have said something at the time but I was kind of blindsided by the whole thing—by how vicious she was."

I flushed a little, part of me not wanting to be reminded of the whole incident, another part of me ridiculously pleased Lottie had taken my corner against one of her oldest friends.

"Well, thanks," I murmured, still surreptitiously looking around, trying to spot Laure or Seb. "Thanks for having my back."

She squeezed my hand. "Of course. I love how real you are, Meg. I'm not here for fake friends, you know? Girls who apparently only want to hang out with me because they want to jump my brother—I mean, *Jesus*—"

Thankfully, at that moment, the choir stopped their dour, paganesque chanting and the lights lowered for the familiar intro of "Last Christmas," conveniently hiding the telltale flush of guilt upon my face.

"*Finally.* C'mon, ladies . . ." Charlie grabbed both our hands and yanked us out onto the dance floor.

A little while later, flushed and overheated with exertion, I found myself desperate for some water. Having no intention of downing the spirits Ollie had so kindly provided us with, I headed to the nearby canteen where refreshments were being served. As I made my way down the dimly lit corridor off the auditorium, I heard low voices emerge from one of the dark classrooms that lined the hall. Assuming it was a couple grabbing some alone time, I kept my head down and continued walking.

Until that is, I heard Seb's voice.

I froze. Part of me was desperate to see who he was with—to confirm it was Laure—while the other part of me wanted to sensibly walk on, head held high, and save myself the pain. We *were* both single, after all.

Feeling like an absolute weirdo, I crept back toward the classroom, crouching down a little so as not to be seen through the high glass windows that lined the room.

Seb and Laure were sitting close together on an empty desk—*unreasonably* close if you asked me—studying a piece of paper. I watched as Laure passed it to Seb, who read it, frowning, then carefully folded it and tucked it in his pocket. Laure rested her head against his chest with a sigh, snuggling into him in a way that seemed familiar—as if it were something she were very used to doing—while his fingers idly sifted through her hair. Even in low light, her face was swollen and flushed, as if she had only recently stopped crying. Seb was talking, his voice soft and reassuring, but too low for me to hear what he was saying, although it didn't take a genius to figure out the tone of it all.

A bolt of violent jealousy jolted through me as she lifted her face hopefully to his, and I fell back against the wall, no longer able to watch.

Water completely forgotten about, I stalked back to the

auditorium, digging the hip flask out of my pocket and taking an enormous swig.

Thanks to the low lights, no one noticed how shaken up I was as I rejoined the others. Seeing me, Lottie pulled me toward her, whooping as I executed a clumsy spin.

"There you are!" she said, smiling. "Connor's been over, hoping to catch you under the mistletoe!"

I glanced over and smiled at him. Who *cared* about Laure anyway? She wasn't one of us anymore. Or, she wouldn't be once I told Lottie what I had just seen. And anyway, she was welcome to Sebastien Wren. Guys who played games were never worth the pain.

I took another large swig of my drink.

An hour later, I was sweaty and exhausted and needed to catch my bus home. I hadn't seen Seb since—thankfully—but Laure had joined our circle at some point, dancing about on the outer fringes, clearly too drunk to sense the disapproval that radiated from both myself and Lottie.

After wishing everyone a merry Christmas (most of them were off to the Caribbean for the winter break) and pointedly ignoring Laure, I headed to the small antechamber off the main entrance, where I'd been directed to put my coat and scarf when I arrived.

Sitting on the bench inside the room, head morosely in his hands, was Seb.

I debated quietly leaving without a word—but it was *freezing* outside. I cleared my throat.

"Uh . . . hi?"

He looked up darkly but I was pleased to see his expression grow warm at the sight of me.

"*Meg.* Shit. I'm sorry—you know, I meant to catch up with you tonight, but . . ."

But you were too busy with Laure.

I nodded blithely. "Yeah, whatever. I heard there's been some drama or something. Anything I should know about?"

He ran a hand over his face. "Honestly, no. It's . . . it's nothing important. Just Laure running her mouth as usual . . ."

Running her mouth?

About what?

About you two? About what's really going on between you?

He glanced ruefully at the stacks of coats hanging from the wall.

"You're leaving, aren't you?"

I checked my phone. "Yeah, actually. I need to head off and catch my bus."

"Always running away from me . . . like Cinderella at midnight," he said, smiling, and patted the space beside him on the bench. "You got a few minutes?"

Literally, I had about one minute, but despite everything, I couldn't refuse him. Not now he was directly in front of me, sprawled indecently on that bench in a beautiful wine-colored frock coat, a paisley cravat lazily untied about his neck, his dark curls disheveled, his eyes hooded and hungry . . .

I sat down next to him, glancing once more at my phone screen. Okay, so maybe I could get a different bus and walk a few more stops—

"Lots told me what Laure said about you the other day—about your family. That was so out of line."

I squirmed a little as he spoke. What I *really* wanted was for everyone to drop it. I didn't want them to treat me like some kind of charity case they felt sorry for—least of all Seb.

"Yeah, well," I replied stiffly. "It was nice of Lottie to stick up for me . . . although I can fight my own battles."

Not for the first time, I felt a cold, smoldering anger toward Laure for bringing this to everyone's attention multiple times. The emotion was immediately extinguished as Seb pulled me toward him, looping his arm around me and squeezing me closer. He smelled as glorious as ever, though the hug was a little sloppy, no doubt due to the alcohol I could pick out, intermingled with his cologne.

"Oh, I don't doubt that," he said.

His voice was low, full of secrets, his gaze flickering to my lips, then back to my eyes. I tensed, my breath catching in my chest.

Sensing my stiffness, he pulled away, sitting up and angling his body toward mine. His dark eyes were full of devilry and mischief, kicking my heartbeat up several notches.

"Where have you been all evening?" I asked softly, curious to see what he would say. Would he admit to speaking with Laure— explain it away somehow? I was desperate for him to, already prepared to forgive him.

He looked away. "Oh, you know . . . with the guys." His eyes flicked back to mine, playfully. "Why? Did you miss me? Were you looking for me?"

Before I could answer, the door burst open, revealing a couple of girls from the year above. Seb immediately retreated, almost falling off the bench in his haste to get away from me.

"Whoops," one called, her eyes flicking between us. "Sorry, Seb, but it's bloody freezing out there!"

They chattered among themselves cheerfully as I stood, also reaching for my coat, intensely annoyed at how quickly he'd leaped away from me.

"Catch you later, then," I called, keeping my voice calm and leaving without a backward glance. "Have a good Christmas."

Desperate for a next step, we located the landline—which was, as Lottie predicted, dead. Aside from that, when it came to finding Laure it turned out there wasn't a lot we *could* do.

It was only early evening but the sky outside was already dark and rain was beating furiously about the house. Cautiously, Seb had opened the back door for another cursory glance outside but the wind had nearly ripped the door off its hinges.

"It's pretty foul out there," he said. "We'll keep trying to call the police. We can take turns every half hour. Then, if Laure still doesn't show tonight, as soon as it gets light tomorrow morning, Ollie and I will head into town to contact the guards."

"The *guards*?" said Joss.

"We're in Ireland—the police," clarified Seb.

"Ooh, hark at the big strong men protecting us," said Saira acidly. "If she doesn't show by dawn, we're *all* bloody getting out of here."

Joss pulled a face, sinking deeper into her fleece hoodie. "Um, speak for yourself. There's no way I'm going *anywhere*, not while the weather's like that."

After yet another fruitless search of the house, we all migrated back to the lounge, crowding together before the fire and fiddling nervously with our useless phones, casting hopeful looks toward the door until Lottie finally got up.

"You know, what we need is some distraction. There's nothing we can do right now, is there? The weather's too filthy to go outside and the phone lines are still down. So . . . I suggest we all head up to the studio. I'll show you the work I was planning on taking to the gallery. Seb, there's a couple of bottles of champs chilling in the fridge. We can make it a proper little celebration."

In the light of Laure's disappearance, the idea of celebrating—of opening *champagne*—seemed a pretty hideous one to me and judging by the confused expressions on everyone else's face, I wasn't the only one to think so. Seb opened his mouth, likely to protest, but Ollie barged past him. "I'll get it."

Obediently, we all traipsed up to the studio, standing around the six covered canvases in an awkward crescent. And when the cloths were whisked away like a magician's trick, I gasped.

The rest of the canvases were all in keeping with the first couple I'd already sneaked a look at, all painted from the exact same viewpoint across the lake—from the folly, I guessed. But together, they told a story—or the start of one—like some horrible children's flip-book.

The woman, who in the first picture was staring across the lake at the house, appeared to move ever closer to Wren Hall in each successive picture. In the third, she was no longer standing on the far bank, but in the middle of the lake itself, her ragged dress billowing around her, her pale face half-turned toward the observer, her mouth open in a horrid black O, revealing elongated yellow canines, her expression best described as *hungry*. Apparently standing on the water like some kind of fucked-up Jesus.

In the fourth, she had reached the bank closest to the house and stood almost hidden amid the drowned statues, her pale hands like snakes in the air as if praying to some unknown dark God. And in the fifth, she stood at the threshold of the house, silhouetted in the light from the kitchen door, her shadow unnaturally tall and slender.

"What's she doing?" whispered Charlie, standing next to me. "What does she want?"

Honestly, I wasn't sure I wanted to know.

In the final painting, she appeared to be heading back across the lake, slipping down the bank, her head bowed, staring down at the suspiciously human-size bundle she carried over her thin shoulder, entirely wrapped in dark cloth.

The line from Seb's tattoo floated unwelcomely into my head in dripping letters.

Fear death by water.

There was a halfhearted smattering of applause and Lottie started to speak, but to me, it sounded as if she were speaking underwater. Her words elongated and distorted. My hands shook as I accepted an unwanted glass of champagne from Ollie; all I could see was that woman in the picture. Why did she look so familiar? A face I seemed to know but couldn't quite place.

Curious, I watched the reactions of the others. Charlie appeared decidedly disturbed while Joss was oblivious, pointlessly tapping away at her phone. Ollie and Saira appeared to be having a discreetly whispered argument, but Seb, like me, could not seem to tear his eyes away from the paintings. He looked sick—his skin green-gray, his eyes haunted.

No—he didn't just look sick—he looked *terrified*.

Then, before I could say anything, before I could ask if he was all right at the very least, he turned and moved toward the stairs, shoving Ollie out of the way in his haste.

19

AFTER THE CHRISTMAS party, I'd avoided Seb like the plague. Clearly *something* was going on between him and Laure, and on top of that, I was terrified that Lottie would suspect how I felt and end our friendship, assuming I only wanted to be friends with her for one incredibly attractive reason. I flushed with embarrassment at the thought of her and her brother laughing at my obvious crush, his arm looped around Laure. Because however much I admired Saira or laughed at Charlie's easy jokes, the truth was—without Lottie's approval—I was alone here at Greyscott's.

A few days after the spring term had begun, I'd been working on a new project in Lottie's studio when Seb walked past the window. I froze, heart in mouth, as he'd rapped on the door, debating for a moment whether or not to hide.

But why? So he'd given me a hug when I'd cried after an accident—it hadn't *meant* anything. By now I'd convinced myself everything else was thoroughly in my head. All it proved was that

Seb was kind—like his sister—and flirtatious by nature. That was definitely *not* a reason to ignore him.

So I opened the door.

"Hey there, Cinders," he said, his eyes flicking coyly from mine down to the ground. "Haven't seen you in a while. I saw your bike outside. Thought I'd just see how you were getting on."

I'd seen him in school a few times this week, and he'd waved casually, but we had no classes together this term. He was now in higher-level streams than me and I'd be lying if I said I didn't find his obvious intellect attractive.

"I'm good, actually." I smiled breezily, shaking back my hair. "Did you have a nice Christmas?"

"Yeah, it was okay, I guess." He gestured past me, into the studio. "Hey, can I come in? I don't want to disturb you or anything. Just for a few minutes?"

Well, I was hardly going to say no, was I? He looked deliciously disheveled, clearly having just returned from Greyscott's, his shirt untucked from his formal trousers, tie loosened and askew. Hoisting himself up on the glossy island, he nodded for me to join him.

An image of him flashed, unwelcome, into my mind as I jumped up: his sitting on the desk beside Laure on the evening of the Christmas party, her head against his chest, his hand in her hair—

"You're brilliant, you know," he said, looking past me to the piece I'd been working on that morning. A handsome face made entirely of flowers that I now realized bore a remarkable likeness to Seb. "I never realized flowers could be so . . . interesting."

I snorted derisively. "Seriously, I don't need the weird attempt at flattery—what do you want?"

He grinned. "All right, fine. Look, this is really awkward, but I wanted to warn you . . ." He paused, holding my gaze this time. "Someone's gone and told Lottie you're"—he winced—"*into* me."

I stared at him, my face heating to dangerous levels of volcanic activity, blinking slowly in horror. "They *what?*"

He chuckled self-consciously, his turn to flush pink now. The first show of vulnerability I'd ever seen from him, although he didn't look away. "Jesus, all right—there's no need to look so horrified. I know it's not true anyway, I mean, we barely even know each other. But like I said, I wanted to prewarn you, in case—in case she mentioned anything."

It *was* a genuine worry. After what she'd said about Laure at the party, there was no way I wanted Lottie to think I was only coming here to see her brother. But then, at the same time, hadn't I been doing exactly that?

I nodded, my manner all business.

"Who? Who's spreading this rumor. And how'd they get that impression? I mean, you barely even acknowledge my existence at school." I hopped off the counter, agitated. I already knew *exactly* who was to blame.

He grinned again, his cheeks still appealingly flushed. "Oh, is that right? Well, I could say the same about you, actually. So, there's this girl—one of Lottie's friends—I think you know her, actually—"

"Laure," I finished darkly. I looked up at him, barely bothering to disguise my disgust. "So you *are* with her, then?"

He frowned, convincingly confused. "What? No—*no*. Look,

between us, she's basically had a crush on me, like forever. Anyway, we went on a couple of dates a while back but it didn't work out."

"Uh-huh. And does *she* also know you aren't together?"

He flushed again. "Yes . . . of course."

"Well . . . you might want to talk to her because from what I hear, Laure doesn't see it the same way you do." I was proud of how cool I was. Unruffled and serene.

He looked directly at me. "Don't you think I *know* that? It's awkward as hell. But I don't care how she sees it. It's the truth."

I decided I may as well go all in. "Someone saw you guys—at the Christmas party—together."

He raised an eyebrow, completely unfazed. "Oh yeah? Well, maybe *someone* shouldn't go sneaking around deserted classrooms, then jump to baseless conclusions."

My turn to blush. He sighed.

"Honestly, I felt bad for her that night. You didn't see what Lottie said to her. I know my sister comes across as all Zen and chill, but when she loses her temper—" He ran a hand across his face and looked so intensely lost for a minute, I wanted to hug him.

"Anyway, like I said, I wanted you to be prepared—in case Lottie said anything. I already told her it was a load of crap, though. Lots speaks really highly of you, y'know."

I nodded, gaining the sudden and bleakly disappointing impression that maybe the thought of anything between us had never even crossed his mind. A cold wash of embarrassment settled over me. What *had* I been thinking?

"Okay, great," I said. "Thanks for the heads-up—and for the record, it's definitely not true."

He chuckled, appearing to visibly relax, and he leaned back on the counter with one hand and regarded me levelly with those sparkling dark eyes. "All right, no need to lay it on quite so thick. You find me repulsive—duly noted."

Well, that wasn't the reaction I had expected. With that comment, that *look*, everything seemed to change around us. The molecules of the air itself re-forming into something new.

Something dangerous.

I relaxed, turning back to him with a knowing smile.

"*Utterly* repulsive. In fact, I can barely even look at you without wanting to throw up."

He laughed again, clutching one hand to his chest in mock pain. "Fuck, Meg—you know how to hit a guy where it hurts."

"Seriously—I mean—can you like . . . *leave*? I'm feeling—oh God." I bent over, one hand outstretched in an effort to ward him away, while pretending to gag. "Please—just get out—now—"

He laughed again, his hand finding my wrist and pulling me toward him and I laughed too and it had been impossible to stop. The giggles bursting from us until we were both gasping for breath. I remember all of it. How the sun streamed through the large windows of the studio. How the air was thick with the heady green perfume of the hyacinths I had placed in a vase, leftovers from an earlier piece. And I'd never wanted to paint a moment more. Then, suddenly, we paused, staring at each other for long seconds, his dark eyes looking directly into mine and I thought he was about to make another joke, but he didn't. Instead he nodded at the vase then leaned forward, pulling me even closer and speaking directly in my ear, softly and quietly.

"I know what they are, at least—

"Yet when we came back, late, from the Hyacinth garden,
Your arms full, and your hair wet, I could not
Speak, and my eyes failed, I was neither
Living nor dead, and I knew nothing,
Looking into the heart of light, the silence."

I laughed, awkwardly, but immediately felt stupid. "They *are* hyacinths. What—what's that from?"

But he didn't answer; instead, he leaned down and kissed me. It was tentative and brief, our lips barely even touching, as if only a trial, as if he were only seeing if he liked it, his face gently brushing against mine, his fingers soft and explorative against my cheek, and I inhaled that deep scent of his: expensive and starchy. Black pepper and pine. He pulled back immediately to lock gazes—I don't know what he had expected to see—but the touch of his mouth against mine, however light, had been scalding, the shock of it clearly showing in my face.

"S-sorry," he said quietly, wrong-footed for the first time I'd met him. "God, I'm really sorry—I didn't mean to—I should have asked—I just—"

But I didn't want to hear his apologies; all I wanted was for him to do it again. I wanted to bury my hands deep in his hair and yank him closer. I certainly didn't want him to be *sorry.*

While I stood there lamenting, desperately trying to put what

I was feeling into coherent words, he jumped down from the counter, the heat of him still on my lips, his scent, the soft brush of his hair against my forehead.

"Wait—*wait*—" I said.

But it was too late. He was already gone.

The desultory "viewing" over, Joss, Lottie, Saira, and Ollie drifted off to their respective rooms to turn in for the night while Charlie and I headed wordlessly into the lounge.

"What was *that* about—" he said, stoking the smoky, dying fire as I slumped onto the dusty tapestry couch.

I shook my head, confused. "I don't think Lottie is . . . handling this well."

"Clearly," Charlie said, collapsing beside me. "And what was going on with Seb? Guy knows more than he's letting on, I reckon."

I frowned. "Do you think? It looked like he was upset by something in those paintings."

"Anyone would be upset by them—it was like horror movie central." Charlie exhaled. Beneath his confident bluster I could tell he was uneasy, amplifying my own fears.

"Do you think Laure's really okay?"

He only shrugged. "I wish I knew. I mean, she didn't look great yesterday, did she? She's not been herself since—" He caught himself. "Sorry."

Tears of shame came to my eyes then, hot and fast. *Was* I the root cause of all this? That night, the first word that had come into my mind, the very moment I'd retracted my hands, had been *sorry.*

But the ease with which I'd managed to justify my actions over the following weeks made me uneasy. What would the police think of me? In recent months, intentionally or not, I'd nearly drowned a girl who was now missing and—depending on who you asked—had willfully *stolen* her boyfriend on top of that.

"This isn't your fault," I heard Charlie say softly as tears spilled silently down my cheeks. I tipped back my head and inhaled a deep lungful of smoky air. Now was *not* the time for self-pity.

Charlie placed a cool, consoling hand over mine. "Right, girl, I reckon we should try and get some rest. Especially if we'll all be wading into town tomorrow morning."

I trailed Charlie down the corridor in the direction of the staircase. When we reached the entrance hall, he stopped dead in front of me. "Shit—what the *hell*?"

I drew alongside him, following his gaze.

The entire hall was ringed with muddy wet footprints, in ragged concentric circles, as if someone had been wandering around parsing a difficult calculation for hours.

And worst of all, the prints were clearly made by bare feet.

Nonsensically, the postcard from my room—Seb's old room—splashed across my vision:

COME ON IN—
The water's DIVINE!

The sodden prints led into the kitchen and the soiled crust of them was also visible in the thick pile of the red carpet that covered the stairs.

A chill like early-morning frost cracked through my chest. "Laure's back?" I suggested, eyebrows raised.

While not at all plausible, it also seemed the only sensible explanation.

"Or it's Seb, back from another dip in that festering pond. We better take a look. I'll look down here, you take the stairs."

Charlie's voice was oddly hushed. Not at all the voice of someone who expected to find a mutual friend in the house. And, frankly, I was feeling the same way. I mean, had Laure just casually walked to the house through the storm, getting soaked in the process and gone directly up to bed?

And *barefoot*?

I glided quietly up the staircase as if in a dream, my mind reeling with unpleasant possibilities as I switched on the lights. There was a low electric hum as the corridor flickered into visibility. "Laure?" I called softly.

The silence was broken only by the sound of someone's gentle snoring. From below, I heard Charlie's heavy footsteps as he prowled through the house.

I could see Laure's bedroom, the door still open and the space beyond it empty. *Not in bed, then.* Wanting to avoid disturbing the sleepers, I crept up to the studio.

It was pitch-black up here even though all the blinds were open. No longer flooded with moonlight like before, the windows brightly reflected my phone flashlight. I looked eerily doll-like—white-haired and black-eyed. Reaching for the light switch, I hastily clicked it on. The was a brief flash of yellow light and then everything around me was plunged back into blackness, even the soft glow of the lights from downstairs.

From somewhere ahead of me, I heard the click of a door.

"S-Seb?" I called, trying to keep the panic from my voice.

"Yeah. Storm's taken out the lights," he called back, his footsteps clumping reassuringly past me and then clattering down the stairs. "I'm just gonna start up the generator. Be a couple of minutes. Hold tight."

Taking a deep breath, I forced myself to get a grip. *All* large old houses were creepy in the dark. It was an actual fact. Holding my phone tightly in my hand, I headed over to the window to wait as a whip-crack of lightning illuminated the forest, followed by a large roll of thunder that boomed across the lake.

"Laure?" I said it softly, unsure now if I wanted a response.

If those footprints weren't Laure's, then whose *were* they? An intruder's? A barefoot one at that? Unwelcome visions of old horror movies exploded into my mind: escaped psychopaths and hook-handed hitchhikers.

Another flash of lightning lit up the sky without warning, revealing the dark blot of the lake and the darker trees behind it. In the reflection of the window I saw a figure behind me, framed in the studio doorway, tall and slender, their face pale.

I whirled around to face only inky blackness again.

"Laure?"

Then, from somewhere at the far end of the studio, close to Seb's room, I heard a soft whispery giggle, the sound smothered by another low rumble of thunder. Helpfully, the light on my phone chose that moment to blink out.

My heart pounded in my chest, painfully hard. It was Laure, it had to be. What was she playing at? Had she been hiding with Seb in his room?

"Laure? God, what are you *doing*?" I hissed, my hand shaking as I fumbled for the flashlight on my phone again. I jabbed at the home button but my phone was dead. I remembered the battery had been low this morning and I'd never bothered to charge it.

Shit—shit—hurry up, Seb.

"Laure?" Using the edge of the center island as a guide, I began to fumble my way toward the sound, bumping against canvases and God knew what else on the way.

The sobbing started quietly. I'd heard it enough times now there was no escaping that it was the same person. I froze, unsure what to do and not at all sure Laure was here anymore.

"L-Laure—is that you? Please stop. Where—where are you?"

As if in response, a blue light flared ahead of me, on the floor, coldly illuminating the space around it.

It was a phone. I recognized the sleek, marbled cover stenciled with the owner's initials in gold.

L W

Laure's phone. But what was it doing, tossed beneath an armchair directly outside Seb's room? I didn't want to touch it, didn't want to go near it. I stopped, staring in dread. The sobbing sound seemed to be emanating directly from the phone, possessing an echoey, tinny quality that I hadn't noticed before.

No. No, that wasn't possible. No—

I backed away, tripping heavily over an easel, knocking it over. As I got closer to where I hoped the door was, the sound got louder, turning almost to a wailing.

"Stop it," I said, putting my hands over my ears. "Please—please stop."

Then the footsteps began. Wet and bare, slapping against the expensive parquet flooring as they got closer. I inched farther back, desperately feeling for the door, barely even caring anymore if I fell down the steep stairs and broke my neck.

"Who are you?" I shouted. "What's—what's *wrong*?"

The sobbing stopped. The footsteps stopped. I could feel someone in front of me. Their breath as cold as the waters on the lake, tattered and wet. The wheeze of someone who had been dead a long, long time. Whose lungs had atrophied, whose eyes were blind and white, whose flesh had slowly liquefied to a squidlike softness in the waters of the lake outside.

The light blinked back on with a buzz. The room was entirely empty. But the floor—pristine in the second I'd switched on the lights—the floor was now ringed with the same muddy footprints as downstairs. Stopping exactly where I stood.

And directly opposite, painted raggedly in dripping black, on one of Lottie's many blank canvases were three words:

YOUR WICKED HISTORY

20

I SAT BEFORE the fire in the lounge, shaking wildly, teeth chattering, as Charlie attempted to poke the dwindling flames back to life. Outside the wind raged and howled about the house and I clutched at the glass of brandy Seb had found for me as if it were a lifeline. It was one a.m.

"Babe, it's no wonder you're freaked out," said Charlie, collapsing next to me on the sofa. "It's probably just Ollie fucking around again—the guy's a menace after a drink."

I took a deep gulp of my drink, wincing as the acrid liquid scalded my throat. But I needed it in order to get out what had been troubling me for ages.

"Something's . . . wrong here," I said, my voice unsteady. "I can *feel* it. This place—this house, the lake—there's something *wrong* with it."

I stared ominously down at Laure's phone, which I'd retrieved from under the armchair once the lights came back on.

"Well, there's no *way* she would have left here without that,"

Charlie said, nodding at the phone, confirming what I already knew.

So, where *was* she? Alone and without her phone. I pictured Lottie, blank-eyed and shivering, walking deep into the black waters of the lake. Had something similar happened to Laure? Was there *really* something in there?

Seb entered the room, pale-faced and sunken-eyed, his voice hollow.

"Well, did you see it?"

I could tell from his face he had.

"What?" asked Charlie, eyes wide.

"Up in the studio . . . someone—someone had painted something on one of the canvasses. It said 'your wicked history.'" I forced myself to go on. "Y'know, like the Ouija board, remember?"

I expected derision. Sarcasm. Laughter. But Seb said nothing, only worked silently rebuilding the fire. Charlie stared at me, his dark eyes wide.

"And, I mean, th-those *footprints* . . . who made them?" I stammered, desperate now. "I keep hearing crying—and screaming. You heard it too, Charlie, and so did Lottie. Everyone around here—the locals—says there's a—a banshee."

Charlie raised an eyebrow.

"A what, now?"

"A *banshee*. It's a water spirit—a woman. She's usually seen crying and when she screams it's meant to mean someone's going to—to die."

"*Harbinger,*" murmured Charlie.

Seb snorted, still not looking at us. "Meg, what are you even talking about? Yes, okay, someone was playing games in the studio for whatever reason, but Jesus, nobody's *died*."

Yet.

"You can't explain everything away, Seb!" I snapped, exasperated. "Obviously, I don't believe in ghosts but there's something going on and it's linked to this lake—this house—that *tower*. You said yourself that Lottie has been acting weird ever since she got here . . . her weird paintings . . . I mean, what about her walking into the lake, her arms full of flowers like some kind of fucking *offering*—did you forget about that? What's *in* there? And those footprints! At the very least there's been an intruder? Maybe they've done something to Laure? Maybe they've—"

I couldn't finish the thought. Seb tossed the poker down and flopped into an armchair, his face flushed pink from the heat of the fire or from anger, I couldn't tell.

"Yeah, I could believe all that. I could believe there's been an intruder. I believe there's something wrong with some *people*. But I don't believe inanimate objects and random geographical features are *haunted*. The lights went out and you had a bit of a scare, that's all. And as for that crap in the studio—Meg, it was clearly one of *us*."

I shook my head. "Are you fucking kidding me, Seb? I was *there*—before the lights went out, it was empty, and then after—there were footprints. Something was in there with me. Something is in this *house* with us. *Something* has happened to Laure!"

Seb regarded me coolly, his arms crossed.

"Look, calm down. You don't *know* they weren't there before—like you said—the fuse blew the moment you switched the lights on. They could have been left earlier, by *anyone* back from a smoke break—my guess is Ollie."

Charlie squinted at me. "And anyways, ghosts don't leave footprints, do they? They kind of waft about rattling chains and floating through walls and shit—"

"I have no idea!" I shouted, verging on hysteria, barely able to believe the content of the conversation myself. "Anyway, like I said, it's a banshee, not a ghost. Maybe it's real—some weird creature, a cryptid living in the lake—like the Loch Ness Monster or Bigfoot or whatever."

"Jesus, Meg, let's think. Who here would get a kick out of scaring you?" said Seb quietly, his eyes meeting mine, almost black in the firelight. "Who would love to see you babble on insanely about ghosts and screaming banshees and dead women? I mean, by all accounts she could still be in the house filming you for A-grade content. Laure messaged *Joss*—maybe they're in on this together? Some crappy revenge plan, I don't know."

I sobered a bit at this. In some ways it made sense.

Except—except Laure had seemed so earnest, so genuine when I spoke to her the evening before last. And almost—almost *afraid.* But afraid of what? Or, more accurately, of who?

"You think Joss has something to do with all this?" I asked.

Seb wouldn't look at me. "Honestly, I don't know. We all know she can be pretty wild. Plus, she was throwing out some strong accusations the other night. Then there's that message—clearly Laure *isn't* at a hotel if her phone is here."

"But why lie?" I wondered aloud.

"Maybe to throw us off," said Charlie, warming to the theory.

"Get us all to think Laure's fine and begin going about our day, business as usual, while they go on with their prank."

"Okay, that's a possibility. But say you're wrong and there is an intruder here—or—or something worse?" I pressed. "What if Laure . . . You don't think anything terrible has happened to her—"

"I highly doubt it." Seb raised his gaze to mine. "I know it looks like an antique, but this place is fully alarmed. Besides, I searched the house—there's no one here except us lot. And I *do* know there's no such thing as ghosts. And so do you, you're just letting this—this situation get to you."

"Exactly," agreed Charlie, brightening at this. He raised his voice. "Right, then, Laure. I'm buggering off to bed now. Ghost or not, I'm knackered. Your game's up, so no standing at the end of my bed rattling chains, you bitch."

I smiled weakly as he got up and kissed me on the cheek.

"Now behave, you two, and give Laure a slap if you see her for scaring my girl."

I half expected Seb to get up and follow him but he didn't. Instead, we sat in massively awkward silence listening to Charlie clump up the stairs and slam his bedroom door.

Disappointment sank in my stomach like a stone as Seb stood too and not only because I didn't want to be alone. But to my surprise, instead of leaving the room, he turned to me.

"Hey," he said quietly, fixing me with solemn dark eyes as he held out a hand to help me up. "Come with me. There's something I've been wanting to show you."

Curious, I followed him through the narrow corridors, past

the kitchen, right to the very back of the house where a small door with a stained-glass panel depicting a wreath of gold and amber leaves was set into the wall.

"It'll be a bit dark in here, but it's worth it, I promise. When Lottie and I were kids, we always used to sit in here during a storm."

Through the door was the vast greenhouse I'd seen the first day I'd arrived. Its frame a complicated skeleton of wrought iron, filled with a million panes of delicate glass. The plants in here were long dead and there was a subtle, unpleasant odor of long-rotted vegetation, but the view was undeniably beautiful. A misty midnight Monet of the lake, the rain deafening against the glass.

There was very little in here other than empty brick-framed flower beds and a bench. He wandered over to the latter and sat down. Almost immediately the entire space around us was lit was a sudden flash of lightning illuminating the sky, the water, the forest—all of them, for the briefest of moments, as bright as a day, turning everything to silver.

It was eerily beautiful.

"See? Didn't I tell you?"

Seb was a monolith before the vast dark expanse of the water. With a soft sigh of defeat, I sank down beside him.

"Are you okay, Meg?"

I gave a humorless laugh. Did he genuinely think I was insane? Seb or no Seb, I couldn't wait to get out of this place.

"*No*, of course not. I mean, are you?"

He looked at me then, his eyes black in the night, unguarded and honest.

"No, not really," he admitted. "I told you I didn't want to come here and I meant it. I don't believe in ghosts or whatever, but I do know that this place. . . . Well, it's old. It has a bad history. It gives everyone the creeps. Being here's not good for Lottie. And inviting both you and Laure was never a great idea either."

I ran my hands over my face.

"Yeah, I'm willing to admit this may not have been the best idea Lottie's ever had. But what do you mean—a *bad history*?"

Seb shrugged. "Y'know, that story Lottie mentioned during the séance. About the woman who died in the lake. Anyway, it's not just that. . . ." He trailed off. "There's—there's a lot you don't know. . . ."

Then tell me! I wanted to scream at him. What's really up with Lottie? What *was* it with you and Laure? Have you *lied* to me the entire time I've known you?

We went on a couple of dates—

She's basically had a crush on me, like forever—

The sky lit up around us again, a sudden loud crack of thunder making me jump.

"Okay . . . well, tell me," I said, forcing my tone to stay even. "What is there to know, Seb? This enigmatic shit isn't nearly as attractive as you think it is. I mean, at the summer ball you—you promised me—you promised—" Pathetically, I couldn't even finish the sentence.

He buried his head in his hands, dark curls gleaming. Around us, the trees creaked alarmingly, the wind rippled the surface of the lake. Faint noises from the house made everyone seem oceans away. It was as if we were sailing off in a glass boat upon the mirrored onyx of the lake, far removed from everyone.

"I know," he mumbled, "I *know* what I promised. And I meant it. I meant everything I said, Meg. And I *still* mean it. These past months have been so hard. But that night—can't you understand why I did what I did? I thought you might understand—I—"

I watched, alarmed and tongue-tied, as his shoulders heaved. Was he *crying*? When he finally spoke, his words were still too muffled for me to tell.

"I thought you of all people might understand. You *know* what she's like. What she did to you. That's why I was so surprised to see you here. Whatever we might have had together—however much I missed you—I knew that in the end you'd be better off out of it. It might not look like it—it might *never* look like it . . . but what I did . . . I did for you—"

I didn't want to hear it.

Because it was still too fresh, too recent, and too painful, like pulling at a ragged scab that hadn't fully healed. Raising his head, he dragged an arm across his face, his delicate features unsuited to a frown.

But also . . . because it rang false. All that talk about gallantly protecting me from someone—from Laure—as if Seb were nobly defending me from his evil ex. It didn't feel that way to me. It didn't feel like he'd *ever* considered me in any of this. Instead, it had felt like a casual shrugging-off. An easy way out.

"Hey, look. We should go back," I said, standing, my voice half-hidden beneath the rumble of thunder. "The others might wake up and wonder where we are."

He twisted to face me, determined now, eyes blazing in the low light, and I was caught like a rabbit in a snare, swinging help-lessly in the dark.

"We won't, though, will we?" he said, his words full of quiet authority. "Not yet. Not now. Stay a little longer—please? Just sit here with me. I don't want to be alone. I can't be alone. And I've—" He swallowed. "God, I've *missed* you, Meg."

His hand took mine, tugging me down gently back to the bench. It was like a spell, our next movements entirely predictable, mapped out as clearly as the night sky above us.

His kiss was obliterating, stealing my breath so cleanly away that for a moment, I was out there, drowning, caught up in the thick weeds of the lake. His mouth was hot and demanding, tasting sharply of brandy, his kisses bruising, almost angry. I gasped and he pulled back momentarily, eyes flicking darkly to mine then back to my mouth. His next kiss was soft, apologetic, and I let myself sink into it. He made a low sound in his throat, his arms encircling me like vines and it was so good. Like a hot bath on a cold night. It had always been so good, between us.

"That day—when you got here," he murmured, his lips warm and familiar against my skin, "when I saw you in the studio—I'm so sorry. I hated myself for saying what I did, especially when all I really wanted was to lock the door, get to my knees, and beg you to forgive me. I wanted to . . . Meg—ever since I met you, you're all I can think about—I swear—"

He stopped himself with another kiss, hungrier this time, leaning over me, his hands framing my face. My desire for him as bottomless as the lake before us, his hands slipping beneath my sweater, so cold on my heated skin. The only cure for a fever that he had started. He leaned back, anchoring himself with one hand and dragging me astride him, almost toppling us both off the bench, reaching for me again, crushing his mouth to mine. I shifted on top of him causing him to groan and pull back with a short breathless laugh.

"*God . . . ,*" he murmured. "Come to my room? Everyone's asleep. If you want, that is."

Everyone's asleep?

And there it was.

Again.

Part of why I'd been reluctant to speak to him, to get close to him again. I'd known this was coming. Like a bucket of freezing water had been dumped directly over my head. Just like the night of the summer ball, where everything I'd ever wanted had been laid out before us, a sumptuous feast upon a golden blanket that he had scrunched up and hastily discarded once he'd taken what he wanted.

The secrecy. The *shame* of it. The unspoken inability to be seen with him. And why? Because I wasn't good enough. Because I never *would* be good enough for Sebastien-fucking-Wren. Because Sebastien Wren only dated the golden girls. Old money. Athletic, confident, and beautiful. The girls his dad would approve of. The girls his mother already knew of.

Meg Green, with her box-bleached hair and swan tattoo. Who lived in a flat in Catford. Who'd never rode a horse and had no idea how to ski. How could she possibly fit into the life of Sebastien Wren?

But at that moment, I had no idea how to voice any of that. Not after that kiss. And a terrible, shameful part of me didn't even *care;* a part of me wanted him so much, so desperately, that I was ready to do whatever he asked, ready to give up everything to him.

I kissed him again, selfishly, open-mouthed and hungry,

moving deliberately in his lap, causing him to gasp, his hands now gripping my waist hard enough to bruise.

"No," I breathed against his neck. "I don't think so. I won't be your dirty little secret anymore, Sebastien Wren." And I got up, leaving him in the dark and slamming the door hard behind me.

21

DAWN WAS TIPTOEING over the forest before I managed to drift off into an uneasy sleep. Every creak and groan the house made in the storm disrupted my dreams, my mind a crazed kaleidoscope of unpleasant images. Lottie's paintings: the gaunt woman carrying the black bundle away from the house. *What had been in there?* The pale figure reflected in the window of the studio when the lights had gone out. Had it been Laure? My imagination? Or something worse? The dark pull of the silent lake, forever waiting beyond the window. Lottie had been right. At night, in the quiet, it consumed my thoughts, drawing everything back to its still, dark waters.

What would be found if they drained it? What had made it what it was? Not just a body of water but something *terrible*. Something hungry. Something that soaked into the mind like an ugly stain.

Then there was the terrible aching, the knowledge I hadn't taken Seb up on his suggestion. That he had *wanted* me, in his room, only a few hours earlier. That there was a good chance he was lying there, sleepless too, thinking about me. Thinking I didn't want him, when he was all I ever thought about. A hunger as deep and as secret, as all-consuming as the lake outside.

And the terrible truth that if I went to him, I would be surrounded by him, and I wouldn't be alone anymore.

I'd been surprised—not to mention *highly* suspicious—when Laure messaged me a couple of days after Seb's and my kiss, asking to meet her at a bubble tea place popular with Greyscott's students. Lately, we'd managed to politely avoid each other at school. My finger hovered over the delete button—I did *not* forget easily, and she'd been nothing but frosty to me since the Christmas party—but then a slyer part of me decided it might be good to get Laure back on my side, if only to find out what the hell was actually going on between her and Seb. Besides, didn't they say keep friends close and enemies closer?

Laure treated me to a massive white grin once she caught sight of me, taking me by the arm and pulling me into the shop, her bracelets jangling madly on her wrists.

"You came! God, you've *got* to try the matcha—it's amazing. How have you *been*, scholarship?"

I stared at her, eyebrow raised, not willing to play this game after our last conversation. Close up, she looked different than she had before Christmas. Her hair lank and unwashed, pulled up into a careless pony. Her freckles prominent against her pale face. Wondering if Lottie had a hand in this meetup, I defiantly ordered a water, unwilling to shell out six quid for a soft drink.

"Sure you don't want tea? My treat?"

Truly, I'd rather had died of thirst than accept her charity. My eyes continued to burn into the back of her head as we made our way to an empty table.

"Good Christmas?" she asked apparently still hell-bent on acting like nothing had gone down between us. I slumped into my seat.

"Okay, Laure, what *is* this?" I asked bluntly. No point in beating around the bush. "I mean, you've been blanking me ever since you decided to randomly slag off my mum. What did I do to you to deserve . . . *that*?" I shook my head. "I thought—I thought we were friends."

At my tone, a wary light gleamed in her eyes, and she sank down at the table with a dramatic sigh, a vortex of spearmint gum, expensive conditioner, and vanilla perfume.

"I know, I *know*. I've been total bitch lately—hence the need for us to talk. I wanted to explain . . ." She stared at my bottle of water, momentarily mortified. "Y'know, if I'd known you didn't like tea, I'd have suggested somewhere else—"

"I really don't care—"

"Meg," she said, cutting me off. "I was wrong. Of course I was. I should never have treated you the way I have. I've just been . . . frustrated and I guess took it out on you . . ." She fiddled with one of the three gold chains looped around her neck, not looking at me, her eyelashes sooty against her overly bronzed cheek. "It's just . . . ugh, Lottie has been so . . . *weird* toward me lately—and on top of that, I thought you and Seb—"

I frowned at her, determined not to blush. "Me and Seb what? What are you even talking about? There *is* no me and Seb."

Telling, how much I enjoyed saying that, though. Liked how

it rolled off my tongue. Me and Seb. Seb and me. Our two names entwined together in our very own little sentence. Liked how it reminded me that the last time I'd seen him he had *kissed* me—*he* kissed *me*—in a room full of sunlight and flowers and—

"And I get that now." She gave me an indulgent little wince. "I guess I was being like . . . overly possessive? I mean, you can see why, right? He's—he's just ridiculous—everything about him—"

With Herculean effort, I managed to give a casual shrug, then took a much-needed glug of my water.

"Whatever," I said flatly. "I still don't get what this has got to do with your character assassination before break, or how rude you've been since?"

Maybe I should have forgiven her—*really* forgiven her. Surely there was a way we could all get along again. And reading between the lines, Lottie and Laure had that kind of forever friendship that went all the way back to pony club at four years old, one that would withstand whatever road bumps my presence presented. But I couldn't just ignore how she'd acted lately. Icing me out of WhatsApp groups, the snide little comments, conveniently "forgotten" invitations. And honestly, it hurt. I'd trusted her, *liked* her, seen her as an ally, when all along she'd just been pretending.

She fiddled with her phone, refusing to meet my stare.

"Plain old jealousy, I guess. Anyway, I've been feeling so crappy about it all. I'm sorry—I know I have a sharp tongue. You've done nothing to deserve it."

I let out a lengthy breath, thinking of the Laure I'd seen at the Christmas party. Swollen-eyed and tearstained, on the outer fringes of the group.

"Okay, well . . . thanks . . . thank you."

Still, my mind was reeling. What exactly had changed? Had Lottie had a word with her? Or had she reconciled with Seb? I hoped it was the former.

"Meg, we've always gotten on so well before," Laure continued. "It's actually refreshing to hang around someone like you! Honestly, Lottie can be *so* pretentious sometimes, right? All that whining on about saving the oceans by boycotting straws when everyone saw the amount of plastic trash generated after her last party. Clearly gets it from her mum, writing all those preachy blogs about clean living, when she's a secret chain smoker, and then—"

I frowned as she went on, not wanting to talk about Lottie behind her back, even if she did make several excellent points.

"Hey," I said, diverting the conversation before she distracted me. "I hope you don't mind me asking, but what exactly *is* going on between you and Seb?"

Laure stopped talking and gave me a sad smile, her eyes glossy with tears. "So . . . you may as well know. He broke things off between us at the Christmas party." She bit her lip, blinking rapidly. "He said he's going through some stuff at home and thought it would be best if we cooled things down for a bit."

I was quiet for a moment or two.

Okay, so which was it? A relationship or, according to Seb, a crush, and a few casual dates? I couldn't exactly tell her what Seb had said without coming off badly myself. On top of that, I got the distinct impression she was lying about something. It was the way she refused to look me in the eye, the way her fingers nervously fiddled with her straw.

I thought back to the day I had fallen off my bike. The idea that Seb had been flirting with me all the time he was with Laure was *not* a comfortable one. I took another sip of my water. Laure continued, hastily rubbing tears away with her sleeve.

"It's—it's *hard*, though. I mean, the thing about Seb is, he's all flowers and soft poetry and heated kisses in dark corners one minute and the next—*nothing*. Nothing at all. He won't reply to my messages like he used to . . . And I can't even talk to my best friend about it because . . . well."

I relented, passing Laure a packet of tissues as she hastily brushed away tears. "Look, I get it, I do." I thought of Seb's warm mouth on mine the other day, in the sun-filled studio, of how he'd jumped away moments later with only a mumbled apology, and of his total silence since.

More than you might imagine.

"Anyway," Laure continued with shaky sigh. "We're planning on meeting up this evening to talk things through. I can't imagine he'd throw away what we had just like that . . . ? Y'know?"

Impulsively, I clutched Laure's hand across the table. "Well, you can always talk to me about it, Laure. I can keep a secret."

The screaming woke me.

I almost closed my eyes to it, so exhausted I half managed to convince myself it was foxes again. But it was different this time. Not the dreamlike, sirenesque wailing of before. No, this was much more human: broken and breathless and familiar. And there were other sounds too, scrambling and scratching, loud panicked voices and footsteps pounding up and down the stairs. Realizing

I was still dressed, I must have passed out with exhaustion last night, I pulled a hoodie over my top and stumbled out of my room in the direction of the noise.

My breath fogged before me as I clattered down the stairs three at a time, every light in the house blazing. That feeling that something was terribly wrong was compounded by the fact the main doors were both wide open and the screaming, coming from outside, was now joined by raised and harried voices.

Below, the footsteps still circled the hall, like a witch's ritual, dried into permanence. And with the rain still sheeting from the sky, I stared.

The scene before me was like a tableau. A renaissance painting, or the funeral of Ophelia by Millais.

Seb stood holding her in the lake, her thin white body draped over his arms. She was wearing the same white dress as she had on Halloween—of course she was, she had never left the house—her red hair drifting across the top of the water like weeds, her skin so pale it shone with pearl-like iridescence.

It was Laure and from the stillness of her form, and the strange blue-white tinge of her lips, I was certain she was dead.

22

TEARS STREAMING FROM my eyes, I staggered down the remaining stairs, accidentally knocking the black cloth from an enormous mirror on my way and confronting myself briefly with the ghost of my own reflection. One thought echoed through my head, compounding the guilt I could never seem to wash away, compounding the fact that even though Laure was almost certainly dead, the first thing I thought of was myself.

They're going to think it was me.

How am I going to get back into Greyscott's now?

A surge of sickening self-loathing shuddered through me and I squeezed my eyes tight shut. God, I couldn't even stand to look at myself anymore.

I ran out to where the others were gathered around her, black umbrellas open like early mourners. We all stood staring for what felt like years as Seb leaned over her, giving her mouth-to-mouth, desperately compressing her chest until everyone knew it was pointless.

Lottie eventually pulled at his shoulder and he walked away, one hand clutched to his brow while Charlie and Ollie carefully rolled her in the sheet. I knelt down, ready to help, desperate to do something—anything. She was cold—freezing to the touch—her skin a mottled shade of blue gray, her eyes cloudy and sightless.

I was glad when they were hidden.

Seb had *definitely* been avoiding me after that encounter in the studio. And I couldn't get a read on him. *Were* he and Laure back together? Is that why he regretted kissing me? I might not have wanted to believe what Laure said about them, but I expected there was some truth in it. Sure, Laure was prone to exaggeration but she wasn't a *fantasist.*

The notion made my stomach weak. On the rare times that Seb did approach our group at Greyscott's—pretty much only ever to speak to his twin—Laure flirted with him outrageously and he did little to discourage her, seeming to tolerate it with a wry smile and occasionally shooting me pained looks. Was he toying with me? Did he feel sorry for me in the same way I knew Lottie sometimes did?

Two could play the avoidance game, though.

If I saw him coming down the hall, flanked by Ollie and some other meat-headed rugby player, I would turn the other way or bury my head in my locker.

Six days after our encounter, four days after my meetup with Laure, I opened my locker one morning to find a note in a scruffy, looping hand. A now-wilted posy of hyacinths wrapped within it.

I'm sorry.
I can't stop thinking about you <3

I stared at it for what felt like hours, my gut immediately telling me it was from him, my head saying no, it was impossible. It was a cruel joke—he hadn't given our kiss a second thought. But if it *was* him—then what did I do next? If I continued to ignore what happened, it would look as though I was genuinely angry with him, which was the furthest thing from the truth possible. And if I didn't—

I was still agonizing minutes later when Charlie loomed up behind me and whipped the note from my hand.

"Shit—that's *Seb's* writing. I'd recognize that childish scrawl anywhere. What's he done this time?"

I hesitated for a moment, causing Charlie's eyes to widen comically.

"No—was it *you* he disappeared with at Adora Rillington's eighteenth?" he said, clasping a hand over his mouth. I scowled at him.

"No—*no*—I wasn't even invited to that. He—he, uh, was kinda rude to me when I saw him at Lottie's the other day. Must be having an attack of conscience." I paused. "Speaking of his love life, though, is he *really* back with Laure?"

Charlie snorted. "Babe, that depends entirely on who you ask." He narrowed his eyes. "But *something's* going on. He's been like a bear with a sore head for weeks now. Anyway, well done for taking a stand. Honestly, the things Sebastien Wren has got away with based on the fact he is unutterably, disgustingly, ridiculously—"

"Like what?" I interrupted, immediately curious. But Charlie quickly breezed over it. Because everything and everyone was perfect at Greyscott's.

That weekend we all caught the train down to Brighton. It was the first warm day of April and the glimpse of cloudless blue skies and feel of the sun on our skin resulted in an impromptu escape to the coast.

We'd spent hours dicking around on the pier, squandering cash in the arcades, eating hot sugared doughnuts while being menaced by seagulls. Ollie had gone to a corner supermarket and returned with a couple of bottles of rosé while Lottie set up Liberty-print windbreaks and designer beach towels on the beach.

We lay there for a while, the eight of us: Lottie and Seb; Saira and Ollie; Joss and Charlie; Laure, and me, as the sun slowly grew in confidence, warming our bones as we drank warm rosé from plastic glasses. Honestly, I couldn't remember a time I'd felt happier.

Seb being there added to it. The frisson between us was palpable now—to me, anyway. I hadn't spoken to him since I'd received his note. I wasn't playing games deliberately—I mean, I *needed* to speak to him. I'd run through endless scenarios in my head: Accidentally bumping into him after rugby training. Studying all night in an effort to join his higher-math enrichment group. Even deliberately falling off my bike again in front of his house. But none of them had felt right. I knew everything was balancing on a knife edge. Did I truly want this? Yes, I wanted *him*, but did I want everything that came with him? With someone who in all likelihood would never acknowledge me in public? Who seemed to be unable to have transparent relationships?

Or was I having a crisis of confidence? He'd never indicated that he would act like that. Maybe I was creating some self-fulfilling prophecy. Maybe he truly didn't care who I was. . . .

"*Right,*" said Lottie, interrupting my rambling thoughts. "I'm fucking braving it. Who's with me?"

She pulled off her vintage Pucci kaftan, revealing her lean athletic body, her sparkling eyes hidden by bright red Ray-Bans, her plain black swimsuit made from recycled plastic.

Beside me, Ollie was half snoring while Joss sat furiously messaging on her phone. Saira, never one to miss out on a sporting opportunity, stood too, whipping off her dress to reveal a neon-yellow bikini.

"Yeah—count me in," she said.

I dithered. I *was* wearing a swimsuit—a simple two-piece—black, of course. And I'd spent hours looking at every angle of myself in the mirror before I left this morning and was reasonably happy. I glanced over at Charlie for support. He sat up with a groan. "All right, then, better work off those doughnuts."

Seb caught my eye. He meant to. I was sure of it. But Laure was there too. Watchful and waiting. Even with her recent apology, things were still frosty between us, and ever since we'd got on the train she'd been watching me like a hawk. So I stood.

"Sure, why not?"

The water was freezing, but I was a good swimmer. Another testament to Mum, who had taken me to lessons every single week since I turned four. It was important, she'd said; drowning was so common it would be wrong not to equip me with the skills to withstand it. Still, opportunities for swimming were rare, outside of the joyless community swimming pool thick with chlorine and leering men in their fifties. So for a while, I forgot entirely about Seb and enjoyed the freedom the water provided, my body quickly adjusting to the chill.

After a while, the questionable combination of doughnuts and wine began to make me sleepy and I floated on my back, drifting on the lazy current, letting it take me wherever it wanted. The hue of the sky was slowly darkening, the sun a blazing orange ball balancing atop the horizon. Above me, seagulls wheeled and screeched. And for a while, I felt completely at peace.

A sudden rush of cold salty water up my nose made me choke, my feet struggling for purchase. Where the hell was I? My toes were still desperately searching for the bottom of the pool. And then I remembered: I was in the ocean. Had I fallen asleep? How far out was I?

I forced the water out of my nose, brushed it out of my eyes, and righted myself, taking deep calming breaths. I must have drifted off for a few seconds, that was all. In the distance, I could see Charlie wading back to shore, Saira a few meters behind him, doing a strong breaststroke.

I exhaled, looking around—embarrassed at my flailing—and prepared to swim smoothly back to shore.

And that was when I saw her.

She was only a few meters away—but in the other direction— farther out to sea. The sun directly behind her made it impossible to properly make out her features, but they were gaunt and shadowed. Her dark hair, sleek and wet as otter's fur, trailed into the water. Oddly, she appeared to be fully clothed and was staring directly at me. She wasn't swimming. She wasn't moving at all. It was as if she stood on some invisible raised shelf beneath the lap of the waves, doing nothing but looking at me—or the shore—I couldn't be certain.

I raised my hand in a halfhearted greeting. "You—you all right?"

A stupid question. Clearly she was all right. She was still, not wasting a breath, the waters moving around her. I began to wonder if she was real. If this was some artistic interpretation of a buoy—we were in Brighton, after all. But then she snapped open her eyes. Bright and shining and silver as starlight. Her gaze seemed to catch mine and sucked me in, allowing nothing else.

I swallowed. The ancient warning systems of my body slowly kicking into gear. A low hum in my ears, my heart beating so fast it left me breathless.

A familiar refrain flashed unwelcome into my mind, a neon sign, a warning.

Fear death by water.

Where had I heard that before?

I needed to get away. Something was wrong. There was no reason for anyone, fully dressed, to be standing in the water this far out, doing nothing but staring at me. I forced myself to turn away, having to almost wrench my head physically with my hands. Thrusting my body forward, I prepared to swim back to shore.

But something caught hold of my ankle.

I screamed—a half scream that turned into a gurgle as whatever held me yanked me viciously down, causing me to swallow half a liter of seawater. Panic gripped me further and I kicked out with all my strength, coming into contact with something spongy and unpleasant that shrank from me.

But I was free.

Gulping air, I kicked frantically, turning in the direction of the shore, gasping for breath. Then I nearly screamed again.

Lottie was no more than a few feet ahead of me, calmly treading water, blue eyes concealed behind her sunglasses.

I struggled to control my breathing.

"Jesus, Lottie, you scared the crap out of me!"

In reply, Lottie's voice was soft and full of concern.

"Are you all right? You looked like you were struggling for a minute. Let's swim back together, hey?"

I nodded, grateful and calmer now. I risked a brief look behind me, but the woman—whoever she'd been—was gone, maybe swum off to scare someone else. So with Lottie beside me, I headed slowly back to shore.

Laure, clad in a red crop top and high-waisted denim hot pants, sneered as I staggered onto the beach.

"Interesting stroke there, Meg. Kinda looked like doggy paddle? Is that how they teach you to swim in the local comp?"

I ignored her, turning to look behind me, searching again for the woman.

There was nobody there. Not even the telltale blob of a swimmer's head. Nothing but the sun slowly melting farther into the ocean.

23

IT FELT LIKE dawn forgot to arrive.

The sky was gray and rain continually fell in endless heavy sheets, bloating the lake outside, only the very tops of the heads of the statues visible now, its waters creeping up onto the lawn, turning it into a bog. On its far banks, the forest was in still shadow; the jagged crenellations of the folly sketched starkly against the darker sky.

As Saira tried desperately to get hold of the police on her phone—which still stubbornly showed zero bars—Seb and Charlie half carried a hysterically crying Lottie to her room. Seb remained with her while the rest of us gathered before the dying fire in the lounge.

"Why's there still no fucking *signal*?" yelled Ollie, slamming his phone on the table in frustration and cracking the screen.

"Calm down," I ventured cautiously. Ollie was always a live wire, but he seemed more jittery than ever these past few days, his glassy eyes darting around the room. When I'd passed him a few moments earlier, I'd noticed he already smelled strongly of alcohol.

"Maybe a phone mast got damaged in the storm. Dad never bothered installing Wi-Fi here," said Seb, reentering the room, his hair awry, dark circles making his eyes look black. "You've seen the weather out there. As soon as it's fully light I'll head straight into town." He swallowed, lowering his voice. "There's nothing we can do for her now anyway."

"Shit—*shit*. This is—is so messed up," said Joss, her voice breaking. "I can't actually believe it. I mean, what the fuck happened to her? What was she doing in the lake? I can't believe it. I—"

Her words devolved into meaningless sobbing.

"We *looked* there," breathed Charlie. "We circled the whole thing at least twice."

"We did," said Saira, placing a hand over Charlie's. "But it's huge . . . and surrounded by all those reeds. It's no wonder we missed her."

"How's Lottie holding up?" I asked, if only to break the tense silence.

Seb shrugged. "Calmer now. She needed some time alone. I left her up in the studio."

Without thinking, I took Laure's phone from my pocket—I hadn't bothered to change clothes before I'd passed out on the bed the night before—and stared at the picture of her on the lock screen. It was a photo of all of us: Saira and Ollie; Charlie and Lottie; Laure, and me, in Greyscott's common room in happier times. Laure's bright green eyes were friendly and smiling. Her overlong fringe falling silkily across her freckled face.

"Um—why the fuck do you have Laure's phone?"

Joss's voice cut through the unpleasant silence in the room. I looked up in shock, remembering I hadn't yet announced my discovery to everyone. Joss was staring at me, her blue eyes near glacial with hate.

"Oh, it—it was in the studio. I found it last night—it was under the armchair—outside Seb's room."

I shrank a little as everyone in the room stared at me.

"Oh?" continued Joss, her voice tight. "And you didn't think to mention that little discovery?"

"I *did*. I found it last night—you were in bed, but I showed Seb and Charlie—and then—then Laure—then *this* happened, and surprisingly enough it wasn't at the forefront of my mind!"

"So you sent that text, then?" she continued, standing up and moving toward me. "*Pretending* to be her? The one saying she was at a hotel?"

"*What?*" I hissed, the adrenaline now spiking through my blood making me bold. "Why would I do that? I *told* you, I literally found it last night. It's locked and I don't know the code, so I haven't sent *anything*. Jesus, if there's something you want to say, just say it."

"Oh, I think you *know* what I'm going to say."

Joss regarded me with overbright eyes, like a tiger ready to pounce on its prey. I needed to get away from her before I did something I'd regret.

Muttering something about checking on Lottie, I stormed upstairs. Breathing hard, I wrenched the open the door to the studio and slammed it behind me. Despite everything, I was proud of myself. I hadn't reacted, hadn't really said anything back—I'd simply walked away. Rain continued to sheet down the large gable windows, blurring everything beyond it into a mirror image of Lottie's large canvases.

Lottie stood before the window, working frenziedly on another painting. The same drab colors. The statues in the lake small white blobs.

"Saira says there's still no cell service," she murmured, barely turning from the canvas. "I—I didn't know what else to do."

She looked terrible. Her face pale, her eyes ringed heavily with bruiselike circles, her usual glossy curls dull and greasy, tied back in a careless knot.

"What do you think happened to her?" I asked, tears welling in my eyes again. "Laure, I mean."

Lottie shook her head. "It must have been the weeds. I should have warned everyone, it's so easy to get tangled up and—"

She ended with a sharp sob. Her words made me think of Halloween.

I live in the weeds—

"Who *is* that—the woman in your paintings?" I asked, needing to change the subject. "Who's she supposed to be, and what's she doing? What's that bundle she's carrying?"

Lottie carried on painting. Heavy, violent strokes of gray.

"I'm not sure. . . . It sounds insane, but I keep seeing her—in my dreams. Every time I'm here I dream of the lake and . . . and her. At first I thought it was just some mad inspiration taking hold—I was telling you before about how connected I felt to nature—to the landscape—when I'm here. And I thought it was always a positive thing—a good connection. But now . . ."

She went silent. The only sound in the room the *slap, slap, slap* of paint on the canvas.

"You've seen her?" I asked tightly. "In the lake? Did you see her the night of the party—is that where you were going when . . . ." I trailed off, a little afraid of how Lottie was looking at me, her eyes overbright and feverish.

"Why? Have you seen her too?"

Had I? Honestly, I hoped not, but then why did she look so oddly familiar? Those flashing eyes; that dark, lank hair. I found myself thinking once again of the strange-looking woman we'd nearly hit in the taxi and the driver's even stranger reaction. That same dark, wet hair, the same listless sobbing that had been haunting my dreams.

For God's sake, Meg. There's enough going on without you seeing monsters in every corner.

"No," I replied decisively. "No, I haven't."

Lottie tilted her head, pausing her work for a moment before turning back to the painting. "Are you all right, Meg? You don't look so good."

Swallowing, I glanced down. "I found Laure's phone in here last night," I said. "It was under the armchair over there. Joss saw I had it and started insinuating that I had something to do with Laure's—with what happened to Laure."

At least my tears were silent this time. I brushed them away.

Would they ever stop judging me for what had happened at the summer ball? The events of that night had been a split-second mistake. Nothing more than an impulse. Lottie had said it herself when she'd called me the next morning. But as the days went on, my phone silent, my nervous texts unanswered—as I had nothing else to think about—the shadowy feeling of guilt began to grow within me like black spots of mold.

You could have killed *her—*
She was drowning—
You held her down—
You wanted this—you wanted it to happen—

Lottie just gave a snort. She put her palette down and wrapped me in a brief, hot embrace. She smelled vaguely unpleasant—stale sweat and damp. Perhaps it was the overalls she was wearing—they looked as old as the house. "*Ridiculous*. Totally ridiculous."

"She thinks I sent that text—the one saying Laure was at a hotel."

Lottie pulled back, releasing me. "And did you?"

"*No*. How could I? For a start, her phone's locked and I have no idea what the passcode is—"

But you *might. Or Seb.*

The thought surprised me. Yet wasn't that what Charlie had suggested—that someone *else* had sent it, someone close to Laure, someone who needed to buy themselves some time after—

What was I *thinking*?

Laure had slipped off the bank and got caught in the weeds, like Lottie said; that was all.

"Well, anyways, I'm about done. What do you think?" Lottie asked distractedly, waving at the canvas.

I stared at the painting again. At the too-tall, too-slender figure framed in the doorway. Was she looking out or looking in? I thought of those muddy footsteps I'd seen the night before and shuddered.

I *knew* that face. I'd seen it, I was certain of that now. In my nightmares. Always near water. But I said nothing. They were just dreams, and Lottie seemed spooked enough already.

What are you capable of?

Lottie stared, still transfixed by the canvas. "Do you remember Samhain? The stuff I said? At first I was making it up, but then it seemed to just, just pop into my head—kinda like an autocue, y'know? Like someone was speaking directly into my ear." She shook her head, gesturing to the painting. "There's this poem Seb's always adored—*The Waste Land*. This reminds me of one of the verses—

"A woman drew her long black hair out tight
And fiddled whisper music on those strings
And bats with baby faces in the violet light
Whistled, and beat their wings
And crawled head downward down a blackened wall
And upside down in air were towers
Tolling reminiscent bells, that kept the hours
And voices singing out of empty cisterns and exhausted wells."

She broke off, pursing her lips, and a shiver ran down my spine. "It's funny, though," Lottie said. "Eimer *hates* these paintings. She refused to come in here after she caught sight of the first one, you know. Dropped all the towels she was carrying and turned the color of sour cream. She's pretty superstitious. Really believes there's a banshee out there and that I shouldn't be painting her."

"And is there?"

Lottie turned to me and smiled. It was a strange smile. Stretched and thin and utterly devoid of humor. "I never used to think so. Thought it was just some crap spouted by the locals. But lately . . . lately, I'm not so sure."

Downstairs, Saira, Ollie, and Seb were readying themselves for the trip into town, while Charlie comforted a weeping Joss in the kitchen. The dried footprints that had circled the hall yesterday were gone. Someone—Eimer, maybe, though I'd assumed she'd left before the storm—must have mopped them up. I planned to look around for her once everyone had gone, if only to have someone sane to speak to. As I entered the kitchen, planning to make Lottie a mug of tea to calm her nerves, Joss glared at me. Even through the dark shades of her Chanel sunglasses, I could see that her eyes were red and sore.

"There's still no service, and the lake's completely burst its banks now," said Seb dully, by way of greeting. "We're going to try to walk to town—or walk at least until we get a phone signal—then let the police know what's happened here, somehow tell Laure's parents." He cleared his throat.

The atmosphere in the room was as thick and as murky as the lake outside. Crossing to the stove, I turned one of the burners on and lifted the half-full kettle onto it.

"Something's wrong about all this, y'know," said Joss coldly. "I mean, did anyone else notice Laure was wearing the same dress she wore the night she arrived? On Halloween?"

"Meaning?" I pressed, never failing to take Joss's bait.

"Meaning she died that *night*, obviously. Maybe she had an argument with someone and it pushed her over the edge. Or maybe she was *literally* pushed over the edge. We all know Laure was terrified of water. We all *know* she couldn't swim."

"How is that possible?" said Seb dully. "She messaged you yesterday." He gave Joss a cold stare. "Or didn't she?"

But Joss wouldn't be fazed. "Yeah, but that doesn't mean it was *her*. Like I said, Meg could have texted from her phone."

"I already told you, I only found her phone last night in the studio," I said, hoping the warning in my tone was clear. I threw the phone onto the table, glad to be rid of the thing. "Hours after she supposedly texted you. See for yourself. It hasn't been unlocked since you called it yesterday."

Charlie gave a humorless little laugh beside me. "You think one of us had something to do with this? Pushed her in? *Murdered* her? Come on, Joss. That's a reach even for you. She must have slipped that night, ended up in that fucking lake and drowned. Maybe she was leaving for the hotel when it happened—you said yourself you have no idea when the text was actually *sent*."

"Lottie said the lake's dangerous," I added. "That it's easy to get caught up in the weeds."

I willed the kettle to hurry up and boil so I could make this damn tea and escape back to the sanctuary of the studio and Lottie's more sympathetic company.

Joss took off her sunglasses and gave me the full force of her stare while pretending to still address Charlie.

"How's it a reach, Charlie? How is it a reach when we all know one of us *did* push her in a damn river already? How exactly is *that* a reach?" She leaned forward, her eyes narrowing. "We all heard what happened that night, Meg. How you went full psycho and

228

tried to drown her. Everyone knows you've been obsessed with her ex since you got to Greyscott's, hanging around him like some dog with its tongue out—"

"That is *enough*, Joss," snapped Seb, slamming his hand so hard on the table everyone jumped. But Joss wasn't done.

"Laure nearly drowned back then, at a party full of hundreds of people, and all because of Meg! Why would anyone be surprised that she finished the job out here?"

I stared at her in horror, utterly speechless, hot tears springing into my eyes.

"Joss, I am warning you—"

Seb again. Or so I thought. Tears blurred my eyes so thickly I couldn't see.

"*What?*" Joss cried. "Everything I've said is true! With Laure out of the way, Meg gets to go back to her fancy school. And as for you, Seb, I don't know what's wrong with you and Lottie either! Why you'd both invite this trash to begin with? This whole Pygmalion act stopped being funny months ago. Fact is, Megan, you being an unhinged lunatic aside, you never bloody belonged here to begin with. And *Laure* was the only one of us with the balls to point it out."

Halfway through her tirade, Joss's words faded, and all I could see was her face, beautiful in repose, but now scrunched up and ugly with hate. *Misguided* hate. Whatever I'd done at the ball had been a split-second decision. Maybe, in my drunken stupidity, I'd thought someone might even see the funny side of it. I hadn't *known* she couldn't swim. Nobody had told me. It wasn't fair—

But I *had* known, hadn't I? I'd known since that day at the beach.

"*Interesting stroke there. . . . Is that how they teach you at the local comp?*"

And Charlie had snorted in response. "*At least she can swim, Laure. Seriously—*"

The guilt swelled within me, a murky black tide.

"Shut *up!*" I screamed, desperate for her noise to stop. "Shut up, shut up, SHUT *UP!*"

Somewhere close by, I heard Ollie snigger. "Better hide any knives that might be lying around. You've properly set her off this time."

I felt someone try to take my arm. Charlie, I think. But I'd had enough. Enough of *all* of them. Laure was right: I *didn't* belong here.

And why would I *want* to? Why did I even want to hang around these people, let alone aspire to be like them? None of them were my friends. Not really. Maybe not even Lottie. If I'd been more like her or like Laure, like Saira, instead of some project she could fix up, would she even have bothered to befriend me?

I slammed down the kettle and wrenched away from Charlie, ignoring the sharp burn as the hot liquid splashed all over my hand. Joss started, shrinking back a little in her chair.

"Fuck *you*, Joss! Just because Laure and I have had our differences in the past doesn't mean I bloody *killed* her. I know I can be hotheaded, but you *cannot* just throw around accusations like that—"

Wringing my hand, I directed my attention to Seb, who was white as a sheet.

"It's amazing you all think I'm some kind of murderer," I said with a harsh laugh of disbelief. "And I'm sorry about Laure, I truly am," I continued, still pointedly looking at Seb. "But I came here to apologize to her and nothing else. I wanted to make amends, and yes, okay I wanted to get back into Greyscott's. I wanted my *life* back, and I needed Laure to forgive me. Exactly what use would she be to me *dead*?"

Pushing roughly past Ollie, I stormed out of the kitchen, desperate to get away from the lot of them.

24

AFTER OUR SWIM at Brighton, we headed to a nearby café to grab some fish and chips. Lottie, Joss, and I ended up falling behind the others, ambling slowly along the crowded promenade, soaking in the late-day sun.

"There she goes, trotting off after him as usual . . ."

I blinked, turning to Lottie, unsure I'd heard correctly. There was a cold venom in her voice I'd never heard before. I smiled at her uncertainly.

"What do you mean?"

She nodded at the others ahead of us. "*Laure.* You've seen the way she acts around Seb. I dunno, it's just kind of . . . pathetic."

Joss snorted. "Um, harsh, Lots, harsh."

And it was, but especially for Lottie. Since I'd met her, she'd always been such a champion of her friends, part of the reason I liked her so much—trusted her. But, now that I thought about it, Lottie *had* seemed different toward Laure lately—ever since the Christmas party. In fact, just different in general. Less smiley and

chill, less full of affirmations to the universe, and more *stretched.*
Like she'd been spread too thin. At first, I'd put it down to the
endless stress of our coursework. Desjardins's art class was intense,
but now . . .

"There's history between them, right?" I asked cautiously. Joss
raised a perfectly arched eyebrow but said nothing. Lottie, on the
other hand, snorted.

"Yeah, Laure would *like* you to think that—would like *everyone* to think that but believe me, that's not the case. She's had a
crush on him forever, like literally since we were twelve or something. It's gross."

"Um . . . I swear down they left the Christmas party together,"
remarked Joss innocently.

I felt my face heat. Jealousy coursing hotly through my veins
remembering how I'd had to leave earlier that I'd wanted that
night.

"Yeah, because he'd promised to drive her drunk ass home. She
threw up all over the upholstery of Dad's new Audi. He was *not*
impressed and neither was Seb after Dad told him he had to shell
out to get it cleaned."

Lottie's expression darkened. "I *know* it sounds harsh but she
won't take a hint. She calls him all hours of the day and he's tired
of it. He says it's harmless but . . . Laure and I grew up together
and I can't help but wonder if she were ever really my friend or if
she just always . . ." She shrugged, leaving the thought unfinished
and linking her arm through mine. "I dunno, I guess people just
grow apart."

Groggy with the sun and wine and full of chips, as the evening set in we'd headed to a club underneath the Victorian arches on the beach. We still had a couple of hours until the last train back to London.

I'd felt subdued ever since my swim. While everyone was being polite to each other, I'd begun to sense an underlying tension between us all, that was only growing as time went on. The club was hectic, full of rowdy stag parties and hen dos. Our group dissipated like smoke, some at the bar, some out for a cigarette or visiting the restroom.

Somehow, at Ollie's suggestion, I'd agreed to buy a round of shots. Looking at the prices, I hoped my overdraft could take the hit. Standing at the crowded bar, desperately trying to get the bartender's attention in a sea of screaming women and roaring men, I heard my name.

"Megan?"

I whirled round, my breath short. My stomach flipped over at the sight of him. Sun-flushed and tipsy. The dark holiday stubble against golden skin giving him a fresh appeal.

"You're avoiding me, right?" He gave a short laugh. "I've been wanting to talk to you forever—but I'm only just drunk enough now."

I smiled despite myself. "Oh, okay? So you need to be drunk to talk to me?"

"To be brave enough to, yes."

He looked back at our table. Ollie was the only one there at present, morosely doom-scrolling on his phone.

"Will you—uh—come for a walk with me?" Seb asked shyly. "We could meet the others back at the station?"

He looked impossibly gorgeous in a crisp white shirt and

belted shorts. Only a year ago my old friends and I would absolutely have cackled at guys dressed like him. But now . . .

"Okay . . . I guess," I murmured, giving him a subtle side-eye.

The beach was much quieter now and we walked along the promenade in comfortable silence, the moon huge and bloated over the ocean. I shivered; there was a distinct chill in the air now the sun had gone down. Without a word, he wrapped an arm about my shoulders. I leaned into him slightly. Conceding.

"So, do I genuinely repulse you?" he asked, his words soft and unsure. Immediately, I stopped walking and looked at him, raising an eyebrow with an ungainly snort.

"Did you *genuinely* just ask that question?"

He smiled, surer now. "It's just . . . after *that* day—you—you totally ignored me. You literally turned in the opposite direction when I saw you next at school."

I wrinkled my nose. Here came the tricky part.

"Well, yeah, firstly, because you *apologized*—as in you seemed to regret it the moment you did it. And then there's this." I gestured to us. "This all seems to be shrouded in secrecy. Is it because you're still thinking about Laure?"

The rosé was making me bold but I was glad. These things needed to be said so they could finally stop spinning around my head at four a.m. every single night.

Seb said nothing for a few moments and we continued walking. The promenade was quiet now, other than the odd intrepid jogger or dog walker, the beach huts casting long striped shadows across our path.

"I didn't regret it, exactly," he said. "But I did feel bad. I want to be honest—want *this* to be honest. I mean, you're one of Lottie's closest friends. I had no right to, y'know." He gave a long sigh. "What I'm trying to say is it's not the best idea to date your sister's friends, is it? As we all found out once things went tits up with Laure. And Lottie *adores* you."

He released my hand and I considered what he'd said. I could see his point. If we got together and broke up messily, it would be difficult for everyone.

"So you *were* with Laure, then?"

He nodded, his expression serious. "Yeah, I already told you. But it was never serious. We ended things not long after I met you—that first time I saw you in the studio. Thing is, Laure took it upon herself to decide we were only on a break or whatever, so I had to speak to her *again* at the Christmas party. Then, only a week or so ago she literally turned up at my house completely uninvited to 'talk about us . . .'"

He gave a heavy sigh. "It . . . it's a lot, actually. And I didn't even want to come today . . . it didn't seem worth it . . . until I heard you'd be here."

He grasped my wrist again. I liked the possessiveness of it. Like he was leading me exactly where I wanted to go.

"*You*, I think, are worth it. And believe me, I've thought about it—a lot."

He looked at me then, his eyes, the same dark blue of the twilight sky, burning into mine, his mouth set in a serious line, all easiness, all humor gone. Then, in one fluid motion, he walked me back into the shadows of the nearest beach hut, pressing me up against the wall, and kissed me.

It was a slaughter of a kiss, expunging everything gentle and delicate and tentative that had gone before it. And for the first time, I felt I got a glimpse of the *real* Sebastien behind the softly joking facade, the easygoing persona. One hand trailed down my throat, while the other kept me pinned me to the door by the wrist. His mouth was scorching on mine and I dug my hand into his hair, wrenching him closer, eliciting a groan. His tongue teased, hot and wet, dancing about my lips, before tangling with mine.

Aware we were on the verge of getting arrested for public indecency, I pulled away, breathing hard and laughing. He kissed my smile.

"I've wanted to do that since the first time I saw you," he said, his lips close to my ear now. "And now I want to do it again."

And I wanted to do a great deal more, but just as he kissed me again, both our phones vibrated loudly.

"Shit," I murmured, reading Lottie's text and quickly replying. "How long have we been? If we miss the last train—"

"We'll have to stay overnight in a hotel through no fault of our own," said a smiling Seb, taking my arm in his. "How terrible."

I smiled, a blush heating my cheeks. "Yeah . . . but we better head back."

As we turned toward the bright lights of the city, something caught my eye, standing on the darkened beach, her dress flowing behind her in the strong coastal breeze. Her sharp light eyes caught and held my own. I nudged Seb, my chest suddenly tight.

"Do you see that woman? I swear she was watching me earlier—in the water."

Seb looked over in the direction she stood. I didn't like her expression. It was stern and disapproving. Maybe she'd caught all of our kiss.

"Can't see anyone, it's dark, Meg. C'mon, we better actually hurry. As much as the hotel situation sounds like bliss, can you imagine the chat at school tomorrow?"

The downpour outside was so heavy it was painful against my skin, needling it with violence. Good job I'd had the forethought to grab my coat before I stormed out the door, slamming it so hard the house seemed to shake behind me.

Good.

I was glad of the rain mingling with my hot tears, cooling them and making them invisible. The unfairness of it all swum round and round in my head as I waded down the long drive to the road and followed the sign pointing toward the nearest town. Lottie would have to make her own tea. I couldn't stay here any longer; I *needed* to get out.

I'd never wanted any of this.

If I stripped it all back, all I'd wanted was to fit in as best I could and focus on my art. Maybe then I could *be* someone. Someone who, unlike my mum, wasn't permanently struggling just to make ends meet. Someone who could one day afford all the things I saw at Greyscott's, the things I spent every day convincing myself I didn't want and certainly didn't need. Box-fresh train-ers and buttery leather handbags. The latest iPhone and AirPods rather than crappy dupes from China. That girl would be smooth and confident and well traveled. Someone who, down the line, might be able to afford a better mortgage, a bigger place for Mum and me. I hadn't wanted anything else—

Except—except for Seb—

And my heart broke for Laure. Despite everything that had gone down between us, there had been a good person buried deep beneath all that insecurity. On top of that, I felt a slinking shame because I was also worried for myself. *Would* this be pinned on me? Joss certainly had a big-enough mouth. Would she name and shame me on social media? Would I be investigated? Would I go to court? What would Mum think? After the ball, she'd wanted me to forget all about Greyscott's, had blamed herself for the aftermath, for suggesting I go there in the first place.

"I knew what they were like," she'd cried as I'd desperately tried to assure her it was a single moment's lapse of judgment and nothing more. A silly prank gone wrong. "I knew what *all* of them were like."

And would they bring up what I did at the ball? It wouldn't look good at all. Almost as if someone had *planned* this—had planned to make me look guilty and—

I forced those thoughts away. Joss was a bitch, but even she wasn't that calculating. It was a tragic accident. And Charlie was right, Laure hadn't looked herself at all the night she arrived here. Thinner and quieter. A shadow of who she used to be. If she *had* slipped into the cold waters of the lake late at night and couldn't swim, then it wasn't hard to see how this could happen. But what had caused that change in her? What had happened in the weeks following the ball? Had she worked things out with Seb? Was that why he'd ignored me, out of some dubious loyalty to her? It was doubtful I'd ever find out.

Deep in thought, I walked along the sodden, grassy edge of the main road. Directly ahead of me was a short, steep rise. I paused to get my bearings once I'd climbed to the top.

The other side, where the road dipped, was completely flooded with the murky brown water of the lake. There was no telling how deep the water was, and despite my confident swimming, the downed power lines lying about the grass verge put me off trying.

Either side of the road, the storm had turned the thick forest into a treacherous, soupy swamp.

I shut my eyes and exhaled shakily, already tired and cold. Not to mention drenched to the bone, my feet sodden and numb. Not sure what else to do, I skidded back down the rise and jogged back to the road sign before the turnoff to the house. The nearest town in the other direction was thirty kilometers away. Still, there had to be a house nearby, or a farm, or *something*.

As I dithered over what to do, a car approached, taking its time to slow beside me. As the window slid down I felt a wave of apprehension, instinctively remembering all the talks we had at primary school about stranger danger. But inside were a smiling middle-aged couple. The passenger, a warm-looking lady with a chic gray bob, nodded at me. "Road to the village's flooded, by the look of things. You need a lift somewhere, my love?"

"Yes—completely flooded," I breathed, relief coursing through my veins as I raised my voice above the drumming of the rain. "And yes, thank you! That would be amazing! In fact—would I be able to borrow your phone for a minute first? We've had an emergency back at the house."

My hopes rose. Okay, this was good. I'd ring the police, they'd come out—somehow—and it would all be left in their capable hands. Whatever I might have done in the past, I was *innocent*. I hadn't done anything here. I had nothing to hide.

The woman's eyes widened with concern. "Well, of course, love. Why don't ya climb in the back out of the rain and I'll— Oh—now, wait a moment. . . ."

Her phone was attached to the dashboard in a plastic holder. I'd noticed the second before she had: No signal. Only a flat line where the bars should have been.

"Now, that's very strange. Fergal—do ye have a signal on your phone there?"

The man beside her began fumbling in his pocket.

"No, actually, that makes sense," I explained. "Seb—one of the guys back at the house—thinks a cell tower may be damaged, as none of us have got any signal back there either. A lift would be great, though."

I nodded over my shoulder at the turnoff to the house. It would be a relief to get away from Wren Hall and speak to someone in authority about everything that had happened before Joss got the opportunity to twist it all.

The woman followed my gaze. Her jaw dropped and she gave the man beside her such a comically dark look it almost made me laugh. No doubt she was about to tell me it was haunted by some mythical banshee. Well, I was way ahead of her.

"You're not coming from Wren Hall, are ye? Horrible, dank place, isn't it? Not been the same since the murder there."

I stared at her, feeling utterly wrong-footed for a moment, wondering if someone at the house had managed to contact the police before me. But Laure hadn't been *murdered*. And neither Lottie nor Seb had ever mentioned anything to us about anyone who had—

There was a soft clunk from the car as the driver locked the doors.

"Murder?" I said. "There's not been a murder."

The woman's voice was harder now, and colder, her eyes fixed on the road ahead.

"A little over a year and a half ago. It might not have made the papers over the water, but it was huge news here. The Donnelly girl—she was only sixteen, poor lass. Whole life ahead of her. She was found floating in that there lake, facedown, drowned."

Fear death by water.

I swallowed, feeling faint and nauseous all of a sudden. The woman noticed my face.

"You didn't know, then? Was a terrible thing. Terrible waste of a young life."

"H-how?" I stuttered. "And who did it?"

The woman shrugged. "No one knows. No one was ever charged. The amount of time she was in that lake put paid to any evidence being found. Should have the drained the whole thing and cemented it over, if you ask my opinion. She was the daughter of a family that ran the place back when it was a B and B. Lovely young girl."

"She was a Wren?"

"No—*no.* She was from a local family—they were looking after it for the Wrens, y'see. They wouldn't dare show their faces now, after all the scandal. People around here don't forget quickly.

But wait—you mentioned a Seb? Do you mean young Sebastien? You're talking about Sebastien Wren?"

It was too late to lie. The woman had already clocked my expression. Her voice dull now, she turned to her husband. "It's a cursed place. No good will ever come of it. Nor from those twins, not from that family. Now then, Darragh, we had better be heading back."

"Wait," I began, panicked, "wait, *please*! Please, our friend's in trouble—if you could just give me a lift to town, then— *Wait!*"

But she had already wound her window tightly back up. I watched, dejected, as her husband executed a violent three-point turn and disappeared into the gray mizzle of the rain.

25

I STARED AT the retreating car, tears mingling with the rain as I watched my ride away from here, my escape from all this madness, disappear into the distance. Not knowing what else to do, I turned back down the drive, defeated.

I'd been walking for a few minutes, the rain making it difficult to even see properly, when, through the trees, I caught a glimpse of a dark figure standing in the distance.

I hesitated. A prickle of fear making my breath short. I turned back to the road, debating what to do. Surely I could walk the thirty kilometers—or maybe even hitch some of it—to the nearest town. There was no one from that damn house I wanted to see anymore, since clearly they all thought I was a *murderer*. As I debated, whoever it was caught sight of me and began to pick up speed.

A cold, slick feeling slid down my spine. An image of the woman from my nightmares crawled unwelcome into my head. The same woman from Lottie's paintings. Maybe she was real after all—maybe it was *her* coming toward me, finally summoned from the lake by Laure's death. Was I next? But as they got closer, I recognized their lanky, easy gait.

"It *is* you—thank God," Seb said. "Hey, *stop*."

I turned sharply, trudging resolutely back to the road, ignoring him as he caught up and began walking beside me, breathing hard. He took my arm, forcing me to a standstill.

"Wait—*wait*. Meg. *Jesus*, we've all been looking for you in the rain for nearly an hour now. Look, Joss was bang out of order—if anything, it's her that should have walked out. Lottie was reading her the riot act as I left—I've never seen her so angry. We all know it was an accident. Hey—hey, would you *stop*—please—"

I did, finally turning to face him.

I was surprised at how relieved he looked. I was so surprised I couldn't even speak when he wrapped his arms around me, warm beneath the expensive waxed jacket he wore. That familiar scent of his sparking the desire I felt for him even now. Releasing me, he gently tilted my chin up so our eyes would meet, his voice soft.

"Are you okay?" he asked. "Do you want to head back now? Some of us are just about to go and get help. You could come with? Whatever you want, Meg—but you can't run away. Not again. Not this time."

I stared at him. Unsure of where this had all come from, his words last night not forgotten. I pushed him away, hard.

"Seb—what *is* this? What game are you playing? After everything that happened at the ball, you vanished from the face of the earth. You happily left me to face *everything* alone. You didn't answer my calls, you ignored my messages. I wasted entire days in bed just staring at my phone, hoping you'd call." I shook my head, my anger rising with every word. "You—you made me . . . *pathetic*. If it hadn't been for Lottie I don't know what I would have done. Answer me this: Why am I only ever good enough for you behind closed doors? When no one else is around? What exactly is it about me you're so ashamed of?" Seb exhaled heavily; raindrops caught in his dark lashes.

"Not this again. Meg, I told you. It isn't what you think—"

I laughed sharply. "Of course it is! It's exactly that! You think I'm not good enough for your perfect gilded life. Because I live in a flat in a crappy part of town. Because, yes, my mum cleans toilets at school. I get it. You're a coward. So you string along other girls who are suitable on paper, like poor Laure, then create havoc between us all because of your—your *cowardice*—" Seb gave a harsh scoff, half drowned out by a sudden crash of thunder.

"Wow. Is that *really* what you think? What you think of me?"

"No, actually. It's what I *know!*"

He took two steps toward me, so forcefully that I flinched, but then his hands, cold with rain, grasped my face, pulling it toward his, and he kissed me, deliciously heated in the frigid rain, his tongue lacing against mine, causing my knees to buckle slightly at the promise in it.

"You're wrong," he said, his dark lashes fringed with raindrops. "I keep trying to tell you—I never cared about Laure. It was all in her head. *All* of it. You're the only one that matters, I swear. And things will be different after this," he said urgently, his words hot against my skin. "I promise, Meg. It'll be different."

I never cared about Laure.

I staggered back, looking at him, the rain distorting my vision. He must have noticed the suspicion on my face.

"God, not like that! I just meant— Look, Meg, is now really the time? We *need* to go get help and—"

"There's no point," I said dully.

"What do you mean?"

"The roads are completely cut off. It's like a—a proper swamp. I saw a car but it drove off as soon as I said I was staying here. Seems like your family has quite the reputation in the area."

Ignoring that comment, Seb ran a hand through his hair in exasperation.

"You're sure?"

I shrugged, already moving in the direction of the house. "Take a look for yourself. We're stuck here until the storm clears up or until service is back up."

As I spoke the words, the unpleasant reality of the situation finally sank deep within my bones. We *were* stuck here. Miles from anywhere, with our dead friend bundled up in the basement, the manner of her death uncertain. Helpless and isolated and—

"*Shit*," Seb swore. "Fine, we better head back anyway. You look freezing and—"

The words came out of my mouth entirely unbidden. "Tell Lottie."

He looked at me, confused. "Tell her what? About the road?"

"About *us*. If you meant what you said, if you ever meant it. If I'm important to you, if you want us to continue . . . whatever this is, then tell her. Why not?"

"You *know* why, we've talked about it. She's your friend—my sister—"

"And you've been leading me on for damn near a year now! I'm beginning to think she's going to be more pissed off at our *deceit*, Seb. You should have come clean at the ball. You told me you would—you *promised* me—and then"—I coughed, trying to disguise a violent sob—"and then you *lied.*"

He set his jaw, looking obstinately away. I felt my heart fracture. But it *had* been so long. Month after month of secret looks and messages, stolen kisses and hiding away, and I was *sick* of it. I knew Sebastien Wren well enough by now that I was determined to have him properly or purge myself of him entirely.

"I hate to remind you of this, but Laure is *dead,*" he said quietly but sternly. "Do you really think now's the time to start shouting about how into you I am?"

I looked away, ashamed.

"But as soon as this is sorted," he continued, softening, "as soon as we're back home, I promise you I will fix this. I will fix it all, Meg. I just need you to wait a little longer."

For all his charming talk, I hadn't properly seen Seb since Brighton. We'd got back and time had moved swiftly on. We'd begun messaging each other, though, even stopping to chat if we walked past each other in the halls at Greyscott's. I could recall the exact time of each meeting, every single occasion I'd analyzed his words, his expression, for meaning.

Then Lottie organized the sleepover.

It was meant to be a cheesy girls' night to bring us all back together a month or so before the end of the school year and the summer ball. One more thing that Lottie apparently deemed desperately uncool but still insisted on doing in the name of irony. We planned to do all the usual things: wear cute pajamas, do face masks, eat pizza, and watch terrible rom-coms. All ready to be militantly added to Lottie's Insta "stories" in the name of content.

Despite laughing along with everyone at the terribleness of it all, I secretly thought it was a fun idea, and the fact I'd be staying in Sebastien's house *overnight* had not escaped me. I didn't imagine Seb and I would *do* anything; just the thought of it was enough.

I arrived early. I'd be lying if I said it wasn't partly on purpose, although the buses out to the Wrens' fancy estate were few and far between. Noticing lights were on in the studio, I headed there first. Lottie was inside, almost manically painting unusually dark swathes of paint over a large canvas.

"Meg," she said, not looking up from her work. "You're early. . . . Why don't you go inside and put the kettle on? I'm just finishing up here. Back door's open." An unusually cool welcome for Lottie, but she was busy and she sounded cheery enough, so I left her to it.

As I rounded the house, I could hear voices floating from the kitchen through the bifold doors. I hadn't set out to eavesdrop, but something in their tone made me stop.

"—what she's playing at? Why on *earth* would she invite that girl over tonight?"

The voice was hissing, exasperated. Lottie's mum.

"You need to calm down. Look—" The second voice was deeper, gruff. Their dad, probably, although I'd never met him. He was always away on business or at the office. He dropped his voice, so I missed the rest of what he said.

Still, my blood ran cold.

Clearly it was Seb and Lottie's parents. And clearly they were talking about me, the lone donkey among the herd of stallions. I bit my lip, wondering whether to slink back to the studio or just go home or—

"Megs?"

Seb emerged around the corner dressed casually in a plaid shirt and joggers, looking surprised to see me. "What are you doing lurking about outside?"

He was smiling, but after what I'd just heard, I didn't really feel like smiling back.

"Lottie told me to put the kettle on. . . . So, are you joining the sleepover tonight?"

I was joking, of course. And in return he feigned shock.

"Wow, pretty forward of you."

I followed him back to the kitchen, now empty of his parents, where he switched the kettle on for me. "But nah. Ollie and I are going to watch the game."

We chatted easily for a few minutes before he left, the usual crackle of electricity between us dampened due to the close proximity of his family.

The evening passed quickly. All of us had worn matching pajamas (provided by Saira's dad, who, I learned, owned a multimillion-pound fashion company): cute satin tops and shorts in baby pink and powder blue. We'd washed off Korean face masks and posed for numerous ironic pictures—pillow fights, hairbrush karaoke—

"Okay, okay . . . truth-or-dare time, girls," interrupted Joss, her long tan legs folded beneath her as she sat on Lottie's vast bed, a wicked smirk upon her perfect lips.

I sighed inwardly. So far the night had been refreshingly drama-free. To my relief, Lottie looked reluctant too.

"*Really*, Joss?" she said in the world-weary tone she reserved for lecturing others about climate change. "Aren't we all a little old for that?"

Laure, who'd been unusually quiet all evening, perked up at this. "Well, I'm down. We're all friends here, right? No secrets between us lot."

I huffed a small, ironic laugh.

"I'll start," said Joss, steamrollering on. "Okay. So, *Meg.*"

I grabbed the nearest pillow and, collapsing to the floor, groaned theatrically into it, determined not to have the night ruined. Quickly sitting up, I faced her directly, ticking off my answers on my fingertips. "Okay, wait, before you ask: No, my mum does not spend all our housing money on flat-screen TVs and weed. No, I have never been arrested for shoplifting. No, I do not only eat frozen food. No, you do not need to watch your belongings around me, *and* my mum did *nothing* to assist with my scholarship other than ask the principal for a bloody application form."

After a beat of awkward silence, I was surprised when Joss just laughed. "Fair play, bitch. Your turn."

I was actually itching to ask Laure about the last time she kissed Seb, but I figured that would raise more questions than answers from the others.

"*I've* got a question," Laure interjected, her eyes oddly bright. She turned to Lottie, who was determinedly scrolling through her phone in an effort to show how done she was with this game. "Lottie. What's the worst lie you've ever told?"

Lottie gave an odd smile without looking up from her phone. "Uh, I don't actually lie."

Saira snorted. "Oh, come *on*, Lots. That answer's a lie in itself."

"Exactly," said Laure, staring fixedly at Lottie in a way that made me uncomfortable. "Play the *game*, Lottie."

Lottie rolled her eyes and threw down her phone, staring directly back at Laure. "Uh, I don't know, probably telling you that my brother thought you were cute all those years ago. Didn't realize how much of an insane *stalker* it would turn you into."

"*Jesus*, Lottie," Saira said, wincing. "This is meant to be fun! What the hell?" But Laure didn't flinch.

"We *both* know that wasn't one-way. And we both know you've lied about worse."

I stared at Lottie, curious to see her reaction. Her face was a rare shade of florid pink—I'd never seen her so riled about anything before—and she bit her lip before uttering only three words.

"Fine, then. *Dare.*"

At around two a.m., when everyone was finally dozing, my phone buzzed angrily beside my head. Blinking, I recovered it and stared drowsily at the screen, my heart beginning to race. Who the hell would be messaging me at this time? Was Mum okay? Then, as I stared some more, a low fizz of excitement flared in my stomach.

Hesitantly, I slipped out of Lottie's bedroom, trying to get my bearings. The Wrens' parents were staying out that night, so thankfully there was no danger of accidentally walking in on them in bed, but then I saw that the door to a palatial family bathroom was open across the wide sweeping staircase, the light flooding into the hall. Taking a cautious glance behind me, my feet sinking in the deep pile of the tastefully gray carpet, I snuck across the hallway as bidden and stepped into the empty room.

Only moments later, I heard a soft tap at the door. I opened it a crack to find Seb standing directly outside, leaning against the wooden doorframe and looking unfairly attractive in checked pajama bottoms and a soft-spun tee, his hair ruffled from sleep. He looked at me brazenly.

"*Oh*, nice pajamas." He smiled, slipping into the room and locking the door behind him, his eyes everywhere at once.

"Thanks?"

"I wanted to chat properly—we barely got to speak earlier," he said, his voice lowering to a whisper. "I feel like you've been avoiding me since we got back from Brighton."

He was making a concerted effort to look me in the eye, but here, alone at night, it felt unwise to meet his gaze. The air between us seemed electric and dangerous.

"I could say the same about you," I replied coolly, forcing myself to look at him. It was a mistake; I knew it would be. He leaned back against the door, his dark blue eyes almost black. Even in the harsh fluorescent light of the bathroom he was beautiful. Tonight there was a sort of casual surrender about him I'd never seen before.

"I know . . . I know," he said. "School's been kinda hectic, right? And . . . honestly, I wasn't sure if all this was a good idea, and it still might not be, but—"

He stepped forward, reached for a lock of my white-blond hair, and twirled it between his fingers. "But it's what I want." Then his hand moved from my hair to gently take hold of my chin, tilting it up slightly as he leaned forward and kissed me softly. I shuddered, tiptoeing to wrap my arms about his neck, dragging him down to me. He chuckled in delight as his mouth met mine again and again.

And then he pulled away, breathing fast, his expression earnest. "It's not nothing—between us—y'know? I know you might think so sometimes, but it isn't. I mean, it's not shallow or casual or—or even like anything I've ever had with anyone else." He kissed me again, his hand trailing my face as if trying to memorize its lines. "Your favorite painting is *Ophelia* by John Millais; you saw it in the Tate when you were twelve years old, and it was then you realized that art was so much more than just *painting,* but if anyone asks you say your favorite is *In Italian* by Basquiat because you think it makes you *sound* better.

"You dress in black; you try to be all dry and cynical; you say you're a nihilist, but you're the biggest optimist I've ever met. You live in the city, but all you ever paint is flowers; you want to make everything flowers, Megan. You take ugly, twisted things and you make them bloom, paint them spilling over with petals and make them so *beautiful*—"

I kissed him, stopping the flow and the poetry of his words before he said something wrong, wanting to keep it pristine and perfect, pinned in my memory like some rare butterfly.

Admittedly, we weren't in the most romantic place in the

world—although, as bathrooms go, it was the fanciest I'd ever seen, with a freestanding claw-foot tub and a pair of enormous marble sinks—but his words, plus the whole forbidden aspect, made this easily the most thrilling experience of my entire life so far. Sebastien took charge, sinking to the tiled floor and molding me around him as I sat in his lap, our kisses hungry, then hungrier. His hand slipped up inside my camisole and he made a low sound against my ear, his curls brushing against my face.

"I *want* you, Meg," he breathed, his lips hot against my throat, surging up beneath me so the truth of his statement was without question.

I had reservations, lots of them, but they all seemed to pop like bubbles the moment his lips met mine. I'm not sure we ever would have stopped had someone not called softly through the door.

"Meg?"

It was Laure. Oddly, Seb seemed to relax at the sound of her voice, his lips curving into a wicked smile as he pulled me back toward him, kissing me again with undisguised hunger. But I staggered away from him, quickly straightening my clothes, my hair. I didn't need Laure starting more unsavory rumors about me, with Lottie only a few rooms away.

"Um—yeah?"

"Are you okay in there?" She was so close, it was almost as if she were in the room with us. I half wondered whether she was peering through the keyhole. "I'm desperate for a pee."

"Yep—yeah—sorry. One sec."

Smothering laughter, Seb climbed into the tub, lay down, and gestured for me to pull the shower curtain. I did, as quietly as I could, and left the bathroom, giving Laure an apologetic smile.

She took much longer than I anticipated to return, evidently discovering Seb, as I could hear the faint sound of their harried, urgent voices as I lay in the dark, touching my lips gently, imagining Seb's mouth on mine.

Somewhere, a door slammed; then Laure's quiet footsteps padded back into the room. I said nothing, praying she'd think I was asleep. But as I lay there, listening to Saira's and Lottie's even breathing, Laure spoke softly into the night, her words unusually hesitant.

"I know you'll think I'm only saying this because I'm jealous or whatever," she'd begun, her words unusually stilted and measured, and I lay there, forcing myself to breathe deeply and evenly as if already asleep. "But honestly—take it from someone who's found out the hard way. He's not the prize you think he is. He'll tell you whatever you want to hear at first. He'll be everything you've ever wanted." Her voice soured. "Until he's bored, that is. Until he's had his fun. Until you're no longer useful. Because that's what the Wrens do, you see. They take and they take and they take. And when they're done"—she lowered her voice—"you won't exist to them at all."

26

BACK AT THE house, Lottie immediately greeted me with a tight hug.

"Fucking *Joss*," she murmured in my ear. "We've had words. Believe me, she won't be saying anything else."

I gave her a wan smile and trailed her into the lounge, my fierce urge to tell everyone about Seb and I immediately dissipating in the suffocating, funereal atmosphere of the house. In the grand scheme of things, after what had happened to Laure, how could I ever have thought it mattered?

"Still no signal," murmured Saira, looking at me curiously. "Did you guys make it into the village?"

I shook my head. "No—the lake's completely flooded the road and the next town is like thirty kilometers away. We could hang about and try to hitch a ride, though?"

Charlie shook his head and nodded at the window. "It's getting dark again already. Fuck's sake—my flight's tomorrow."

Seb snorted. "You can't just jump on a plane and fuck off back to England, Charlie. Laure is *dead*. The police will want to investigate. I doubt any of us are going anywhere for a while."

I winced at his words. Mum had saved for weeks to afford this flight. I wondered whether I'd be cursed to stay in Ireland forever until I could pay my way back to England. I imagined the excuses I'd have to make to Lottie and Seb to explain why I wasn't coming to the airport with everyone before they cottoned on, exchanging those sympathetic glances I'd come to hate.

"So what are we going to do?" I asked. I wasn't sure I could face another night trapped in this house with a dead body and whatever else was lurking within its grounds.

"Try to rest?" suggested Lottie. "Everyone looks exhausted, and if we're planning on trying to walk to town at some point, we're going to need energy. Seb and I will rustle up something to eat and give everyone a shout when it's ready."

I stared at Lottie, then at Seb, who wouldn't meet my eye. Lottie looked far better than she had earlier. What was going on with her? Was she on medication? Why was she acting so *normal* now? One of her oldest friends was currently wrapped in a sheet in the basement, and here she was taking people's dinner orders. Would she be nudging past Laure's dead body to get to the larder?

"Okay," I murmured, keen to leave the lounge and its odd atmosphere. "Okay."

Upstairs, in the quiet of my room, I attempted to piece everything together.

Laure had drowned—that was a fact—and someone else had

drowned in the same lake just over a year ago. Another young girl found floating facedown. The Donnelly girl. Was there a connection? The only immediate connection I could see was Seb and Lottie. So why hadn't they mentioned it to us?

An image flashed into my mind: Seb pounding down the jetty and completing a perfect swan dive into the lake's still waters. And what had that woman meant about the Wrens not showing their faces around here? Perhaps the drowning had been due to some negligence on their part. Perhaps the lake should have been fenced off. But if the girl had drowned by accident, then how could it be *murder*?

I picked up the postcard from where I'd left it on the desk the other day.

Come on in, the water's full of corpses.

A love letter—to Seb, seeing as this had been his room—from E. Who was E? A random holiday romance? Or someone else—E Donnelly?

Beneath the trees where nobody could see

What *was* it with Seb and his bloody secret romances?

Lastly, the folly—was that where these secret meetings had taken place? I thought of the blanket on the floor.

Place is a death trap.

Was it possible that someone drowned Laure deliberately? I thought back to how she looked that night in the kitchen. Hollow-eyed and pale. But who else could possibly have a motive—other than me? Could there have been some psycho stranger wandering about the woods that night? I recalled the statistic about most murders being committed by someone the deceased knew. And what about the text Joss had received? If Laure did drown in the early hours after Halloween—which made sense, considering what she was wearing—it would have been impossible for Laure to have sent it herself. So who *had* sent it? Someone who had known her passcode. Had Laure been forced to give it up? *Had* someone wanted to buy themselves some time, to make us think Laure was fine when all the while she was . . . And what *had* Seb and Laure been discussing the night before she died? I remembered the agitated hiss of their voices.

You don't know what she's capable of.

Who? I'd assumed they meant me—but had they?

The pool of guilt within me widened, became bigger than the lake. Of course they'd been talking about me, who else could they have possibly meant? I'd spent this whole year trying to change, trying to struggle free from this tight cocoon of anger, but why would anyone believe me. Still, at least my concerns about getting back into Greyscott's had lessened—now I was more concerned about being accused of *murder*.

I ran my hands over my eyes, exhausted and unable to think straight. Lying down on the bed, I tumbled into an uneasy sleep.

It was the morning after the summer ball, and the insistent buzz of my phone gradually drew me out of an uncomfortable half sleep. My head pulsed dully with pain and my mouth was sour and tacky. Groaning, I picked up the phone, sure it was Seb. After last night, after what had happened there, things between us were serious now—he'd said so himself, hadn't he?

But it wasn't Seb. Instead, I had six missed calls from Lottie. That was unusual.

Slowly, I sat up, my pores seeming to weep stale alcohol, and, swallowing my nausea, chugged a glass of water. There was a bucket beside my bed, obviously put there by Mum. I flushed hot with shame. God, how drunk had I *been* last night? Wiping my bleary eyes, I tried to piece together the events of the evening. It had started well enough—

Beside me, my phone began vibrating again. Immediately, I picked it up.

"Hey . . . Lots."

My voice was sandpaper scratchy. She didn't reply immediately, and a strong sense of unease began to crawl over me, compounded by the blankness of my memory.

"*Meg.* Thank God—I was so worried; I've called so many times. I—I wanted to know if you've heard? I wanted—wanted to check you were okay."

Her voice was insistent and sober.

I frowned, taking another glug of water, desperately trying to recall how last night had ended. My memories were fuzzy and disjointed—just flashes, really. The sticky-sour taste of the too-strong punch, the warm twinkle of a thousand fairy lights, the salt-sweet tang of popcorn, the frigid waters of the river—

"Yeah . . . I'm fine. I mean . . . Why—why wouldn't I be okay?" I gave a feeble laugh. "Actually, scrap that. I have the world's worst hangover. Like seriously bad. When Charlie said the punch was spiked he wasn't wrong. So, um, what—what should I have heard?"

There was another long pause. The sense of unease I'd been feeling in the pit of my stomach, the unspoken knowledge that something was very, very wrong, turned to a clutching, griping dread. I almost cut the call. If I didn't hear it, if I didn't know, then maybe I could pretend whatever it was hadn't happened. . . .

"Meg, I didn't want to be the one to break this to you . . . but you need to know. You've"—she swallowed, her voice shaky—"I'm so sorry, Meg, but you've been suspended from Greyscott's."

I remember I laughed. Surely Lottie was joking. But her voice was solemn in a way I'd never heard it before, and deep down I knew it was true.

"What? *Why?* How?"

Lottie's breath hitched. I realized she was crying.

"Seriously, Meg. Do you not remember anything? Nothing at all?"

I remembered some things. The way Seb had smiled at me in the woods—a smile I'd never seen before—wolfish and wanting. I remembered the heat of his body against mine—

Suspended?

What had I *done?* I swallowed back a mouthful of bile, my breathing shaky and fast.

"Lottie—I was drunk . . . *so* drunk. I don't remember the end of the night. I . . . I don't even remember getting home. What— what happened? What did I do?"

There was an uncomfortable moment of silence, during which I began to recall glimpses of the evening, each image viewed under a darkened lens.

Laure slipping into the inky waters on the river like a seal, panic flaring in her eyes.

But that wasn't me. Couldn't have been. Maybe a year or so ago, but I was different now. I would never have—

Lottie's voice was stilted when she finally responded. "You and Laure were arguing on the jetty. You—you pushed her into the river and—and tried to like . . . hold her *down*. She can't swim— she almost drowned, Meg. Everyone knows—God, it's such a mess. I'm so sorry. I—I said you were drunk. I told them—"

Another loud sob, then the phone went dead.

Immediately, I'd tried to ring her back, but the call was cut off, with a text following moments later.

> Meg. Sorry, but I need some time. I'll call you later,
> okay? We can get through this. I'll speak to Laure and
> we'll work it out. I promise--xx

I'd never been so grateful for a friend.

Soft shaking woke me. It was Lottie. I sat up hurriedly, embarrassed that I'd drifted off, given the circumstances.

"Hey, you," she said softly. "Coming downstairs? Food's up."

When I arrived at the table, I wasn't surprised to see that no one was eating; they were only morosely pushing food around their plates. I had absolutely zero appetite. The mere smell of the slightly charred frozen pizza made me want to gag.

Laure was *dead*. What was Lottie playing at, organizing cozy meals? After a few minutes of this farce, I cleared my throat and spoke up.

"So, while I was out looking for help, I found out a girl died here a couple of years ago. Murdered, according to the locals. Do you guys know what happened—since this is your family's place, right?"

Lottie's fork clattered to the table, and Seb immediately paled.

"What the hell?" said Ollie, his eyes alarmingly bloodshot. "What kind of question is that? How about you read the *room*, Meg?"

"It's only a *question*," I said coldly, staring steadfastly at Seb as Ollie got up and left the table, nearly careering into the door as he did so.

But it was Lottie who spoke, picking up her fork and avoiding eye contact. "Yeah. Yeah, actually it's true. It happened. Nearly two years ago now. There was a girl who worked here—her parents took care of the place for us. She was found floating facedown in the lake one morning. Except she wasn't murdered—honestly, the locals are so dramatic. No one knows what really happened to her." She cleared her throat. "I mean, if you can't swim, all bodies of water are dangerous."

Fear death by water.

Beneath the trees where nobody could see—

I nodded nonchalantly. "Huh. And who'd have guessed that only a couple of years or so later there'd be another body floating in the lake. You guys should probably think about fencing it off."

"Jesus, Meg," muttered Charlie. "That's *Laure* you're talking about. Our *friend*."

"Our family wasn't even in the country when it happened," said Lottie, her breezy mask back in place. "People love to gossip—let's face it, there's fuck-all else to do round here."

An uncomfortable silence followed, broken only by Ollie staggering back into the room. He collapsed into a chair and stared accusingly at Saira.

"Why'd you leave the taps running in our room?" he murmured. "Damn sink was overflowing."

Saira sighed, not even looking at him. "I have no idea what you're talking about. And where *is* Joss?"

I'd been relieved she wasn't at the table at first. I couldn't say I'd missed her. In fact, I'd have been grateful to never see her again as long as I lived, but now her absence made me uneasy.

Lottie shrugged. "I knocked for her, but I think she was napping—I could hear her snoring. Think she took a sleeping pill earlier."

I decided I'd go and speak to her after dinner, if only to set her right about the absurd notion of me murdering Laure and try to forge some temporary peace.

"The rain's not stopped all day," said Saira, her brown eyes huge in her face. "What's the plan if the flooding gets worse?"

Seb sighed, resting his head on his hand, toying with his food. "I'll try to head out again tomorrow. There must be some point that's easy to cross, even if I have to bloody swim."

"So why didn't you do that today?" Saira pushed, her tone agitated. Seb put down his fork, his food untouched.

"Because I was too busy looking for Meg, as it happens."

"Shame you didn't look as hard for Laure, isn't it?"

I looked up at Saira, surprised at the poisonous tone of her voice.

"Maybe because nobody knew anything was up with Laure,

whereas Meg was literally accused of being a murderer?" shot back Seb.

"That's not true, though, is it?" said Saira, a cold light in her eyes that I'd never seen before. "Most of us knew quite a *lot* was up with Laure. We all knew how upset she was ever since you decided you didn't want her around all of a sudden. Makes me wonder exactly how *much* you didn't want her around."

I looked across at Lottie, shocked, but Lottie only stared down at her plate.

"Is that right?" replied Seb with worrying calm. "Now that she's dead, Laure's suddenly your best friend? How convenient."

"We *were* good friends, as it happens. I've known her since primary school, and I got to hear every single detail of how badly you treated her, Sebastien."

"Oh yeah? You mean the part where I repeatedly told her I wasn't interested?" His face was flushed pink. "And I really *doubt* she told you every detail of her personal life, Saira, or are you genuinely the doormat everyone says you are?" Seb's eyes glittered dangerously. "Because if we're throwing out Laure-related accusations here, you might want to look a little closer to home."

Across the table, Ollie paled considerably, placing down his food-laden fork and clearing his throat.

"Hey, come on now, Seb, that was just a vicious rumor—"

Saira got up immediately, thrusting her chair under the table with barely concealed violence while Ollie called halfheartedly after her. Lottie sat, head down, staring fixedly at the table. I didn't know where to look. There had been rumors about Laure and Ollie fooling around at a party around the same the time I started at Greyscott's, but I quickly learned there were rumors about Ollie and literally *everyone.*

Seb swallowed, immediately looking sorry.

"Wow. That was pretty low, Seb," Lottie said quietly.

"What do you *expect*?" he murmured. "She outright accused me of having something to do with this. Fact is, no one here had anything to do with this other than Laure herself."

"You know, I thought that at first," piped up Charlie from beside me. "But there's a lot that doesn't add up. That text message, for starters. Definitely seems like someone was trying to buy themselves some time. . . . Makes me wonder which one of us knew Laure well enough to have the passcode to her phone."

"Anyone could have it," muttered Seb darkly. "And especially someone who knew her better than they let on. Someone who might have wanted to *delete* incriminating things from it."

I realized that once again this was directed at Ollie, moments after the wineglass he had been greedily refilling from the moment he'd sat down smashed in his hand.

"That is *enough*!" he roared, making everyone jump. Blood dripped from his hand onto the white tablecloth but he barely seemed to notice. Lottie immediately got up, running to the sink, and holding a towel under the cold tap. "I didn't kill *anyone.*" He slammed his good hand down on the table. "Not *yet,* anyway."

Seb looked immediately chastened. "Hey, I'm sorry, man. Think we're all on edge. Understandably. I mean, we're all just *stuck* here and"—he cast an odd look in the direction of the basement door, behind which lay Laure's body—"and I don't know about anyone else, but it's starting to fucking get to me."

I watched in amazement as Ollie began picking fragments of glass from his palm without even wincing. Lottie came over to help clear the glass away, applying a wet towel carefully to his hand.

"It's getting late. Tomorrow we'll get help, one way or another," said Lottie with a calm I was frankly in awe of. A flash of memory—how she'd acted in the direct aftermath of the ball, her face relaxed, her voice strong and steady. I felt grateful she was here. "We just need to hold it together until then and remember we're *friends*, for God's sake—not bloody serial killers! What happened is *awful*, but come *on*, none of us are to blame for this."

I think she meant it as a joke, but of course nobody laughed. And I wasn't even sure the last part was true. Not anymore.

27

AFTER DINNER, OLLIE retired to his room, no doubt to placate
Saira, while Seb and Charlie pored over some dusty-looking
ordnance survey maps they'd found in a kitchen drawer. Needing to feel busy, I helped Lottie scrape full plates of food into
the bin.

"Hey, where's Eimer lately?" I asked suddenly. "Do we know
if she made it back to the village before it flooded? I mean, if she's
living nearby, maybe she can help us? Her family might have a
landline we could use or something."

Lottie nodded. "Great idea in principle, but she lives in town
and left the day we arrived."

I stared at her. "No she didn't. . . . I spoke to her during the
party. After Laure got here."

Lottie gave a humorless laugh, her expression confused. "Er,
no you didn't? She had an appointment with the osteopath the
afternoon everyone arrived—as she loved explaining to me in
graphic detail—and then the weather turned and I told her not to
come back if she was still in pain."

Something caught in my mind. "The osteopath?"

"Yeah, I keep telling Daddy that he really needs to retire her, but—"

I stared at Lottie. Clearly something was being lost in translation.

"*Retire* her—what? She must be about our age or younger—"

Lottie spluttered a laugh. "Meg, I don't know who you're talking about, but the Eimer that works here is pushing sixty-five."

Seb suddenly spoke up from where he sat at the kitchen table, an odd look on his face. "What does she look like, this girl you saw?"

I shrugged. "I dunno. Around our age, maybe? She's pretty—thick blond hair, green eyes. Local accent. Really friendly. Why—who is she?"

Why indeed?

But Seb had got up, slamming his chair hard under the table and jabbing his finger at me with uncharacteristic violence as he passed. "I don't know what game you're playing here, Meg. But we are in some major *shit* already, and we don't need you making things worse."

I stared back after him, then looked at Lottie. "Jesus. What was *that* about?"

Lottie stared back at me, white as a sheet. "I—I don't know. Excuse me a sec. I'll go see if he's okay."

I made polite chat with Charlie for a few minutes, but the whole Eimer thing was playing heavily on my mind. If that girl I'd chatted to *hadn't* been the housekeeper, then who the hell *was* she? Some random chancer hanging around the house looking to rob it? And she must be local—she knew about the lake—about the folly—

An unpleasant thought entered my mind. Could *she* have been involved in Laure's death somehow? Had she been the one to take her phone? To message from it?

But *why*? If she was a stranger, it made absolutely no sense. The idea that she was another girl Laure had mercilessly bullied crossed my mind, our being in an entirely different country making it only slightly less plausible.

And what had *Seb's* reaction been about?

I don't know what game you're playing here.

I stared at the postcard lying discarded on Seb's old desk.

E

The Donnelly girl—she was only sixteen, poor lass.

E Donnelly?

Seb in the forest that day, the look of shock on his face.

It's pronounced Ee-mer, *not Emma.*

But I'd known deep down I was right. That girl I'd met, out by the lake, she'd clearly said her name was Emma, not Eimer.

Emma Donnelly?

She was found floating in that there lake, facedown, drowned.

I rubbed my eyes, feeling a monster headache coming on. Whoever Emma was, she certainly wasn't *dead.* She was as real as I was. I'd chatted to her, helped her with the bins. I thought again of Seb's odd reaction—had she been some ex of his come to say hello? Maybe she'd also been forbidden to talk to anyone about their relationship, like some kind of fucked-up Wren family nondisclosure agreement—

Beneath the trees where nobody could see—

I toyed with the idea of finding Seb and asking him what the deal was, but he'd made it pretty clear the topic was off-limits.

With a groan, I forced myself off the bed and drifted down the corridor in the direction of Joss's room. I didn't really want to speak to her, but at the same time I had a strong urge to clear my name. To make it apparent to her that whatever I might have done in the past, I was a different person now. I would never push anyone into any body of water ever again.

I rapped at her door.

"Joss?"

I rapped again louder, but there was no sound within, not even the gentle breathing of sleep. Feeling a momentary spike of panic, I grasped the handle, meaning just to open the door a little, check she was okay—

The door was firmly locked.

"Hey, Joss?" I called again, deliberately rattling the handle. Bending down, I squinted through the large old-fashioned keyhole. The curtains were closed, and all I could make out was an untidy dresser, its surface littered with skin-care bottles and clothes.

A soft noise from the other end of the corridor made me start.

Turning toward the sound, I watched the door to the main bathroom quietly shut. After a final rattle of Joss's bedroom door, I followed the sound to the end of the corridor. Maybe Joss was taking a bath or something. I paused outside.

"Hey, Joss, you in there?"

I knocked gently, and after there was no answer, I tried the handle. To my surprise, the door swung smoothly open with almost a flourish. I flushed, an embarrassed apology already on my lips, until I saw that the large room beyond was completely empty.

A deep porcelain bathtub with elaborate clawed feet dominated the room, decorated with trickling rust stains. A white-framed sash window that looked out over the lake trembled in the wind, and what must have been a mirror hung over the gray marble sink, covered with a black dust sheet similar to those in the entrance hall. The battered wainscoting was painted a deep bottle-green, and above it, the walls were papered with a crumbling ivy print.

Wasn't this the bathroom Lottie had said was out of order the day I'd arrived? It looked fine to me—and though Joss wasn't in here, I was suddenly overtaken with the urgent need to pee.

As I shut the door behind me, an acrid smell filled my nostrils. It wasn't actively unpleasant; in fact, it seemed strongly floral and cloying, like an older person's perfume. Probably just some cheap air freshener the housekeeper had put here.

After emptying my bladder, I washed my hands—or did the best I could with the dried sliver of yellowed soap and stiff towel—then padded back across the smart marble tiles to the door. As I placed my hand on the key, I heard a soft, subtle noise behind me.

A sifting sound, followed by a soft *flump*.

The sound of a cloth slipping to the floor.

I swallowed.

Okay, the cloth had fallen off the mirror. No doubt I'd disturbed it somehow when I'd washed my hands. Big deal.

If it's no big deal, Meg, then why won't you turn around to check?

My hand tightened on the key. Around me, the house seemed

unnaturally silent, the only sound the persistent rattle of the window frame. It was as if everyone had taken a taxi out of here and left me alone, stranded here beside the lake and the endless forest.

Fear death by water.

Yes. Fear death by lakes—dark and weed-choked—or bottomless oceans—or swift-running rivers, yes, but not *bathrooms*. That was ridiculous. *Seriously—*

I remembered arriving here, walking upstairs with Lottie for the first time.

Eimer likes to keep them covered. Some old Irish superstition.

But if the mirrors *weren't* covered, if they uncovered themselves, what happened then?

For God's sake, just turn around, just look—

I recognized the smell then. That sickly floral scent. It was hyacinths, I was sure of it. An intensely green smell as if the flowers were on the turn. Sickly and wilting, slowly changing to speckled brown slime within a vase.

You gave me hyacinths first a year ago—

Yes, hyacinths. From the poem that Seb liked. The one he'd whispered to me before we kissed. No. Just a purple air freshener—I swear I saw it by the sink—just turn and *look* for God's sake—it's only a mirror—are you afraid?—why would you be AFRAID—WHY—

I *was* afraid.

Relaxing my grip on the key, I forced myself to turn around.

I'd expected to see my own face, pallid and tired, reflected in the large gilt-framed mirror above the sink. A mirror much too big for a bathroom, stately and grand as it was.

But reflected instead was the back of someone's head.

A woman. Her hair, water-dark, saturated.

I chewed my lip. So it wasn't a mirror at all then, but a clever portrait. A trompe l'oeil or whatever Monsieur Desjardins had called them in art class that day, when we'd all marveled at John Pugh's murals.

But then . . . it *moved*.

Seeming to take one slow step in my direction, away from the mirror and toward the door, toward *me*. Around it, everything was reflected as normal. The corner of the window, gray and streaming steadily with drops of rain. The old-fashioned pink bath mat. The cobwebbed vase of desiccated pampas grass in the corner.

Me, standing shaking by the door as the figure approached.

It's not real it's not real it's not real—

This was why the mirrors were covered. Why hadn't Lottie warned me? Did she *know*? Had she seen this herself? Had this happened to her?

Some ancient part of my brain was throbbing with warning. Vibrating rhythmically like a phone left on silent. I needed to go. I needed to get out of here. But a newer part—a dangerous, curious part—wanted to see what happened next.

The figure in the mirror took another step toward me. Slow and precise, as if she were playing a game. Grandmother's footsteps. That game where you could only move when no one was watching, lest you'd be *caught*—

Who are you? I wanted to ask. What are you trying to tell me? You're facing me, but why can't I *see* you? What happened here? What *keeps* happening here?

But all the words in my head turned to dust when I tried to voice them.

The corners of the mirror seemed to dim. I noticed the figure's dress, the same somber black it always was (a maid's dress? a peasant's dress?), her hair straggling to her lower back in wet rattails. And a soft sound penetrated the thick silence, breaking my gaze away from the mirror.

The gentle patter of running water.

Was there a leak in here? The roof, maybe?

No. No, I knew what it was. I forced myself to look over and confirm it. Someone had placed the plug neatly in the bath, and both taps were furiously running, filling the deep tub with indecent haste.

I took a step toward it, automatically going to turn off the taps.

Fear death by water—

And then—oh, and *then* I saw it.

Lottie or Seb coming up here an hour or so later. *Anyone seen Meg?* they'd ask. And so they'd search the rooms again. Just like before. Just like with Laure. And I'd be in here the whole time, quietly floating facedown beneath the surface, my hair drifting like seaweed. The only sound in the room the regular *drip-drip* of the tap, sending ripples out across the quiet water—

A noxious, oily wave of pure fear made me gag, the shock of the noise setting me into action. I physically made myself turn around, my hands trembling so much I couldn't even grip the key. I watched in despair as it tumbled out of the lock and onto the tiles. A soft sobbing issued from behind me. I'd always thought the sound was sad—mournful, even—but now I recognized a low tone of mocking within it. Forcing myself to focus, I managed to grasp the key and work it back into the lock. I gripped my right hand in my left, forcing my nails deep into my palm, using pain to pull myself together. With a gasp, I managed to twist the key and wrench the door open, slamming it hard behind me and clattering down the staircase.

28

THE KITCHEN WAS empty, the sky outside the window rapidly darkening, the rain increasing in violence as the light faded. I took a bleak look at the closed basement door and immediately left. No one was in the lounge either, only an empty whisky bottle giving any clue to who had been in here. The ticking of the clock, distractingly loud.

Had everyone gone to bed already? I couldn't stay down here, not alone, not with Laure down there in the pitch-black basement and whatever I'd seen in the bathroom—

I rapped hard on Lottie's door and was relieved when she answered immediately, stepping outside her room and closing the door behind her. Curiously, I noticed she locked it, twisting the old-fashioned key in her hand with a sharp jerk. I suppose we were all extra jumpy—inclined to grasp as much control over our surroundings as we could. She frowned, looking more closely at me.

"Meg. You all right? You're pretty pale."

Weird question. Surely we were all as far from all right as it was possible to get. We needed to get away from this house, and if I could truly trust anyone here it was Lottie and Charlie.

"Hey, this is going to sound pretty . . . strange, but I thought I saw something in that bathroom down the hall. I thought I heard Joss go in there—but she wasn't—in there, in fact, I'm not sure where she is." I took a breath, aware I was babbling. "I think we need to *leave*, Lottie—I think there's something *wrong* with this house."

Lottie's brow furrowed. "The bathroom, you say?" she asked. "The one at the end of the hall?"

Was that a glint of fear in Lottie's eye? I nodded.

"Okay," she replied hesitantly. "Well, let's check it out together."

Feeling more and more silly the closer we got to the room, I went from desperately wanting everything to be normal when we got there to hoping there'd actually be something to see.

The bathroom looked as it always had, the black cloth placed neatly back over the mirror. And how had I taken the sickly synthetic smell of the cheap plastic air freshener for hyacinths?

Extreme mental stress. I knew it could affect the mind. Make you see things that weren't there. Hear things. That was what the doctor had said, after Mum had insisted on taking me. After the ball—

I shook my head. The woman I thought I'd seen—had I just made her up?

Well, one thing I *hadn't* imagined was Emma. I'd spoken to her, plain as day, both outside and inside this house.

Was she the housekeeper's daughter, lending a hand in her spare time? Maybe she'd had something with Seb at some point—that would go some way to explaining his overly dramatic reaction, anyway.

In the shade beneath the trees—E

"It's an old house," Lottie said, drawing me back to the present with a forced smile. "It's always creaking and settling—it likely just spooked you. And as for Joss, she's probably ashamed of showing her face after what she said earlier. We're all proper on edge at the moment."

"Lottie," I said, shifting subjects. "I was confused earlier—about Eimer. The person I was talking to—the girl that was here, the night of the party—*was* actually called Emma. Do you or Seb know her? It's just, when I brought it up, Seb, he—"

Lottie frowned. "I know *of* an Emma, but I know for sure that's not who you were talking to—"

"Okay." I drove on, undeterred. "So could whoever this Emma is have something to do with all this? I mean, why was she hanging around your house, *in your kitchen,* without permission? She seemed to know a lot about your house—the lake and the folly. Could she—could she be dangerous?"

Lottie gave me a sympathetic look, placing a soft hand on my shoulder. "You look so pale. How about I go down and make us both a cup of tea and we sit in the studio and talk about this? I'm not tired either. I mean, it's not exactly surprising we're all finding it hard to sleep."

Gratefully accepting the offer, Lottie's soothing presence was a gift, not to mention the fact she might finally provide some answers—I climbed to the top floor as Lottie made her way down to the kitchen.

I knew something was wrong before I even opened the door. It was the smell. Acrid and familiar.

Paint thinner.

I clamped a hand over my mouth.

Every single one of Lottie's canvases had been completely destroyed. All had been slashed at repeatedly with what must have been a knife, shredding the canvas to gloomy ribbons, paint thinner liberally squirted over the remains. All were unrecognizable now. Just ragged strips of green-gray wash.

Who would do such a thing? And *why*?

I heard soft quick footsteps coming up the stairs behind me and, panicking, whirled around, and pulled the door shut behind me.

"Meg?" said Lottie, only her bright eyes visible in the low light as she stood on the stair below me. "What's up?"

I swallowed. "Someone's—um—I'm sorry—your *paintings*—"

Immediately, she shouldered roughly past me and pushed open the door. There was a dreadful few seconds of silence; then she fell to her knees with a guttural sob, the mugs of tea tumbling to the ground beside her.

The door to Seb's room flew open and he stood across from us, taking in the sight before us with evident shock.

"What the fuck—"

"Who *did* this?" wailed Lottie. "This is *hours, days* of work—this is—is *important*. God, I can't believe this! *Seb?*"

Seb and I looked at each other, neither of us knowing what to say.

"It wasn't like this when I came up," said Seb, holding his hands up. "I think I must have dozed off . . . but I didn't hear anyone out here."

"Ollie," muttered Lottie, a dark expression on her face. "It must have been him—revenge for what you said earlier. He was off his face on whisky. When I find him—"

"Hey," said Seb more sharply than I'd ever heard him speak to her. "*Hey*, you need to calm down, okay?"

He threw a pained glance at me.

"Just . . . just leave us a minute—I'll deal with this. Just—just try and get some rest, okay?"

Rest? The idea was laughable.

Twenty minutes later, I lay in bed—Seb's old bed—and thought back to the first night in the house, when I'd gone to sort the fuse box. There'd been someone down there—in the basement— the figure I'd convinced myself I'd imagined. Someone who'd got caught in the rain, by the sounds their shoes had been making. Could it have been this Emma, hiding down there? Had the girl that had drowned in the lake two years ago been related to her? A sister or close friend? Had she been waiting down there in the darkness to take revenge?

Some logical part of my brain suggested I should go and take a look.

No.

I imagined Laure lying down there on the stone floor, cold and bloated. Not Laure any longer.

What was I thinking? There was absolutely no *way* that was happening.

From somewhere above me came that soft familiar noise that filled me with dread. The sobbing. It *had* to be Lottie. Had to have been her all along? But *why*? What was *wrong* with her?

And then there were her paintings. That *woman*. The same woman I kept dreaming about—and now was seeing lurking in mirrors—whose face I could never fully make out. Was she linked to this drowned girl too? Or was there some truth to all those legends? About the mother who had drowned in the lake. The banshee?

Your wicked history—

The first night I had heard screaming was the night before the Halloween party. If Laure *had* drowned the next night, then wouldn't all that screaming-that-foretells-death stuff make sense? And what *had* Lottie been doing, wading into the lake the night of the party? Had she been lured out there too? If Seb and I hadn't been nearby, would it have been her found floating facedown in the water next morning? What *was* in there?

Harbinger—

Ridiculous. Why was I letting myself tumble down this particular rabbit hole? All it was, was stress and lack of sleep. I hadn't slept properly since I got here, no wonder I was seeing ghouls in every corner. I imagined explaining everything that had gone down to the doctor I'd been seeing. Imagined what they'd say.

Why, yes, of course, Miss Green, it does indeed sound as if the house is haunted by a screaming banshee. Your prescription is to get the hell out of there.

I stifled a half-hysterical giggle.

If only I could.

What I should really have been afraid of was the truth behind Laure's death. That wasn't some phantom dreamed up by my exhausted mind. If Laure hadn't wandered into the lake herself, which, for someone who was afraid of water, who couldn't swim, seemed unlikely, then someone else—someone *real*—was responsible.

Faces floated before me in the darkness: Emma, her friendly grin now seeming almost sly. Ollie, clutching his glass with such violence it smashed. The hurt etched clear on Saira's face. Joss and her wicked tongue. And then there was Seb. What exactly *had* he and Laure been arguing about that night?

I got up and locked the bedroom door.

Eventually, I drifted into an uncomfortable half sleep, and at some point during the night the rain stopped. The silence, the lack of water constantly drumming on the eaves, must have woken me.

Moonlight flooded through the window, bright and silvery. Wide-awake now, I got up and walked over.

Far across the lake, at the top of the folly, a light flickered within.

Was someone *in* there?

I stared.

Could it be Emma? Was that where she was hiding? Was that why she'd warned me away from the place? I remembered how I thought I'd heard someone up there, the day we looked for Laure—okay, so Seb had gone in after me to look around, but maybe Emma had been hiding, or worse, maybe Seb already knew she was in there. Maybe she held the key to all this.

By now, I was utterly sick of wondering. The constant what-ifs were causing me to question my sanity, and things were too real now for me to sit around writing a thesis about all the things I thought *could* be happening. At this point, I needed answers, needed to *know*. And if I could solve this one thing, if I could somehow prove that "Emma" was as real as everyone else in this house, then that would go some way to proving I wasn't losing my mind.

I dressed quickly, pulling on a light raincoat I found in the porch and taking an industrial-size flashlight from the kitchen before leaving. I hesitated by the knife drawer. Laure had *died*. There was a damn good chance I was in some danger. But I forced myself to walk past it. Mum always told me knives did more harm to the innocent than the guilty. I'd just need to be careful.

Beneath my feet, the ground was like a heavily sodden sponge, making my progress around the lake slow and exhausting. But the night was almost balmy, the air warm after days of heavy cloud cover. Ahead of me, through the trees, I could still see the light flickering in the windows of the folly, drawing me ever closer like a lonely moth.

As I approached slowly through the wood, I began to hear something. I froze at first, praying it wasn't the sobbing that seemed to have dogged my entire trip, but as I got closer, I realized it was the gentle ringing of bells. Curiously, I raised the flashlight. In the clearing around the tower, dozens of tiny golden bells had been affixed to the branches and were jingling almost merrily in the night breeze.

The door to the folly was wide-open. I knew it would be, through some weird sense of dream logic, although I wasn't dreaming.

I stepped through the door into the tower.

Candles had been lit in every window, their wax dripping poetically down long white stems. Carefully, I half climbed, half hoisted myself up through the first three floors, each bathed in their own pools of golden light. And I kept on climbing this time, passing floor, after floor—I think I counted ten in all, unable to stop until I reached the very top.

Up here, the floorboards were sturdier. Thick slabs of polished oak instead of the gray scratched boards of the floors below.

The room blazed before me. Candles had been lit on every spare inch of floor and sills, in ever smaller concentric circles. I hesitated on the stairs, unsure now as to whether or not I should step into the room. It felt as if I were about to enter a sacred place, a private temple, like my stepping into that space would somehow violate it. Who had lit all these candles? What were they for? Who were they for? But I was here now. The only way forward was up.

As quietly, as delicately as I could, I hauled myself into the room, quickly dusting off the cobwebs I had accumulated on my climb up and clumsily dodging the myriad flames. Close by me, in the middle of the room, positioned like an offering was a slip of paper.

I picked it up.

It was a photo, the edges yellowed and creased. It was of a younger Sebastien, his hair a little longer, his dapper short curls looser waves, his body lean with youth, but unmistakably him. His eyes sparkled as he affectionately wrapped his arm around someone, pulling them close.

That someone would remain a mystery, as whoever it was had been scratched out of the picture, their face erased by black ballpoint pressed so hard against the paper there were just ragged holes where the eyes should have been. With shaking hands, I turned the photo over. Taped to the back was a shriveled flower.

A hyacinth.

With shaking hands, I carefully placed the photo back where I'd found it and raised the flashlight, curiously taking in the rest of the room, I sucked in a shocked breath. Affixed to the stone walls were a series of large paintings done in dark oils. Five of them in total. The odd thing was, despite being painted in the style of Holbein's sixteenth-century portraits, appearing to loom out of a stygian darkness, they were all of the *backs* of people's heads. All with long hair, their faces turned away from the artist. Beautiful in their way, but the overall effect was disturbing.

Why were they here? In some abandoned old tower. It didn't immediately strike me as Lottie's work—she'd never been into portraits. Some strange vintage find of the Wrens, perhaps? I circled them with the light. It was impossible to guess who they were meant to be. All I could see was hair: blond, red, brown, black. A little unsettlingly, the hair in the last portrait looked like mine, an unusual shade of silver-white in a loose plait tied with a black ribbon. It could just as well have been an elderly lady, perhaps, but something about the parts of the face that were visible—the very edge of the profile, the tip of a snub nose—still struck me as familiar. I walked closer, raising the flashlight to get a better view.

At that exact moment, from far below, I heard the door to the folly creak open and then quietly shut. An undeniable sound. The sound of someone being careful. Stealthy.

I froze, somehow knowing I couldn't get caught here. I *shouldn't* be here. The photo—the paintings—these were somehow things I should not have seen. There was a sense of inherent *wrongness* about the whole tower, and I needed to leave.

Panic rose within me as I heard hushed footsteps making their way upstairs. Wildly, I looked about the room. There was nowhere to hide. There was only one way out: down the same stairs the intruder was currently climbing. That, or through the window.

Only a few floors below now, cupboards slammed and footsteps pounded as the intruder gave up on silence.

29

I LOOKED AROUND frantically, trying to formulate a plan.

Although the tower was tall and impressive from a distance, its circular rooms were cramped, barely accommodating any furniture, let alone hope of a hiding place. In desperation, I gazed out the window. I was ten floors up, high above the tempest of trees, in the middle of a raging storm. And far away, across the lake, the house watched impassively.

Then I caught sight of something that gave me hope. I unlatched the window with fumbling fingers, praying that the storm wouldn't catch hold of it and shatter the glass against the stone of the tower, immediately alerting whoever was in here with me. The hinges were stiff and opened with a yawning creak. I leaned out, the wind barreling in at me. Running a couple of feet below the window was a sturdy-looking stone ledge that seemed to ring the entire tower. It was only about twenty centimeters wide, but if I could balance on that, even for a minute or two, then I had a chance of remaining hidden.

I weighed up the impossible choice: stay and face whoever was in here with me, or climb out the window of a hundred-foot tower. If I slipped, it would mean death. We were way past the height where I'd escape with a broken bone at worst.

Maybe I shouldn't have felt so compelled to hide. Possibly someone had seen me slip out of the house and had followed me to find out what I was up to—maybe it was even Seb, hoping for a clandestine liaison.

But Laure was *dead*.

And it wasn't just Laure. It was everything else too. That constant feeling of being watched that had only intensified lately. That sobbing I couldn't escape. The odd things I was seeing—*thought* I was seeing. And the fact that it wasn't just Laure, someone *else* had died here, almost two years ago.

A noise from a floor or so below chilled my blood. A laugh, deep and unpleasant, that slowly turned into a low, undulating wail. Summoning all my courage, I hoisted a leg over the low sill, slowly lowering it until my foot met the reassuring strength of stone. Exhaling heavily, I followed with my other leg, awkwardly turning so I was facing the room, my fingers clutching the stone sill for dear life.

Gingerly, I straightened, pulling each pane carefully toward me, until the window closed with a gentle click. Then, scrabbling for handholds on the gray stone before me, I crouched and waited.

Around me, the wind howled and bayed, whipping my hair into my eyes with furious violence. The tower felt unstable, seeming to lean and sway with the wind. My hands were shaking so much I was afraid I wouldn't be able to hold on. And how long would I need to wait here?

The urge to look down was impossible to resist. The forest stirred in the blustering wind far below, the creaking of the trees alarming. Wren Hall looked like a dollhouse in the distance. I could see lights in the studio. A welcoming orange blaze a million miles away.

From somewhere within the tower came heavy footsteps, and the sound of crates being carelessly tossed about. I risked a glance up at the window a few centimeters above my head. The panes were dusty and scratched, so it was unlikely I'd be seen. But what about my hair, floating about my head, made wild by the wind? What if the intruder saw it, thrust open the window, and shoved me off the edge? It would take next to nothing to destabilize me in this gale.

I forced myself to look at the ledge, solid and sturdy beneath my feet, the stone cut with pleasing regularity. I deepened my breathing, in and out, slow and easy. Only minutes more. That was all I could stand. Panic was threatening to drown me.

A sudden flurry of freezing rain lashed against my face with biting cruelty. I swore, tears of frustration welling in my eyes. What was I *doing*? Why had I come out here? Regardless of who was inside, at this point I needed to take my chances.

Then, a reprieve. Far below, far, far below me, I heard the main door shutting. Through the thinning trees of the clearing I could see someone in a heavy black mac leaving the tower, their hood pulled low over their head, a thin yellow beam from an electric flashlight illuminating one gloved hand, and in the other, something that flashed silver.

A knife?

Not a banshee, then. Not a monster. Not a ghost. A person. And possibly someone who'd come to shut me up. There were no clues as to who, though. The raincoat was anonymous—not one of the expensive goose-down jackets or pricey hiking fleeces piled on the hooks in the front porch.

Slowly, I raised myself from my crouched position, my knees screaming, and pulled back one of the windows, hurling myself over the sill and back into the darkness of the tower. The candles had all gone out. Either the intruder had blown them out or the wind had seen to them. For a moment, I lay on the floor, pressing my face against the dusty floorboards in relief. Then, gathering myself, I stood.

For a moment, I considered shoving the photo in my pocket and taking it back to the house, but then I looked once more at the candles, arranged so carefully around it in a ritualistic pattern, and decided to leave it. Whoever had done this, it was clear they hadn't expected anyone to see it—and they might not take kindly to me waving the picture around.

Because whoever they were, it was looking more and more likely that they were in the house with me.

30

DAWN'S SILVER FINGERS were creeping over the low hills by the time I got back. In contrast to my hammering heart and clammy skin, the house felt almost serene, as if it were sleeping along with everyone else. But there was no forgetting Laure, wrapped in a black sheet and lying in the basement. Or the intruder I'd glimpsed, the silver flash of what could have been a knife visible in the moonlight. A heady flush came over me, a dizziness that threatened to drown me.

No. There was no serenity in this house. Only death.

With shaking hands, I retrieved my phone from my pocket. *Still* no signal. Just an obstinate line where the bars used to be. There was no time to waste. I had to tell someone about what I'd seen, but as I couldn't be sure who it was, stalking the tower out there in the darkness, I was reluctant to wake the whole house.

Running lightly up the stairs to the upper floors, I bypassed my room and continued to the studio, where I'd noticed the lights from the tower. I paused outside the door, listening intently. I couldn't be *sure* I was in immediate danger; I couldn't be sure the person who'd entered the tower had seen me, or even if they had carried a knife. But that meant I couldn't be sure I was safe either. Despite the crushing weight of my eyelids, there was no way I could rest now.

Around me, the house slept on.

Gently, slowly, I twisted the handle. The lights still blazed but the room was empty. There'd been an attempt at tidying some of the destruction from earlier.

I padded over to the room at the end of the studio, desperate to share the knowledge of what I'd just seen, and knocked softly on Seb's door.

"Meg—hey—Meg—I've been looking for you everywhere. Why are you hiding from me?"

His voice is soft, whispered in my ear as he catches both my hands and pulls them behind me. His breath is hot and laced with the sweet sharp smell of liquor. He twirls me around to face him, like a ballet in which we are doomed lovers. I look up at him and he smiles at me and it isn't a smile I've ever seen before. It is darker and full of wickedness. Something sparks within me, burning higher than the flames of the bonfire. I see it mirrored in his indigo eyes, as secret as a midnight ocean.

He slips his hand down to encircle my wrist, and drags me into the twinkling woods like a wolf in a fairy tale. I am too drunk on him to take notice of the path we follow, of how far we head in. Too drunk to remember that wolves are dangerous.

We stop, eventually, in a clearing. A picnic bench has been thoughtfully provided for us, but it's still so shadowy. The twilight sky barely visible between the canopy of leaves overhead. The lights and noise of the summer evening an entire world away now.

He turns to me, breathless, and grins, although, like me, I think he feels less sure now.

"I wanted to tell you . . . you look amazing tonight. I couldn't stop staring when you walked in."

You'd never describe me as the most confident person, not when it comes to boys like Seb, but tonight at least he is right. And I want this. Consciously, unconsciously, it was there, foremost in my mind as I applied a glittering cat eye, as I painted my lips—the color Carnelian Spell—as I slipped into this spiderweb of a dress.

I am nothing like Laure. Boring, needy Ophelia.

I am Queen Mab. Dark and resplendent.

I say nothing because I don't know what to say. Do I return the compliment? He always looks amazing. It is a fundamental part of who he is. Effortless and expected and as natural as breathing for him. Byronic and dark—dark curls and darker eyes—tipping almost into pretty.

I laugh. A million cautious questions shimmer through my head like quicksilver. I notice he has a backpack slung over his shoulder from which he is extracting a plaid picnic blanket. He has planned this. How long did he plan? Has he done this before? Have other girls lain on this blanket with him? But the rest of the questions, fluttering moths in my mind, are obliterated by his nearness. I step closer, fixing my eyes on his. None of the answers matter anyway. They won't change the fact I want this. I've always wanted this.

He pulls me down to my knees and we kiss, softly at first, and even that is like dying. My veins are liquid fire leaving me restless, knitting at his arms like a cat. I pull his face to mine with both hands, loving everything about this: the scratch of his stubble against my skin, the intoxicating scent of him. I'm almost afraid he will run away, like a deer glimpsed through trees. Surely this is too perfect to have. He kisses me again with a low groan, and we tumble into abandon. He pushes me back until I am lying down, helpless, his heavy weight on top of me welcome, his hands busy at his belt, at my skirt, a moment ago so pretty, now only annoying.

"Are—are you sure?" he breathes, stuttering kisses against my lips.

I nod furiously, a strangled mm-hmm *leaving my lips. His breathing quickens, his hands are burning brands against my thighs. He pauses once more.*

"Hey, have you—you know—have you, um, done this before?"

He must sense how I freeze at his words, because he sits up slightly, his pupils huge in the dark, his breathing heavy and labored.

There's no point lying, I know he might be able to tell anyway, that my body might give me away. But in the moment, I'm unsure how to answer because I don't know what answer he wants to hear. I'm not inexperienced but I've always stopped short of this.

In the end, my hesitation gives me away. He sinks down again, propping himself up on one arm, tilting my chin toward him, kissing me gently now, tempering the dark storm of our want.

"I'll be careful," he says, "I promise," and here, in the darkness, on this balmy night, a secret summer breeze playing on our skin as we lie hidden deep within the forest, I believe him.

For precious minutes, stretched infinitesimally into the dusk of the wood, we lay together, our skin touching, his heart thumping in tandem with mine, his hands clutching me close.

But then, the *after*.

The disentangling, the disengaging, the disposing; the dissipating of whatever magic had seized hold of us before. He righted himself with impressive speed, brushing burrs and leaves from his velvet jacket.

Was I meant to say something now? Compliment him? Was *he* meant to say something? Compliment *me*? I mean, did we *thank* each other? I couldn't think of anything that would convey the world-shattering impact of what just happened. All I could do was stare at him. He chuckled at my expression and kissed me, brief and affectionate.

"Hey, are you okay? You look a bit . . . shocked."

I smiled; it came easier now. "Yeah, yeah, of course, I, uh—yeah."

"There's a couple of things I need to do tonight," he said, his eyes sliding away from mine in a way I'd understand later to mean he was lying. "This stupid crowning nonsense, for starters. But I'll call you, first thing tomorrow, I promise."

"The crowning," I repeated. "With—with Laure?"

He winced at the sound of her name. "Unfortunately, yeah. Don't worry, I'll be there for the obligatory photos, then I'm gone. I promise. You know how it is. . . ."

No, I wanted to say. A curious possessiveness that hadn't been there before now rising in me. No, I *don't* know how it is. Since the first time I met you, I have been yours. It's *that* simple for me. Why isn't it for you?

But despite the fairy tale of our surroundings, I knew it wasn't that simple. Nothing was simple for Sebastien Wren. His popularity, his wealth, his family name meant there were expectations he had to uphold at Greyscott, whether he wanted to or not. Expectations of exceptional grades, of sporting prowess, of decency. Expectations that extended all the way to who shared his bed.

Yet I still trusted him. His gentleness just now, the vulnerability I never saw him show at school, those weren't lies. They were the truest thing about him.

"All right," I said.

But he'd already gone.

Seb didn't answer, and I was becoming ever more suspicious of the silence behind the door. Turning the handle boldly, I entered his room. It was, as I suspected, empty. The bed unslept in, still neatly made. His clothes in an untidy heap beside his suitcase, laptop and headphones discarded on the dresser.

Where *was* he?

Thoughts ran through my mind like vapor. Was he downstairs sleeping on the sofa? Was he looking for me? Could he have been the person out at the tower? Or was he with Ollie? With Lottie? With *Joss*? With—

Laure is *dead*.

I swayed on my feet, for one insane second considering sinking down on his bed and sleeping. No. I needed to tell *someone* what I'd seen. Charlie, then.

"*Meg.*"

The voice was a short, sharp whisper. Impossible to recognize.

I hurried out of Seb's room as above me, the bright studio lights gave an increased hum and then flicked off insolently, leaving me in utter darkness for a second before blinding me again with white brilliance. I swallowed a gasp.

Lying in the middle of the central island was a sturdy-looking paint knife. I swiped it without thinking, slipping it into my jacket pocket. I wasn't sure what use it would be, but its presence calmed my racing heart a little.

I made my way back to the studio stairs, listening for whoever had called my name.

"Me-eg—"

The voice was singsong, almost teasing. I paused at the top of the stairs, listening intently. Was it the intruder? "Emma," or whoever she really was? The rational part of my brain was telling me to go back to my room, to lock the door, and throw the covers over my head; nothing good ever came of whispers in the darkness.

Except that was a lie, wasn't it? I knew it firsthand.

I held my breath, listening intently.

"There was a woman and she lived in the lake—"

It sounded like someone singing quietly, contemplatively, to themselves in the hallway below. Lottie, maybe? The voice was light and soft.

"A weila wailya—"

Unable to stand there anymore, wondering, I padded carefully down the steps. Below me, the door to the hallway was shut. Before I opened it, I put my ear to the door and listened again.

"Down by the river Saile—"

The singing was drifting down the corridor, away from where

I stood, concealed behind the door to the studio and in the direction of the house's main staircase. Was someone else being lured outside to the lake to take their last swim? Urgently, I opened the door, my breath unusually cold, drifting from me like smoke, and slipped down the upstairs corridor in the direction of the main stairs, my fingertips trailing the peeling wallpaper. The hallway lights were low, buzzing intermittently like angry insects. I paused before turning the corner, afraid of what I might see on the staircase. Unwelcome images flashed through my head: Lottie dressed as a banshee again, standing at the bottom of the stairs, that strange, disconnected grin on her face. Laure, dripping wet and gray-skinned, weeds plaited into her hair, rising to meet me—

Jesus! Stop it, Meg.

There was nobody on the staircase.

Silvered dawn light shone through the transom window above the main door, turning everything to frosted pearl. The heads of the newel-post figures remained respectfully bowed in prayer at the bottom of the stairs, the checkerboard floor obediently deserted.

But the singing continued, much nearer now.

"A weila, weila, wailya—"

An Irish folk song, by the sound of it. I glanced around frantically, looking for its source—an old radio, perhaps, or someone's phone, someone playing a trick. The faces in the somber paintings hung along the wall looked back at me, dour and stern. The mirrors stared blankly, still covered with their funereal black cloths—

Mirrors?

Impulsively, I tugged at the corner of the nearest black cloth. It fell heavily to the ground in a crumpled heap, silencing my gasp.

Reflected in the age-spotted glass was not myself but a girl around my own age, with a sheaf of golden hair braided neatly back from her face. She was dressed in a sober gray shift (a uniform of some kind?) and walked dreamily down the staircase, softly singing to herself. I couldn't quite make out her face from where I stood, but there was a familiarity about her movement, the color and style of her hair, that made me sure I knew her.

Emma.

Was I dreaming? *Had* I fallen asleep on Seb's neatly made bed, exhausted, spent from fear?

I followed her down the stairs, step by step, softly pulling the remaining cloths from the mirrors as I went, slowly imitating her progress, her nimble fingers dancing along the banister as she sang.

"She had a baby, three months old, a weila, weila, wailya."

Then she stopped, pausing on the landing halfway down, as if noticing someone in the hall below. She smiled, as if listening.

"Does it *always* have to be the lake, now? You know I'm not fond of it. They say something lives in there—a bean sí, the spirit of a local girl who drowned her child there. They say she's always found by the water. They say there's a darkness in that lake, and if you stare too long into its waters, it *changes* you. . . ."

She paused, no doubt listening to whoever was answering her, their voice silenced, then laughed gaily.

"Well, we happen to like our little legends around here, mister!"

Without warning, Emma whirled to face me, her eyes filled with sadness, her skin gray and bloated, her golden hair now a sopping mouse brown. I gasped at the sight, clutching wildly at the banister, my knees sagging, nearly tumbling down the stairs toward her. Her voice became an unpleasant throaty, gargle.

"It's true what I told you—when you hear her *scream*—"

Water began cascading out of the mirrors, dark and brackish, foaming and brown.

A scream lodged in my throat and somehow I managed to turn and half stagger, half crawl back up the stairs until I reached the very top of the house, the studio.

The view from the many windows immediately drew my attention—a perfect panorama of the woods and the water. The folly rose out of the trees, an accusing finger pointing to the heavens. People had died to build it. The woman who lived in the lake, her husband had been one of them, leaving her and her children starving. And for what? Some rich aristocrat's amusement?

And *she* stood on the far bank watching; half hidden beneath the trees, the only thing giving her away the silver coins that were her eyes, her dark sodden dress blending in with the gloom of the forest.

Dressed in nettles . . .

She was always watching. Had been watching us since we got here.

I'm sorry, I tried to tell her. *I'm so sorry for what happened—for what they did to you—but please—please stop this.*

But she was long past hearing. Had been for centuries. And she opened her mouth, a hopeless void, and screamed her unhappiness into the world. I jammed my hands over my ears, squeezed my eyes shut, anything to block out that terrible *noise,* and around me, the world faded to darkness.

31

I WOKE WITH a start, back in my narrow bed, gray light seeping through the thin drapes, with no idea of how I'd got there. Was it possible I'd never even left?

Head pounding, I sat up. Memories flooded into my mind, blurry and half faded, like watercolor paintings. Had *everything* that happened last night been some kind of fever dream, brought on by fear, exhaustion, the ever-present damp of the house—even the trip to the folly? I thought of the odd things I had found there—the scratched-out photo, the bizarre portraits . . .

My thoughts were interrupted by a terrible, twisted cry, low and keening, like an animal in pain. I scrambled out of bed and tore open the curtains.

Outside, there was only Seb this time, all alone in the silver dawn. Last night's storm had melted away, leaving only a gentle rain, the weak sunlight turning his dark curls auburn. His hair was plastered wetly to his face, his T-shirt clinging to his body as he dragged something pale up the bank, then sank to his knees over it, his body racked with sobs.

I live in the weeds.
Blond hair streamed out behind the pale figure.
My voice the ebb of the bloated river—
Joss.

When I finally found my legs and made it downstairs, the kitchen was a mess and so was everyone in it. Saira was sobbing hysterically. Lottie sat catatonic, her face an unhealthy shade of white, like soured milk, her whole body shaking. Charlie was busy retching noisily into the sink.

"What the—what *happened*?" I said urgently. "What *exactly* happened?"

"It's Joss—"

"So she's—she's dead?"

Lottie gave a disbelieving shake of her head, then looked at me with wide glassy eyes and nodded.

Saira raised her head. "The fuck? *How? How* is it possible both her and Laure—"

"It isn't possible," I said quietly. "There's no way they both accidentally drowned. And this isn't the first time people have died in there, and something tells me it won't be the last. It's meant to be cursed—there's a woman in there—"

Over by the sink, Charlie turned and stared at me incredulously.

"For fuck's sake, Meg!" snapped Saira. I flinched. I'd never once heard her swear the entire time I'd known her. "Have some bloody *respect*, would you? Is now really the time for this spiritual woo-woo shit? Two of us—our *friends*—are dead!"

"Wait . . . hold on," said Charlie slowly. "What do you mean?

You said something about this the other night. Haunted by what? What woman?"

"A banshee—it's an Irish legend. She wants *revenge*, I think— she's always found by water, and when she screams it means some- one's going to die."

"Harbinger," murmured Lottie slowly.

I nodded. "Yes. On Halloween, I one hundred percent did *not* move that planchette—and if no one else did, well, maybe it was some kind of warning. I mean, it even spelled out Laure's name, right? Years ago, a woman drowned herself and her child in that lake—they were both starving, she'd run out of hope—so now she's meant to haunt it and carry people into it, and . . . and I think it's who you keep painting, Lottie. There's something else too. Last night, I—"

I knew my voice was becoming shriller and faster but I couldn't stop. I was on a runaway train to crazy town, passengers: one.

"That is *enough!*" Ollie spoke from his place at the table, his voice hard and commanding, all trace of louche Labrador now gone. "Two of our friends have *died*—so if you think I'm about to sit here and listen to this absolute *shit*, you're wrong." He stood un- steadily. "Seb and I are going to walk into the village right now and get the police. You can explain all your batshit theories directly to them when they arrive and see what kind of reaction that gets you."

I ignored him, looking directly at Lottie.

"Wait . . . *wait*. I'm not saying I *believe* it," I tried again. "I *know* how it sounds. But it's not just Laure and Joss, is it? There was that other girl that drowned here, two years ago or so. There's no *way* it can all be a coincidence. Something's *wrong*." I moved closer to Lottie, pleading now. "That girl I told you about, who I saw in the house on the night of the party—who said her name was Emma—she was the one that told me about the banshee. I think she might be staying in that tower over in the woods. What if she has something to do with this? The police need to know."

"What girl?" asked Saira sharply.

"Some girl Meg thinks she's seen around the place," murmured Lottie. "Odd that no one else has seen her, don't you think? Megan, the lake is *dangerous*. I warned you all the first day. Haunted or not, it's completely choked with weeds. If you get caught in them and you're not a strong swimmer—"

"Oh right," I snapped. "So Laure and Joss—neither of whom I'd describe as the most athletic of people—just upped and decided to go for a midnight swim and accidentally drowned within days of each other?"

Lottie shuddered, turning away to stare into the fire.

"Perhaps they were lured out there," said Charlie, his voice hushed.

"By whom?" asked Saira.

My eyes slid over to Seb, who stood behind Ollie in the doorway. He looked ghost white and was visibly shaking.

"I don't know for sure, but what I *do* know is that I've heard sobbing or screaming every night since I've been here, and I'm not the only one," I said. "Maybe Joss and Laure went to investigate, and whoever was out there . . . well . . . This girl could be using the whole banshee thing as a cover to get revenge."

"Revenge for *what*?" asked Charlie incredulously.

"For Emma Donnelly's *death*. Lottie, you said it yourself the other day. Emma also drowned in that lake. What if her sister, or friend, or some other relative, is hiding out in that tower, trying to scare us all—only it went too far, and now . . . now we're all in danger and—"

"Right, let me get this straight . . . the only person who's seen this mysterious girl is *you*?" said Ollie, a sneer marring his pleasant features. "How convenient. You've never liked Laure, and then you had that big blowout with Joss—also not your greatest fan. I mean, fantastic"—he gave a humorless laugh, throwing up his hands—"guess that makes me next, right?"

The entire room silenced; even the crackle of the fire and the wind outside seemed to die down. Five pairs of eyes slid toward me. Ollie took a step closer to me, his playful brown eyes now glittering with menace.

"Banshees *aren't* real. Mysterious girls who can only be seen by *you* . . . not real. But I'll tell you what *is* real, Megan. Jealousy. *Rage*. Loss of control. People who are known for not being able to handle their temper. People who can't be trusted around water."

The words "I'd *never* drown someone" were on my lips, but how could I possibly say them? They all knew what I was capable of in my worst moments. How could I ever convince them I'd changed?

White-knuckled, I clutched at the kitchen table, right now the only thing holding me up.

"Oh, please, Ollie," said Seb dully. "If we're playing that game, we all know there are reasons you'd have been absolutely okay with both Laure *and* Joss disappearing."

"Whatever you're implying, we all make mistakes. Fact is, I

got on great with both of them," Ollie fired back. "And given how you've treated Laure, that is *rich*."

Charlie looked up from the sink, wide-eyed. "What the fuck, guys? Come on, what are you saying? You don't *actually* think it's one of *us*?"

My mind raced.

Wouldn't that be the most logical explanation? Had all these local legends, Emma's unexplained appearances, and the weird, pervasive atmosphere of the house blinded me to the truth? My eyes flicked from Lottie to Seb to Saira to Oliver to Charlie. Was it possible one of us had been wearing a mask all along? Was it truly possible one of us was a *killer*?

"It's paranoia, that's all," said Charlie. "We're all trapped and slowly going mad. We need to get out of here."

"Yeah," agreed Ollie, still glaring at me. "Before it happens again."

Saira spoke up firmly. "It's not paranoia once people start *dying*, Charlie." She stood. "I agree—if we stay here, who'll be the next one of us to be found out there? We need to leave right now and speak to the authorities. I say we *all* walk to the village."

But Seb shook his head. "No, it's not safe. There are power lines down and the road's blocked by trees. Going through the forest means potentially walking through deep areas of marsh, and—"

"Oh *right*," snapped Saira. "Something only *you* can do. Fuck's sake, Seb. I'm coming too. There's absolutely no way I'm staying here like some sitting duck."

"Okay, but someone *needs* to stay back at the house," argued

Seb quietly, shooting a meaningful look at his sister, who sat on the floor beside the stove silently rocking, clearly not in a fit state to go anywhere. I quickly weighed up the odds. Out of everyone, I trusted Ollie the least. And he was strong too, Greyscott's prop forward, stronger than Seb. If any one of us was able to hold someone underwater for a prolonged period, it was him.

"Fine," I said. "Charlie and I will stay with Lottie while you three go get help."

Needing to get out of the oppressive darkness of the kitchen, I left through the back door into the misty pale light of the morning. Despite the welcome reappearance of the sun, now glinting playfully on the water, it felt dangerous to even look at the lake. I glanced at the dark ribbon of forest beyond, half expecting some girl to emerge, running toward me from the direction of the tower, brandishing a knife and screaming, but there was nothing, only the trees swaying silently in the breeze, keeping their mysteries.

After that conversation in the kitchen, I was beginning to think Ollie was right. It wasn't a ghost or spirit that had led Laure and Joss into the lake. It was far more likely to have been one of us. *Someone* had pretended to message from Laure's phone to buy themselves time. *Someone* had messed around with the Ouija board the night of the party. *Someone* had destroyed Lottie's paintings.

Not a ghost—a person.

I forced myself to stop thinking. My head was pounding, filled with unpleasant images, like buzzing flies. Strolling over to the patio, I perched on one of the few unsubmerged benches and stared out over the water, rippling silently in the bitter wind, closely guarding its secrets.

Soft footsteps approached behind me, and I managed a half smile as Lottie sank down next to me. I was relieved to see she'd emerged from whatever trance she'd been in earlier.

"Honestly, I can't believe this is even happening," she murmured. "This trip—it was meant to bring us all back together. It feels unreal, what's gone on. Just the idea that they're—that Laure's—Joss—that they've *gone*—"

She gasped and wiped an arm over her eyes.

"God, I can't even talk about it. Not yet. But what I do want to say is how grateful I am that you're here, Meg. What would I do without you?"

I gave her a wan smile. "I'd like to say I'm grateful to *be* here, but that's a total lie."

She casually threw an arm over my shoulder. Her closeness felt comforting and she smelled good—a fresh citrus scent. "I know you think it's one-way sometimes, Meg. That you think you should feel grateful for my friendship or some shit like that. But you're wrong. You mean the *world* to me."

I leaned into her.

"*Okay*, but how many times have I lent *you* a Dolce dress?" I teased.

She stroked my hair.

"Stuff like that doesn't matter—it's literally just that—stuff. What matters to me is loyalty—trust. I was friends with Laure forever—but I never really had that with her, y'know? I always knew she'd drop me in a hot second if Seb asked her to. If she was asked to choose between him and me. It took me a while to realize it, but our friendship was never real."

I felt my face heat slightly. That familiar swell of guilt rising within me.

"No? I mean, couldn't she like you both?"

Lottie looked away and shrugged.

"She wasn't right for him. He never saw her in that way. She begged me to make her head girl at the ball, y'know—his *Titania*. She had this vision of her and Seb as Greyscott's power couple, and she wouldn't let it go. We *wanted* to go for Callum and Ade. I mean, if we weren't allowed to abolish that outdated popularity contest, at least we'd go out with a bang." She sighed. "Seb was all for my idea, of course, but Laure's dad is head of the Friends of Greyscott's. You know the type, right? Tory donor. Has pretty conservative views."

Lottie cleared her throat.

"Seb told me he spoke to her the night she arrived here. Told her pretty plainly that he wasn't into her. Asked her to stop . . . *harassing* him, really. He's been pretty stressed lately."

I remembered the hushed urgent voices coming from his room.

"Really?" I swallowed. "Oh *God*. You don't think that might have led her to—"

Lottie shook her head, cutting me off. "*No*—no, of course not. I mean, I don't know for sure, but I don't think so, not if I know Laure. She seemed . . . angry rather than upset. You spoke to her after, didn't you? Did she seem devastated to you? Like she was prepared to do something like . . . like that? And anyway, that doesn't explain Joss . . ."

Lottie was right. Laure hadn't seemed heartbroken or even particularly pleased to see Seb. There'd been none of her usual flirting; instead, she'd appeared determined, filled with a cool, righteous anger.

I need you to tell the truth. . . . Everything that happened.

It occurred to me now that there might have been a clue there. That she'd been trying to tell me something. What had she wanted to me to say? Was it possible someone had wanted to shut her up? I swallowed, barely able to put the unspeakable into words. "Seb was suggesting that Ollie might have reasons to—"

Lottie gave a shake of her head. "I've known Ollie longer than anyone here. He has his problems, but he's not capable of this. None of us are—I don't and can't understand it—"

She broke off, pulling away from me and rubbing her hands over her face, still not looking at me, staring into the water before us. "Look . . . I think . . . you might have guessed, Meg."

I looked at her, surprised. A chill dancing up my spine. "Huh? Guessed what?"

She nodded in the direction of the folly. "About what happened that summer, a couple years back. But . . . I don't think you know it *all*."

She placed a firm hand on my arm. "And I think, given what *I* know, maybe you should."

32

"FROM THE FIRST time we met the Donellys' daughter—a couple of years ago when daddy dragged us all over for a family holiday—I *knew*." Lottie's eyes flicked to the lake and she gave a rueful smile. "You didn't need a crystal ball—or a bloody Ouija board—to figure out what was going to happen the moment Seb laid eyes on Emma.

"The Donnellys were a local family that Daddy had employed to run the place while we were in the UK. Seamus—Mr. Donnelly—was very handy at maintenance, and Dad liked the fact they had links to the house that went way back. Turned out some of the earlier Donnellys had actually helped build the house—and the folly."

She sighed, staring down at her hands.

"I don't know how much you know about follies, but they cropped up all over Ireland around the time of the famine. Apparently, rich families just wanted to give their tenants something to do when there was no work. Terrible, I know. And they've pretty much no purpose. I mean, look at the tower over there." She gestured toward it absently. "It's so narrow, you could barely lie down in it, let alone put any decent furniture in it.

"Anyways," she went on. "We were about to turn sixteen in a few months, and neither of us wanted to be here. I mean, who actually wants to go on holiday with their parents? Okay, maybe if it was Bermuda or St. Kitts—but *Ireland*? But Daddy forced us, blathering on about we still needed to keep in touch with our roots—roots that in actual fact we should *not* be proud of."

She gave a rueful little smile before continuing. "Of course the Donnellys came out to greet us as usual, only this time they'd brought their daughter along to help. Emma was around the same age as us and *gorgeous*." Lottie emphasized the word, her eyes widening. "She looked like Rapunzel, with this thick golden hair that hung to her waist and sharp green eyes that didn't miss a thing. She had a wicked sense of humor too. Seb and I were both pleased we'd have someone else to hang out with it. But it didn't take long before I worked out it wasn't going to be that way. I got sidelined pretty much immediately."

She huffed. "I mean, you of all people know what he's like, Meg," Lottie continued, rolling her eyes. I looked at Lottie in surprise, adrenaline sparking in my veins at her words. How much *did* Lottie really know? But she refused to look at me, her gaze remaining fixed on the far side of the lake as she continued to speak. "When he wants something, he's charm personified and very hard to refuse. And he wanted Emma and she wanted him. A charming holiday romance. Or so my parents thought. Although I wonder if they'd still have thought that had they known exactly what they'd been getting up to for hours at a time in the folly. My brother's never been reticent in *that* area."

My cheeks heated. Okay, so I had no illusions about Seb's innocence, but something about the way Lottie framed it made me feel . . . embarrassed. *Used*, even. Like I'd been an idiot to believe I was special or different or any of the other things he'd promised me. When in fact all I was, was just another girl for Sebastien Wren to fool around with and toss away once he was done.

"Anyway, after a few weeks, it was time for us to go back— thank God. Before we left, Seb muttered something about saying goodbye to Emma, but he was gone so long Dad ended up storming out to look for him. Neither of them looked pleased when they returned. I don't know what had gone on," Lottie added, shrugging. "You know Seb and I are close, but to this day he's never told me what happened.

"Back in England, I knew she sent him letters and postcards almost daily, and he'd cast a quick eye over them, then chuck them in the trash. I read a couple—I know I shouldn't have—but let me tell you, the poor girl was in deep. Then, all of a sudden, he stopped even reading them, saying Emma was obsessed with him. We were meant to go back at Christmas, but Seb outright refused. So we didn't."

Lottie paused for a long time, so long I thought she'd finished. But she gave a shuddering sigh and continued.

"It was a week later, on New Year's Day, when we found out," she said, her voice thicker now, laden with a dark emotion I couldn't identify. "Dad called us into his study, grim-faced, and told us Emma had drowned in the lake over Christmas. No one was entirely sure why or how. Only that her father had found her in there one morning, floating facedown. We were sad, of course we were, she was so young. But honestly, we'd only known her a couple weeks. Dad then asked to speak to Seb separately. Again, I don't know what was said, but Seb was crying when he came out."

Lottie looked at me. "So that's why I've been reluctant to talk about it. It's a pretty dark and crappy event and Seb gets all uptight and upset every time it's mentioned. I can't blame him. Because the cause of death was unexplained, I think sometimes he blames himself. Like she was so sad he didn't write, she did it on purpose." Lottie wiped silent tears from her face. "Course, the papers around here had a field day with it, coming up with all kinds of dreadful speculation. When we get back, I hope to God Dad sees sense and this place is filled in."

I've thought about you every night since you left.

I was silent for a long moment. A smiling face with clever green eyes still clearly etched into my memory. *No.* The girl I'd seen was a relative, a sister, a cousin—that was *all.* A member of the Donnelly family or even a similar-looking daughter of another disgruntled local playing a sick joke on the Wrens and their friends—or worse.

I recalled the journal I'd found that day in the folly. The words of a young girl giddy with first love. A scratched-out face in a photo. A dog-eared postcard.

Imagined you adorning my hair with hyacinths.

Perhaps I shouldn't tell you that.

"Lottie," I said urgently. "Remember what I said earlier? That girl I saw—what if she's a relative or friend of the Donnelly family pretending to be Emma? What if she's come here for *revenge*?"

"You can't be serious" was all she said, avoiding looking at me.

"Of course I am!" I replied, exasperated. "I mean, what other explanation is there? Either it's one of us or—or—I mean, do you really think Laure and Joss threw themselves into the lake too just because . . . because Seb rejected them? I mean, come *on*, Lottie. Do you *really* think that?"

Lottie looked at me, her blue eyes wide with surprise.

"No, of *course* not." She shook her head. "That's not at all what I'm saying—you know it isn't. I have no idea what's going on. But the lake . . . I think you've been right about it all along. I think there's something in it. Something dark and unpleasant. Something that could make someone do something they'd never dream of doing normally, you know?"

I stand at the edge of the woods, my mind crowded and unfocused. I want nothing more than to leave this stupid party, to get on the bus back to Catford and shut my bedroom door, to lie on my bed and re-play all of it. I quickly swallow the cup of punch I'm holding, enjoying the burn of it down my throat.

Everything about Sebastien Wren is intoxicating.

I'd be lying if I said I wasn't hurt. I'd imagined us leaving the woods, arm in arm, ready to confront Lottie and the whole of Greyscott together. No longer a couple in hiding, but united in plain sight.

But he could barely wait to be gone.

I wipe a shaky arm across my wet eyes and wander back among the trestle tables, no longer full of a faerie's feast but littered with sticky paper cups and scattered crumbs. While I'm there, I pick up another cup of punch. Like some magical fairy brew, the more I drink, the better it tastes. I want to forget but I also don't.

Truth is, I don't know what I want anymore.

I head down to the dock. During the summer, the boating team train on the river in preparation for the posh universities they'll attend. I'm hoping to find Charlie. The need to tell someone what happened a driving force within me. A dark bubble rising inside me waiting to burst.

That's when I see them, silhouetted like dark devils before the black expanse of the river. It's like some hellish tableau from Bosch. A bastardized version of Klimt's The Kiss. *Him bent over her, her leaning back in supple submission, her auburn hair cascading to the floor, his mouth on hers.*

His mouth on hers.

His hands, which less than an hour ago were all mine, are comfortably at her waist. Like they're used to being there—like they belong there. He wears a stupid plastic crown at a rakish angle. Her circlet of flowers has fallen over one eye, petals preternaturally bright in the lights strung about the pier.

They look perfect.

Him, the dark faerie lord; her, the elegant fairy-tale princess. Greyscott's golden couple, both destined for greatness.

There are a few drunken whoops from the small group gathered before them. Sightless, I move in their direction, not truly believing what I'm seeing. Not now. Now after everything we just did. After everything he promised—everything he told me.

Surely it's impossible for anyone to lie that well.

How could he?

Objections come from around me as I elbow my way through the dwindling crowd, most people immediately heading back in the direction of the candle-strewn dance floor now that the crowning is over. The noise causes both of them to look at me. The difference between their expressions is comical. He looks worried, already half shaking his head at me in warning. She looks nothing but triumphant, her eyes glittering with a dark glee.

"Oh—amazing—your stalker's turned up," she says dryly, one hand pressed possessively to his back.

Most everyone else has gone now. Joss, Charlie, Ollie—none of the others are here. It's only the three of us.

Somehow, in a strange way, it's fitting.

"Meg—" Seb ventures awkwardly. He begins the sentence but I know he can't end it. There is nothing he can possibly say to justify this.

"You lied to me," I say to him, my voice so broken I wonder if anyone can hear me.

Laure laughs humorlessly. I see the uncertainty in her eyes: she knows. The knowledge is what tipped her teasing into cruelty.

"You lied," I say again.

Still he shakes his head at me, eyes pleading. But Laure won't shut up.

"Hey, can someone call this psycho's mum? You'll probably find her emptying the bins round the back—or cleaning up sick in the toilets."

Why is she like this?

All the hate he deserves, that he is due, why does she want it for me? Why is she so full of spite?

Even as I ask the question I know the answer. The reason is standing beside her with pretty curls and an intimate smile.

"Seriously, bitch. Get lost—the grown-ups are talking."

And that is enough. It is all I can take. Pure hate propels me. I see fear blossom in her eyes. I see the realization hit that this time she has pushed me to my limit. That too much has happened tonight for me to accept another sharp dismissal.

I shove her chest hard: once, twice, three times, until she staggers back, landing heavily on the wooden dock. I know I should stop now, that I've humiliated her, that already I've gone too far. But I can't. I need to wipe that smug expression from her face. I advance on her and she crawls desperately away from me, until her hands reach only air and she's slipping off the edge and into the river.

A smile of triumph splits my face. My problem now erased. And I stand there watching her struggle, watching her stupid white dress tangle in her legs. Watch her face disappear, the black water folding over her, erasing her.

Her clothes spread wide; and, mermaid-like, awhile they bore her up.

"She can't swim! She can't swim— You idiot! What are you doing?"

Familiar voices scream around me. There is an explosive splash as someone dives in after her.

And then I see her, in the reeds on the other side of the river. At first I wonder if she's a passerby, but she's standing on the water. Her face is pale, her eyes as dark as the water itself.

I think she's crying.

Lottie was still talking, but I had long stopped listening. The memory of that summer night still as painful as a fresh wound.

"Meg. Look, I know we don't talk about it, but I'm sorry you got mixed up with him. I didn't even know you guys had even *met* before it was too late—let alone everything else. If I'd known earlier, if I'd even *guessed,* I would have talked to you. Let you know what he can be like."

I swallowed; her words stirred a whirl of emotions so strong, my eyes filled with tears. How had she found out? Had Seb told her?

"I didn't *get mixed up with him,*" I murmured. "We were— We *liked* each other. We still do."

"Okay, but who doesn't like Seb?" she replied quickly.

I didn't appreciate her tone. Soft and knowing, bordering on condescension. As if she'd been here before.

"That's what he *does,* Meg," she said in that same quiet voice. "It's all a game to him. I don't know about you, but when I was younger, I got warned about boys—*men.* You know what I mean, right? Your mum, your gran, random aunts, all offering their own archaic advice. Don't get too drunk alone in their company, keep your wits about you walking home late at night, don't wear short skirts—all that victim-blaming shit. But what they *don't* warn you about is boys like Seb. Those guys who are nothing but flashing eyes and charm and gentle words whispered in your ear for you and for you alone. Who keep hearts in trophy cases. Who have memories and feelings like quicksilver. Who break and break, over and over, because it's never *their* fault. It's not Seb's fault girls fall in love with him, obsess over him, except . . ."

She shook her head, her palms upturned, weak sunlight streaming through the willow tree behind us. "Except it *is.* He is full-on. You're his sun, his everything at first; he'll whisper poetry, bring you flowers, pretend he can't help himself from falling for you. But it never lasts.

"Y'know," she said with a harsh bark of laughter, "sometimes I *loathe* him. When it's one of my friends—and it usually is—*I'm* the one left to pick up the pieces. That's why he was so keen to hide you, to keep you quiet. Not because he was *ashamed* of you—Sebastien doesn't appear to feel shame—but because he knew I'd be furious. After the last time, after Laure, I made him swear my friends were off-limits. It's not as if he's ever stuck for options." She pursed her lips bitterly. "But it was a stupid idea. Not being allowed something only makes him want it more. And as for you two *fighting* over him publicly"—she shook her head—"he couldn't believe his luck."

I stared at her.

"You make him sound like a *monster.*"

She wouldn't meet my eyes.

"Yeah? Well, maybe he is."

33

I FOLLOWED LOTTIE back into the house in a daze.

Was what she told me *true*?

Did Seb hurt people for sport? Love-bomb them, then leave? Emma, Laure, and now me? Was he as heartless as she made out?

I couldn't help feeling that what Lottie had told me was slightly overblown. And as much as I liked her brother, I had zero intention of chucking myself into a lake because he'd rejected me.

Unless—unless Lottie was insinuating something far darker.

You don't actually *think it's one of us?*

Was Seb really capable of that? It some ways it made sense. The only person who could be linked to all three—to Emma, Laure, and Joss—was him.

My breath came shorter.

I needed to get out of here. I needed to *go*.

That morning, the last morning before the ball, I'd deliberately gone to the studio to see him.

My heart was half sardonic stone, half squidgy putty for Sebastien Wren. There was no point in trying to convince myself otherwise, especially since the night of the sleepover, aka the hottest moment of my life so far. But he kept. Playing. Games. He had my number but only ever used it to message me obscure lines of poetry or snapshots of Renaissance paintings. Pretentious, yes, but compared to messages from previous guys, *lord,* I was here for it.

His was the only car parked in their immaculate gravel driveway. And I knew Lottie was busy at school this morning, helping Monsieur Desjardins show prospective students around the art department.

I wavered halfway between the studio and the house. Should I just knock on the door? I was sick and tired of being so *passive.* At first, I'd allowed him this secrecy—as if we'd both silently accepted I wasn't worthy of Sebastien Jago Chatto-Wren. But the more Laure revealed herself, a trash bag dressed in Gucci, and the more the two of us actually spoke about *everything*—art, writers we admired and those we didn't, movies, games—I realized I was actually worthy—more than worthy—and that this *wasn't* shallow, wasn't based on attraction (well, not entirely, anyway).

I pressed the doorbell, anxiously eyeing the camera above my head. A bronzed button set into an enormous arched doorway, flanked by neat mini-topiary. But nobody answered.

With a sigh, I went to the studio, messaging him anyway, my words always so pedestrian following his (*license my roving hands*) to let him know I was here. And only minutes later, as I busily mixed paints, deciding I might as well work on my end-of-year project while I was here, the door opened.

The smile on his face was wicked, and my stomach flipped as he briefly turned to lock the door. His eyes flickered from me to the painting I'd been working on. A twelve-foot-square canvas of carnivorous, sly-eyed plants wrapped about a building suspiciously similar to Greyscott.

"Shit, that is *good*, Meg—though not exactly subtle."

I grinned, heat warming my face. "Thanks. It's meant to be . . . beautiful, but kind of horrible at the same time."

Like you, a too-honest part of my brain whispered.

"So, training was canceled today," he said, moving closer. "Turns out I have the whole morning free."

"Maybe we could go get, um, coffee?" I suggested half-heartedly. I didn't *want* coffee. Nope, I wanted exactly what I saw reflected in his eyes, but some kind of public outing would be a good test.

He pinned me to the counter, his arms on either side of me.

"Oh, but I can think of something so much better than coffee," he murmured, one hand suddenly buried in my hair. "Y'know, you always smell *so* unusual, in the best way—like moss, like the darkest parts of the forest." He kissed me, lazy and open-mouthed, and I pulled him to me. He was all heat and want, one hand already unbuttoning my dress, the other traveling beneath it. But the thought was still buzzing in my brain like a wasp around a perfect picnic, and sensing it, he withdrew.

"Hey, is this okay?" he murmured, his breath tickling my ear. "You seem kinda distracted."

I pulled away; it was now or never.

"What *is* this, Seb? I mean, what are we doing?"

His smile darkened. "We-ell, I could draw you a diagram, or better yet, show you?

I scrunched my nose. "You *know* what I mean. Why all the secrecy?"

Please don't say it's just fun—just messing around—please. Please don't say, in a roundabout way, that you're ashamed of me.

He looked away, his expression serious, his eyes seeming to harden. But I refused to appease him, to soften or back down.

No. I wanted him properly or not at all.

"I *want* to be with you, Meg. You know I do. And there's no-body else. Thing is, though, it's—it's difficult—"

"*Why?*" I said, exasperated. "I mean, do you really care that much about what Laure thinks? Or Lottie? Or is it something else? Because I'm not rich like you guys?"

He slumped a little, bowing his head and resting it tenderly on mine.

"No—*no*, of course not. And it's not Laure," he admitted. "I keep telling you, there's nothing between us anymore, she's not even a *friend*. It's—"

Behind us, there came a soft ssound. A key turning neatly in a lock. Seb whirled round and staggered so far away from me he nearly tripped over an open tin of paint as Lottie appeared in the doorway, a confused smile on her face. She looked from me to Seb, back to me again. I was achingly aware of my disheveled state, the button-down black sundress I knew Seb liked, now much more buttoned-down than was appropriate, the strap slipped entirely off my shoulder.

"Hey . . . guys? Seb? I thought you had training this morning."

As her gaze slid to her brother, I quickly righted myself, smoothing my hair and clearing my throat.

"It was canceled," Seb answered. "I thought you were helping out at school."

Their words were light, almost playful, but there was an undeniable undercurrent in the room, a squall ready to break, clouds lowered and bleak.

"I *was*—fewer students turned up than we predicted." She looked back at me, her eyes as light as ever, the smile still on her face, but there was a blankness to her expression that I'd never seen before. It unnerved me. "And, I, uh, thought you had stuff on this morning, Meg?"

I smiled back awkwardly, hating myself for lying to her. "Ah, yeah . . . but it— My plans fell through, so thought I'd come up and get this finished." I nodded to the canvas, grateful the counter was scattered with paints.

Lottie's smile warmed just a fraction. "Good idea, but I'm sure you don't need my brother here distracting you."

"I was just passing by," he said, now standing beside his sister, clutching the door handle, looking as if he would rather be anywhere else in the world. "Saw someone was in here, so I popped my head to say hi. Anyway, I forgot, Ols said he was on his way over, so I better go. Catch ya later, Megs."

He gave me an apologetic glance before he left. Lottie was still staring at me quizzically.

Should I just come clean? I asked myself. Okay, so the whole situation wasn't ideal, but surely it was better than *lying* to her.

Lottie walked over, stopping incredibly close to me. She wore a pair of high-waisted, wide-legged cotton pants and a black crop top—all ethically sourced, no doubt—accessorized with gold-rimmed glasses, and was every bit as beautiful as her brother. She smelled delicious, of fresh meadows and daisies, unhurried summer afternoons. She bit her plump bottom lip gently, her voice teasing.

"*Megs*, huh?"

I smiled nervously, deciding what to say. She was smiling too—maybe it would be okay. Maybe I could come clean and—

"Y'know, I could have *sworn* I left the door unlocked when I headed out."

I recalled Seb only moments ago, leaping away from me like I'd delivered him a thousand-volt shock. No, he would need to break it to her, not me.

"Weird," I said. "I didn't lock it."

She didn't look in the least convinced, her smile thin and wary as she tucked a dark curl behind her ear.

"My brother is the most terrible flirt. And thinking about it, Meg, you're exactly his type—arty, smart . . . *different*." She smiled more broadly now, her eyes flicking down to the three undone buttons on my sundress. "But he doesn't mean anything by it. . . . It's all a game to him—a challenge, you know?"

I tried to give her an appeasing smile. "Oh, believe me, I know. Laure's told me everything—"

I flinched a little as her hand moved to my face, tracing a line down beside my lips, still moist and swollen from where her twin had kissed them moments ago.

"Laure's a hopeless case. But you—you're smarter. I hope you're smarter, anyway."

The sound of a car squealing up the drive, scattering gravel everywhere, broke the spell, and she moved quickly away.

"God, that's Ollie. Better go and say hi. Catch me before you go, okay?"

I nodded, keen to escape her X-ray gaze, letting out a long breath of relief as she shut the door behind her.

He messaged me later that day. Not random lines of someone else's poetry but his actual words. I must have read them a thousand times.

At the ball. We'll tell everyone. I promise, Megs.

A cloud passed over the sun and from somewhere downstairs, I heard a door slam, probably Charlie coming back in from a smoke break. Now was the perfect time. Lottie had recovered and once I made it to the village, I could send the police back to the house and they could deal with everything from there.

Fear was proving a pretty useful tool for putting things into perspective. My mum might be pissed off about stumping up for an earlier flight, but I'm damn sure she'd prefer me coming home alive than found floating on a lake.

I jammed my clothes into my suitcase, throwing my toiletries bag on top, then thrust down the lid with both hands. I didn't trust Ollie, and after talking with Lottie, I didn't even trust Seb. Something about his dire warnings didn't ring true now. Even if a power line was down—or a tree or two—how exactly would that prevent me from leaving, from walking to the village?

I paused before the door, listening for sounds in the corridor.

328

I felt faint and sick. Shaky and insubstantial. I didn't want to see anyone before I left. I didn't want to say goodbye. For the very first time I felt truly done with them all. Entirely done with Greyscott's. No amount of potential success could ever compel me to hang with this bunch of sociopaths again.

Deciding the coast was clear, I lugged my suitcase down the stairs and quietly slipped out the door.

The rain had begun again in earnest. Fat heavy drops that splashed into the deep puddles of the driveway. Pulling my hood over my head, I carried my suitcase by the handle, not wanting the crunch of wheels over gravel to give me away.

My tears ran into the rain, and I was glad of it. This way, it was like they didn't exist. I'd head to the forest path, keeping the road in sight, and make my way up onto the road once it began to get really boggy.

Up ahead, I heard the loud crack of branches underfoot and saw a flash of dark brown. Just an animal or—

Seb.

I froze, like a scared deer.

His face was pale, glistening alabaster in the rain. His eyes flashed in the gloom of the forest as he caught sight of me.

There was no time for me to do anything now.

"Meg? What— Where are you going? And on your own? I'm not sure it's safe out there—"

He crashed toward me. I'd always loved the fact he towered over me, but right now it seemed threatening. And I'd never noticed how broad he was. How *strong*. How easily he could overpower me. Hold me down in a lake or—

"Wait—*wait.* Where's Saira and Ollie?" I asked in confusion.
"Where are the police? What's going on?"

I began to back away as he continued walking toward me,
slowing his pace and picking his way carefully over fallen branches.
"Ollie and Saira are still with the police in the village," he said.
"I said I'd come back and let you guys know what's going on. I
thought they'd be here by now, but they must be having trouble
getting through."

I kept walking away.

Were they with the police, or were they lying somewhere face-
down in the forest? Or floating beneath the surface of the lake?
Dropping my suitcase—there was nothing I needed in there, what
I *needed* was to get to safety—I turned and began to run.

"Meg—what the fu— Meg—*wait!*"

Footsteps pounded behind me. The fact that he was *chasing*
me made my lungs burst with fear. I tripped over my feet in my
desperation to get away. He grabbed for my hand and missed,
getting a handful of my coat instead. I staggered forward, arms
pinwheeling wildly, then fell to the ground. He must have tripped
too, landing half on top of me, warm and solid, knocking the
breath clean out of me. His eyes met mine, full of shocked surprise, and, pink-cheeked, he got up immediately, reaching down
and pulling me up with him a second later. Considerate. He'd
always been so outwardly considerate.

"What the *hell,* Meg? What's going on? Why—why are you
running away from me?"

As he said the last part, he didn't meet my eyes. He knew
something, at least. Knew I had some reason to be afraid.

"Lottie told me everything," I said, my voice trembling. I had nothing to hide now. Nowhere to go. And still, a traitorous part of me wanted to confess so he could convince me I was wrong.

He frowned. "Told you what?"

Again the uncertainty in his voice, filled with dread. There *was* something. Something bad they both knew and I didn't. I was sure of it now.

"You *know* what. About Emma. About Laure. About *everything*."

He exhaled, crossing his arms.

"Oh, is that right? And what about them, exactly? I'd love to know—really."

His lips were curled in a slight sneer, a tangle of black curls hanging over one eye, more wolfish than I'd ever seen him. Not for the first time, I thought of Red Riding Hood, led astray, away from the path. What was I doing here again with him, in the deep shadow of the woods? Had I learned *nothing*?

But then he relented, his body softening with defeat as he walked away and sat heavily on a nearby tree trunk, felled by the storm, no doubt. I watched in alarm as he buried his face in his hands and let out what sounded like a sob of despair. I stared at him, utterly unmoored now. My instinct screamed at me to go to him, but I was afraid of what would come next.

"It was such a fucking *mistake* to come here," he murmured, his voice muffled by his hands. "I *knew* it. I *told* her. Everything here has always gone *bad*. Emma used to say it wasn't just the lake that was cursed, but everything the Wrens ever touched. Y'know, I laughed at her back then—I remember that—but she didn't laugh with me. She only looked worried."

"Yeah," I said bitterly. "I heard all about Emma. The one before Laure, right?"

Seb exhaled slowly and raised his head.

"Meg, how many times do I need to tell you this before you believe it? It was never serious between Laure and me. She had a crush on me or whatever. I should have just left it well alone, and you have no idea how much I regret the fact that I didn't. And I explained to you already about the ball. . . ."

I shook my head sharply. "No. Whether you wanted to take part in that or not, you still *kissed* her, I saw it. You kissed her, and you *know* I saw—and approximately, what, ten minutes after we—we—"

"It was a mistake. I just got caught up in the moment. . . . But it meant *nothing*. I've had more meaningful kisses from my dog." He exhaled, not meeting my eyes. "You *don't* understand. You've never understood *anything*. It's like . . . you actively try not to."

He grasped my hands in his, warm and familiar. Pulling me to sit beside him.

"Listen, that day I first saw you, on your knees in the studio, surrounded by flowers . . . There's never been anyone else since. And that night at the ball was one of the most amazing nights of my life." He gave me a small guilty smile. "Well, the first part, anyway. We *have* something—something real, Megan. A connection—and I know you feel it too. Do you know how *shit* I felt ignoring your messages after? Do you know how many times I almost replied?"

"But you *didn't*." I practically spat it out.

He sighed. "I *know*. I know I didn't. But that was a choice I *had* to make. I needed to deal with Lottie—with what she had done. And however it looked that night—and I know it didn't look good—I wasn't about to let you take the blame for it all. I told her I'd tell the principal the truth if she didn't come clean about it. But you don't know my sister—not really—not like I do. I . . . I needed time."

He sighed, burying his face once more in his hands. He looked exhausted. "But I underestimated her. By the time I'd worked out what to say, what to do, she'd already invited everyone here, including you. And"—he swallowed—"I tried to make sure you'd stay away—hence how I acted when you got here. But by then, it was too late."

"Wait—wait, wait," I interjected, slowly taking in his words. "What do you mean, 'the truth'? Let me take the blame for what? What did Lottie *do*?"

I thought back to Halloween, Laure looking at me with sad green eyes.

You need to tell the actual truth.

Every single detail of that night.

Seb's hand slipped from mine, and he brushed his wet hair back from his face impatiently. "Jesus, Meg—the *truth*. Are you telling me you've been covering for her so long that you've forgotten what *really* happened that night?"

34

I'D HAD WAY too much punch.

Charlie, knowing I wasn't much of a drinker, had warned me it was spiked, but it must have been about 90 proof. I'd had a couple cupfuls before I met Seb. Not because of any last-minute doubts—God, I'd never been surer of anything in my *life*—but because I was a raging ball of hormonal nerves and was already considering the hundreds of ways I was going to mess *it* up. Then I'd had a few afterward because—because Seb and I and Seb and I and Seb and—it was a *lot*.

Then I found them. Together.

And after witnessing that kiss, I'd been floored. I'd never guessed he'd go through with it all. He'd literally promised me he wouldn't.

And there was something else I'd forgotten. There had been four of us there, at the jetty. The others had melted away, perhaps going to alert a teacher it was all about to kick off.

But Lottie had been there too. A crucial detail that was missing from the bruising recollections I'd worked so hard to push away, those bleak, painful memories that left me sweaty and shaken. But had I truly forgotten, or had I *wanted* to forget? Had I wanted to let Lottie—capable, confident Lottie—take charge like she always did? Because it was always easier being under her sway, swimming along with her tide. Her voice on the phone the morning after, concerned and shaky but telling me again and again that it would all be all right, it would all be all right. She knew people, her parents knew people. She could fix it for me. Her tone becoming slightly stern when I attempted to correct or question her about certain details, kindly insinuating I was too drunk to remember the finer details, that other people disagreed with my recollected version of events. Convincing me it would be all okay, it would be fixed if I just did as she said.

She'd been standing there in her designer silk jumpsuit, grinning away, snapping pictures of Laure and Seb with her phone for the school paper. Was she pleased for them? A further betrayal. It didn't matter. By then, I'd had it. I wasn't going to wait for him forever.

But as I got closer, despite my inebriation, I'd sensed the fizzing tension in the air, secrets kept too long, nerves frayed too thin.

"Right, all done," Lottie had said with businesslike efficiency. "Seb, we gotta go—there's an Uber waiting."

At that, Laure's face had darkened. "Both of you can't keep avoiding me forever, y'know." Her voice was dark and thunderous, her speech slightly slurred.

"Fuck's *sake,* Laure," said Seb. He looked tired, his cravat loose about his neck, and more than a little drunk. "I'm so over all of this. I don't know how many times I have to tell you. Anyway, you may as well know that I've been—"

"Laure. You can't blackmail someone into being with you," interrupted Lottie, her voice clear and perfectly sober.

"That's *not* what I'm doing!" Laure said, one hand on her hip, her stance at odds with her elegant fairy regalia. "Why do you always need to get *involved*, Lottie? Your brother has his own life. He should be able do what he wants without you breathing down his neck. This is nothing to do with you—"

At this, Seb had given an exasperated laugh.

"You *don't* understand," Lottie had said patiently, but with an edge of steel in her voice I'd never heard before. "Our family is going through some real shit at the moment, and—"

"Oh, I *understand*," said Laure, her voice dangerously low. "I understand perfectly. If it's in the papers, it's not exactly a secret, now, is it? I read the whole article, Lottie, and found it pretty interesting. Especially the part where your dad swore in court that you guys were all in the UK when it happened."

Lottie seemed to freeze at her words at the same time Seb noticed me, his eyes lighting up.

"Hey Meg!" he said, giving me a louche wave. "You lied," I'd said quietly.

"Say that again?" hissed Lottie, ignoring Seb and me and taking a step closer to Laure, as tall as her brother, towering over Laure's slight frame.

Laure gave a nervous laugh and then noticed me too. "Oh—amazing—your stalker's turned up. Hey, can someone call this psycho's mum? You'll probably find her emptying the bins round the back." She turned away from me, apparently deciding I wasn't worth bothering with. "Lottie, you heard exactly what I said. That girl, over in Ireland. I double-checked the dates. They said no one was there, but that isn't true, is it?"

"You lied," I'd said again.

And Seb had rolled his eyes, just briefly, but I saw it all the same. *That* I remembered, like a knife pushed hard between my shoulder blades. That casual shrugging off. The clear evidence I was nothing to him.

"Look, Meg, I know I'd said we'd chat, but now is *not* the time—"

Seb turned his attention back to Laure. "Laure—what in the *actual* fuck? Look, I know things might not have worked out between us in the way you wanted, but I told you when you brought that bullshit to the Christmas party to keep out of—"

"I'm talking to you," I'd called. Louder this time, interrupting. Refusing to be quieted.

Seb had given me a thunderous look, but it was Laure who'd spoken. There'd been a jittery edge to her that had unnerved me but that I'd just put down to me ruining her plans with Seb.

"Seriously, bitch, get lost. The grown-ups are talking."

I didn't even hear the rest. The steady pounding of blood in my ears, the liquor running like fire through my veins, drowned out everything except my rage. Enough was *enough*. I was not going to sit here and be her punching bag anymore.

Stumbling over, I shoved her hard in the chest once, twice, three times—deaf to anything anyone was saying—until she staggered back, surprise evident in her wide eyes as she landed heavily on the wood of the dock. It felt deliciously good. The tension I'd felt since the start of the evening already leaking out of me. She crawled desperately away from me, until her hands reached only air and I watched as she slipped off the edge and fell soundlessly into the river.

Seb blinked at me in horror. "She can't swim! She can't swim— You idiot! What are you *doing*?"

What *was* I doing?

A chill wave of shame washed over me, causing me to shudder violently. Not *again*. Think first and act *later*, Mum had always said when I'd miserably relayed something I'd said in anger, but this—I'd never done anything like *this* before.

"I—I didn't know. I—I—"

A hot wave of nausea washed over me and I swallowed down a mouthful of bile.

But I did know.

I just wanted her to shut up.

Lottie moved so fast I didn't think anyone realized what was happening before it was too late. We both thought she was diving in after her. To rescue her, I thought in my drunken state, with a flush of relief. But as I stared down into the water, I saw Lottie looming over Laure, her hand wrapped around Laure's pale throat, forcing her under again and again as she writhed and wriggled frantically to get free, gasping for air, like a fish on a hook. It seemed to go on for hours; I couldn't look away but I couldn't move—all I could do was watch.

Another splash. Seb—it must have been Seb, but I couldn't look. I couldn't look anymore. I remember falling to my knees, struggling for air that wouldn't come—my chest tight—iron bands across my ribs—my stomach forcing a violent somersault as I threw up the liters of sticky punch I'd downed into the wet grass.

Next thing I knew, Laure was crawling up the bank, coughing up half of the river. And Seb's hands were in mine, warm and reassuring. His eyes huge and dark. His words like silk in my ear.

"Breathe—*breathe*—you're okay. Hey—hey, look at me—*look* at me. It wasn't your fault, okay? You were drunk, you didn't mean it. You didn't *mean* to push her in."

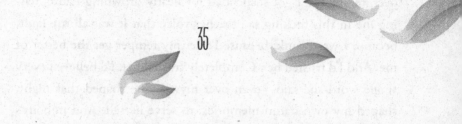

35

I GOT UP, immediately backing away, but he kept coming, and despite having no idea what I was doing, I swung for his face, putting my entire weight behind it. My fist connected hard with his cheekbone, sending a burst of bright pain through my knuckles. Seb cursed and staggered back a few paces, clutching his face and staring at me in disbelief.

"Meg! What the *fuck*—"

"You blamed *me*," I hissed, shaking out my hand in pain, still barely able to believe the truth of it. "All of you blamed me! You made *me* the scapegoat because of who I was, when all along it was—it was her!" The unraveling, the realization stunned me. I wanted to collapse to my knees and sob, I wanted to laugh hysterically at my utter delusion, wanted to scream and scream at Seb, at Lottie, at all of them, until I was hoarse.

Seb stayed where he was, holding his face, looking at me warily. "You still pushed her in? And you *knew* that—Lottie said you were happy to go along with it. Why are you acting like this is some kind of surprise?"

"I was absolutely *wasted* that night, Sebastien! I was an emotional *wreck*. . . . I had a damn panic attack immediately after—I was a *mess*! You—you slept me with and then you immediately left to go and find Laure! How do you think that made me *feel*? Then Lottie calls me the next morning, when I'm dying of a hangover, telling me I got suspended for nearly drowning Laure, telling me in this fucking sad teacher voice that it was all my fault, because I was drunk, because I'd let my temper get the better of me. And I'd trusted her. Completely trusted her. I'd believed every single word she said—even over myself. She shaped that night, shaped my own damn memories, to serve herself. And nobody's spoken to me since!"

And I had been properly, dangerously drunk. So much so that I still had no recollection of how I'd even got home, waking up at midday in a bleary daze with a pounding head and cramping stomach, my mum's worried face looming over mine.

"Fine, you were a bit drunk. Lottie said you were happy enough to go along with it—with the story—until we'd sorted everything out. Dad was going through some stuff, and the last thing he needed was Lottie acting out again."

I shook my head, unable to even take in what he was saying. Bile flooded my mouth at the truth of it. The sheer deception of it all.

"I didn't know I was going along with anything! And I wasn't a *bit* drunk, Seb. After you just *left* like that, I literally drank all the alcohol I could get my hands on. I barely remember anything that happened later that night—just fragments. You *used* me. Both of you did. You knew my history—I'd told you, been vulnerable with you both—and you . . . you *weaponized* it against me. And *going through some stuff*? What—do you mean covering up for you and Lottie again? I mean, what exactly *did* happen to Emma? Oh my *God.*" My breathing came quicker now. "You took every opportunity to ruin my *life.* Greyscott's was my one shot, Seb, and you *all* knew it! Fuck your dad, fuck Lottie—fuck you! I *needed* the opportunity. Both of you are set for life whatever you do, whatever mistakes you make—but you both decided to blame all this on *me*?"

I stared at him. He was a stranger before me. And I'd never felt so *stupid.* So righteously angry. The Wrens had all happily let me take the fall for Lottie's behavior. That was why Seb had completely ignored me for three whole months. That was why Lottie had immediately inserted herself back into my life—now the only friend I had left after my terrible actions that night—to make sure *her* version of the story was the only one I heard. That was why Laure—God bless her, for all her faults—had wanted the truth to come out.

Because that's what the Wrens do, you see. They take and they take and they take.

She knew what Lottie had done, but she was afraid too.

"You're *poison. Both* of you. You don't care who you hurt! Who else knows the truth? Charlie? Saira?"

Seb shook his head, his dark eyes focused on the ground. "No—only you, Lottie, Laure, and me. We were the only ones there."

I nodded, harsh laughter escaping me. "And now Laure is dead. Did Joss know? Did she find out?"

Seb ignored me. "Lottie and I—from the moment it happened, we were always intending to make amends," he insisted, his expression hyper-focused, verging on manic. "That's why we're all here, isn't it? You were going to apologize to Laure—she was going to accept and the school would take you back. It was going to be fine. My dad had had a chat with Laure's. It was all sorted. We weren't ever going to let you take the fall, Meg. We care about you. *I, especially,* care about you."

I buried my head in my hands, still barely able to believe it, even though I knew it was the truth.

"But Laure wasn't happy, was she?" I said, more to myself than him. "She might not have been my biggest fan toward the end, but she wasn't comfortable with me taking all the blame."

"What?" said Seb, looking genuinely confused.

"She told me—on Halloween—that she was willing to forgive me if I told the actual truth. That's what she meant. She meant for the whole truth to come out. The truth about what Lottie did." I stared at Sebastien, things slotting unpleasantly into place. Things I couldn't even voice yet. "And then—then she died."

You make him sound like a monster—

Seb gave a short harsh laugh. "Wait. You can't possibly think that—"

I turned to look back at the house.

"I don't know *what* I think anymore."

A pathetic part of me wanted to cry. After everything I knew, everything I heard, I had still wanted to believe I was special, different from all the other girls. But no, the bitter truth was, I was another in a long line of Wren family secrets. It wasn't anything to do with his unwanted star-student status or his worries about his sister. No, Seb was just an opportunistic dick. A coward and a liar.

And worse than that, a quiet voice in my head warned me, quite possibly a murderer.

Before I could do anything, he was on me. His hands hard around my arms, trying to restrain me, calm me down—before what? Now that I was certain of the truth, now that I was no longer a convenient scapegoat, was I about to find myself floating in the lake too?

"You won't get away with this," I spat at him. "Two people are *dead*. You can't hide the truth forever."

"You need to *calm down*," he said, his grip on my arms vise-like. "We'll go back to the house—we'll talk—and we'll wait for the police. Like I told you, they're on their way. We'll tell them everything and let them take it from there. Okay?"

"Seb—you're hurting me—"

He sounded calm, he *looked* calm, but I wasn't about to take any more risks, especially knowing how easily he'd been willing to dispose of my future only three months ago. I wrenched away my arm, my hand scrambling to my pocket and around the handle of the knife I'd stashed in there earlier that morning. Grabbing it, I thrust wildly at his shoulder. It wasn't as sharp as I hoped and his waxed jacket proved as effective as armor, but the shock of the move, the force of it, was enough to make him stagger away, clutching his arm.

I seized the opportunity, doubling back to the house at speed.

36

I BURST THROUGH the kitchen door.

I might not trust Lottie as far as I could throw her, but Charlie was still here, and Charlie was my ally. I just needed to tell him what I knew and get the hell out of there.

But the house was strangely silent. Lottie sat alone at the vast kitchen table, her hands clutching a mug of steaming tea. She barely looked up as I entered.

Something was very wrong.

"Where—where's Charlie?" I said urgently.

Slowly, she raised her head to face me. She looked different. Her face gaunt and so ghost pale it was almost gray; her eyes hollowed and sorrowful. Her dark curls greasy and lank, slicked away from her face.

Like the banshee in her paintings—

"I don't know," she said mildly. "Where did you go? I noticed your stuff is missing from your room. Your suitcase. Everything. Here—I made you some tea."

The last thing I wanted was to play teatime with either of the

Wrens. But something about Lottie's expression—the emptiness of it—frightened me to my core. *You don't know what she's capable of.* So, sitting down, I accepted the mug and took a small sip. Wanting to play things safe, not wanting to escalate the situation before I needed to. The tea tasted bitter. I glanced down at it. There was something unpleasant floating just beneath the surface. Like pondweed. Hurriedly, I put the mug down.

What had Laure *meant* that night at the ball? The article she'd spoken of, the dead girl—she had to have been referring to Emma. But why would that have angered Lottie? As she'd said to me herself, the death was a distant tragedy to her and Seb, something that happened very far away, to a near stranger. I remember the evening of the pajama party, and the twins' parents' agitated conversation:

Why on earth would she invite that girl over tonight?

I'd assumed they were talking about me. But what if they'd actually been talking about Laure?

What had she found out?

Like a phantom, Laure's voice sounded in my head. *They said no one was there, but that isn't true, is it?*

My heart thumped in my chest. Did she mean . . .

"The police are on their way," I said, my voice much bolder than I felt. I had no idea if it was true but it sounded good. Seb was probably much closer than the police, lurching back to join his twisted sister. "You see, I know the truth now, Lottie. I remember. Yeah, Laure fell into the river because of me but you jumped in to finish the job. Then you thought you'd pin that on me—you *and* your bloody brother. Don't think you're going to get away with this—"

I wasn't sure what I was expecting in way of a response. As

I spoke, I'd stood and edged away from her, closer to the knife drawer. But Lottie only laughed, a sound of genuine amusement, high and musical.

"I have to hand it to Seb—he really is something. And you'd believe anything he said, wouldn't you? I know for a fact that if Seb has anything to do with this, the cops won't be here anytime soon. Nope, it'll be just you and me and Seb. The way it should be. The way we need it to be."

"Where *is* Charlie?" I insisted again.

She gave me a wide grin. "Keeping Laure and Joss company," she said, and my blood froze within me. "Don't worry, you'll join them soon enough. She's always *watching*, you know? Wherever there's water—the lake, the sea, rivers, even fucking *bathrooms*—I can't escape her. You see, she's waiting. I don't blame her, poor thing, it's been so long. I know she's lonely. She cries and cries and screams and wails, and it's all I can ever *hear* in this damn place. And the only thing that stops her—and even then, only for a while—is someone joining her."

I stared at Lottie, barely even believing what I was hearing. What had happened to my friend? What had been hiding beneath her unruffled surface for the past year? She gave me her familiar, wide-eyed grin.

"I couldn't believe my luck when both you *and* Laure agreed to come here. I had a feeling Laure was going to come clean—tell you what really went down at the ball while you were staggering about, pissed. She never could keep her mouth shut, and she'd been avoiding me for ages. But with *you* here—angry little Meg with her utter lack of self-control—well, no one was going to believe it was *me* who shut her up for good, were they?"

I tried to speak, but for some reason, my voice became lodged in my throat. Sweat sprang to my forehead at the same time as the whole room seemed to recede from me like the tide, the corners of my vision darkening.

"Ah," I dimly heard her saying, her tone bright, as if revealing some fun plans for the evening. "Fab. That'll be the meds kicking in. I was prescribed half the contents of the pharmacy after all the *shit* that happened with Seb and that girl back here—that poor Daddy had to take the fall for. They work all right but you need a shitload of them to have the desired effect."

I staggered helplessly toward the table, scrabbling for purchase, dimly aware I was bringing the tablecloth crashing down with me, and the darkness rushed in.

I honestly couldn't tell how long I'd been awake for before I realized I was sitting in pitch-darkness. I think I'd gradually become aware of my limbs, tied up and sore against the concrete floor beneath me. Around me was nothing but the darkness and silence. My head throbbed painfully.

Was I dead?

No.

I *was* breathing. I could feel my chest rising and falling, could hear my breath, a thin strange-sounding whistle, could feel my skittering heartbeat. My arms were tied painfully behind my back, but that was all, and I was somewhere very dark and very quiet. Even the folly let some sunlight through its blinds. Was it night already? Was I in the cellar?

The idea of being held down here with the drowned bodies of Laure and Joss ignited me. Frantically, I jiggled my wrists together, the rope chafing my skin, until finally there was some slight give and I could begin to slip my wrists out. Halfway through this process, I had to stop to lean over and retch, the pressure in my head intensifying to a crescendo as I did so.

But soon my hands were free.

It took a while for me to stand up properly. I was wary of collapsing to the ground and knocking something over, alerting the twins to the fact I was awake. If it hadn't been for the imminent danger I knew I was in, I would barely have believed what was happening to me. Only days ago I had been so excited about coming here, my whole future ahead of me, bright and shining, with Lottie or Seb—ideally both—by my side.

And now, here I was locked in a stuffy basement, trying to stay alive while Lottie and Seb apparently wanted me dead.

Somewhere in the dark ahead of me, I heard a soft shifting sound, as if some kind of fabric were gently troubling the floor. I got down to my hands and knees. All I needed to do was to find the stairs. But if Seb and Lottie were still in the kitchen waiting, watching the door . . .

I felt desperate tears spring to my eyes.

I had no clue what to do. No plan. Nothing. A quick pat of my pockets revealed that my phone had of course been removed. Sniffling quietly, I crawled along the concrete floor, feeling my way in the pitch-dark, until I found a wall. Perhaps there was another exit down here—but it was impossible to tell without being able to see.

Trying to quell my rising panic, I sat for a minute, trying to formulate a plan. I had no choices that I could see, other than finding the stairs or a light switch. Without either one, I was screwed. Standing tremulously, I fumbled my way along the cold, damp paintwork of the wall, scouring the surface for a switch.

After several minutes of shuddering through enormous cobwebs and unseen insects skittering across my hands, I finally found
something switch-shaped. Bracing myself for either a sudden
movement overhead, footsteps thumping heavily down the stairs,
or worse, a deranged screaming or wailing, I flicked the switch.

The lights buzzed on. Bright fluorescent tubes overhead. Taking in the scene before me, I jammed my hand into my mouth to
stop myself from screaming out.

Three figures, each wrapped in the same black cloth that covered the mirrors, lay slumped against the wall. Part of the cloth
had come away on the figure closer to me, revealing skin so blue-
white it didn't seem real, and a tendril of dark red hair.

I turned to face the wall, forcing myself to focus on my
breathing—in and out, again and again—until the panic lessened. They were dead, that was all, and it was a tragedy. But they
couldn't hurt me.

I took in the basement. It was cluttered with box after box of
junk—tattered books and broken furniture, old lamps and mildewed bedding. Things that might have been useful when the
house had been a B and B.

And, set into the far wall, half obscured by a rusting shelving
unit, was what appeared to a be a small hatch. Hope leaped within
me like a flame. Could it be another way out of here? I'd need to
move fast, before Lottie realized I was awake down here. I edged over,
avoiding the overflowing boxes. The hatch was locked with a long-
rusted padlock that looked possible to break. I glanced around for
some kind of tool I could use among all this junk. I began opening
boxes and dusty plastic tubs at random, desperate for a wrench or—

Bingo. At the bottom of a tub of light fittings I found an ancient hammer, its head rusted beyond repair. It would do the trick, though. I heaved it out, trying not to look at the hideous insects that scurried out of the disturbed innards of the box.

As I hit the padlock, from directly behind me came a swift, slithering sound.

I turned, fully expecting to see Lottie behind me, that insane smile on her face, glimmering knife raised in triumph.

But I was still alone.

However, something about the basement was different. One of the black wrapped figures was no longer propped against the wall and was now lying across the floor, blocking the stairs that led to the kitchen.

I swallowed. Dead people can't hurt you, I reminded myself. And they *definitely* can't move. Zombies and ghosts aren't real—

And banshees?

A low gurgling moan came from the body. I stifled another scream, my entire body shaking in fear. Part of me wanted to run, but if there was a chance Joss, or even Laure, might still be alive . . . With shaking hands, I approached and ripped the cloth away.

"Shit—shit—*Charlie!*"

His eyes were fluttering back in his head and a terrible choking sound came from his throat. Dimly remembering a long-ago first-aid course, I rolled him onto his side, trying to clear his airway. He gave a terrible retching cough, then shut his eyes, clearly not quite conscious. But his breathing was soft and easy now.

Above me a door slammed violently.

"I'll come back for you," I vowed, heading hastily toward the hatch. "I *promise* I'll come back for you."

37

THE HATCH CREAKED open and a damp wind blew in, followed by a torrent of dark brackish water. Once the flow ebbed, beyond a thick patch of yellow reeds, I could make out algae-stained flagstones. I almost cried with relief when I realized I'd emerged onto the patio, the waters of the lake now lapping into the basement. Shutting the hatch behind me, I crawled through the filthy water and lay boneless on the ground while I regained my breath.

It was nearly dark, the sky above me a deep twilight blue.

In the distance, on the far side of the lake, I could hear a low sobbing sound. The hair on the back of my neck rose sharply. It was fully dark over there.

I squinted. Was it my imagination, or did I see a slim dark figure slowly descending into the deep water, barely causing a ripple—

Did I see a black bundle carried in their arms—

It's all in your head.

Getting ahold of myself, I forced myself to stand. I needed to decide what to do, and quickly. I couldn't go back to the house; I wouldn't be able to overpower both Seb and Lottie. That left me with only one choice: head into the village—even if I needed to bloody swim there—and alert the police.

I tried to gather myself, sitting up on the bank, my teeth chattering violently, the evening air frigid against my sopping clothing. But I was okay. I was conscious. And, I reminded myself firmly, every step away from the house was a step closer to safety.

I turned, ready to skirt the steep bank and head deep into the forest, where I was less likely to be found. It would mean staying uncomfortably close to the lake, but I was far more afraid of the very much alive Wren twins than of anything that might be lurking in these waters.

Something grabbed my ankle then, hard and fast, sending me completely off-balance and yanking me straight into the depths of the lake. I didn't even have the chance to scream; dirty water immediately filled my mouth, cold and bitter, choking me. For a brief second, I bobbed back to the surface in time to gasp a blessed mouthful of air before I was dragged down again. I kicked desperately at whatever had hold of me, faintly hearing a gasp of pain. Momentarily free, I whirled round as I tried to gain purchase on the muddy bank.

Lottie was behind me, only her sleek dark head visible above the water, a ghoulish smile on her ghostly face.

She bobbed a little closer to me, her glittering eyes never leaving mine.

"Y'know, I didn't believe it for the longest time—"

I looked toward the bank again, edging away until my feet finally found solid ground.

"Stay—stay away from me. I know all about you. I know what you did."

What are you CAPABLE of?

"—believe all the rumors about you and Seb, I mean. Laure told me first, but I thought she was just being paranoid—you know how obsessed she was with him. I mean, sure, you're pretty, they're *always* pretty, but you're nothing out of the ordinary. I thought—I thought with everything that came with you—all your baggage—and after the last time—after *her,* after everything that happened here, the trouble he caused—" She paused, swallowing hard. Her next words were harsh, almost choked out.

"I *thought* he'd learned his lesson. But he never does. He. Just. Can't. *Help* himself."

"You tried to drown Laure," I said, never surer now. "Yes, I pushed her in—but you jumped in after. You—you wanted to *kill* her. She found out about Emma—about what happened here— she even showed the article to Seb at the Christmas party. And she came here to tell the truth about that night—she wanted to *help* me—wanted everyone to see you both for what you really are. And then you killed her, right? To shut her up."

Lottie smirked. "Oh, come *on,* don't act like it was some big loss. She was a bully and borderline *stalking* my brother. Another of his frequent lapses of judgment. He played it all down when he told you, right? Acted like he was horrified—like I was insane— but you didn't see him that night, you didn't see how *amusing* he found it all. How he laughed about her face—mimicking the way her eyes bulged as she struggled to breathe but all she could do was swallow more water." She inched nearer, sending ripples through the water. "And as for *you*—doesn't he play the wounded twin act to a tee? He *used* you, Meg, the same way he uses them all. If you hadn't been there, simpering all over him, ready to do absolutely anything he asked, how else would I have got away with it?"

I stared at her in disbelief.

"I mean, think about it. If he cared about you—even as a friend—do you honestly think he would have screwed you on a forest floor, immediately left to get it on with someone else, happily blamed you for an attempted murder, and ignored you for three entire months? I mean, *fuck,* what is the bare minimum for you, Meg?"

Bile rushed into my mouth, hot and thick. Nothing she said was a lie. In fact, she was right. He had done all of that and I had happily let him.

"But, Lottie—*why?*" I managed, spitting out bitter lake water as the waves rippled forward. "Both Laure and Joss are dead! They're not coming back. And for what reason?"

I needed to hear her say it. Needed her to confirm what I was finally starting to see, the picture that was falling into place . . .

"Because of the mess he always makes," she says, her voice harder and far away now. "They are *all* wrong. Emma, Ava—although lucky for her, she moved away once she got the measure of him—Laure, and now *you.* As for Joss—well, she started putting things together a little too quickly. Accused the wrong twin, of course, but Seb and I come as a pair. None of you are right for him—for the *Wrens.* Our family *owned* this land. We were aristocrats, once. And as for you—Jesus, you're most unsuitable of the *lot*. I swear he set his sights on you just to spite me. So you need to go. To *disappear*. I mean, honestly, other than your mother, would anyone really miss someone like you?

"And when you stupidly agreed to come here—I couldn't actually believe you'd accept—but when you did, I knew I'd got you. It's perfect. You see, everyone knows what you're like, Meg. Your track record speaks for itself. No one would ever believe I had anything to do with all this—with Laure, with Joss—not all the time *you're* here."

Lottie nodded over my head, her gaze fixed on something behind me, something in the darker waters where the forest met the lake. "She's lonely, Meg. She's been alone for years now. She needs company. And now she'll get it. Don't worry, she'll look after you. She looks after them all—the same way she looked after her child."

"And all those paintings in the tower—was that you?"

Lottie smiled again and began advancing toward me, her long dark curls splaying around her perfect face in the still water.

"Those were my promises to her—my gifts. The ones I'd bring her. It doesn't even matter where, so long as it's by water. I *know* you see her. But I've seen her for *years*. Ever since Emma." Lottie laughed, low and harsh. "She wanted her so badly, and Emma was pathetically easy to lure here. All it took was some half-assed note from Seb and there she was, waiting patiently, like a puppy for its master, back there in the weeds, conveniently hidden from view. I know you've heard her too. There's no refusing her, Meg."

I couldn't bear to listen to her madness anymore. Tears streamed down my face at the loss of her—a person I'd loved, who I'd thought was my friend. I scrabbled at the bank, but it was slick with rain and mud and any purchase was impossible. Lottie grabbed my ankle, twisting it painfully, and I screamed, my body jackknifing in the water. The second I emerged, wiry hands clamped onto my shoulders, her eyes—now more black than blue and dancing with a terrible glee—bored into mine as she wrestled me with impossible strength.

Managing to gulp a last lungful of air, I was driven into the filthy silent world beneath the lake.

This was the last thing Laure would have seen—and Joss and Emma—before their final breath ran out. I forced open my eyes, desperately kicking out against Lottie as my ability to hold my breath became painful, but I couldn't reach her. I swallowed a lungful of water, choking, my lungs on fire.

What are you capable of?

Well, now I knew exactly what Lottie was capable of. And so had Sebastien, all along. Unfortunately, I had found out far too late.

Then, for a moment, Lottie's grip on my shoulders eased, just slightly, and some survival instinct I didn't know I possessed kicked in. I rose to the surface with a burst of adrenaline, took in a deep, racking gasp of air, and caught Lottie in the chest with a kick. She staggered back, tripping, submerging for a moment and immediately resurfacing, cursing, her eyes blazing with a hate I couldn't fathom.

And I should have used this time to swim away, to drag myself up the bank, but I couldn't. My entire body had turned to lead, and all I could do was stare. Stare at what had risen behind Lottie, out of the lake.

She rose slowly, pale and terrible. Her skin an unhealthy gray green, her once-glorious yellow hair now drenched and streaming with pondweed. Despite everything, I recognized her face.

I live in the weeds—

"Emma . . ." She wore the same gray shift dress I'd seen her wearing in the mirror, once some kind of uniform, now blooming with algae, the material long rotten.

The sun-starved ditches—

She didn't say the words, but I heard them in my head just the same, like a clamoring bell.

I KNOW—

Instinctively, Lottie turned, immediately losing her balance in the thick dirty water, her eyes comically wide. "No . . . No . . . not you. Not *you* . . ." Despite what I saw—what I thought I was seeing, because, no, I couldn't really be seeing that—relief flooded through me as I was free to slip away.

I KNOW YOUR WICKED HISTORY.

Fear gave me a much-needed foothold on the slippery bank and I waded heavily toward the lawn, violently coughing up water.

Dressed in nettles,

My voice the ebb of the bloated river.

Behind me, I could hear Lottie. Her voice no longer assured and confident, but uncertain, stammering. Afraid.

"You're . . . you're . . . dead. No . . . What—no. I didn't mean it. . . . I was only trying to make things right. . . . You . . . you *knew* he wasn't right for you. He could never have made you happy—"

It was the girl who had once been Emma Donnelly; the girl whose only mistake had been to fall for Sebastien Wren. A girl who had hoped for some kind of future with him, however fleeting, before his sister stole away that possibility. Stole away every possibility she'd ever have.

She moved toward Lottie, gliding effortlessly through the water, reaching to take Lottie's hands, pulling her toward her in what appeared to be a warm embrace—if it hadn't been for Lottie's frantic screaming, that is. The terrible sound richocheted about the lake—a sound I'd been hearing for days now, even in my sleep—turning quickly into a terrible gurgle as they both disappeared into the soupy depths of the water.

I watched the surface of the lake; I don't know how long for. Until the bubbles stopped and the brown waters were once more stagnant and still.

38

THEN, STILLNESS. THE breath of the wind over the lake, the ripple of the leaves on trees, the soft cooing of wood pigeons. A gasping, shaking breath escaped me.

An agonized cry split the silence, and I watched in alarm as Seb thundered down the dock, dived into the water, and emerged only a yard or so from me, gasping for air, his eyes wild.

"Where *is* she? Where's Lottie? What—what happened? Who *was* that?"

I stared at him, and when I spoke my voice was uneven over the chattering of my teeth.

"She—she tried to drown me—she tried to *kill* me—"

Rain began to fall heavily, fat droplets exploding into the water around us. Seb disappeared once more, diving once more into the foul water. Was it possible Lottie was still alive under there? And if she was, would I feel a terrible pull on my ankle, yanking me back down—where Laure, where Joss, where Emma had all lost their lives?

Turning, I staggered toward the bank, constantly losing my

footing on the slippery, weed-choked lakebed. There was another splash as Seb reemerged.

"Lottie!"

The pain evident in his voice made me wince.

"Seb, it's no good—you need to get out of there—there's something *in* there," I implored, tears rolling down my cheeks and mingling with the rain. "There's something wrong with this lake!"

"You don't understand. She's my sister—my *twin!*"

She was also a murderer. How long had she worn that mask of hers? Sunny, reliable Lottie, with not one person aware of the dark undercurrents beneath? Had she been bewitched or influenced by whatever was in the lake? I thought about the things I'd seen—at the beach, here in the lake—always by water.

Not one person? I looked at where Seb had disappeared beneath the water. He had known what happened to Laure that night, at the ball. What else did he know? How far did their allegience go?

I scrabbled up the bank and lay on my back in the reeds, waiting to catch my breath. A terrible sobbing filled the air, but I knew it wasn't her. No. She was satisfied—for now. Some soft instinct urged me to slip back down the bank, wade over to Seb, and comfort him. Tell him it was all okay now. That we could finally be together. That I would be safe. That I was here for him and would do anything I could to make him feel better. To heal his broken heart.

But that was a fantasy now. Even if he wasn't as murderous as his twin, I deserved so much more than Sebastien Wren had to offer, with all his half-truths and glib poetic declarations only ever uttered in secret. Something cold and thick had grown over my own heart, like the weeds in the lake. The endless splashing and calling behind me began to fade, the only sound now that of my own breathing—heavy and rasping—and the world slowly gave way to darkness.

After what must have been hours, I regained consciousness.

I was lying on the ground just outside the folly, the moon shining brightly through the canopy of leaves.

I got up, staggering through the trees toward the bright lights of the house.

Charlie.

I needed to find him—make sure he was all right. A terrible well of darkness spilled open within me. Had I left it too late?

In the dusk, flashing blue lights set Wren Hall into stark relief. The moon had risen large behind it, yellow and bloated and full. Several police cars had been hastily abandoned in the gravel drive while men in scuba suits were preparing to enter the lake.

Thank *God.*

I gasped with relief when I saw Saira, tired and drawn, speaking to an officer while Ollie sat, white-faced and still, in the car behind her.

But Seb saw me first, clad in a foil blanket, his eyes wide at the sight of me.

"Meg—*Jesus,* it's—it's—Meg! You're okay—thank *God*! I thought—I thought—"

I flinched away from him, staring fixedly at the house, my head throbbing, my eyes streaming, my lungs raw. A brief stab of guilt pierced me as I noticed his shoulder, now neatly bandaged. He ran toward me, then stopped, noticing my expression.

"Did"—he swallowed, the hopeful light in his eyes already dimming—"did you see her? Did you see Lottie out there?"

I didn't have the words for him.

All I could do was shake my head.

He crumpled then, falling to his knees on the ground and letting out a deep, guttural sob.

Instinctively, I moved to comfort him. He looked broken, collapsed there on the ground, crying bitterly. And after all, *he* hadn't drowned those girls. He'd had to live with his sister and all her problems, forever secreting away potential girlfriends due to suspicions she might—

I froze, my hand halfway to his shoulder.

But how much *had* he known? Could he have even suspected what might happen to Laure and Joss? To *me*?

I straightened, forcing myself to walk past him.

I walked past the police cars and into the house through the kitchen. Relief flooded me, so violent it left me unsteady on my feet as I saw Charlie seated at the table speaking to a sympathetic-looking policewoman. Thank *God* someone had looked in the basement. He saw me and stopped speaking midsentence, immediately standing.

"Meg!"

He clasped me in a bear hug and I let out a violent sob against his shoulder.

I told the guards everything I knew. I told them everything Lottie had said. The only thing I left out was what truly happened out there, in the lake, at the very end. Truth was, even I couldn't fully accept it, let alone trust myself to relay it to a stranger.

So I said we'd struggled in the water and Lottie must have got tangled up in the weeds somehow. I'd been too desperate to get away, too afraid to help her. But it still felt like a lie, felt odd in my mouth as I voiced it.

"And you're sure of that part, Miss Green?" the policeman had said sternly, picking up on my uncertainty. "You understand there are three dead girls out here and you, one of the only ones left alive, are drenched with lake water. It's important that everything you say is the truth." He was a cold-looking man in his fifties with gelled-back gray hair and hard blue eyes. Beside him was a rounder, softer-voiced accomplice. Good cop, bad cop. Like in the movies.

I swallowed, feeling faint.

"It's true," came a soft voice from the doorway. I looked up, surprised. Seb stood there, looking like a ghost himself, shaken and drawn. "Everything she said is true. I saw it all— from the far bank—I was coming to help but I was too late to— My sister, she"—he swallowed—"she tried to drown Meg. I saw it. Saw Lottie push her repeatedly under the water. It's all true."

I stared at him, entirely lost for words. He dropped his head then, and I watched as he staggered forward, to be caught by the paramedic standing behind him.

"Right then, fella, you'd better come with me and get yourself checked out."

I wanted to follow him, to acknowledge he'd finally come

through when it counted. But the police were still watching me closely.

Composing myself, I turned back to face them.

Hours later, as the police were winding down their questioning, I found him. He was sitting on the benches in the gray morning rain, staring out at the lake. I hurried a little when I caught sight of him, part of me afraid of what he might do.

He didn't move when I collapsed next to him.

"Thanks," I managed.

He dropped his head and sighed. "What for? It was the truth, wasn't it? It's about time I finally started telling the truth, I think."

"Look, I *have* to ask. How much did you know, Seb?"

He shook his head. "Barely any of it. I didn't even guess. Stupid of me, really, but I didn't think we had any secrets between us." He sighed. "She'd taken what happened to Emma—and subsequently what happened to our family—badly, I knew that much." He sighed. "Emma and I, we had a . . . holiday fling, I guess you'd call it, a couple of years ago. I mean, I thought she knew it was never going to work out—she lived over here and . . . Well, she took it pretty hard when I told her. I ended up having to tell Dad all the . . . details, and then a couple of months later she *died*. An accident, Dad said, but there were all these rumors swirling . . . threats of a lawsuit. Sure, Lottie had been over here at the time; she'd spent a few days over the Christmas holiday setting up the studio and painting the views from the folly. Even when Laure showed me that article, it never crossed my mind that Lottie had anything to do with Emma—with what happened."

He took a shuddering breath. "Lottie had a pretty spectacular breakdown just before you started at Greyscott's—it was blamed on all the stress our family was going through. And then there was what went down at the ball . . . That's when I began to suspect that maybe her dislike of who I dated was more than just the fact there was overlap with her friend group. That there might be something deeper . . . darker . . . going on. When you got here, I tried to get you to leave. And Laure . . . I tried to warn her that Lottie wasn't herself right now, that she should just stop bringing up what happened at the ball, but . . . but, Meg, she was my *sister*—my twin. I just never believed, never *dreamed* she'd be capable of—of what she did."

His voice was thick; I realized he was crying. I took his hand.

"I mean—I thought there was a possibility Laure had walked into the lake drunk that night—that it had been a tragic accident," he said. "But when Joss"—he swallowed, his shoulders shaking—"the night before she died, I overheard her and Lottie arguing. I couldn't hear exactly what they were saying, I just assumed Lottie was sticking up for you again, you know what Joss is—was—like. And then"—he rubbed his eyes roughly—"and then after that, after she drowned, well . . . I began to suspect something was up. That was why I was so desperate to go and get help."

I sighed. If only he'd voiced his concern earlier.

Seb turned to look at me, still beautiful despite the pallor of his face, the shadows around his eyes.

"There are some things—some things you can't bring yourself

to even think about—you know? I don't think any one of us—not even Mum—knew how ill Lottie really was."

"You'll tell the police, though. You'll tell them everything?" He took a deep shuddering breath.

"Of course. And I'm so sorry, Meg. You deserved an apology *long* ago, but I *am* sorry. Again. Sorry for ever dragging you into all this." Then he laughed. "But then part of me isn't really sorry at all. Because I'm happy I met you, despite everything, despite all this horror, all this *death,* I'm still happy I met you. Does that sound messed-up? Selfish, even?"

"Completely." I laughed too, now crying a little myself. Because I knew that this was goodbye. Because whether or not I ever got a second shot at Greyscott's, I knew Seb would never go back. I knew he'd be taken away from all this, from us, from me. Knew he'd be scrubbed clean of this mess and given a second chance at things somewhere far, far away, where, after a year, maybe longer, he'd be Seb once again.

I rested my head on his shoulder, and we continued to stare in comfortable silence at the water as the dark clouds finally broke and the autumn sun shone in glorious majesty above the forest.

The air about the lake felt different now. A serenity about its dark waters that was absent before. A bird, long-necked and grace-ful, swooped down from the sky to settle on the water, busily dip-ping its head beneath its wing.

It had been a long night, but after I'd told the police everything we knew, several times, we were allowed to leave. The sun was high over the forest as the taxi finally pulled up hours later.

Charlie climbed in beside me, thankfully he'd emerged un-scathed, although, like me, her was still thick-headed from the drugs Lottie had slipped us.

"Fancy a swim before we go?" he said mildly, nodding at the lake. I elbowed him sharply in the ribs, not managing even a ghost of a smile.

I watched the house through the rear window as we left for the airport, and I couldn't be sure, would never swear by it, but from the top floor, I thought I saw someone wave at me. A glint of golden hair caught in a stray beam of sunlight. A perfect inver-sion, reflected in the lake's still waters.

ACKNOWLEDGMENTS

My greatest thanks go to my agent, Claire Friedman. As a cynical Brit, it feels weird to say "she made my dreams come true," but, Claire, you literally did. If you'd told thirteen-year-old Amy, constantly bashing away writing trashy horror fan fiction on an electric typewriter, that one day her books would be published by one of the big four publishers and stocked in actual bookstores, I would have rolled my eyes and muttered *"Whatever."* Your fierce intelligence and keen editorial eye are so, so appreciated. I never forget how lucky I am to have you on my side.

The other person fabulously complicit in making my dreams come true is the wonderful Lydia Gregovic. Not only does she have excellent taste in reality TV, she also has the *very* best taste in literature. This book in particular is very close to my heart, and I cannot thank her enough for her skillful guidance and sensitive insights, and, most importantly, for truly understanding the story I needed to tell.

Thanks as ever to the wonderful team at Random House

Children's Books for all their hard work, particularly Beverly Horowitz, Colleen Fellingham and Anne Heausler for their copy-editing skills, Cathy Bobak for the beautiful interiors, Tamar Schwartz, Barbara Marcus and Judith Haut, as well as the RHCB Publicity and Marketing teams.

Please can we acknowledge this cover! Thank you to Liz Dresner and Marcela Bolívar for creating the cover of my dreams! You bet I am going to have this gorgeous art blown up and displayed on my wall (as well as printed on a T-shirt, tote bag, fridge magnet . . .).

Thank you as always to all the fellow writers who have helped make me feel like I'm not alone in this one way or another; thanks to Skyla, Lyndall, Zeynab, and Jenni, who have all read early versions of my work and given me the positivity passes I've genuinely needed. Special thanks to Kat—truly, I am so grateful for our friendship. You have been there through the roughest times of my debut year, offering support and wisdom, and I appreciate you so much.

To all the authors who shaped me growing up, whose deliciously creepy stories have inspired and comforted me throughout my life: Stephen King, Peter Straub, M. R. James, Shirley Jackson, Ramsey Campbell, Daphne du Maurier, and Ray Bradbury.

More personally, enormous thanks to the Cremins: Emer, Susan, Ruth, and especially Gaye, whose warm hugs and endless hospitality have made Ireland feel like a second home.

Thankful forever for my parents, who always did their very best for me, particularly my mum, who, like Meg's mum, has always worked so hard to support my brother and me while Dad worked long shifts. Both of you are always my biggest cheer-leaders. Whenever I spy my debut cover sticker on your phone cases, I honestly want to cry (happy tears).

And of course to Neil, Ciara, and Rory, the beating hearts of my own story, without whom none of this would be possible.

ABOUT THE AUTHOR

Amy Goldsmith grew up on the south coast of England, obsessed with obscure '70s horror movies and antiquarian ghost stories. She studied psychology at the University of Sussex and, after gaining her Postgraduate Certificate in Education, moved to inner London to teach. Now she lives back on the south coast, where she still teaches English and spends her weekends trawling antiques shops for haunted mirrors. She is the author of *Those We Drown* and *Our Wicked Histories*.

Underlined

Where Books Are Life

your favorite **books**

your favorite **authors**

all in one place

Share your love of reading with us!

getunderlined.com

1470E